PRAISE FOR *THE SECRET WORLD OF CONNIE STARR*

'*The Secret World of Connie Starr* will set the literary firmament ablaze. This brilliant, quintessentially Australian ode to difference transcends time and place. Written in sublime prose, filled with drama, humour, tragedy and astounding beauty, it's an achingly lovely tale that shines long after the last page.'

Karen Brooks, author of *The Good Wife of Bath*

'A perfect novel, poetic, evocative and hopeful. Your heart will break and then heal for Connie Starr.'

Victoria Purman, bestselling author of *The Nurses' War*

'Robbi Neal has written a book of pure charm, full of heartache and warmth. The writing is vivid and the action moves apace. This is a story both intimate and grand, of Australian history through the eyes of Ballarat families down the generations. Neal finds intrigue and beauty in everyday life. The rich detail of Connie's world and those around her kept me reading right til the very last page.'

Emma Harcourt, reviewer for *The Australian* and author of *The Brightest Star*

PRAISE FOR ROBBI NEAL

'This book takes off and flies, thanks to some lovely writing ... One of the books of the year – I devoured it in two days.'

Carol George, *Australian Women's Weekly*, on *Sunday Best*

'What sets this story apart ... is the telling of it. [The] narrative voice is neither pedestrian nor sensationalist ... subtle and finely balanced ... it is at once intimate and polished.'

Lorien Kaye, *The Age, on Sunday Best*

Robbi Neal has lived in country Victoria, Australia, for most of her life and lives only a couple of blocks from where this novel is set. When Robbi isn't writing, she is painting, or reading or hanging out with her family and friends, all of whom she adores. Robbi loves to walk down Dawson Street past the church her grandfather preached in, the same church with the columns that appears in this book. She loves procrasti-cooking, especially when thinking about the next chapter in her writing. She also loves cheese, any cheese, all cheese, and lemon gin or dirty martinis, the blues, and more cheese.

Also by Robbi Neal

Non-fiction

Sunday Best

Fiction

After Before Time

The Art of Preserving Love (writing as Ada Langton)

THE SECRET WORLD OF CONNIE STARR

ROBBI NEAL

First Published 2022
First Australian Paperback Edition 2022
ISBN 9781867207825

Published by
HQ Fiction
An imprint of Harlequin Enterprises (Australia) Pty Limited (ABN 47 001 180 918),
a subsidiary of HarperCollins Publishers Australia Pty Limited (ABN 36 009 913 517)
Level 13, 201 Elizabeth St
SYDNEY NSW 2000
AUSTRALIA

A catalogue record for this book is available from the National Library of Australia
www.librariesaustralia.nla.gov.au

Printed and bound in Australia by McPherson's Printing Group

To Peter, who, when he got to the end, said
he didn't want it to end – just like us.
And to Asher, Seth, Indea, Zane and Maia,
I am so proud and lucky to be your mama.
You make my life extraordinary.
And to Jules, Sterling, Sorin and Remy —
who are joy, more joy and laughter.
I thank your lovely mamas, Kylie and Clara, for you
and hope there's still a dusty copy on a
bookshelf somewhere when you're old enough to read this.

Contents

Connie's World xi

Prelude: When evil is approaching Ballarat *Monday, 2 April 1934* 1

Part One: 1939 to 1940

When Nero keeps his lions at bay *Monday, 7 May 1939* 13

When Joseph catches his reflection *Monday, 7 May 1939* 23

When Connie tells a fib *Monday, 12 June 1939* 31

When the manse suffers an invasion *Monday, 4 September 1939* 34

When Birdie starts it *Sunday, 29 October 1939* 40

Let's go back to when Birdie had high hopes *Monday, 4 March 1929* 49

When Hazel makes a silly decision *Sunday, 12 November 1939* 56

When Aubrey is in a pickle *Monday, 20 November 1939* 65

When Birdie finds hope in a duffle bag *Monday, 20 November 1939* 76

When Birdie holds on too tight *Monday, 27 November 1939* 83

When the children catch a demon *Sunday, 10 December 1939* 89

When Cecil has to get home *Sunday, 10 December 1939* 99

When bitter tea is served *Sunday, 17 December 1939* 103

When Thom and Lydia think on what could have been *Sunday, 17 December 1939* 111

When Connie finds a secret *Monday, 18 December 1939* 115

When Corporal Tuddenham dreams of early retirement *Tuesday, 19 December 1939* 125

When Dr Salter has his Christmas Eve ruined *Sunday, 24 December 1939* 132

When Birdie knows better *Monday, 25 December 1939* 144

When there is a commotion *Thursday 28 December 1939* 147
When Flora takes advantage of her position *Sunday, 1 January 1940* 157
It's the grand old Duke of York *Monday, 8 January 1940* 162
When Flora comes to the rescue *Wednesday, 31 January 1940* 169
When Flora sees Hazel dance *Tuesday, 5 March 1940* 178
When changes happen like whispers *Friday, 3 May 1940* 188
Part Two: 1941 to 1943
What Birdie did *Friday, 1 August 1941* 193
When Thom takes a train or two *Monday, 1 December 1941* 204
When Thom learns new skills *Monday, 5 January 1942* 208
When Thom takes a shower *Thursday, 19 February 1942* 213
When something is stolen *Sunday, 12 July 1942* 219
When Birdie gets a visitor *Sunday, 12 July 1942* 231
When Joseph is given an ultimatum *Sunday, 2 May 1943* 240
When Joseph gives an ultimatum *Sunday, 9 May 1943* 244
When Lydia dances *Saturday, 15 May 1943* 249
When Lydia takes flight *Saturday, 15 August 1943* 254
The weight on Lydia's shoulders *Sunday, 16 August 1943* 264
When Lydia gets a promise *Sunday, 15 August 1943* 274
Part Three: 1945 to 1947
When Gunter's long journey begins *August 1945* 281
When Birdie and Aubrey dance *Monday, 1 October 1945* 289
When the war fails to end *Monday, 5 August 1946* 296
When there are cuts and bruises in Ballarat *Saturday, 10 August 1946* 299
When Connie can't see what's right in front of her face *Monday, 2 September 1946* 303
The dribs and drabs *Friday, 6 December 1946* 309

Part Four: 1947 to 1948
When a journey ends *Saturday, 4 January 1947* 319
When Connie dances *Saturday, 4 January 1947* 324
When Gunter chooses his path *Saturday, 4 January 1947* 329
When Hazel knows a thing or two *Friday, 7 May 1947* 334
When Birdie takes what's hers *Saturday, 8 May 1947* 336
When lemon marmalade is not enough *Monday, 10 May 1947* 342
When Manny looks at death *Saturday, 5 July 1947* 347
When Greg shows Connie his treasure *Sunday, 6 July 1947* 350
When Flora makes a mistake *Sunday, 6 July 1947* 355
When angels make an almighty racket *Saturday, 22 November 1947* 359
When Joseph loses everything *Saturday, 22 November 1947* 363
When Danny gives Connie what she needs *Sunday, 23 November 1947* 367
When Flora sees everything *Monday, 24 November 1947* 373
When Connie turns fourteen *Friday, 2 April 1948* 382
When so much is invisible *Wednesday, 12 May 1948* 387
When the manse is a prison *Monday, 17 May 1948* 394
When a million frogs sing *Monday, 5 July 1948* 397
When the world is a lonely place *Saturday, 28 August 1948* 402
Part Five: 1950 to 1952
When Connie makes a decision *Monday, 17 July 1950* 411
When Connie goes to the pictures *Saturday, 4 November 1950* 415
When the mayor gets a shock *Friday, 15 December 1950* 418
When Connie can't tell one voice from the other *Friday 29 August 1952* 421
When the Yarrowee flows fast *Friday, 29 August 1952* 431
Acknowledgements 437

Connie's world

The Starrs
Joseph *b*.1890
Flora *b*.1910
Thom *b*.1924
Lydia *b*.1925
Danny *b*.1929
Connie *b*.1934

The Mabbetts
Aubrey *b*.1900
Birdie *b*.1910
Michael *b*.1929
Gabriel *b*.1932

The Mitchells
Claude *b*.1871
Elsie *b*.1875
Viola *b*.1925

The Finchleys
Cecil *b*.1882
Mabel *b*.1882
Manny *b*.1917

O, what may man within him hide,
Though angel on the outward side!
— William Shakespeare, *Measure for Measure*

Prelude: When evil is approaching

Ballarat, Monday, 2 April 1934

Connie Starr was always a difficult child.

Her mother, Flora, would tell everyone that when Connie was born she brought the war with her. This wasn't actually true as Connie was born on the first Monday in April, 1934, at twelve noon exactly – a good five years and five months before Australia was to plunge itself into the Second World War. But Flora knew as soon as Connie entered the world and opened her lungs to scream that there was more chaos in the world than before and that the chaos Connie had brought would work its damage until the day Connie left the world, which she would not do until her ninety-second year – though Connie would spend the last thirty-two of those years declaring to her children and grandchildren and great-grandchildren that this would be her last Christmas.

When Connie came into the world there was no time for Flora to get to the hospital. Her husband Joseph knew that was certain because he'd seen three babies birthed by his previous wife, so when Flora's waters spilled in a pond on the kitchen floor, he took Flora to their bedroom, where he ripped back the apricot bedspread with chenille tufted rows and tossed it to the floor where it landed in a crumpled knoll, soon followed by the woollen blankets, and Connie was born on their bed, on the lemon flannelette sheets. Within an hour of the waters breaking she had slipped easily into the world, there were no contracted pains, no writhing and crying out. Joseph had been ready with a damp flannel to wipe the sweat from Flora's brow but there'd been no sweat, and already it was as if Connie had always been there. As if all it took for her to be birthed was for them to notice her.

As they gazed at their newborn, Connie gazed back, not with the milky eyes of a baby but with eyes sky blue that could see things no one else saw. Flora saw her accusing eyes and felt a shiver run through her. But Joseph saw himself in the sky-blue ponds.

'Put her to your breast; it might settle her,' he said, so Flora picked up the baby, awkwardly, as though she was a lump of wood and not a soft fleshy newborn thing, and Flora held her nipple to the baby's mouth, but Connie turned her head away. Flora held the baby tighter and Connie squirmed for freedom. Flora pushed her nipple into the baby's mouth and Connie bit down hard with her gums. She had surprising strength and Flora cried out.

'She bit me,' Flora said to Joseph. There were tears at the corners of her eyes. She took the baby away from her breast and balanced Connie on her legs.

'Cup of tea, love?' Joseph asked, thinking the baby and mother would soon settle into each other.

'Maybe when we've changed the sheets,' said Flora, thinking she could really do with several cups of tea and maybe a scotch. But there was no scotch or any alcohol in their teetotal home (apart from the brandy Flora hid in the laundry to make Christmas pudding each year). Joseph never touched alcohol and would not have it in the house. Alcohol was the ruin of many a good man and thereby the ruin of his family.

Joseph held Flora's hand to give her support as she climbed out of the bed and he put Connie back in her arms, but the baby squirmed and instead of enveloping the new baby, Flora stiffened and recoiled and was uncertain whether the child would ever accept her; the baby wasn't happy in her arms. How was Flora to know that Connie would never be happy with where she was and would always want to be in the next spot, doing the next thing?

Connie let out an almighty holler. Flora rocked her and cooed but nothing quieted her, so Flora knew that before she had even begun, she had failed to be the mother Connie was hoping for. A cavity had opened between them, where each felt rejected by the other. It sat and gnawed at both their hearts.

Joseph didn't notice the chasm widening between mother and child because he was busy scooping the placenta into the bedpan that lived hidden in shame under the bed, and then he pulled the bloodied mucous-y sheets from the bed and scrunched them up in his arms with the unused flannel so his arms were full of a sheet cloud striped with a vivid blood sunset. He headed to the laundry at the back of the house next to the toilet.

Flora put Connie on the stripped mattress and stood against the wall with her arms tightly around herself, shivering in her soiled nightdress until Joseph came back with two clean sheets. She picked up the baby and Joseph laid the sheets out on the bed; their crisp ironed creases divided the bed into neat rectangles. Connie put the baby back on the bed and waited. Joseph brought a bowl of warm water and a fresh flannel and he gently pulled Flora's nightie over her head and dropped it to the floor. Then while Flora stood shivering and empty he ran the flannel over her pink skin, tenderly, lightly, as if she might dissolve if he rubbed too hard. He cleaned the blood and birthing fluid away, he touched the warm flannel between her legs, barely touching her skin because he didn't want to hurt her. She let him wipe everything away until she was newer than the baby lying on the crisp white sheets. He dried Flora with soft pats of the towel, every pat a kiss on her skin, and then he got a clean nightie from her drawer, and she held her hands up as he slipped it down over her. He got her tortoiseshell comb and ran it ever so carefully through her bobbed caramel hair, breathing in its scent as he combed.

'Done, I think,' he said, standing back.

'I'm still bleeding,' said Flora, who knew nothing about birthing.

'It's normal,' said Joseph, thinking of his three older children. Flora walked to her dresser and took a fresh pair of cotton pants from the top drawer and she went into the bathroom and took the terry rag from where she hid her rags at the back of the drawer and pinned it to her underpants. She slipped the undies up her legs and walked back to the bedroom. She lifted the baby from the bed and, balancing her in her arms, she clambered into the bed and held Connie tight and hoped the crisp sheets would signify a fresh start for them as mother and daughter, and Joseph plumped the pillows to make her comfortable.

'I'll get the tea,' said Joseph.

'The children will be home soon,' said Flora, and she wriggled so that Connie was resting again on her legs. 'There's sliced ham in the ice chest for sandwiches.'

Joseph picked up the bedpan. He wondered if he should tip its contents down the toilet pan to be collected in the darkness of the night, but then he decided he would bury the birthing under the new lemon tree in the side yard. He had planted it at the end of the summer, but it was a straggling thing that refused to grow. No matter how much he peed on it to nourish it, the tree curled its dark green leaves inside themselves, as though it might die at any moment. Perhaps what had nurtured the baby all these months would make the lemon tree grow.

The three older children, all from Joseph's first marriage, were Thomas, who was nearly ten and only answered to Thom, and like his namesake doubted everything; Lydia was nine and filled with a bitterness that you could see around the corners of her mouth; and Danny, who was five and woke every morning amazed to find himself still alive with a place in the world. The children arrived home from school every day at twelve-thirty and Flora would have something hot ready for their lunch, which they gobbled down quickly before going back to the school at the end of the block for the afternoon classes that began at one-fifteen.

Flora and Joseph had discussed Joseph's first marriage only once, when they first met. He had come as the new pastor at the Baptist church and before he arrived the gossip had done its rounds and everyone knew he was a widower. When he stood up behind the pulpit the congregation saw a tall, proud man who was in control of his world, but Flora saw a melancholy man who was lost and was perhaps the saddest man she had ever seen and knew immediately that she was the only one in the entire world who would be able to heal him.

He had reasons for being sad. For an entire year he'd been on his own with three little children. But as he stood in the pulpit on that first Sunday, as he introduced his first hymn – 'Be Thou My Vision' – Flora could see the river of his sadness ran deeper through his veins than the loss of his wife; it was in the blood weaving through his heart. She could see he was filled with failure. He couldn't be who he wanted to be. She could help him.

Deacon Finchley had asked for a young lady to volunteer to care for the new reverend's children while he preached and Flora had thrown up her hand. Joseph had to be at least twenty years older than her, but she didn't let that put her off. He needed her and she liked nothing more than to be needed, and when the children's hymn was sung she'd picked up the twelve-month-old baby who was sitting on old Missus Hooley's knee, taken the three year old's hand in her spare one, and motioned for the other child to follow her and she took them to the crèche room and squished all three onto her lap as she sat cross-legged on the floor and read to them from the *Illustrated Bible for Children*. Six months later Joseph and she were married.

When Joseph met Flora he knew immediately she was exactly what he needed. He could feel that his life would regain purpose and direction if she was in it. She was much younger than him but he didn't let that put him off.

'I need her, I can't manage without her,' Joseph said to her mother, who was a foot and some shorter than Joseph in height but a foot and some taller in determination. Flora was a change of life baby and so her parents were older than most. Her father had died three years previously and her mother couldn't bear the thought of Flora going off to live with the new pastor and his ready-made family.

'Employ a nanny then,' said Flora's mother Constance Pottage, 'but you can't marry Flora without my blessing until she is twenty-one.'

'Well,' laughed Joseph, 'that's only a six-month wait.'

So Joseph employed Flora as the children's nanny until they could marry and Constance was furious because she hadn't meant Joseph should employ her actual daughter. But Flora stood her ground against her doting mother and for the next five months and three weeks she arrived at the manse each morning at 7.30 to give the children breakfast and left after feeding them dinner and putting them into their pyjamas at 6 p.m. and two days past her twenty-first birthday, on 31 July 1931, she braved the sleet that fell like shards of glass and the rain that fell like impending doom and she married Joseph, who was then forty-one.

Joseph's hair was black and thick without a trace of grey in it. He had a voice that washed over his congregation in waves of warm sweetness as though someone was baking bread, making everyone declare he was possibly the best preacher they had ever heard, or at least second-best, not as good perhaps as Reverend Rose whom he'd replaced but pretty close; you would have to listen to them side by side to really compare. But he was very good, they agreed, despite not being able to remember one word he'd actually said.

Flora was short, only just five feet tall. Her hair fell in soft tawny curls and Joseph was so pleased she hadn't succumbed to the modern styles that he found harsh and blunt. After the service each week the congregation stood around the columned veranda and in the street and chatted while the women prepared morning tea and then they poured into the church hall. Flora would have a saucer with two shortbreads balancing on the edge and three sugars in the tea, just the way Missus Gleeson liked it, in Missus Gleeson's trembling hand before Missus Gleeson had even asked for it. As soon as Danny opened his mouth to bawl she knew he felt lost and motherless and in no time he was balancing over her arm where she could put pressure in just the right place next to his heart to calm him.

'Oh, they never ever fight,' everyone said of their marriage.

'Flora is the most submissive wife a man could hope for,' said the men to each other. 'Joseph has all his needs met in that little lass,' they said.

'Joseph just adores his wife,' said the women as they dried dishes in the church kitchen.

'I bet he does anything and everything she asks of him without grumbling and whining like our useless lumps of husbands,' they agreed.

Everyone looked at their marriage with envy, but most of all Birdie Mabbett.

Joseph came back into the bedroom with the tea on a tray and the three older children following him. Flora looked up and smiled and the children stood at the door cautiously staring at the new baby that had entered their lives. Flora beckoned them and they threw themselves onto the bed beside her and scrutinised their new sister.

'Look what the postman brought with the morning mail,' said Flora, and she looked up at Joseph. 'Isn't she lovely?' she said, but she could hear the hesitant tremble in her voice.

'What's her name?' said Lydia, not at all impressed by the new baby girl.

'It's Constance. Constance Faith Starr,' said Joseph.

'For my dear mother who passed away so recently,' said Flora, and tears fell from her eyes. Her mother had died only six months ago; she was an orphan now. And when does a girl need her mother most if not when she herself has become a mother?

She reached to pick Connie up so the children could each take a turn to hold her and the baby flinched at her touch. Grief filled Flora's heart as she knew Connie would never need her. And more than needing love, Flora needed to be needed.

PART ONE

1939 to 1940

When Nero keeps his lions at bay

Monday, 7 May 1939

Each morning the wireless broadcasts broke the tempo of Flora and Joseph's household like an overbearing aunt talking ten decibels louder than everyone else. The gleaming new AWA Skyscraper bakelite radio sat proudly on the mantelpiece as if it was too good for the rest of the house, too good for the furniture that had seen better days, too good for the post-Depression meals of cabbage and tough meat that were put on the table. After all, the wireless was modelled on the Empire State Building that sat across the seas in New York. It had been a wedding present to Joseph and Flora from the church deacons. The varnished wooden clock that sat humbly next to it had been a wedding present from Flora's mother, and every half hour the clock protested it was just as good as the radio as it sang out its chimes. Each morning the wireless slowly came to life and crisp words, vowels rounded and consonants clipped, came into the Starr kitchen through the steam from the kettle and the ringing of cutlery hitting china.

In March Prime Minister Joseph Lyons had been broadcast. '*We want goodwill, cooperation and understanding*,' he had insisted, his voice crackling through wirelesses across the country, but on the seventh of April he'd upped and died, and on the twenty-sixth of April, Robert Menzies, who everyone in Ballarat said must be a good bloke because his mother was from nearby Creswick, took over running the country. Many hoped he would be a less congenial fellow and would, with the help of Mother England, stand up to these overseas bullies, Japan and Germany, who were threatening the get-along nature of the rest of the world, which had been hard fought for after the Great War.

But Menzies disappointed, and no one was surprised because he was first and foremost a politician. '*Peace and goodwill*,' he boomed through the wireless speakers. He tried to speak with authority but he wasn't fooling anyone because everyone could hear his voice trembling and faltering and it wasn't just the distortion of the broadcast.

News of impending war in Europe could not be avoided. Pope Pius XII had sent delegates to London, Paris, Berlin and Warsaw. The pope had stood with his robes fluttering in the breeze and waved off his most trusted diplomat, the Jesuit Father Peltro Tacchi Venturi, to plead for peace with Mussolini. The pope had high hopes that Mussolini would listen to his pious messenger. And everyone, including Mussolini, did politely listen and then everyone, including Mussolini, ignored the religious emissaries who had come from their gilded cage in Rome in their expensive robes from an era long gone.

The foreboding of war was in people's skin, it birthed new worry lines in foreheads and weighed shoulders down; it made food tasteless in their mouths and turned beers warm. The skies were grey and the air was chill and still. The clouds, crying for the state of the world, had set a new record for April, unloading buckets of rain on Ballarat day after day after day until the rain filled the streets like rivers. Boys had dragged out dinghies and manoeuvred them up and down Main Street like pirate ships, using their hands for paddles and splashing each other, uncaring as they became drenched in the cold muddy water.

The Yarrowee River flowed fast and gushed over its banks. Twelve-year-old Joe Gleeson, rushing home for forgotten schoolbooks, collected them and decided to take a shortcut back to Mount Pleasant Primary School across the river. He yanked up his shorts and in bare legs, with the water swirling around his thighs and his toes clutching slippery riverbed stones for grip, he waded into the river. Two days later his body was found half a mile downstream, washed into some bracken. As the discovery of his young body was announced, it seemed an omen of all the young deaths that were to come. Gloom was what people woke to and took to bed. The hunger and desperation of the Depression had barely had time to leave people's bodies. Memories of the last war were fresh and raw. Was it just yesterday? It seemed so. They had been promised it was the war to end all wars. And now here was another one waiting for its moment, greedy and angry and hungry for more young men, and everyone felt the bitterness of having been duped.

Five-year-old Connie couldn't understand half of what they were saying on the wireless as it boomed over the breakfast table, but she knew when her pa was cross and she always assumed he was cross at her because she always had something to hide. This morning she peeked up at him and saw he was staring at her and she squirmed and tried to think of the bad things she had done most recently: she'd climbed up on a chair and stolen a cream biscuit from the rosella tin on the mantelpiece; she'd taken a tortoiseshell hair clip from Lydia's drawer and lost it in the garden; she'd not said her prayers last night. Her pa's eyes moved to Lydia, who was sitting next to her. Connie sighed with relief and looked at Lydia and said, 'Lydia wants to be anywhere that isn't here.'

Lydia walloped her arm and Connie cried out even though it hadn't hurt. She waited for either of her parents to tell Lydia off for hitting her, but they didn't. It was terribly unfair because she'd only said what was true.

As far as Connie was concerned, Lydia got everything she wanted from Ma just because she was older, whereas she Connie got nothing and got into trouble for everything. Pa was looking at her brothers Danny and Thom now. They sat next to each other on the other side of the table. Danny, like Lydia, was in his school uniform and Thom was in his work overalls. They were both shovelling porridge into their mouths like they hadn't eaten since the start of the Depression, which Connie didn't remember but which was mentioned daily by every adult she knew and was the reason she had to eat brussels sprouts and cabbage and why she could only have one pair of hand-me-down shoes and couldn't have extra desserts. It was why they had a vegetable garden and horrible pecky chooks in the backyard. Everything bad in her life could be attributed to the Depression, whatever that was.

Pa looked over at Mister Ellis, who smelt like sardines and was sitting next to Mister Huntington, who had nostrils big enough for Connie to see right up them. They were sitting at the other end of the table. Messrs Huntington and Ellis had both slept in the vestibule last night on the rickety stretchers. There were always visitors staying in her home. This too was because of the Depression. Connie wished her parents wouldn't let every stray person stay over. Sometimes she said so and Ma would hold her firmly by her arms, look right into her and say, 'Connie, it is our duty to take in the lost and the needy.'

The radio presenter's voice announced, '*Wuthering Heights* *has been released in America to brilliant reviews but sadly I have to inform you that the film will not reach our shores of sunny Australia until December.*'

Lydia, who was now fourteen, groaned. December might as well be forever away. Until December she could only sit swooning over the pictures in magazines of the handsome and arrogant Lawrence Olivier, who played Heathcliff, and dream of him gloriously pronouncing his love for Cathy.

Connie watched as her pa stood up and turned down the wireless. He looked at her ma and said, 'Flora – we are Christians and Christians always turn the other cheek and so we shall turn the other cheek to Hitler, we shall take the higher road, the narrow road, and by our example we shall avoid war.'

Miss Mitchell, Connie's Sunday school teacher, had told them what it meant to turn the other cheek. She had flicked her head from side to side and her brown hair had swished across her face. Then all the children had to swing their faces from side to side pretending to take slaps on each cheek one after the other like Jesus said they must if they were to be good Christians.

'Whatever you think, dear,' said Flora, as though it was now settled. As though Joseph's words alone controlled the future of the world. Only Connie saw the rigid set of Thom's jaw as he braced against his father's words and she had her mouth open ready to declare Thom's mutiny, but Thom glared at her and she clamped her mouth shut and Pa turned the wireless back up and they listened to the weather forecast in silence. After the weather Pa stood up and turned off the wireless and Connie said, 'Can I be excused from the table?'

'May I be excused from the table?' Joseph said. 'You can be excused from the table but you may not.'

'But you haven't finished,' said Flora, looking in her bowl.

'But I want to go outside,' said Connie.

'You may but you must brush your teeth, wash your hands and go no further than the corners of the block,' said Flora, 'and wear a coat and take a hanky.' Flora didn't sit down to breakfast, she ate toast while she prepared sandwiches, made more tea, washed and dried dishes as they appeared. Connie held out her porridge bowl and Flora scraped the scraps of porridge into the chook pail and put the bowl in the sink to wash. Connie manoeuvred her body out from the table and walked past her father and he grabbed the edge of her frock and pulled her to a stop in front of him.

'You've got to learn to finish things,' he said, 'and not always be rushing off to the next thing.'

'I did finish my porridge,' said Connie, and looked to her mother.

'I'm not talking about your porridge, Connie. I'm talking about your life.'

Connie felt her frock fall free from his grasp and she fled before he could start a sermon, through the living room and up the stairs two at a time to her bedroom. She got her hanky from under her pillow and her coat from the hook behind the door and then she jumped down the stairs two at a time and went into the bathroom. Connie watched herself in the chipped bevelled mirror as she ran the toothbrush over her teeth, swiping left once and right once, and figured that would put her just inside her mother's command. She wiped away the dribble of paste running down her chin and cleaned her hands on her washing frock. Connie had two frocks, her washing frock and her Sunday best. Next year when she went to school she would have her uniform as well. Connie tried to brush the smeared toothpaste from the bottom of her frock but it had already dried.

She trailed her finger along the oily black crayon lines on the hallway wall left by some other child who had lived in the house before them and which no amount of whitewash would cover and, according to her ma, no amount of scrubbing would clean away. Then she was out the front door, jumping over the three porch steps and leaning on the fence that divided her home from the monstrous church next door, her father's church. She was near the front of the fence where it nearly met the street and it dipped down and was short enough for her to see over and she climbed up onto the first cross bar. The church had massive white columns that held up the veranda; those Corinthian columns could just as easily have been at the Colosseum. Just the other day Thom had told her it was at the Colosseum that Nero had set loose his ravenous lions to tear the limbs off Christians and that the sand in the arena had turned red with Christian blood. They had been sitting on his bed in the room he shared with Danny. Thom had shown her a drawing of Nero and the lions and the Colosseum in the *Illustrated Bible for Children*. In the drawing the Christians knelt praying in the sand.

Thom said they stayed true to the end and the Lord took them home. He said if she was true to God and always told the truth then she would one day be taken home. Thom sounded just like their pa when he preached his sermons in church and she said she did always tell the truth and Thom had sniggered and said, 'Yeah, like I said, Con, you have to start telling the truth.'

There were many things Connie was afraid of, including lions that ate Christians, though she wasn't baptised or anything because you had to be nearly an adult to get baptised, but she was afraid that even without being baptised, Nero might set his lions on her. She was afraid of war, too. She had seen drawings of the Israelites fighting the Canaanites with swords, so she knew war was about swords and heads getting chopped off. After Thom had closed the book she had run outside to the columns, which were exactly like the ones in the book.

And then she had seen him, playing his fiddle, calling in the demons, and following them came the angels, ready for war.

Connie peered over the fence now to see if he was still there but he wasn't and she looked up into the sky and it was filled with angels and demons. Then she looked back at the enormous church columns and there he was. There on the church veranda stood Nero, leaning lazily against a massive white pillar playing his violin, a slight smile on his lips, his long fair hair dancing in the wind and his green eyes sparkling as he gazed over at her and gave her a slight nod. She shivered because even though he was handsome and looked a lot like Lawrence Olivier, she knew he was a wolf in sheep's clothing. She knew his handsome looks hid his black heart and he killed Christians. Nero was wearing a white dress with a tan leather tunic over the top; a leather strap went across his chest and around his waist. There were medals pinned to the strap over his chest like her pa's war medals. His legs were sturdy and he was wearing sandals strapped up to his knees, his arms were muscly and strong, like drawings of Popeye, and as he played faster and faster, his green eyes turned dark with flashes of lightning.

Safely behind the fence, Connie stood with just her eyes peering over the top of it. She took her gaze away from Nero and looked up into the sky where the angels were fighting with the demons. The angels wore white robes tied at the waist with cord and they had golden curling hair; their massive white wings glinted with gold flecks as they beat back and forth. The angels let loose their arrows, some hit demons, who withered and shrank, and some arrows disappeared into the clouds. An angel banged a demon on the head, catching the demon's stunned face in the net of his harp. Another angel lashed about with his trumpet, bopping demons on the head. The demons wore black long johns and had tails like monkeys and grinning faces. They laughed and cheered as though the whole thing was a great game and it mattered not one iota who won. They had forked spears that they prodded furiously at the angels and they threw hammers that boomeranged back to them.

The angels and demons swirled and dipped and tussled. They rose into the sky, then swooped, sometimes flying quite close to Connie as they fought, so that she ducked right down and put her arm over her head to protect herself from any wayward blows, and when the angels and demons tumbled over each other and tumbled away again, she stood back up. One angel plunged in quite close, taking aim at a demon who was prodding another angel with his pitchfork. The angel fired his shot and the demon laughed as he dissolved into black smoke and his laughing died away with him. The angel turned and looked at Connie.

'Ah, Connie Starr,' he said. 'You can't sit on the fence, you know.'

'I'm not,' said Connie, because she wasn't, she was standing safely behind the fence.

'You must make a decision,' said the angel, 'one side or the other.'

'Are you going to turn the other cheek?' asked Connie.

'What? No,' said the angel. 'The time for turning cheeks is well past.'

'What's your name?' she asked. It would be Gabriel or Michael. All angels were called Gabriel or Michael. Connie knew that because Missus Mabbett had named her two boys Michael and Gabriel and told everyone they were named after the archangels because they were angels. Michael might be an angel but not Gabe; Gabe was definitely a demon with an angel's name.

'What name would you like me to have?' said the angel, swatting away a demon with his huge wing. The demon rolled off into the clouds to fight with someone else and the angel's wing blew back Connie's hair as it cut through the air.

Connie thought hard. She loved her brother Thomas the best so she said, 'Thom.'

'Archangel Thom it is then. Remember, Connie – you must choose a side.' The angel went back to fighting the demons and Connie looked back at Nero, who smiled and fiddled faster and louder on his violin so that Connie hardly heard her pa calling to her from down the driveway.

When Joseph catches his reflection

Monday, 7 May 1939

If you asked anyone what kind of man Joseph Starr was, they would look at his actions and their assessment would be that he was a gentle man who had control of his destiny. If you asked Flora she would say her husband was tender because he was devoted to her, never once losing his temper with her.

If you asked his children, they would say he was a fearsome father, but when they grew up they would say he was fair and kind and was only harsh when their behaviour called for it.

But the children knew, from some intuitive place deep inside them, that their father's restraint was a fragile thing and the softer their father's voice became, the angrier he was and if his voice quietened to barely more than a whisper, their minds flustered, wondering what sort of punishment they were in for and how they could get out of it and whether or not it would involve the thick rod that Flora used to stir the clothes in the copper as they bubbled in the hot water and soapy Rinso flakes.

If you asked Connie what she thought of her father Joseph Starr, she would shrug her shoulders and look up to the sky and eventually she would remember you were waiting for her answer and she would say, 'He is an angel dressed as a devil or a devil dressed as an angel.' And you would walk away thinking, *What a strange child.*

But perhaps what matters most is not what others think of us but what we think of ourselves, and if you asked Joseph Starr what he would say of himself, he would stop and look at the ground, run his finger down his fine straight nose and then say that he was not a naturally gentle man. And you would be stunned because that is the exact opposite of what everyone said about him. But Joseph knew that he only achieved gentleness through constant effort, and if you had to work so hard for it, was it real?

He aimed for meekness and humility, but he was neither a meek nor humble man. He stood tall, his olive skin was flawless and his eyes were deep and dark. His face was beautiful and made women gaze at him longer than they should, and he towered over other men in the church and they admired him. Joseph held his shoulders straight and if you saw him out of his dog collar, walking down the street with firm purposeful steps, you would swear he was a politician or a supreme court judge or some other important person rather than a humble church minister.

Joseph's words were soft and clear, a skill he had gained from the elocution lessons his mother had insisted on. To his Ballarat congregation his voice was exotic, almost English, like the ones used by those mystical ABC wireless men who were heard but never seen. His voice was seductive and compelling and he remembered to speak softly and to only raise his voice to drive home a point in his sermons. To the rest of the world Joseph was a sovereign of his church and his family.

Only Joseph knew the work it took for him to be that person. Joseph had a darkness filling his soul with dread and when he looked at himself from afar, he saw a solitary figure, parched and beaten, raging helplessly in the middle of a vast desert. He blamed himself for losing his first wife. He was a man who couldn't hold tight enough to life and so the important things slipped through his fingers. In those moments Joseph sought out Flora, and he would fall into her arms, weak and lost and panting for water. She was his source of nourishment. When he breathed in her ear she would wrap her arms around his neck and any storm within him calmed. It was she who shared her gentleness with him, let it eke into him while they slept side by side under the blankets. Without her, he would lose his temper easily. And when his temper was lost, his control of his life and the world vanished with it.

Joseph clung to his faith as though it was his lifebuoy and he kept the words of the book of James always in his mind: *Ye see then how that by works a man is justified, and not by faith only.* So Joseph opened the door of their home to the bedraggled men with grimy unshaved beards and worn-out clothes as any good Baptist reverend would. Though he knew it was Flora who understood their pain and filled their hungry bellies with her food, who warmed hot water bottles for them on cold nights and placed them in their stretchers to soothe their bruised feet, and it was her words that moistened their dry skin.

For six days of the week Joseph was devoted to his congregation. He visited the sick and lonely, he counselled the battling spouses and the grieving, he gave communion to those unable to attend church, he went to the hospital and to the jail cells at the police station and he pondered his next sermon. For six days of the week he wore his black suit and starched white dog collar that bit into his neck, but on Mondays the day was his and on his day off he wore a pair of old trousers that Flora had darned at the knees, a flannelette shirt that he left open at the neck with the sleeves rolled up to his elbows, he wore his old boots and his old akubra and on this day, because it was May and it was cold, he put on a cardigan Flora had knitted for him. On his day off he would do quiet, peaceful things that would enable him to be the man he should be.

He sat at the kitchen table taking his time to read *The Courier*, while Flora kept his teacup filled and he read aloud to her and to Mister Huntington and Mister Ellis, who both knew they should be on their way but were loath to leave the warmth and the toast and tea that Flora put in front of them. And so they had sat on even after the children had left for school and after Connie had gone out to play. Joseph read out Canon Needham's article that was on page seven:

> '... *many Christians are pretty flabby Christians, and if Christians don't pull up their socks and work together, Hitler and to a lesser degree Mussolini will take over the world and all who are not of a certain class will be wiped out. Only the Anglican church led by myself and the Baptist church led by Reverend Starr have agreed to cooperate with each other. If we do not work together, blood will run like rivers across the world and we will not have a world worth fighting for.*'

'It's nice that he mentioned you, dear,' said Flora, wiping her buttery fingers on her apron, and she picked up the kettle from the stove and refilled the teapot and twirled it around three times in one direction and three times in the other and then filled Mister Huntington's and Mister Ellis's teacups and they silently prayed they would never have to leave the Starr home and go back to cold nights on the roads looking for work. Joseph didn't like the feeling of pride that was bubbling in him, pride that the canon had mentioned him, that he alone was willing to work with another denomination and that he had had the good sense to marry Flora. So he found a distraction, he looked out the window and saw the low grey clouds hovering over the world on its precipice of an apocalypse and decided the weather was finally cold enough to begin the grafting.

'Grey clouds,' said Joseph, and he looked at Messrs Huntington and Ellis and said, 'Where do you have to reach today on your travels?'

'Ararat,' said Mister Huntington, pulling at his ear. 'I want to reach there by nightfall,' he lied, not wanting to go anywhere at all.

'I've already packed my bag,' said Mister Ellis. 'One more cup of tea and I'll be off.' Though he had nothing to pack and no destination to be off to.

Joseph reached in his pocket and pulled out two one-pound notes, put them on the table and pushed them over the timber towards the men.

'Oh no, you've been kind enough,' said Mister Huntington.

'You must,' said Joseph. 'It's not from us, it's from the Lord. It's funds the church sets aside specially to assist people on their way,' and he reached over and pushed the other note closer to Mister Ellis, who thought of his bag of nothing that was waiting for him in the vestibule, and took the paper note and folded it into a tiny square and hid it in his palm.

Joseph hoped to heaven that both men were as decent as they seemed and the notes weren't going to the nearest pub when it opened.

'I'm going to get Connie to help with the grafting,' Joseph said to Flora. The child needed to learn peacefulness; she was a torrent of tides smashing against each other, sending her off in all different directions at the same time. He worried that if she didn't learn calmness she would be swept away and drown. She was too much like him.

He stood up and shook Mister Huntington's and Mister Ellis's hands and wished them godspeed. He bent over and kissed Flora on the forehead and he stood at the end of the driveway buttoning his cardigan against the cold. Seeing Connie leaning over the side fence that divided the church and the manse, he called out to her. She was off in her own world as usual and he had to call three times before she looked in his direction, and when she did look at him she did so as if she was looking at a complete stranger and it knocked him and he pushed his hands firmly into his trouser pockets to steady himself.

'Connie,' he called, 'I need you to help me. You need to get me some old newspaper from the stack in the woodshed.'

Connie jumped down from the cross bar on the fence.

'Is it important?' she asked, walking towards him. She only wanted to help if it was important.

'Oh yes, I think so,' he said. She smiled at him. She rarely smiled and for a moment he was off balance again, then he realised she was deigning to do what he asked, rather than doing it through any sense of obedience.

'Well, off you go,' he said and she ran off towards the shed and he watched as her long ringleted ponytails bounced against her back. Her hair was black and thick like his.

Messrs Huntington and Ellis came out and he shook their hands again and wished them well and watched as they dawdled down the driveway forcing one foot in front of the other. He thought it would be an awfully sad thing to be on the road with nowhere to go.

Connie was back with two newspapers from the pile and she waved them in front of him so he forgot about Mister Huntington and Mister Ellis.

'Now take them to your mother in the kitchen and wet the paper under the tap – not too wet so that it falls apart, just so it's damp. But get your mother to help.' He knew she wouldn't ask Flora for help. If she determined to do something she just barrelled in without caution. Soon she was back carrying dripping soggy wads of paper that left a grey river behind her.

Joseph looked up at the sky as Connie stood holding out the wet paper. 'Now, Connie, it's going to drizzle soon which is just perfect for our job, but go and put on your gumboots and raincoat or your mother will have words with me.' He watched her go to the back door. 'You can leave the paper at the door,' he called out just as she was about to drag it dripping through the house. He followed her into the house and scowled as he stepped carefully through the muddy puddled kitchen floor. She had run upstairs to where the children's bedrooms were. He went into his own on the ground floor and rugged up in his Driza-Bone and scarf and waited for her at the back door. Flora came in from outside carrying the mop and bucket.

'Sorry,' he said. 'I told her to get help from you but you know Connie, won't do a thing she's told.'

'It's only clean dirt and water,' said Flora and he bent and kissed her and pulled away when he heard Connie coming. She stood expectantly in her raincoat and gumboots, gloves, hat and scarf. He took her hand and walked to the orange tree in the middle of their backyard. The drizzle was falling, fine enough to seep into his skin, his coat, his hat. There was something dishonest about this wetness that was not rain. He preferred the upfront honesty of decent proper rain, of splashes big enough to bounce right off you. The air was damp and grey and settled in his pores so that his chilled nose began to redden. It was only May; it would get colder yet. At this rate it may even snow come July. The grass was already becoming slushy under his feet and he trod carefully so as not to slip and held Connie's hand tight to support her. Then he inspected the branches of the tree and Connie stood silently watching. Finally, he picked a slender branch that met his criteria perfectly.

'What do you think, Miss Connie?' he asked, holding the branch out so she could see it. He knew she had no idea what he was doing but she nodded approvingly anyway. He pulled a knife from his pocket and quickly sliced through the branch, separating it from the tree.

'Come on,' he said. 'Isn't this exciting?'

Her face contorted and he saw her make an effort to look excited but she only looked pained. He took her hand again and they collected the wet newspaper from the back door and he sat on the step.

'Now wrap the branch in the wet paper, carefully like it's a baby,' and he watched as she wrapped the soggy paper around the branch. 'Now we put it in the ice chest and we have a nice cup of tea and a milk arrowroot biscuit to dunk. And every morning, Connie, before breakfast, before we turn on the wireless, you have to test the paper. You have to make sure it hasn't dried out and if it has you must sprinkle some water on it to remoisten it, but not too much. It has to be damp not wet.'

'Like christening a baby,' said Connie. 'I will be the grand duke pope archdeacon christening a baby.'

'No,' he said firmly. 'We don't christen babies and we don't sprinkle. It's not true to God's word. Where did you learn about this, anyway?'

Connie shrugged. She learnt everything from listening when she wasn't supposed to but she didn't want to get into trouble so she wasn't about to admit it.

When Connie tells a fib

Monday, 12 June 1939

A month later Joseph switched on the wireless and waited for it to warm up and begin broadcasting. The theme tune sputtered through the speakers in broken pieces and gained strength until the orchestra boomed into the kitchen. '*This is the ABC News broadcast for Monday 12 June 1939.*' Joseph sat at the kitchen table and Flora filled his teacup.

'I nearly have enough Lipton's tea coupons for a new rotary beater,' she said. 'Ours has gone rusty. So drink up – the more you drink, the sooner I get the new beater and the sooner I get the new beater the sooner I can make a sponge.'

'And what did women use before rotary beaters?' asked Joseph and got a smack on his arm. 'So I am doing you a service by drinking lots of tea.'

'Assuredly,' smiled Flora.

Joseph watched as Connie took small spoons of porridge from the side of the bowl where it would be cooler and pretended he didn't see when she quickly spooned extra sugar on. The sugar melted in the hot porridge and formed translucent sticky rivers and ponds around the oaty hills. The wireless talked about the coming months – '*The outlook isn't good, it seems highly likely that war cannot be avoided*' – then, guilty for raining depression on listeners so early in the morning, the voice pepped up to show the world that everything would be okay. '*King George and Queen Elizabeth enjoyed a lovely dinner of hot dogs and beer with Franklin and Eleanor Roosevelt thus proving to the world that royalty can be just as ordinary as the next fellow – if they so choose.*'

'Beer and hotdogs,' said Joseph, 'and they had to pretend they liked it.'

'*While on the other side of the world, Hitler has forbidden his young brigade from eating ice-creams while in uniform because he thinks slurping ice-cream is an undignified sight*,' said the announcer.

'Just lucky you aren't a child in Germany,' said Joseph, 'or there would be no ice-cream.'

'How mean could a person be to deny ice-cream to little children?' said Connie.

'*England is trying to broker a compromise with the rebellious Germany*,' said the wireless, '*and its strange little leader who doesn't like ice-cream, so that peace can be assured.*'

Joseph wasn't so sure that peace could be so easily gained. He thought of the Prussian statesman Otto von Bismarck, who had said, 'One day the great European War will come out of some damned foolish thing in the Balkans.' And he had been right. The Great War, which Joseph had fought in, was started by a simple wrong turn causing the Archduke Franz Ferdinand and his adored wife Sophie to drive straight into the path of the surprised assassin, who was taking the same corner from the opposite direction. And because of this one mistake, so many men lost their lives. Wars were so easy to start but so hard to end. Joseph kept these worries to himself; he didn't want Flora or the children becoming upset or afraid. He knew from the last war that the longer the war dragged on the laxer the army's requirements became until in the end they would take a man with one leg and one arm and turn a blind eye.

He looked at his two sons, Thom, who was growing into manhood, and Danny with his pale blue eyes, and his insides wilted. He looked at Lydia and wondered if they would call up women – surely not. He looked at Flora, who he never fought with because she was so accommodating, so cheerful about everything he asked of her. She had brought contentment to him and his three older children and now they had Connie as well. No, he couldn't bear it if a war came and ruined it all. He felt the darkness approaching and he reached out and grabbed Flora's apron and pulled her to him and put his arm around her as if giving her strength for what was ahead, but knowing it was really she who gave strength to him.

He cheered up when the wireless said, '*On Saturday the Saints beat the Kangaroos by a mere 14 points.*' Joseph slapped his leg and smiled at Flora, who shook her head and loosened herself from his arm and went back to the kitchen bench where she was wrapping sandwiches in paper. She couldn't work out how men got so worked up over sport. '*It will be a cold, damp but rainless day,*' the announcer continued, and Joseph and Flora looked out the window at the falling rain and Joseph stood up and turned off the wireless.

'Let's hope he is as right about the war as he is about the weather,' said Joseph. Then, turning to Connie, he asked, 'Have you checked the paper around the cutting this morning, Connie?' and she hadn't and quickly jumped off her chair to do it.

She felt the icy paper; it was dry and brittle and a corner broke off and fell like a snowflake to the bottom of the ice chest. 'It's wet, Pa,' she said. 'What do we do next?'

'We wait for spring,' he said.

When the manse suffers an invasion

Monday, 4 September 1939

Joseph didn't hear the announcement of war because the radio was never, ever listened to on a Sunday – the Lord's Day – but he heard all about it from his congregation at the evening service, and on Monday morning it was played again and he listened, with his arm around Flora, and he saw the world becoming desolate. Hitler had invaded Poland on three sides – the west, the north and the south – and on the third of September 1939 England could no longer turn the other cheek, because it appeared that Hitler had an ego and thought he was entitled to the entire world, and if he wasn't stopped everyone might die anyway.

'Poor Poland,' said Flora as she spooned fruit compote into bowls and passed one to Joseph and one to Missus Whitehall.

'My bedroom has been invaded,' said Connie, glaring at Missus Whitehall and her two children, Frankie and Jane, who had stayed for the last three days, displacing Connie to a wad of blankets on her parents' bedroom floor. She hoped to get the same level of sympathy as Poland.

'Connie, apologise to Missus Whitehall,' said Flora, but Connie didn't have to because Prime Minister Menzies's announcement of war was played yet again and they listened as he said in sombre tones that it was his melancholy duty to inform the country that because of Hitler's actions against Poland, Britain was at war, which meant Australia, her child, was also at war. Menzies asked that the Mother Country and God in his mercy would deliver them all from the agony that was to follow, but with the Mother Country being so far away, it wasn't terribly reassuring. How far could the Mother Country's arm reach in a pinch?

So the rationing of oil and fuel that had begun in the Depression would continue; food and commodities would be next. Without waiting for the weather report, Joseph turned off the wireless and opened the paper. *The Courier* filled its front page with bombs and battles and fighting for freedom. There was the king's hope that the war would be over in months rather than years like the last one and the Prime Minister's melancholy speech was printed in full but amid this catastrophe the paper made room for Joy of Life kid shoes selling at Faull's for a whopping thirty-five shillings. War or not, women needed shoes for their feet.

'Can't I have a pair of Joy of Life shoes – in blue, please, please,' said Lydia.

'Thank goodness you're too young to join up,' Flora said to Thom.

'I'm not,' said Thom with a mouth full of vegemite toast.

'You are,' said Joseph, his voice low and quiet. 'You have to be twenty-one, and thank the Lord you're a long way from twenty-one,' and he held a prune in his spoon and stared at it suspiciously. Thom tore off a resentful mouthful of toast. If the war could go on for long enough, he would certainly be able to join up.

'Look,' said Joseph, 'the sun has come out. It's so warm this year that we can ignore the plight of the world and finish our grafting, Connie. Finish up your porridge and we'll do just that.' Joseph stood up and looked out the window where the sun was warming a cold and belligerent world that didn't deserve its light and affection.

'So I can't have a pair of new shoes?' said Lydia, knowing that of course she couldn't.

'There are more important things than shoes,' said Joseph and he stepped outside. Finding the air warmer than he expected, he went back inside, past Lydia sulking at the table, past Thom working out exactly how long until he could join up, past Danny lining his marbles up on the table, and past Connie who was trying to fit more sugar into her porridge. He took off his cardigan and left it over the kitchen chair, then he went to the garden shed and, reaching to the top shelf, took down the sharp knife he kept hidden there in its leather sheath.

Back in the kitchen he said, 'Flora, love, get some gauze and bandage my thumb, will you.'

'Have you cut yourself?' she asked, holding his hand to the window to inspect it in the light.

'It's for protection,' he said. 'The grafting knife is sharp enough to slice through a man's neck if need be.'

'I could kill Hitler with that knife,' announced Connie, 'and then German children could have ice-cream.'

Joseph leant over to where Connie was eating sticky spoonfuls of dissolving sugar and with his elbow on the table he held the knife upright like a sword in front of her nose and said, 'Under no circumstances do you touch this knife.' He waited until she nodded solemnly but her eyes were bright and he knew she was wondering how soon she could try the knife out and what she could try it on and he sighed. His warnings were lost on her and he worried where this would lead her.

'Now as soon as you've finished, get the branch from the ice chest. I need some cotton sheeting,' he said to Flora.

'Will the cotton rags I use for Connie's hair do?'

'They will do perfectly,' he said.

So Flora bandaged his thumb into a thick mummy wad and he took the cotton ribbons that were once a bed sheet in one hand and took Connie's hand in the other and with her holding the orange tree branch in its newspaper blanket they went outside to the small lemon tree that stood in the garden between the driveway and the fence separating the manse and the church.

The sun was getting warm for September. In a normal year September was pleasant enough, as long as you had on a jumper, a coat and a hat, and as long as you could find places without the shade that murdered the sun's warmth. At four in the afternoon the sun would disappear and all the cold damp that had fermented through history would roll up from under the ground, through the grass and weeds, past the bushes and scrub, and would settle around the townsfolk's chests, chilling their bones and making them hanker for exotic tropical places like Cairns or Townsville. But this year it was unseasonably hot and no rain had fallen since the middle of August.

Connie plonked herself down on the ground. She watched her father intently, not saying a word, which was unusual because normally you couldn't shut her up.

He nodded at her.

She looked at him with those penetrating eyes of hers.

'This lemon tree is five years old, the same age as you,' he said. 'It was planted not long before you were born and when you were born I planted your afterbirth under it. So the same nourishment you got growing inside your mother has nourished this tree. This tree – it has a part of you, Connie. You are intrinsically linked.'

'It looks dead to me,' she said and broke off a curled brittle leaf.

'Looks can be deceiving,' he said. 'It may well be strong on the inside and if we marry it to a piece of the orange tree, perhaps the two together can grow into something the lemon tree on its own can't achieve.'

She nodded. It didn't mean anything to her.

She watched as he took the knife and with the precision of a surgeon, cut a wound into the lemon tree. Then he took the small orange tree branch Connie was holding, unwrapped it from the wet paper and cut into it in the same way he'd cut into the lemon tree. Then he took the cotton rags and bound the branch to the tree.

'The branch is called the scion, that's the thin, new branch, and we are binding it to the root stock, that's the lemon tree,' he explained to her.

Joseph wrapped the bandaging around and around the tree and when it was firmly in place he gave some rags to Connie so she could have a go.

'One tree is too sweet, the other too sour,' he said. She stopped bandaging and looked up at him. Her gaze was unnerving.

'We have combined an orange tree which is sweet with a lemon tree which is sour to create a new tree.'

'Are you sure you're not God?' she asked.

'Don't blaspheme, child,' he said, 'and start listening to your Sunday school teacher! I didn't make the lemon tree or the orange tree. I am just bringing two of God's creations together like a marriage.'

He picked up the leftover rags, the knife, the wet newspaper and took her hand as they walked back into the kitchen.

'It's your tree to look after, Connie. You must water the tree every single day – unless it rains – which I doubt. Make sure you don't miss.'

'I will make sure it grows big enough for me to sit in,' said Connie.

'I doubt it,' he said. 'Lemon trees don't grow that big.'

'But I can make it grow big,' she said. She imagined the tree growing, becoming bigger than their house, its top high enough to talk to the angels and its branches low enough to look down on the rest of the world and hear all the forbidden whispers. She saw a limb strike out from the trunk, and stretch and uncurl into one strong branch with a dip in the middle where she could sit.

When Birdie starts it

Sunday, 29 October 1939

By October the sun had gathered its strength and become extraordinarily hot; the winter sleet that slithered through the warmest coat, and the frosts that froze the grass to brittle glassy shards were distant memories.

A few blocks away from the church in Dawson Street was Humffray Street South, and at the back of Humffray Street ran the Yarrowee River canal, where Connie and Danny and Danny's friend Mike and his brother Gabe would clamber down into the bluestone canal and run up the middle of it until it turned into a proper river at Darling Street, and there they searched for mud frogs and unbearably noisy crickets and fossicked for nuggets of quartz they convinced themselves were real gold. In winter when the canal was full the children ran along the side of it until they reached the point where it widened into the river and they swung off ropes into the icy water and pushed each other in.

In autumn and spring Gabe and Mike's father Aubrey would sit on his back porch and marvel at his luck to rent a house with such a view. But in summer the nearly dry canal brought flies and mosquitoes that bred in the puddles of soupy water left by the hot sun, and then his wife Birdie complained non-stop about her bites and itches and his lack of sense in renting by the canal and she chased the insects with wire swatters and he filled the poison can with kerosene and sprayed the buggers who hid high in the corners of the room and in the dark spaces under the furniture.

On this Sunday morning the sun shone hot so that at breakfast Birdie said to Aubrey, 'Summer is already upon us. You better keep the kero topped up.'

He looked out the window at the cloudless blue sky and said, 'Perhaps.'

Birdie got up from the table and took the kitchen step stool to the bedroom and pulled down the box of summer clothes she kept on top of her wardrobe. She put the box on her bed and opened it and took out two neatly folded shirts for her boys, seven-year-old Gabe and ten-year-old Michael, that she had made during winter in preparation for summer. Gabe was most like his father, Aubrey: raucous one minute, charming the next. Mike was the gentle one; he held all her hope for the future.

The shirts were identical sailor shirts, white with navy stripes around the sleeves and a large handkerchief navy collar that tied in the front. She had sewn the bias binding stripes on by hand with tiny invisible stitches and she had made them matching shorts. She took the biggest shirt, the one for Mike, and walked into the kitchen. The boys were both slurping porridge and Aubrey, sitting in his singlet and boxers, was reading the paper, a cup of tea in his left hand tilted so the tea was at the brim, ready to spill in a waterfall to the floor. Birdie held the shirt out in front of the boys. She saw Aubrey glance up at the shirt and then scrunch up his nose in distaste.

'Why do you dress them like pansies?' he muttered.

'For church,' she said to the boys, ignoring Aubrey. Then she said hopefully, as she did every Sunday he was home, 'You could come?'

'I'd rather pull my own eyeballs out,' said Aubrey and he laughed and pretended to do so and the boys laughed with him.

Gabe looked back at the shirt and drawled, 'Do we have to wear that? Connie Starr is gonna bust my chops.'

'It's too hot,' said Mike.

Birdie felt crushed. She made the boys new outfits every summer and until now they had always loved them.

'I'll leave them on your beds ready for church,' she said, and her disappointment filtered through her and settled in her gut where it was lost in all her other disappointments.

Birdie Mabbett's life had been one of constant disappointment and she saw no reason that should ever change. Eric Homer lived next door and had never married; he was alone and sad and Birdie sometimes invited him in for a roast dinner and each time he said her chicken was the most tender and succulent he had ever tasted and her potatoes were the crispiest and slapped her husband Aubrey on the back saying how lucky Aubrey was to have a woman like Birdie and if he Eric could only find a woman half as good he wouldn't be so miserable. But Birdie could only feel disappointed that the potatoes were burnt not crisp and that there had been a lump or two in the gravy.

Birdie cajoled the boys into their outfits. 'Just wear them this once, so people can see, and when we get home I'll make you custard,' she promised and the boys relented but as they walked to church they made a show of how uncomfortable they were by tugging at their collars all the way.

After the service Nola Turnbull and Dulcie Whittaker pulled at the material of her dress, tugging her thin frame in opposite directions.

'Ooohh,' said Nola, 'your dress is so pretty, Birdie.'

'I saw one just like it the other day in Harry's department store, only it was an exorbitant sum, ten shillings,' said Dulcie.

'Oh, I couldn't possibly afford that,' said Nola.

'No, not with all the trouble approaching,' said Dulcie, and she turned to Birdie and said accusingly, 'However did you manage it on Aubrey's wage?'

And Birdie, who would only think of a response to this rudeness hours later, said quietly, 'Oh, I got the material at an oddment sale for one and ten and made it myself.'

'Oh my, Birdie,' said Nola, 'why aren't you selling these creations? I would buy one in an instant, wouldn't you, Dulce?'

'Absolutely,' said Dulcie, running her fingers over the beautiful even stitching on the pockets, but Birdie could only think about how she should have used a contrasting pattern for the pockets and trim and how the machine had caught on one side and pulled the stitching when she was doing the hem. So really the dress was a failure and she didn't look half as good as they did in their shop-bought dresses that shimmered in the soft October sunshine.

Birdie walked off to find Flora, who was standing at the end of her driveway watching Gabe and Danny chasing Connie around the lemon tree.

'I can't tell if she likes being chased or if I should intervene,' said Flora. 'I never know with her what I should do.'

Birdie's eldest, Mike, was sitting up against the thin trunk reading his Zane Grey book.

'Your boys look so sweet in their matching outfits,' said Flora and Birdie said, 'They hate them.'

'Are you coming into the manse for lunch?' asked Flora.

'I must go; Aubrey will be waiting for me to get him sandwiches. I have some silverside left over,' said Birdie, and her marriage to Aubrey compared to Flora's marriage to Joseph filled her with disappointment. Birdie felt that there was something terribly wrong with her that she felt this way. That she couldn't be happy and contented with what she had. With her husband who had thick glorious hair that curled cheekily at the ends no matter how many bottles of Brylcreem he poured into it and his eyes that were always glinting with ideas of something he wanted to do but shouldn't.

There were only two things in Birdie's life that weren't a source of dismay and they were her sons and her looks, in that order. With golden natural curls that never needed ragging, large blue eyes that always looked on the verge of tears so that men wanted to sweep in and cart her off to a castle where she would be eternally protected behind a wide moat, dark lashes and full red lips that didn't need a touch of lipstick and cheeks that didn't need rouge, she had been dealt a good hand in the looks department. And Birdie adored her two sons – they were perfect, they were God's angels on earth, Mike with his golden hair like hers and Gabe with his dark unruly curls like Aubrey.

But that was where contentment began and ended for Birdie. Aside from being pleased with her sons and her looks, she was filled with a sense of knowing that no matter what she gained in life it was either not what she needed or was sure to be taken from her. So she never allowed herself to feel really happy. Feeling happy was too big a risk.

When Birdie got home she took off the much-admired frock and put it on the hanger in the walnut wardrobe. She hated the frock now because she could only see its faults. She would never wear it again. She undid her rayon stockings and carefully slipped them over her legs, flattened them out and folded them into a neat envelope and took off her garters and put them and her stockings in her dresser drawer. She put on her plain green housedress with shell buttons up the front and then she tied her green half-apron tight around her waist. When she wore these Aubrey sometimes looked up at her and said, 'God, you're enough to send a man packing. I don't know why you insist on wearing such drab rags.'

She went to the kitchen and took the leftover silverside that they'd eaten the night before with white sauce and cabbage, and the cheese from the ice chest and cut thick slices of the meat and thin slices of the cheese and put them on a plate on the table, along with the mustard pot and bread. She called the boys down from the loquat tree and ignored the fact she had told them to change out of their sailor suits into their Saturday clothes and that they hadn't and now their new suits were covered in grass stains. She never saw their disobedience. It simply didn't exist. She called Aubrey from the living room where he was reading the paper in his chair.

Then when they had all gathered in the kitchen, she sat at the opposite end of the small kitchen table to Aubrey, the boys sitting either side. She made a sandwich, cut it in half and gave one half to each of the boys and then half filled their glasses from the milk jug. She stared at Aubrey, allowing her disillusionment with him to fill her up, and it settled in her belly like cement so she couldn't eat and she pushed away her plate. He never came to church with her and the boys. Why couldn't he at least do that? Half the church must think she was divorced or even worse, living out of wedlock. They never went anywhere as a family, she never got to proudly walk around Lake Wendouree with her arm linked in his, their boys skipping along in front. She never got to show off her little family to the town. He never promised his undying love, he never wondered at her beauty or made her feel alive, but most of all Aubrey hadn't rid her of her discontent, and she had really thought he would. She had married him and then woken the next day with the same dread she always had; it filled up her brain and travelled through her till it settled heavily in her stomach, swirling and churning in a stormy sea of fluids that made her want to sink to the bottom of the ocean where she could lie invisible to all.

As he ate and slurped tea, Aubrey was unaware that a storm was brewing in their kitchen. And when it came, the dangerous words spilled out before Birdie could stop them.

'If only you could be more like the reverend,' she said.

Aubrey dropped the half-eaten sandwich that had been on its way to his mouth and it fell apart as it hit the plate. 'Bleedin' hell?' he said.

She grimaced but ploughed on regardless. 'I'm serious, Aubrey,' she said, ignoring the impending danger. 'The way he looks at Flora, he's always mooning over her, putting his arm around her. Watching out for her. If she trips he is suddenly there, a reassuring hand under her elbow, holding her up. When she sings in church he closes his eyes.' Birdie stood up, closed her eyes and swayed in the middle of the kitchen, her green dress and green apron rustling from side to side. 'He just forgets where he is; he's so filled up with love for her.' She opened her eyes and looked at Aubrey, who sat clutching the end of the table. 'One of the deacons has to cough to remind him to carry on with the sermon. Why can't you be like that with me?' challenged Birdie. 'You used to, when we first met.'

'Because, Birdie,' Aubrey stood up from the kitchen table, his chair scraping backwards on the linoleum with a resentful squeal and leaving a dark grey streak. He took three large steps and he was right in front of her. He held her chin tight between his fingers, lifting her face to his, hurting her with his pinch, 'I'm not some ball-less ponce that's going to let his wife wear the trousers and I know what you need, Birdie. You think that religious twat knows what a woman like you needs?'

The boys, knowing their father's anger, once unleashed, was unpredictable and could land anywhere, slunk down in their chairs, hoping he wouldn't turn on them. Gabe twisted the navy tie of his shirt around his fingers.

Birdie braced herself. This time it was her fault; she had started it and she would have to see it through. She deserved what was coming; her unhappiness was her perversity, not his.

But Aubrey had been in a good mood until the fight started and he had plans for where he wanted to take his good mood that afternoon and he wasn't about to let any tiff with Birdie stop him. So where normally he might have lost his temper with Birdie and then possibly the boys as well, he instead took the fight as the perfect excuse to get out of the house, to chase what he was after and not come back for some days. He smiled at his boys, a big broad boyish smile that invited them to have fun with him. The boys' shoulders relaxed slightly and they grinned back at their father. He picked up his trilby from where it sat on the kitchen dresser, slowly spun it on his finger and then put it on his head and walked out without another word.

Birdie stood as though she was standing in the middle of the cosmos and there was nothing in the universe that existed but her and her guilt. Once again she had driven him off. She and her dissatisfaction. And her loneliness.

Then he came back and stood for a minute at the end of the table. She couldn't read him; his face was expressionless so she didn't know what to brace for and she stiffened. He leant over and ruffled Mike's hair and he put his hat on Gabe's head, then he walked around the table, past Gabe, and swept Birdie into his arms. He leant her back as though they had tangoed and kissed her hard and long and she felt herself forget all her anger and melt for him.

'You think the reverend kisses his wife like that?' he growled in her ear. Then he took his hat back from Gabe's head, said, 'Thank you, son,' and walked out. She stood for a moment in the kiss and then she remembered he was probably off to another woman or to gamble or to drink.

'Eat your crusts, boys,' she said, and they didn't.

Let's go back to when Birdie had high hopes

Monday, 4 March 1929

Once Aubrey had treated her like there were no other women in the world. When Aubrey wanted to marry nineteen-year-old Birdie he told her that her curls were like sunshine and that her small waist was just right for him to encompass with his hands. He told her she had bowled him over backwards and he would never recover, he would never look at another girl because her beauty had blinded him to all others. His voice tripped over the words like he was singing her a song and she'd believed every word. Birdie knew his reputation and ignored all her misgivings. When she fell in through the front door breathless from the kiss he had given her on the porch, her father Claude had frowned at her and said, 'He's a skirt chaser and too old for you.'

She'd said, 'He's a larrikin, that's all.'

'A philandering one,' said Claude, and shook his head sadly. Birdie believed she had the power to change Aubrey where others had failed, and she wasn't the first or last girl in the world to think that about a man. So on the first Monday in March in 1929, a blistering day, she had put on the yellow dress that she had sewn with little daisies all around the bottom and held out her hand and he had lifted her up onto the 8.06 train and she'd taken off her straw hat and put her head out the window, ignoring the ashy steam and smoke that stung her eyes to tears and settled in her hair and clogged her skin and she let the wind cool the hotness rushing through her veins as the train hurtled towards the city of Melbourne. At Spencer Street Station he took her hand and led her to the Registry Office of Births Deaths and Marriages in Collins Street and, standing in a room with timber panelling and a window that needed washing to let the light in, and smelling smoky as if she had been barbequed, she had married Aubrey Mabbett, knowing it was against her parents' wishes because her parents, Elsie and Claude Mitchell, knew, like everyone else knew, that those Mabbett men could be as charming as a prince, which is why they were so good at sales, but they were as reliable as the weather reports on the wireless, and had tempers that would scorch the skin off a kangaroo.

Birdie had thought that even though they were getting married in the Registry, there would still be an organist, there would still be confetti and a bouquet, but what she got was a balding man with a sniffle who asked her to say she would honour and obey and pronounced them married and all it took was three minutes and twenty-seven seconds. As they left the office and walked down the stairs Aubrey must have seen the disappointment in her face because he said, 'Don't worry, Birdie sweetie, we'll have a proper church wedding back in Ballarat.'

'I'll sew a proper wedding dress, in silk, and I'll have my sister Viola as a bridesmaid.'

'Sure,' he said, 'if you think that dowdy religious sister of yours would make a good bridesmaid?' and before she could be shocked he had been so mean about her sister he put her arm through his, patted it and took her to a dark little hotel in Spencer Street, opposite the train station, where she followed him up creaky stairs to their room. Inside there was a bed pushed up against the wall and a dresser with a water jug and bowl for washing and a window that looked out onto a brick wall with an advertisement for Rinso Soap Flakes. Before Birdie could register her dissatisfaction, Aubrey was stripping her clothes from her with urgency, muttering her name over and over and she thought that without her he would dissolve and be nothing and, sure that this was the moment of his change, she forgot about the ugly room. He made love to her on the creaky bed and she could hear the men downstairs at the bar whooping as they drank too much beer and a train whistled from over the road signalling the new life that was conceived inside her.

Aubrey lay back and said, 'Oh, Birdie, what you do to me.'

And she said, 'Yes.'

Overall, though, she was disappointed both with her wedding and with the consummation of it. She wanted the church wedding with old Mister Hooley on the organ and a honeymoon somewhere delightful like Queenscliff, where one Saturday she had splashed in the sea as a child until she had stepped on a sharp piece of driftwood and cut her foot from one side of the sole to the other. And she had expected making love for the first time would make her feel like she could be someone new, that he would fill her up with himself and she would never feel empty again, but all she felt afterwards was that she was the same old Birdie.

On Tuesday they got back on the train and when they arrived in Ballarat on the 11.24 they walked to the little house in Humffray Street that he had rented for them at ten shillings a week. It was so small it seemed to Birdie to be a dolls' house next to the houses either side. His mother Gert had put a corned beef in the ice chest and a loaf of bread in the cupboard and she had left them a kettle, some Lipton's tea, a teapot and two plates, two sets of cutlery, two teacups and a bread knife. Birdie got them out; they were hungry and hadn't had breakfast and it was just past lunchtime. She sliced the marbled beef into jagged pieces with the serrated bread knife and she asked, 'So when will we do the church wedding? It needs to be soon, perhaps in a fortnight. Or a month; my mum would like a month to plan.'

And she scratched at the mozzie bite that had already swollen to a red lump on her arm and it bled. Aubrey didn't look at her, he looked at his corned beef sandwich instead and after too long he said, 'God has no place in my life, Birdie, and neither does any Luddite Baptist wowser church! I'd rather die of diphtheria before anyone gets me inside that mausoleum in Dawson Street.'

'Even to marry?'

'Especially to marry!' he'd said.

She sat in the only other chair and refused to eat. Food never satisfied her anyway so it didn't matter to her if she ate or not. When she had stayed like this for some hours and refused to speak to him, he became frustrated and he didn't know what to do with her blackness. She looked ugly now and not the bright yellow girl he had married, so he threw things.

She ducked.

As he threw things, his temper built. It started small, just a breeze and a solitary dark cloud that warned of more to come, and it built into gusts, which became a storm, and he let it because he wanted an excuse to go to the pub and drink away the sharp edges of her that he hadn't seen before he married her. He had thought her the most beautiful girl in Ballarat, a sparkling girl with white eyes and pale smooth skin. He had drunk in her legs, which curved so softly at the calves, and her small feet tucked into fashionable but still sensible blue and white saddle shoes. They were honest shoes and he saw that she didn't have any tricks up her sleeves like most of the women he had sex with; she was naive and refreshing and with her he was sure he could turn over a new leaf and become a good man, the man she thought he was.

But now he looked at her, he saw sharp edges everywhere. She was thin and her bones protruded, her mouth was pursed tight in a harsh streak, her eyes were sad and empty. What had possessed him to run off to Melbourne and marry her? He could have married any number of women.

Because it was the first time she'd seen him lose his temper, Birdie didn't know to stay out of the way and he swung his arm out and punched her in the jaw and her lip split and blood stained her yellow daisy dress. They were both shocked it had happened and he, horrified because he had sworn not to be his father, left the house, slamming the door behind him, and she thought he was leaving because he was horrified by her. She wouldn't be able to go out of the house for two weeks in case anyone saw the bruise. On Wednesday, Gert, seeming to know exactly what had happened without being told, let herself in the back door.

'Don't worry, he'll be back,' she'd said encouragingly, holding a chunk of ice wrapped in a hanky against Birdie's blackening jaw. 'His father was the same. You have to learn, love, not to set him off.'

His mum was right. Aubrey did come back. He came back three days later on Friday with wildflowers he'd picked down by the river that drooped with the shock of being yanked from their idyllic life watching taddies playing hide and seek and fat white-faced herons wading like children on the water's edge. Aubrey knelt on the floor and looked up at her from under his thick lashes; the curls on his forehead refused to kink up towards the sun and hung penitent and lank over his sad dark eyes.

He held the flowers in front of him and said, 'I won't lie, Birdie, you know I've been out and about drinking and whatnot but I'll never look at another woman again, I promise. I'll look after you and at least I'm honest about it, Birdie, and that's got to be a good thing, hasn't it? I can't live without you, Birdie – you know that, don't you? Marrying you was probably the best thing I've done, Birdie. You've made a man of me, Birdie.'

And she'd thought about the last three days when he'd been gone. The emptiness of the house had been loud and her heart had withered at its edges as she'd realised he wasn't there. The bed was too big without him in it and she'd felt she was shipwrecked on tides and what a dreadful failure she'd be if she was unable to keep her husband after only one day. She'd thought of the shame she'd feel in front of her parents who didn't approve of her running off and marrying him one little bit and about what his mother had said and how she must stop driving him away. She'd looked at him and saw how pleading his smile was and how desperately he wanted her forgiveness but was too proud to ask for it and she was filled with guilt and didn't tell him the flowers were actually boneseed weeds and she'd reached out her hand to take the injured flowers and completely forgot about her own bruises.

Nine months later the labour pains started and when she went to the hospital, Aubrey went to the Unicorn to celebrate. She named the baby Michael after the archangel. When Aubrey came to visit her two days later, he was plastered and furious that she had given his son a religious name. She lied and said she'd already filled in the registration forms and the hospital clerk had already sent them off in the post and there was nothing could be done about it now. Then when the next son was born the same thing happened again. He went to the pub and turned up three days later and Birdie had named and registered the boy after another angel, Gabriel. She hoped with two sons Aubrey would settle down.

Fatherhood didn't change Aubrey.

Not one iota.

But Birdie now had two things in life that didn't disappoint her. They were Mike and Gabe. When Aubrey was in his moods it was Mike and Gabe who made it possible for her to get out of bed in the morning, to make the porridge with salt and butter, to wash his white work shirts and the baby's nappies, to breathe the air. When Aubrey hit out at her she stood and took it and when he hit out at the boys she threw herself in front of him to protect them. Sometimes he would push her aside and lunge at the boys and afterwards Birdie would take the boys straight to the doctor, making sure to not use Doctor Litton or Doctor Quimby because they went to the church. She took them to Doctor Salter, a Catholic, so that no one she knew would find out what was happening in her house and Doctor Salter would patch up her and the boys without a word. It wasn't his business how another man ran his castle.

This was her marriage to Aubrey Mabbett. A seesaw of rage that rose till it overspilled and he stormed out, then a quietness when he came back full of love for her and her golden curls and they both forgot the storms. When it was bad she thought she couldn't keep going, but she couldn't leave him because the shame would be too great. And what would she and the boys live on? When it was good she thought she was the luckiest woman in the world because he really did act as though she was the only one.

When Hazel makes a silly decision

Sunday, 12 November 1939

By November, summer had landed with madness. The pavement was sticky, the ground brown, the grass crisp and brittle, and men in Ballarat felt justified in having a few more Ballarat Bertie's bitters to cope with the heat. The women in church waved paper fans or hymn books in front of their faces and Joseph prayed for rain. But God didn't hear or was concerned with other things and the temperature soared to over 40 degrees Celsius and on Sunday the heat cooled but only by two degrees to 38.

With the heat everyone was short tempered, even Flora. On Sunday afternoon after lunch Joseph could see Connie was particularly annoying her mother, so he said she could go with him to visit ill members of his congregation up at the hospital.

'It's always cool in the hospital,' he said. 'But you have to be quiet and only speak when you're spoken to.' He put on his hat and slapped it down.

'I don't know how you can think of going out in this heat,' said Flora.

'The sick still need ministering to,' he said. 'Come on, Connie.'

Despite the heat she skipped alongside him, trying to match his strides, up Sturt Street to Drummond Street. The streets were empty, everyone having scurried home to their electric fans and darkened rooms after church. They came to the hospital, a big red brick building that sat imposingly on the corner. Connie couldn't wait to be inside the cool building; perhaps she could pretend her throat was sore and one of the nurses would give her jelly or an icy pole.

Just as they were about to walk inside she saw Gabe's father standing beside the rose bush smoking. She called out, 'Hello, Mister Mabbett,' and he barely waved back. He didn't tip his hat and walked off as though he'd only stopped for a moment on his way to somewhere else. Connie didn't see him about-turn as soon as he was sure she and her father were inside. But she was soon peering out the second-floor window and staring down at him there beside the rose bush as her father gave communion to Missus Jensen, who'd had another baby, which thankfully was in the nursery so Connie didn't have to pretend to like it. She watched Mister Mabbett as demons danced in the sky above him and kept the angels from coming near. That's how she knew Mister Mabbett was up to something no good. Mister Mabbett waved to someone on the floor below her and then he scurried off and Connie, bored, had to find something else to amuse her. The hospital wasn't as exciting as she'd hoped it would be.

Aubrey was a man who needed space in every part of his life. Without space and freedom, he couldn't breathe properly. This is what he told himself as he took out a second smoke and lit it beside the rose bush that offered no shade. For the last two

Sundays he'd fought with Birdie over lunch. She'd started one and he'd started the other, and those fights had led him to this spot by the rose bush both times.

God, he must be a mad dog standing out in this heat, but there was something different about her, something that had made him willing to wait. He hoped she would see him soon through one of the hospital windows; he could get out of this blasted heat and get his reward and finally make her dance. And then, well, then he would probably forget about her like he usually did. He rubbed the pink hot skin of his bare arms and didn't notice Connie watching him.

He hadn't been standing there long when Hazel walked over to the window in Ward 6 on the first floor and saw him. She smiled and adjusted her uniform and apron, pulling them tight over her hips, and the four men in the beds watched appreciatively as her luxurious bottom wiggled from side to side. Hazel never wanted to be a nurse. She wanted to be a ballet dancer with her unruly red hair pulled smooth and tight into a bun. She had read everything she could about dancing in the book *The Dancers Technical Manual and Dictionary of Ballet* and she knew all the positions by heart and practised them daily.

Sadly, Hazel didn't have a dancer's body. As a child she had been a freckled solid girl with a large friendly smile who stomped through the world in her boots and landed with a thump when she tried to pirouette. Her mother, not wanting her to have dreams that would only let her down, had ignored Hazel's pleas for dance lessons.

Hazel grew into a young woman with inviting hips and strong arms and at her mother's insistence she moved from the family cottage in Daylesford to the nurses' quarters in the Ballarat Base Hospital, taking a position as a nursing student. Becoming a nurse was three years of training and sitting exams in Melbourne every

January. Hazel had three months to go until her last exams. At twenty-two she still lacked the body of a dancer. But she did have the personality.

Hazel loved to be on show – well, really she loved to *be* the show. She was forever in trouble with Matron Strickland for wearing lipstick on duty, for having powder on her face and clips in her hair, for turning a step into an arabesque as she swept into a ward, which wasn't easy in her starched nurse's uniform. The other nursing trainees were reduced to trembling whimpers as soon as Matron Strickland came into a ward or passed them in a corridor, but Hazel held her head high and firm and controlled her nerves, knowing she was the most promising trainee of their small cohort of four, the one who got the highest marks in the exams.

The three other nurse trainees in Hazel's year, Mary, Beatie and Ena, hung around Hazel like puppies hoping to catch some of whatever it was she had. They lapped up her drops of attention, and asked her advice on boys, clothes, make-up and life, and the more attention Hazel had, the more she bubbled and shone. The boys they walked out with thought Hazel was exceptional. But Hazel didn't want to tie herself to a boy. She wanted to go somewhere and she wanted a man to take her. None of the boys had a clue that to Hazel they were only boys and she, secretly, had a man, a real grown fellow in his thirties, maybe forties.

He'd come into Emergency on a Friday night about a month earlier, holding his hand up high as blood dribbled down to his elbow, giving his white shirt a red trim.

'Been out fighting the Gerries, have you?' she said crossly.

'As good as,' he'd said and he'd looked at her and smiled gently as though he was a humble war hero whose heroic deed had just been found out despite his efforts to conceal it. She nearly fell into the delusion and had to shake herself and remember he had simply been in a pub brawl.

'Well, let's have a look at you – this way,' she'd said. She took him behind the pink curtain and sat him on the wooden chair in the cubicle. She took his hand in her own and turned it over and he unclenched his fists. His knuckles were red and open with cuts and he had a gash across his palm.

'Looks like an ordinary pub brawl to me,' she said. 'It's not what we're here to do, you know. There are people with real injuries.'

'This other fella,' he said, 'claimed Hitler could be reasoned with. He said the war was unnecessary and, well, that's when I lost it, I suppose. I threw him onto the billiard table at the Unicorn. Can you really blame me?' he said as he looked up at her through thick black lashes.

Certainly not Hazel. She could see him as a hero, she could see him punching Hitler straight in the snout and ending the war.

'Well, I admire your honesty in admitting what caused your injury,' she said.

'You do?' he asked and he smiled again and she felt her bones just melt into that smile.

'It looks like it needs stitches,' she said, and she turned and walked out of the cubicle leaving him and his smile back in hero-land.

She found Doctor Blagg in the pharmacy room and told him she had a patient who needed stitches. He groaned and said, 'The six o'clock swill – the ruin of this country. We didn't have this problem when pubs closed at the same time as work. Now they race from work to the pub and down as much as they can in the forty-five minutes left to them before the pub closes. I have no patience for them. Well, come on then.' He walked out of the pharmacy and Hazel followed him back to the cubicle where he hurriedly put two stitches in the man's deepest cut, taking no care to be gentle, but the man only grimaced and still managed to wink once at Hazel.

A week later he'd come into Outpatients saying his stomach hurt and Doctor Blagg was puzzled that even though the man was doubled over in pain he could find nothing wrong with him. Hazel stood in the corner of the cubicle waiting for Doctor Blagg to prescribe a remedy which she would fetch and administer. Doctor Blagg acted as though she was invisible; she was just a nurse, and a trainee to boot, so it was beneath him to acknowledge her. She served no purpose other than to know what he needed and to pass it to him before he needed it.

Now he said, 'A good dose of heroin cough syrup, nurse, and a glass of stout.' This was Doctor Blagg's remedy for anything he couldn't diagnose. Doctor Blagg patted his coat pockets to make sure he had picked up all his equipment and she looked at the man, whose name she still didn't know, and he gazed at her so intently that she knew for certain he was there for her, claiming her, and as soon as the pink curtain had swung shut behind the doctor she'd turned a little pirouette in her nurse's uniform and he'd clapped and she'd hurried out to get him his dose of Bayer heroin hydrochloride and a glass of stout, holding her arms tight over her chest to control the beating of her heart against her ribs.

Two weeks ago he'd stood by the rose bush, his smoke dangling from his lips, and an hour later when she'd finished her shift she'd looked and he was still there. She'd gone out to him and he'd taken her by the arm and walked her around the lake and asked her all about herself and no man had done that before.

But when he'd whispered in her ear, 'Your name?' suddenly she hadn't wanted to say her name. She wanted to be someone else.

So she'd said, 'Giselle.'

He had reached out for her hand and bowed like a knight. 'Giselle,' he'd said, 'I am your duke.'

Last week he'd been there again, and again they'd walked around the lake and when they'd got back to the door to the nurses' quarters he'd pulled her to him and kissed her and her heart had danced. She thought it might be true love.

This hot Sunday afternoon she looked out the window at him standing by the rose bush. He looked up at her from under his fringe of black curls, drew on his cigarette, and she felt her heart leap towards him. She caught his eye and then tapped her watch. Her shift would finish in thirty minutes. She pointed to the back of the hospital where the nurses' quarters were and he nodded. All men with the exception of doctors or priests were strictly forbidden in the nurses' quarters.

She kept an eye on her watch as the minutes ticked down, then ran to the back door and opened it to him. He tossed away his smoke. She put her fingers to her lips and whispered, 'Shhh.' He followed her up the stairs to her tiny room. As soon as they were both inside she quietly shut the door and he took her wrist and spun her towards him and she felt her feet fly up as she twirled into him. He leant the length of his body against her, pushing her up against the door. She could feel the heat of his bones and muscle as he leant into her. He took her wrist and lifted her arm above her head in fifth position and kissed her as though he was starved for her and only she could keep him alive and Hazel thought, *This is what it means to be a woman*, and she felt she was ready for it.

He lifted her up as though she was nothing more than a little bit of a thing and she flung out her arm with her fingers held just right and her toes pointed perfectly as he carried her to the single cast-iron hospital bed that was pressed up against the wall of her small room and it groaned as he laid her weight onto it. She swept her finger gracefully through the air to her lips to shush the bed and he, realising the bed was untrustworthy and would give them away, lifted her back up, his hands tight against her waist, and kissing her he held her up against the wall and lifted her leg until it curved gracefully around his back and for a moment he held her foot in his hand as though he was holding her heart.

Hazel had waited her entire life for this dance. His kisses trailed down her body until he was kneeling before her, softly kissing the inside of her thigh, up up where it was warmer warmer closer closer to her soul. He undid his trousers and stood up and they fell around his legs, a discarded costume. He was ready for the next act – he held her tight in his arm and with his other hand he reached down and pulled up the soft silkiness of her slip and as he did so his fingers brushed against her bare skin and the softness of his touch made her heart leap in a grand jeté and then he was inside her and she cried out with the surprise of it but he quickly put his hand over her mouth to stifle her cry, so they had a silent stifled love. He moved rhythmically and she was sure she could hear the orchestra playing *Giselle My Giselle* for her as they danced together. He moved his hand from her mouth and again held her arm over her head and he kissed her over and over and then he sighed and shook and she realised they had reached the coda and the dance was over, he had withdrawn, he was letting her go and she felt so sad and empty and wished they could have danced forever.

She wanted to talk, to say so many things to him, but she dared not make a sound. They all knew Matron's twitching nose could sniff out when her rules were being broken. Hazel rested in his arms on the bed, both lying as still as they could so it wouldn't squeak, and her mind filled with the repercussions of what she'd just done. Would she get pregnant? What if he didn't really love her? What if he didn't marry her? She realised finally that she, a single girl with a career, had placed her future in his hands. She got up and opened the door and looked out into the corridor and seeing it was empty she motioned for him to arrange his clothes and to follow her back the way he'd come.

Aubrey had not expected to be her first man. She had seemed so worldly, her red hair so fiery. He was filled with guilt and saw all the expectation in her eyes for a future.

'We'll marry, Giselle,' he promised, completely forgetting about Birdie.

She smiled like the sun.

When Aubrey is in a pickle

Monday, 20 November 1939

Even Connie could have told you that if you were silly enough to open a shop on the north side of Sturt Street you were sure to go broke.

No one knew why this was the case. Was it because the Ballarat winter came without warning and overstayed its welcome by a good four months? And during these long bitter winters the sun struggled to warm the north side of Sturt Street, and shoppers, already shivering in their coats and rubbing their hands together or holding them in their armpits for warmth, didn't want to shop in the dark iciness that was the north side. Was it because in the short blistering summer the shade was a lie that provided no relief and so shoppers felt cheated before they even looked at the price of merchandise?

Or was it because the shops that mattered had, without any real thought, established themselves on the south side where they were lined up side by side in a neat long row of tantalising windows, whereas on the north side the shops were broken up and scattered willy-nilly between other businesses?

In winter people who lived on the north side would scurry across the vast main road of Sturt Street, the blustering winds cutting their cheeks red, their eyes smarting with salty tears from the icy blasts and their noses purple and dripping. With one hand they held their coats tight across their chests as a shield against the gusting gales and with the other they held onto their hats that desperately tried to fly to freedom, pressing them down hard on their scalps. In summer they crossed Sturt Street still with their heads down to protect themselves from the angry sun that wanted to burn the flesh from their faces, and they held their hats against the vile north winds that whipped against their bare arms and legs. People who lived on the south side commended themselves on their good sense in living on the south side so they didn't have to bother to cross Sturt Street to shop at all.

The streets to the south and the north of Sturt Street had the same names differentiated only by a 'South' or 'North' tacked onto the end of the street name, and the houses had the same numbers in both the north and south ends, so mail often landed where it wasn't meant to land and both sides were united in complaining about this stupidity of planning. However, despite all its setbacks, the north side of Sturt Street had its own right to pride because it could claim at least two pubs, if not more, in every block. So when the men who lived in the streets ending in 'North' had drunk Ballarat Bertie's until they were blind, they didn't have to risk their lives crossing Sturt Street, enormous like a sea, its curb somewhere far away on a blurry horizon. The south-side men did have to cross and they set off like Moses crossing the Red Sea. They tottered and stumbled, swaying into each other as they traversed the immense main thoroughfare. There was nothing to grab hold of to keep them upright except each other until they made it to the other side and fell gratefully against a lamppost, which they clung to for dear life.

Sturt Street, wide as it was, narrowed at Grenville Street and became Bridge Street. If Sturt Street was fat Jack Sprat then Bridge Street was his lean wife. Bridge Street was a modest little street that rose unassumingly to Bakery Hill, where ten thousand miners had protested against the mining licences, their harsh working and living conditions and, forgotten by the history writers, they also protested the planned closure of many of the eight hundred or so illegal pubs that existed in the town centre alone. Yet now all that history from a mere eighty or so years ago had been replaced not with monuments to bravery or reminders of the dogged heroism that initiated the country's political democracy, but with shops. Because Bridge Street was small, all the shops had done well regardless of which side of the street they were on.

Mister Faull's shoe shop at number 20 cherished customer loyalty alongside value and quality. In Faull's, customers were provided with plush velvet seats to ease their bottoms while they put their feet into shoe after shoe, umming and ahhing and tossing up between the shoe that was ugly but comfortable and the shoe that was fashionable but bit at their toes. Connie sometimes lingered outside Faull's while Flora was at the grocer's, her nose pressed up against the window, and she dreamt of getting a brand-new pair of red leather mary janes instead of always wearing someone's hand-me-downs. Even her Sunday shoes were hand-me-downs, usually Lydia's old shoes, or shoes passed on to Flora by one of the church women. Sometimes Mister Mabbett would see her standing there and he would wink and come outside with a sticky boiled lolly and she'd open her mouth wide and he'd pop the sweet right in. Then he would go back inside and she'd watch through the window as he put shoes on women's feet, laughing and smiling with them until Flora, having finished her shopping, called her to come and help carry.

The shop ran the length of the block and had two entrances: its main entrance on Bridge Street, and a back entrance on Little Bridge Street right opposite where the Coliseum Theatre had once proudly sat. This meant Mister AT Faull insisted on two sales staff working the back end of the shop and two at the front end, and each day the teams rotated.

Aubrey Mabbett arrived for work at Faull's at 8.00 a.m. sharp as he had done every morning since he had begun his apprenticeship at fourteen. As a fourteen year old he had been given chores like washing the windows, sweeping floors and unpacking deliveries in the storeroom. Now he was head sales clerk, and no one in his family had ever been head anything, so Aubrey felt he had done all right. Aubrey had a key to the back entrance because as head sales clerk he was often the first to arrive and the last to leave, so he always let himself in through the Little Bridge Street entrance.

As he made his way to the staff cloakroom, he took the opportunity to walk through the shop, looking at the displays as if he was a customer. He checked that every pair of shoes was looking straight ahead as it sat on its shelf; if not, he stopped and adjusted the shoes so they stood proudly to attention. He trailed his fingers across the leather to make sure no shoes were where they shouldn't be, that all the men's shoes were on the right side of the shop and the women's on the left and the children's in their own section at the back, where there was also a jar of Brown's boiled lollies, which he gave to the children, telling the good ones the lolly was for their excellent behaviour during their fitting and telling the bad ones the lolly was because their mother was so pretty.

After his inspection, Aubrey stood in the middle of the shop and breathed deeply so the leathery smell filled his lungs. There was no perfume, not even sausages cooking, that smelt better to him than the smell of leather. It made him feel as though he was more than he was.

Mister Faull liked to have two female sales clerks and two males. He believed some male customers didn't like to be served by women and some preferred it and the same with the women customers, some of whom preferred a male and some a female assistant. And some customers like Missus Freeman would refuse to be served by anyone other than Aubrey. Aubrey liked that. Aubrey understood women and their shoes. Sometimes when he was in the storeroom alone he would take a cardboard box, lifting it carefully in both his hands, his fingers resting against the corners of the box ever so lightly so as not to dent it. He would carry the box to the wooden unpacking table and, after setting it down, would slowly open the lid, then he would gently, with just his fingertips, lift back the tissue paper nest and reveal the shoes. He would lean down close and breathe in the leathery perfume of the new shoes, he would suck those smells of virgin leather right down deep into his lungs, until the odour of leather wafted around his bones like smoke around a fire. Then he would run his fingers along the soft kid, he would trace the circumference of the gleaming metal button at the side of the shoe and then he would pick the shoe up and feel the weight of its heel in his palm. He would run his finger over the seam of the toe cap and the suppleness of the tongue, along the crisp edge of the topline and the smoothness of the quarter. Just before he put the shoe back in its bed he would hold it up to his nose and once more breathe in the warm woody fragrance of the shoe.

Oh yes, Aubrey knew all about shoes and he knew that all you needed to know about women could be learnt from their shoes. And he had learnt it all. He would say this sometimes to the junior sales clerk, Clancy, when, in their breaks, they stood smoking in Coliseum Walk: 'My female customers never leave without buying at least one pair of shoes.'

Aubrey knew that Missus Freeman always bought the sensible court shoes but secretly hankered for gleaming patent leather mary janes like the ones she'd worn as a young girl. He knew that Missus Trebilcock always wanted the shiniest latest shoes but once home was as dissatisfied with them as she was with her husband and would be back the next week for more. He knew that Giselle, who he had bedded again just yesterday after another fight with Birdie over why he couldn't be more like the reverend, needed shoes light enough to let her dance. When Aubrey was kneeling at a woman's feet as she tried on the shoes he suggested for her, he was Prince Charming and only their foot would do. He made each and every one of them a princess no matter if their ankle was thick or thin, bony or plump, no matter if it was sweet young Lydia Starr who he knew couldn't afford to purchase any of the shoes she tried on, or tumbly, giggly Missus Sackmore who was a friend of his mum's and called him Young Aubrey and always greeted him with a pat on the cheek and 'My you've grown into a handsome young man'.

At nine he opened first the back door and then the front door and there was Missus Trebilcock already mooning over the Joy of Life shoes in the window. He noticed her floral dress that hung low over her breasts and clung to her hips and her bright red lipstick. As he pushed the door open and secured it in place with the stopper she smiled and ran her tongue slowly along her teeth, partly for him and partly to make sure no lipstick lingered there. A gust of dusty hot air filled Aubrey's lungs. Missus Trebilcock put her hand on the glass window – he'd have to get Winnie to clean the greasy imprint later – as she bent her leg up behind her and fiddled with her shoe as though it was the most uncomfortable shoe in the world. He had sold her that shoe only last month.

He had delivered it to her home and Mister Faull had said how lucky he was to have someone like Aubrey who was always willing to go the extra mile for customers and he had laughed his deep crackly laugh and said, 'Home delivered shoes – fresh baked – hah hah.'

Aubrey had home delivered a lot of pairs of shoes over the years he had worked at Faull's. If Missus Trebilcock was buying new shoes this morning she would want them home delivered later in the day and that was a problem because Aubrey was already in a pickle as it was. He'd been stewing for a week. A week and one day, to be precise.

A week ago he'd promised Giselle they'd marry. It had given him a bit of a shock that he'd done that. No one else had had that impact on him – apart from Birdie, of course. But with Giselle he was a different man. With Giselle he could be decent and loyal, he just knew it, and he just had to have both of them – and why not? He'd heard in some religions a man could have as many wives as he needed and could love them all. There was nothing Aubrey loved more than women, apart from shoes. But now he was in a bit of a sticky situation given he was already married. He would sort it out somehow. He always did.

'A pair of those nice Joy of Life shoes, please, Aubrey,' said Missus Trebilcock, walking past him. He watched as she angled her ample bottom and held it for a moment, partly for him and partly to position herself to fall into one of the plush velvet seats. 'If you think they'll suit me.'

'In which colour?' asked Aubrey, as though he hadn't noticed her bottom.

'What colour do you think would suit me best?' she said, looking straight at him from under her lashes as she crossed one leg slowly over the other.

'Blue, I think,' he said, ignoring her demanding gaze.

'It's already awfully hot out,' she said, taking off her hat and flicking her hair out in black rushing waves. Aubrey took a deep breath as she arched her back and let her hair fly from side to side, her thin summer dress stretched over her bosom, her lips parted, but right at this moment he had enough on his plate with a wife and a fiancée. He escaped to the darkness of the stockroom. He stood for a moment to gather himself. She would think he was looking for the shoes but he knew exactly where they were. He took some deep breaths and then reached up for the box he needed. When he carried it back into the shop she had her stockinged foot out mid-air, waiting for him. He knelt down and took her foot in his hand. From under the stocking he could feel the warmth of her skin soft against his fingers and he slipped her foot easily into the indulgent blue shoe.

'The treasurer says we must tighten our belts because of the war,' said Missus Trebilcock.

'A beautiful woman always needs shoes,' said Aubrey, but he knew that there would never be enough shoes for these feet.

'Oh yes,' she said eagerly, taking his words as permission to ignore the country's treasurer.

She leant forward and put her hand gently on his arm and let it rest there. 'I'll have them home delivered.'

Aubrey stood up and put his hands in his pockets to secure himself to the spot.

'I'm sorry, Missus Trebilcock, but with the belt-tightening I can no longer do home delivery.' He watched her face turn ashen.

'Are you sure?'

He wasn't sure and he teetered back and forth on his soles. He really did love women but he was in his pickle, he'd barely been able to consume anything other than beer for a week and didn't need any more complications.

'Jocelyn,' he leant over and whispered in her ear, 'I'm quite sure,' and he thought not of Birdie but of Giselle.

'But I've only come for the home delivery,' she said like a thwarted child, and she took her foot out of the Joy of Life and put it back in her own perfectly good shoe, picked up her bag and strode out of the store with large angry steps.

Young Clancy was at Aubrey's side in a moment. 'Mister Mabbett, what happened? You've never lost a sale.'

'Turns out,' said Aubrey, staring at the empty doorway, 'I still have something to learn about women. Turns out that you can't give all the women what they want all the time.'

Aubrey was disorientated and could barely think of anything other than his two problems: Giselle and Birdie. At lunchtime he opened *The Courier* and read it while taking a bite out of the egg sandwich Birdie had made for him. The egg tasted bitter, perhaps it was turning. He scrunched it up in its greaseproof paper, turning it into a cricket ball, which he tossed across the room into the bin. He slurped his hot tea and continued to read the paper. Two boys had started a wrestling match in front of Messer and Opie's clothes shop and had gone through the window. Silly buggers. He laughed and turned the page, He read the treasurer's plea, *Australians must be warned against undue optimism. Belts must be tightened. There is no place for indulgence in rosy and impossible dreams in this time of war.* Bloody lot a rich pollie knows about belt tightening. He turned the page on the treasurer and right in front of him was the answer he was searching for. It was so plain as it stared out at him; why hadn't he thought of it sooner? He could have saved himself a week of pain. He folded up the paper and went back to work and at 3.00 p.m. he was fitting Missus Grant, who hadn't had a pair of new shoes in just forever and she knew it was a luxury given the treasurer's call for austerity what with the war and all but a woman must have some shoes mustn't she because after all one couldn't go barefoot.

'No, certainly not a woman of substance like yourself,' said Aubrey, knowing the pair she'd had on her feet when she walked into the shop were only purchased a mere three months ago and he had delivered them himself. When he'd carried her to her couch she had giggled like a schoolgirl and he had watched as her eyes filled with light, pleased with himself that he'd put the light in them. Now he gently clasped her foot in his fingers, he gently massaged every stretched tendon and every tight muscle and he heard her sigh as all her worries for her son, who had signed up, lifted from her and she didn't have to worry any more and Aubrey slipped her foot into the black Joy of Life shoe where it belonged and she wiped the tears from the edges of her eyes and looked at him and smiled.

'I'm so sorry, Missus Grant,' he said, 'but I must get Nancy to ring you up.' Missus Grant's shoulders slumped, taking back the weight they had come in with. He kissed her hand so as not to leave her without anything.

He saw the Starr girl standing outside the shop as she sometimes did, her nose pressed hard against the window and he grabbed a handful of the boiled lollies. 'Put your hands together and close your eyes,' he said and she did and he dropped the handful of lollies into her palms and laughed at her delighted shock. 'Wait,' he said, and he got a piece of brown paper for her to wrap them in.

Then he scooted to the stockroom where he found a pair of size 8 Joy of Life shoes in russet and slipped them under his jacket. He knew the shoes would be the right size. He could tell a woman's foot size with one look. He went upstairs and put the shoebox into his lunch satchel. He felt the pain of the beautiful cardboard box as he squished and dented its sides to fit it in the satchel, but he got them in. Then he went next door to the office and knocked on the door and when Mister Faull opened it, Aubrey stepped inside and resigned without notice and given the circumstances what could Mister Faull say apart from how much he would miss Aubrey and how Aubrey would always have a job at Faull's once this darned nasty business with Hitler was over.

When Birdie finds hope in a duffle bag

Monday, 20 November 1939

Aubrey walked to the Army Enlistment Office that had been set up at the School of Mines and stood in the queue. There were three men in front of him and then it was his turn. He stared at the government poster on the wall: '*I've joined up. What about you?*' When he got to the front of the queue he looked down at the balding head bent over a typewriter and said, 'I am here to enlist in the City of Ballarat Regiment,' as though he was the only man in Ballarat to have done so. The clerk didn't look up at him, he just pulled a new sheet of paper from the pile beside him, fed it into the typewriter and began typing, only pausing to ask Aubrey questions.

'Name?

'Age?

'Place of birth?

'Occupation?

'Are you a natural born British subject?

'Next of kin?

'Have you been convicted of a criminal offence?'

The man asked the questions in a bored monotone and it was hard for Aubrey to keep his optimism in the face of the man's obvious dejection, but Aubrey was determined to enjoy this moment of giving himself to country and king and escaping the pickle he'd got himself into. The man pulled the sheet of paper from the typewriter and the typewriter groaned. Still not looking at Aubrey, he placed the form in front of him, then put a fountain pen on the paper.

'Sign here and here.'

Aubrey did and the man also signed.

'Take the form to that queue for your medical,' said the bald head, his finger pointing to the left, and Aubrey joined the next queue and was declared fit for class A1, which Aubrey was sure had to be the best. At the next queue he watched as clothes were stuffed into a duffle bag.

'Your kit,' the soldier said, dumping a duffle bag heavily onto the trestle table between them. 'Report back here next Monday morning at 6.00 a.m. sharp.'

Just one more week and Aubrey's problems would be solved. He stuffed his lunch bag with the shoes inside the duffle bag and walked home to Humffray Street, going down Grant Street and then straight up Peel Street. With his kit slung over his shoulder, a smoke dangling from his lips, his final pay in his pocket, he was already a hero. And being a hero, he just had to stop at the Centenary and then The Grapes and let the boys know he had joined up.

After he had spent his pay, he visited his mother and her sobbing caused him to leave quickly, so he continued home and congratulated himself on choosing Birdie as his wife. She was beautiful, there was no denying that, and he knew she would never cheat on him. He could trust Birdie to wait while he was away. Giselle was the opposite of Birdie. Life was a great dance for Giselle and

Aubrey desperately wanted to dance with her. She could make him a different man; he wasn't angry when he was with Giselle, she filled him with floating peacefulness. He would see Giselle at least one last time, maybe two, before next Monday.

As he walked, his shoes tapping on the road, he thought of the women who came into the shoe shop. Once he had just made it out of Missus Hunt's back door as her husband walked in the front, and Judyth Yarrow had dug her nails into his skin and bit at his neck and left marks that if he wasn't careful he'd have to explain to Birdie. Jocelyn always had a whisky ready for him as she pretended for an hour that he was her husband and not fusty old Selwyn Trebilcock who had whiskers growing out his ears and squinty eyes that made it impossible for him to see anyone's needs but his own.

None of those women would be trustworthy. But Birdie would be, he could see it in her. She would maintain his home and care for his sons; she would keep them safe. His father had always said to him that when he took a wife he should look for his mother. And he had, he realised, and he smiled at the trees, sullen and drooping from the day's heat. Just as his mother had looked after his father no matter what, so would Birdie look after him.

He determined then and there that he would give up Giselle, break it off with her before any real damage was done. He'd see her one last time, though. Frustrated that he couldn't find a way to have both of them, he kicked at the dirt on the road. He turned into his street. How lucky he was to have Birdie to come home to, and as he was thinking these sweet thoughts about Birdie, he walked in the back door through the laundry and into the kitchen and threw his duffle bag onto the kitchen table. Gabe and Mike were at the table eating mutton stew with large chunks of potato that sat like islands in the stewy sea and they shuffled their plates, their chairs and themselves further up the table because they couldn't tell what sort of mood he was in. Birdie was stirring custard on the kookaburra stove top. Her hips and bottom swayed gently with the stirring of the spoon and even in her godawful grey-green dress he felt himself wanting her. He waited for her to turn around; she was taking her sweet time about it, punishing him for coming home late.

'How's it going, boys?' he said. 'I see you started dinner without me.'

Birdie turned then. 'Well, if we waited for you we'd never eat, would we?'

Her blue eyes were dark, almost black.

'Now, now, Birdie,' he said. 'Don't be like that. I'm here now, aren't I? And you're exaggerating, as usual.'

'You're gone more than you're here,' she spat.

'Well, I can be gone again if you can't be nice,' he said.

'For how long?' she said, her hands on her hips and she glared at the duffle bag. She knew what it meant. 'How long are you here for this time?'

'As a matter of fact I –'

'I wasn't actually asking,' she said. She got a bowl from the dresser and slammed it onto the table and poured a ladle of stew into it. 'You'll have to move that bag if you want to eat. You know the war's only just started. It could be over before you finish your training. I don't know why all you men are so eager to rush off. It's as if any excuse is good enough to get away from your responsibilities at home.'

'Now, now,' said Aubrey as he propped the bag up against the wall. The smell of the meat, the turnips, carrots, onions and potatoes wafted around him, making him dizzy, or perhaps it was the beer he'd drunk.

'God, Birdie, I'll miss your cooking. You're a good woman, Birdie, you know that, you've got it all. You've got looks, you can keep house, you gave me two fine sons.' And he meant it. He didn't know why he lost his temper with Birdie sometimes. He couldn't bear to even glimpse himself when he did. Hitting her was cowardly and cruel and after doing so, he would make sure not to catch his reflection in the shop windows on his way to the pub because if he did he didn't know what he would say to himself. But he couldn't control it; it would come on him without warning, just as it had with his father. 'It's just what us Mabbett men are like,' he told himself. Only drinking could numb his shame and it wasn't just the drinking that made him feel better. At the pub the men slapped each other's backs, laughed as though the world and everything in it was theirs. 'Kings of our castles,' they agreed with each other. 'It may not be much of a castle but each and every thing in it is mine.' And by *things* they meant their wives and children. They talked about keeping their missus and kids in line, about how women were indeed the weaker sex and didn't understand the responsibility placed on them, the men, who had the thankless task of being the leaders of their households, the workforce, politics and the world, and with all these burdens, well, sometimes a man just had to let off steam. By the time Aubrey had spent a good few hours at the pub he knew that he was a good husband, a man who wore the trousers and had acted in the only way he could. He was a man who needed outside interests to help him cope with his burdens and he would take a room at the Unicorn for a few days.

But this was the night of his enlistment and he deserved a nice time with Birdie; it might be their last in a long time. After the children went to bed Aubrey took Birdie's hand and even though she strained away from him, he pulled her into the bedroom, lifted her onto the bed, removed her house shoes, the ones he had got at the end of the season, on sale and even cheaper with his staff discount, and he gently placed his hands around her feet and massaged away all her misgivings and resentment. Then when he saw her soften and a smile begin at the corners of her lips, he said, 'You know I love you, Birdie. You know there'll never be anyone but you,' and he leant her back against the pillows and kissing her feet, then her calves, then kissing the inside of her thighs he felt her melt into him and he couldn't wait to take off their clothes so he pulled aside the silky panties she had made herself so he could fill her with himself and he said, 'It may be the last time, Birdie. Who knows what will happen at war?' And then he wished he hadn't said that because she began to cry.

While Aubrey slept the sleep of a man who had spent himself and solved a problem, Birdie, who hadn't slept at all, crawled out of bed and, ignoring the chill in the night air, pulled her nightie around her chest, slid her feet into her chenille slippers and crept down the hallway to the kitchen and flicked on the light. The kitbag was still leaning against the wall like a visitor waiting to be asked to sit and have tea and she grabbed the drawstring top and hoisted it rudely up onto the table. She glared at the bag, giving it the full weight of her anger. Aubrey must have lied about his age. He was thirty-nine years old – four years too old to sign up. Leaving her alone for days at a time wasn't good enough for him. Now he had to go and leave her good and proper with two little boys to raise when there was no good reason he should. He might not be a perfect husband like Joseph Starr but Aubrey was still her husband and many girls would be glad of him.

She hated that duffle bag and everything in it. She held down the toggle that clasped the drawstring and loosened it, opening the bag up, and reached inside its darkness and pulled out Aubrey's leather lunch satchel. She sighed. If she didn't empty it, any left-over food would start to smell, so she undid the buckles and reached in for the greaseproof paper she wrapped his sandwiches in and any old fruit, but instead pulled out a shoebox. She opened the box and there, in the electric light, glinting with all her hope, was a pair of new ladies' shoes. Just like she'd seen advertised on the front of *The Courier.* Thirty-five shillings a pair. Over three weeks' rent. They were reddish brown, a sunset sky when the sun is saying its last hurrah before the moon takes over to quiet the world, before everyone is offered a new beginning.

She held the shoes to her heart and felt the warmth of the leather against her skin. This was her new beginning; he had never bought her such a beautiful gift before. He would go away to war and when he came back they would start again. And in that moment, as the sunset shoes warmed her sad heart, she felt that life could indeed be something to look forward to.

When Birdie holds on too tight

Monday, 27 November 1939

He woke her at five-thirty the following Monday morning. The sun would still sleep for another twenty-three minutes, missing its chance to wake her by bursting through her thin curtains and dancing on her eyelids. She blinked and rubbed her eyes, trying to see more than his dark silhouette. He stood up straight, at arms, waiting for her to applaud him, to tell him how handsome and brave he was, to tell him he was her hero. But in her sleep she'd forgotten the shoes, which he still hadn't given her, even though it was a week since he'd brought them home. Instead she felt alone, and so she wouldn't give him the satisfaction.

'I'm off then, Birdie,' he said disgruntledly. Why couldn't she be proud of him? Why couldn't she see how smart he was in his uniform?

She didn't answer.

'Come at nine-thirty,' he said, and he swung his duffle bag over his shoulder and she watched the dark shadow of him leave the room. She threw the blankets over her head and was solitary in her cave. She didn't want to face the world. She and Viola had often thrown the blankets over their heads as children, then they had drawn letters on each other's bare backs with their fingers and tried to guess the letter. She reached her hands around herself, holding the skin of her back, and tried to pretend it was someone else holding her, but it didn't work and she felt no comfort.

The sun made its way further into the room and she ignored it, keeping herself covered by the blankets even though she was too hot. Then at seven the boys woke up and she heard them run outside. Their yells and laughter echoed into her cave. They weren't allowed outside in their pyjamas. They would tell her they had forgotten and she would immediately forgive them.

She threw back the blankets, pulled her grey-green dress from the wardrobe and then remembered the shoes and chose her orange polka dot dress instead. She hadn't worn it in years but it would be perfect for the shoes Aubrey was going to give her. She should have kissed him goodbye. She buttoned the dress closed at the side as she walked down the hall to the back door. The air coming through the screen door was hot and dry. She peered into the backyard.

'Boys, what would you like for breakfast?' she called out.

'Can we have custard?' Gabe asked from the loquat tree.

'Why not?' she said and she went into the kitchen and took a saucepan from the shelf. She lifted down the jar of cornflour and put in two tablespoons and two tablespoons of sugar, some vanilla essence and then two cups of milk and stirred it over the kookaburra stove. She put the custard into two bowls and knelt down and looked to make sure they were equal, then while it cooled she made herself tea. Then she called the boys in and was surprised when Aubrey's mother Gert came in with them.

'How long have you been here?' she asked.

'Not long,' said Gert. 'Gabe has ripped his bottoms.' Gabe turned around and poked out his bottom.

'What time are we going down to the barracks?' asked Gert.

'Nine-thirty,' she said and poured another cup of tea.

She and the boys were dressed and almost ready to leave when Gert looked at her and said, 'Of course you and the boys will come and live with me.'

Birdie wondered what that would be like. She looked at Gabe's pained face as Gert fussed over the buttons on his shirt.

'I'm sure we'll be right,' said Birdie. 'I'm sure Aubrey will send enough home for us.' She looked at the clock on the mantle. It was nine. 'Okay, boys, let's go see your dad off.' Aubrey might give her the shoes when she got to the army depot, so she brought the string shopping bag to carry them in. He would probably give them to her in a flourish, at the last minute, to cheer her up at his leaving – that was just the sort of thing he'd do – that was the sort of thing that made her love him.

Mike and Gabe chased each other down Humffray Street; they turned into Peel Street and then up Curtis Street, where she was surprised to see a crowd had gathered – maybe a hundred people. Birdie hadn't expected all these people; she had thought it would be just a few men and their families. She grabbed the boys' hands but they wriggled free and darted through people's legs to the front of the crowd. She followed, apologising all the way. Her parents and sister came and stood next to her.

'We've come to see the boys off,' said Claude. 'And to see you, of course, with Aubrey going.'

'We come every week,' said Elsie. 'It's nice, you know – to let them know …' and she finished there because she wasn't sure what she was letting them know. That they might not ever see them again? That life would go on without them?

'Aubrey's in there somewhere. Can you see him?' Birdie asked.

'He's gonna be a hero,' said Gabe.

Birdie stood on her tiptoes, trying to find Aubrey among the uniformed men. The men were lined up, ready to march. She spotted him in his new uniform, his hair shining in the beating sun, his cheeks flushed with anticipation.

'They're going to Mornington for training,' said Dulcie Whittaker, standing beside her. 'Your Aubrey certainly is a looker in his uniform. I'm going to miss him at Faull's.'

Birdie looked at her. 'Why?'

'Why what?' said Dulcie.

'Why would you miss him?'

'Well, no one fits a shoe like Aubrey. My, that's a lovely frock, Birdie. I suppose you made that one too.'

But Birdie was thinking about Aubrey. He had never fitted her for a shoe but he had held her foot in his hand and tenderly outlined the shape of her arch, he had cupped her heel and massaged her toes and told her that her foot reminded him of a perfect leaf on a tree. She bet he hadn't done that to any other women. Birdie looked past the people to Aubrey who saw her and winked at her. The Ballarat City band played the national anthem and Birdie stood to attention and sang with everyone else to ask God to bless the king and send him victorious, though the king was probably not going anywhere near any danger, unlike Aubrey, who may never come back. Then the band played 'Wish Me Luck As You Wave Me Goodbye' and everyone sang much more enthusiastically for their boys than they had for the king, and the women took out their handkerchiefs to wipe away their fears for their sons and husbands, who they would follow as far as the railway station in Lydiard Street, which was not far enough at all.

Birdie took her handkerchief from her pocket and dabbed it to her eyes, even though she wasn't crying. Instead she felt numb and wondered if her heart had stopped beating. She was in such turmoil over him, one part of her grief-stricken and the other part of her relieved. At least in the army she knew where he was. Her mother linked their arms and Birdie said, 'It seems silly to be crying when all the boys are doing is catching a train.'

But it wasn't just a train and now Birdie cried real tears. She didn't want Aubrey to die. She wanted him back so they could begin again. She looked for the boys and saw her father Claude had Michael and next to him, her sister Viola was holding onto Gabe, who was nearly pulling her over. Whistles were blown and orders yelled and the band stopped playing so the whistles and orders could be given again and actually be heard this time. The men began marching forward, ragtag and out of step because three hours' training wasn't enough.

Birdie pushed through people and grabbed Mike's and Gabe's hands from her father and Viola and ignored the boys' squirming protest as they fell in with the crowd who followed the march up Sturt Street and down Lydiard Street and then everyone crowded onto the station platform, pressed in so tightly they were back to back and arms and legs tangled and no modesty was maintained as bodies pressed against each other. Women threw themselves into their soldier-lovers' arms, lips pressed hard against lips, hearts pressed hard against hearts, no one caring who saw. Birdie felt a pinch on her bottom and turned to face a young grinning soldier. 'You're not old enough to join up,' she said, but before she finished speaking he was lost in the crowd, washed away like a buoy at sea. She saw a young nurse in her starched uniform, her flaming red hair refusing to be bound by her nurse's cap, who was crying.

'I can't see him to say goodbye,' she said.

'Me neither,' said Birdie, not knowing they were looking for the same man, and she kept a tight grip on her sons. She stood on her tiptoes trying to find Aubrey, to hold him one more time, so he could give her the shoes that would mark the beginning of their new life, so her love would keep him safe because he had never been further than Melbourne. The boys were crying because she was holding their hands so tight as she manoeuvred towards the edge of the platform looking constantly for Aubrey. Then the whistle blew and the soldiers, smiling as though off on a school excursion, loosened themselves from their lovers and mothers and jumped on the train and Aubrey never had the chance to give her the sunset shoes.

When the children catch a demon

Sunday, 10 December 1939

It was almost Christmas and still the world was at war. So much for peace and goodwill. The world was an asphalt schoolyard where a small push could result in a bloody knee. America complained that Britain was playing unfairly with Germany because Britain was confiscating and prohibiting Germany's products. Britain said it was just trying to stop Hitler on his relentless march across the earth and what right did America have to complain when they weren't even playing the game? After all, Hitler wasn't trying to invade America, but he clearly had his sights set on England. And if Hitler took England then his best mate Japan would have Australia as its bounty. What no one outside Germany yet knew was that the Nazis had begun their mass murders, gathering together one thousand and forty-three disabled patients from hospitals and sanatoriums and filling their lungs with gas.

If he had known about this atrocity, Joseph, who had fought in the last war with its trenches of hell and gases that sucked life from a man and fields of crying barely alive boys scattered and left for dead, he would have clenched his black hair in his tense fingers and narrowed his eyes and said quietly that this war is the devil himself stomping across the earth. When Jewish refugees began to escape, Australia opened its arms to seven thousand of them, thinking they were escaping because they were losing land and businesses and completely unaware they were escaping genocide, and as the refugees brought stories of death, the chest of every man and woman in Ballarat was constricted with icy terror as they wondered what shreds of family and life they would be left with when the war was over.

On Sundays Joseph had no choice but to force his dread down below his stomach so he could preach hope and victory for the Allies. Each week he saw more wives sitting alone in the pews, managing their bored children. There were more young women weeping into white lace-edged handkerchiefs saved especially for Sundays. The men who came to church were too old or too young to join up and they stood around after church and discussed the politics of it all. The too-young were full of the stories of heroes from the last war and saw themselves slotting into the role easily and talked in quiet voices their mothers couldn't hear about how and when they would run off and join up. The too-old said if the young men knew what they would be walking into they would never join up at all – a man's duty was a heavy load, they agreed.

The girls wondered if enough boys would come back for them all to marry and if there would be a role for them to play in the war other than knitting beanies and socks, and the mothers and wives baked Christmas puddings and packaged them in boxes for the soldiers. And they fed the remaining men sturdy food like date loaf and rock cakes to ground them to the soil of Ballarat; there were no flights of fancy like cream sponges or fairy cakes or chocolate éclairs put out for morning tea. The women put the food on the trestles after church with sombre faces, barely speaking, scarcely able to contain the edges of their hearts, which were frayed with worry. The children ran around the trestles, sneaking food before they were allowed to and chasing each other out into the yard, barely aware of the dangers in their futures.

Connie never ran around with the other children. A fog existed between her and them. When she spoke they looked at her as though she was speaking a foreign language, as though she was a creature they had never encountered before, and they would shrug their shoulders and wander away from her so she just gave up and in her separateness she hated them for their rejection.

She loathed Sundays; it was ridiculous her pa called Sundays the day of rest because they were always extremely busy. From having to wear her Sunday best, a gingham dress with a prickly lace frill at the bottom, and her white socks that wouldn't stay up, to having to spend nearly the whole day doing church things. First there was church itself. The children sat in church until after Pa gave his children's talk, which was followed by the children's hymn, and in the last verse the children would follow their Sunday school teachers out to Sunday school and Connie would follow Miss Mitchell, who was her teacher.

Connie didn't mind Miss Mitchell, even though she was Gabe Mabbett's aunt, and she hated Gabe Mabbett the most of anyone in the world. When she saw him, she could feel revulsion well up from her feet; it was enough hatred to send her straight to hell, but that would be a small price to pay for hating Gabe Mabbett. But his aunt, Miss Mitchell, was kind to her and had a soft sweet voice that was always on the verge of a little laugh; sometimes she would laugh at the end of her sentences like a trickle of cool water. In Sunday school they sang songs and coloured in pictures of Jesus. After Sunday school Connie would go home for lunch, where she would have to balance on an upended fruit box squished between Gabe and her brother Danny. Her mother invited so many people for lunch each Sunday that they were jammed in around the formal dining table.

At three her father went visiting the ill at the hospital, but for her it was back to the church hall for Christian Endeavour, where she would have to learn psalms and the books of the New Testament by heart ready for the annual exam (if she passed she would get a silver-plated pin to wear on her chest), and then it was home for supper and singing around the piano and then the evening church service. But she wasn't allowed to go to the evening service until she was fifteen. Instead she had to go to bed.

There was a constant stream of visitors in and out of her home, and Connie could never remember their names. She had to be polite to them or she would get in trouble from Ma, but she stamped hard on their toes and said, 'Ooops, I'm so clumsy.' She put salt in their tea and slaters under their pillows. There was never enough food to go around as far as she was concerned and since his father had joined up Gabe Mabbett had come every single Sunday for lunch with his mother and brother Mike. Gabe sat behind her in Sunday school and pulled her long ringleted pigtails. One morning he took crickets to Sunday school in a condensed milk tin and then released them up the curled tunnel of her pigtails. They were sticky and quickly became tangled in her hair and she had screamed and rolled around on the floor sure she was going to die. Miss Mitchell had run and collected her ma from church and Ma took her to the kitchen and plucked the crickets out one by one and said, 'Well, Gabe has his own problems and no harm was done.' But harm was done, because those crickets were going to go all the way up her pigtails and then once they reached her head they would burrow through her skin and into her brain and kill her. She'd probably only had seconds to live.

Now the women were cleaning up after morning tea and the men were discussing the war, while the children chased each other around the church buildings. Connie lay next door on the grass under the growing lemon tree. Each year tiny white buds formed that she was pretty sure were baby lemons or flowers, she couldn't tell until they grew into one or the other. It had branches filled with new verdant green leaves. She could hear Gabe yelling, 'I'm coming!' and Mike running past on the other side of the fence saying, 'This way,' and Dan saying, 'I know a good spot.'

She ignored the pain of the enormous space between her and the other children and looked through the branches of the tree to the blue, cloudless sky that was so so close she could almost reach out and touch it. Connie reached under her frock and scratched her sticky sweaty skin then she closed her eyes, let her head and arms flop to the side and pretended she was a dying soldier. She felt the sun shrivelling her skin and sucking out her soul and she held her breath until she could hold it no more and she let go with a big gasp and opened her eyes and he was standing over her, blocking the light so all she could see was a huge shadow of him. His stupid grinning face was directly above hers. He might dribble spit onto her or do something terrible to her hair so she sat up and scowled and held on tight to each of her pigtails with their yellow Sunday ribbons. Danny and Mike were soon standing either side of Gabe, all three of them looking down on her, silhouetted by the sun. All she could see of their faces was their enormous toothy grins. Connie could feel her heart thumping hard against her ribs. What torture had they concocted for her?

'We're going to the river, wanna come?' said Gabe.

'Really?' she asked. They never invited her on any of their adventures.

'Really,' said Mike, and he held out his hand to help her up. She took his hand and he lifted her up and she held her pigtails together in her other hand to be sure.

Gabe picked up a stick and started hitting at the lowest branch of the lemon tree.

'Don't!' she said, standing in the way. 'That's my tree.' Gabe looked at Danny and he nodded and Gabe dropped the stick.

'So, you wanna come?' said Mike.

'P'raps,' she said, controlling the excitement tingling in her fingers and cheeks at the thought of being on their adventure. The boys began walking down the driveway, so she skipped after them. Her frock bounced and she felt a cool breeze around her legs that had burnt pink in the sun. She followed the three boys down Dawson Street, skipping and running to keep up with them. They went past the church men, past the deacons and her father Joseph as they stood in groups on the church veranda, discussing the state of the world so intently that not one of them noticed the three boys and the little girl tagging along after them as they went down the street on a mission of their own.

The boys turned the corner and were out of sight so Connie ran to catch up with them, and out of breath followed them down Dana Street for several blocks before they all cut across the empty paddock to the canal. Mike, Danny and Gabe scrambled down the bluestones into the canal, which had only a dribble of thick brown water at the bottom. There they were hidden from adult eyes. Danny and Gabe ran up the middle of the canal, stomping in the brown puddles. But Mike stopped and came back to where Connie was still standing at the top.

'Hang on, old girl.'

Connie stared down at the base of the canal. It was too far for her to get down without help.

Mike held out his hands to catch her. 'Come on,' he said, 'it's easy. I'll catch you.' She looked up the canal to where Danny and Gabe were watching. She couldn't chicken out in front of Gabe, so she jumped and crashed into Mike and they both wobbled, nearly falling over, but he straightened them up, let go of her, and they ran to Gabe and Danny. Then all four of them ran to where the canal became the river again.

The Yarrowee River snaked its way through the town. It curved around the backs of houses and dipped under bridges. Even though it boasted tributaries that ran into it, this was in fact the humblest of rivers and was constantly insulted by being called a creek. In the gold rush the Yarrowee had run like a shimmering yellow path that made the sun grimace with envy as panning and mining made its waters sparkle and shine with gold filaments.

As the gold mining had become busier, businesses established themselves along the river's banks. The soap works, the fellmongery, a woollen mill, the gasworks and a collection of other factories to fill miners' needs – as well as the jail – were built along the banks and the Chinese set up their camps and they all spilled their waste into the Yarrowee without a thought for its wellbeing. The river turned murky green with scum sitting on the once-golden water. In summer the sun, ever competing with the river, sent down its heat, which caught on the north wind and attempted to burn the river dry, emptying it until its rocky bed was visible and its fish were easy picking for the magpies, but in winter its banks would overflow and children disobeying parental orders not to go near the churning water would smash its icy covering to pieces with sticks and throw each other in, and fish would breed in the deeper waters.

Now the four children plunged through the overgrown weeds, every so often having to dislodge their clothing from where it got stuck on a thorn or blackberry bush until they got to where the river was shaded by trees that stopped the sun from evaporating the water, which was a foot deep. Not far upstream from where the children were playing, red blood from the meatworks and blue dye from the woollen mill poured through drains into the river.

The red blood and blue dye swirled and churned until the two colours turned to purple. The Yarrowee was delighted to have the children and welcomed them with its magical purple water. The children splashed and threw stones and laughed and completely forgot their mothers and their lunch as the gentian violet water stained their clothes and their skin. Excited by the children, the river ran fast for them, in and out of pebbles, burbling and bubbling white like soap bubbles and the children squealed and whooped and tossed water at each other and then Gabe, simply because he couldn't not do it, reached out and pushed Connie into a deeper part of the water and she fell backwards with a crash.

She lay there on the stony bed, the water coming up to her ears, taking gulps of water and spluttering it back out. She shut her eyes to keep the water out of them, she felt the sharp rocks cutting into her back, punishing her for landing on them so heavily and without care and she could hear Gabe laughing and every sinew in her body was rigid with hate for him. She would drown. Even though the water only came halfway up her head, still it splashed and bubbled over her face. She blinked her eyes and opened them and there was a hand reaching out to her. Once she realised she had a saviour and she was safe, she began to cry.

'Come on, old girl,' he said gently, and stretched his hand out further.

She reached out her hand, wet and purple, and he took it firmly and pulled her to her feet and as he did so she kept her eyes on him and his pulling her out of the water was slow. She memorised every second. She had seen her pa pushing people backwards under the warm water of the baptismal bath that was hidden under the pulpit until the deacons removed the pulpit and the timber floorboards to reveal it. The baptismal candidates would come up looking shocked and her pa would announce they were born again, they were a new person. Connie knew that once she was upright she would be born again and would be a new person. The sun glinted on his blond curls in a halo; it buried itself in his eyes making them bluer than the cloudless sky. He was her angel come to save her and every bone she had in her body and every breath she breathed would love him for the rest of her life. She felt the water drain away from her face and her feet found a solid spot among the stones of the riverbed to root her and hold her upright.

'There you go, old girl,' he said as she got her balance. She felt him try to pull his hand away but she clung to it and gazed at him and she realised that he and her angel were one and the same. She had given her angel the wrong name. He was Archangel Mike. She didn't want to let his hand go but he wriggled away and the loss of his grip on her made her feel as though she might faint back under the water. Still she gazed at him and he smiled at her; it was a kind smile.

'Steady now,' he said, and thank goodness he took her hand again. 'Just take it easy till we get to the bank; don't slip on the stones.'

'I've found a frog,' hollered Danny, and Mike and Connie reached the bank and ran over to where Danny had scooped a muddy frog into his cupped hands. Connie looked at Mike and saw the frog captivated him and she quickly held up the edges of her wet purple dress to make a pouch and Danny dropped the startled frog in. All three boys scrabbled in the mud looking for frogs and when one was found Connie ran over and the frog was dropped into her dress pouch to join its kin. Soon her dress was full of frogs clambering over each other but too terrified to jump out.

Mike said, 'We better get back. It will be time for lunch.' They had completely forgotten about lunch and walked back in their muddy clothes, Connie still carrying the abducted nation of frogs. The boys laughed about Connie falling on her back and she laughed with them and didn't remind them that Gabe had pushed her because she was just so pleased to be included. None of them thought about what to do with the frogs or what they would say to their parents until they were standing in a row at Connie and Danny's front gate. They stared down the driveway like worn-out soldiers back from a mission.

'Have you got a bucket?' said Gabe.

'We do, in the shed,' said Danny and they went into the shed, quietly, so as not to attract attention from inside the house. Danny dragged two metal buckets from where they hid in the corner and Connie emptied half her dress into one and half into the other and then Mike took one bucket and Danny the other and they put the buckets under the garden tap and put a bit of water in the bottom. They hid the buckets back in the dark corner of the shed. Only then did they look at each other, taking in the mud and the purple stains on their soaking wet clothes and skin and realised they had no idea how to deal with the adults.

When Cecil has to get home

Sunday, 10 December 1939

When Flora invited Mabel Finchley and her husband Cecil to lunch, Cecil particularly had been very glad to accept. His Mabel had been the one to always pick and change the church flowers each week, to make the largest apple cake for morning tea, to get the cups and saucers out with Flora before the other women arrived. She swept and mopped her own floors every day and she had a laundry full of jars of fruits she preserved in summer for eating in the winter months. She cooked solid stews and her husband and son were the only men she knew of who got two hot meals a day. Cecil had been scraggy and empty after the Great War and doing his articles when she married him and now he was content and soft with her food. Her son Manny had taken after her with his ginger hair, blue eyes and stringy bones, but with her hot meals he had grown soft and malleable like his father.

She had cried and pleaded with Manny not to join up but he and his father had prattled on about duty as though they had no duty at all to her, and he had left on the same train as Aubrey Mabbett. So it was that Mabel no longer baked any cakes or preserved any fruit. Instead she made sandwiches and soup for her and Cecil and because Manny was at war she fed his portion to his black labrador Snowy, and Snowy, who had once been lithe and sinewy, was quickly becoming fat and lazy. Her house gathered dust and daddy longlegs in its corners and the dishes got done when there were no more to eat from. Cecil was sick to death of soup and sandwiches, so lunch at Flora's was very welcome indeed.

Flora had prepared corned beef and salads of lettuce, tomato and hardboiled eggs. She'd made Connie collect the eggs from the chook pen, which Connie had complained about mightily. She put out two bottles of freshly made Air Raid Apple Chutney and there were loaves of crusty bread. All this, except the chutney, which Flora had made months earlier, was prepared on Saturday so that Sunday would be free for her duties as the pastor's wife. Birdie Mabbett had also been invited to lunch along with her two sons. But the children hadn't appeared, even though Flora had called for them. Flora and Joseph's two older children, Thomas and Lydia, shared the piano stool at one end and there was Mister Little, who had left his family in Ararat to try and find work in Ballarat and was staying for a few days with the reverend. Next to him sat Birdie Mabbett and at the other end sat Joseph and Flora and on the other side were Mabel and Cecil. Mabel was glad not to be sitting next to Birdie, who usually fussed endlessly over her boys and was at this moment worrying about where they could be and imagining all the harm that could come to them.

Mabel said, 'You worry too much, Birdie; just thank the Lord they aren't at war,' and then wished she hadn't. She'd heard the accusing tone in her words and it wasn't Birdie's fault her boys were just children. Flora stood up and Mabel felt Flora's hand gently rest on her shoulder and a calm came over Mabel and she said, 'Don't worry, Birdie, children are children and they'll be off somewhere fighting Indians or robbers or they'll arrive just as they think it's dessert time.'

'Or Germans,' said Thom, 'something I wouldn't mind having a go at. Manny's lucky he's old enough to join up.'

'It doesn't feel lucky when you're his mother,' said Mabel, and she felt tears sting her eyes.

'Here,' said Flora, putting the large china teapot in the middle of the table, 'hot tea for everyone,' and she poured Mabel a cup and passed it to her and sat down in her seat again and rested her hand on Mabel's arm. Mabel sipped the tea and its hotness went down her throat into her chest and warmed her sad heart.

Once Mabel Finchley would have thought Birdie ought to pay more attention to the goings-on of her husband, rather than her children, and would probably have said so. Mabel had seen him come out of three different women's houses over the last few years and she knew all of them happened to have husbands who were out at work at the time. Birdie said he had joined up, but who knew with that man? But none of this was significant to Mabel now, she just didn't have the energy to worry about other people's lives. Manny was twenty-two and their only child. His only interest was maths and he had studied hard for three years to become an accountant. What good was he to the war effort? What sort of fighter would he be with his soft edges and round innocent eyes? He could never kill anyone, not even if they were an enemy.

She felt Cecil nudging her skinny ribs and she remembered that he insisted on listening to *Dad and Dave* at three on Sunday afternoons. He couldn't miss it. Missing *Dad and Dave* was the one thing that got him agitated and she just couldn't cope with that. Cecil liked to sing along with the opening tune, 'The Road to Gundagai', and Snowy would force himself up from his position in front of the stove and lie across Cecil's feet. Mabel moved her arm from Flora's and even though it was hot and dank with everyone in the dining room, her arm suddenly felt cold and she rubbed it. 'Thank you, Flora, for the lovely lunch.'

'I don't think we'll be up to the evening service tonight, Joseph,' said Cecil, and Joseph stood up and reached over the table and they shook hands.

'Of course,' said Joseph, starting to walk them to the door.

'Sit back down,' said Cecil, 'finish your tea. We can let ourselves out.' And Flora and Joseph sat down and Mabel walked through the vestibule, past the stretchers that slumped in their middles from overuse and she opened the back door and came face to face with the four dishevelled children who looked like they had been at war after all.

'Oh, Flora,' called Mabel.

When bitter tea is served

Sunday, 17 December 1939

The sun beat down on Ballarat through the middle of December. Politicians bickered and parried and the League of Nations took action and told the Soviet Union they were out of the gang if they didn't stop their hostilities towards poor Finland. The Soviets laughed – along with Germany, Italy and Japan, who had already quit the League. Now England and France were the only members left to discuss if you could have a League of Nations if you only had two members.

On the front lines boys' blood gathered in ponds on brown soil, then ran like rivers to the sea, where it dribbled to the ocean floor. The boys cried out for their mothers as they died on the damp earth and in the wet seas and in the grey skies over Europe. *The Courier* was careful to follow government instructions and didn't report the torn skin or the burnt organs or the dismembered bodies. It reported that artillery fought valiantly, submarines launched strategic attacks, and planes heroically defended the skies, and for the sake of mothers and lovers it didn't mention the boys who manned this war equipment.

While war raged in the world, the state's politicians argued about whether or not motor vehicles should be included in the *Larceny Act.* Mister Alured Kelly stood in his suit and tie and asked how stealing a motor vehicle was any less of a crime than stealing a wireless set. The other politicians murmured and yelled a bit and Mister Kelly lost his temper and said, 'We have to do something about these young scamps that are stealing cars for Sunday afternoon fun and yet suffer no consequences. The law needs updating to include motor vehicles!' And the politicians murmured and then yelled at each other some more and no decision was made for the present time and so the scamps were left to their Sunday afternoon fun and the politicians went on to discuss if the school leaving age should be raised to fifteen.

In Ballarat the sun scorched the grass and made the tar on the roads sticky so it stuck to the soles of shoes like gum and in the middle of Sturt Street women had to reach down on wobbly bent knees and pull at the heels of their shoes to free them from the tar. The older men pulled their hats down tight over their burning noses as they played Tru-Go or True-Go or Trugo – no one could agree on the spelling – wiping the sweat from their necks with their hankies and walking to the shade of the trees where they stood not any less hot and swore about the heat and muttered 'only Englishmen and mad dogs' while the next bloke took his turn. The women watching the men play Trugo whispered to each other as they fanned themselves and the men playing glared up at the sun and said, 'We'll have another Black Friday like last year if this keeps up and what will happen then with all the fit young men away at war? Who will be left to fight the fires at home?'

The trees had brittle brown leaves that snapped like thin bone china. The Yarrowee River had dried to no more than a trickle for the thirsty birds and fish to suck at and the frogs died as the river mud hardened like concrete – but not the frogs kept safely hidden in the corner of the shed as Connie added twigs and rocks to the buckets for the frogs to climb on and water to the buckets each day and the frogs lived happily on a banquet of mosquitoes and flies. While everyone else wilted like plucked flowers.

The one thing that thrived in the summer heat was an enterovirus. A week earlier when the children had been playing at the river, splashing and taking gulping spluttering mouthfuls of water, the virus, hidden in the contaminated water, had seized its opportunity and silently entered their mouths and travelled to their guts, where it began a journey that would take it seven to fourteen days as it worked its way towards their nervous system. No one knew the children were facing an enemy as dreadful and as cruel as the Nazis, so they had gone through their week in blissful ignorance from one Sunday to the next when the children were once again sitting in Sunday school looking up expectantly at Miss Mitchell.

Viola Mitchell was fourteen and a half years old. There were fifteen years between her and her older sister Birdie. She'd been teaching Sunday school for six months. Her father Claude was the Sunday school superintendent and had been in this role for nearly twenty-three years. Her mother Elsie played the organ when old Mister Hooley couldn't do it and her older sister Birdie had married Aubrey Mabbett.

When Birdie had eloped with Aubrey, Claude and Elsie hadn't yelled or even given Birdie the silent treatment. It had been much worse than that. They were disappointed and overnight they grew more wearied and more wrinkled. Viola was going to make sure she never disappointed her parents like that. She would choose the best husband, a good upright man, one her father liked and her mother admired. Viola knew Birdie was filled with guilt over her marriage; she could see the cracks in Birdie and how the weight of her guilt was making her crumble and bend like an old woman and Viola wished she could mend Birdie.

Viola had her young nephew Gabe in her Sunday school class. She preferred her other nephew, Mike, but she would never tell anyone that. There was no point at all in hurting people's feelings. If a decision she made was going to hurt someone – well, she just absolutely couldn't make the decision and didn't realise that sometimes not making a decision hurt people anyway. Viola also had Reverend Starr's daughter Connie in her class. When Viola looked at Connie she saw a lame bird that needed special care. So when Connie stood proudly in class and told some outrageous story, Viola didn't get cross or exasperated or accuse Connie of outright lying like other teachers might. She said kindly and softly, 'Thank you, Connie, for your contribution.'

And there was Connie's big brother, Thomas. He was the sort of boy who, if she married him, might erase the lines in her parents' faces. But Thomas had a bad effect on her. Every time she saw him her heart throbbed against her ribs until it hurt and her hands became hot and sweaty and then she became ill as though she was going to vomit and she had to rush away from him to calm herself. She began to hate him for causing this reaction in her. It was getting worse over time, not better, like an allergy, but despite this she found herself standing near him after church until she was a trembling mess and when Lydia, her friend and his sister, asked if she wanted to come to the manse to study or if Missus Starr asked her parents to Sunday lunch, she would hear 'Yes please,' jump from her lips before she'd even thought to say the words. No matter what he did to her insides, she was a moth to his flame.

Viola tried to put Thomas Starr from her mind and focus on the children in her class. 'Now, good morning, boys and girls,' she said and they chorused 'good morning' back. Then she asked, as she did each week, 'What has the Lord done for you this week? Not all at once, put your hands up please.'

'Janet,' she said.

Janet stood up and straightened her skirt. 'We got a letter from my brother so the Lord kept him safe while he is away at the war.'

As soon as Janet sat down the children threw their hands up again.

'Verity.'

Verity stood up and said, 'The Lord gave me peace.'

'Peace?' said Viola.

'Yes, in my heart,' said Verity and she clasped her hands to her chest like an actress in the throes of – something.

Connie was throwing her hand up in the air like she had a violent twitch. Viola was avoiding letting her speak but after three more children Connie was frantic, her bottom going up and down on her chair in time with her arm and Viola sighed, feeling she had no choice but to say, 'Connie – your turn.'

Connie jumped from her seat, ran to the front of the class and stood right up next to Viola in her teacher's chair. Connie swayed from side to side and her Sunday frock brushed against Viola's knees and the lace scratched at her skin. Viola watched as Connie took a deep breath and wondered what she would say this week. It was never anything you could anticipate. 'Here we go,' she said to herself.

'This week,' said Connie, and she put her hands behind her back and clasped them together as she swayed from side to side, 'this week the Lord brought our kitten back to life.'

Viola gulped.

'You don't have a kitten,' said Gabe from the back of the class and Viola shushed him and said, 'Let Connie tell her story.'

'We do too,' said Connie, standing rigid like her father in the pulpit, 'and the Lord brought it back to life.'

'How did this happen?' asked Viola, turning in her seat to face Connie.

'Well,' said Connie, taking another deep breath and looking out over her audience, 'I found the kitten frozen on our doorstep in the morning. It had frozen in the ice overnight.'

'But it's been very hot, Connie,' said Viola quietly. She didn't like to point out the girl's lies in front of the whole class.

'It's cold at night,' said Connie vehemently, 'and the kitten was frozen to death and so I prayed over it and the Lord sent my angel and he made the kitten alive again.'

'Where's the kitten now?' said Gabe.

'It ran away,' said Connie. 'It was alive so it ran away.'

'Well,' said Viola, 'I don't know what to say. That's quite something, Connie. You can sit down now.'

Connie strutted back to her seat, terribly pleased with her excellent example of the Lord's intervention that absolutely outdid any other story that day. Viola watched her sit down and then Connie squealed and Viola suspected that nephew of hers had just pulled Connie's hair, which he did often, and Connie yelled out that he had, so Viola scowled at Gabe but Gabe looked at Viola with such large innocent eyes and she saw all his self-doubt and all his loss and she understood that he blamed himself for what he didn't understand but could sense was wrong in his home, and his father leaving. Rather than being the brash arrogant boy everyone thought he was, he was just as lame as young Connie.

'We'll sing "If you're happy and you know it clap your hands",' said Viola brightly and the children sang and clapped and then she prayed and Sunday school was over. Viola stood up and straightened her dress and saw Birdie standing in the corner of the room, just inside the door, scratching at her arms, looking as worried as ever. Viola walked over and put her arms around her and said, 'It'll be okay, Birdie, I'm sure he'll come back safely. He can wangle anything, that Aubrey of yours.'

Birdie shrugged and Viola saw the tears in the corners of her eyes and Birdie's ambivalence and said, 'I'm just going outside to get a spot of sun; why don't you come out? Your arms are cold.'

Birdie shook her head and Viola felt useless to help Birdie and somewhere inside of herself, in some secret place she was looking for Thom. She kissed her sister's cheek and went outside and he was standing in the road under a spindly tree talking to his sister Lydia. Viola and Lydia would finish the intermediate certificate this year and Viola would like to leave school then and work at the Lort Smith Animal Home in Melbourne, caring for all the lost and injured animals. She only felt whole when she was caring for broken things. But Melbourne was too far away, and she couldn't leave her mother and father – or Birdie, for that matter. All of them, she knew, needed her care. So she would become a nurse instead and that way she could stay at home.

She leant against the fence between the manse and the church and saw Connie in the manse driveway on the other side of the fence, muttering away to thin air. Perhaps the child was mad. She felt Thom glance over at her and she twisted her hands inside each other and realised it really was far too hot to stay out in the sun and she scurried inside and leant against the cool brick wall of the church hall to get her breath back.

'Are you all right, dear?' It was Missus Starr, resting a hand on her shoulder.

'It's just the heat,' said Viola.

'Are you all right, Viola?' said Birdie.

'Of course, Birdie. Really it's just the heat. You don't need to worry and fret.' Thom and Lydia walked past and Lydia, seeing Viola trembling, turned back and took Viola's arm through her own as Viola fell further down the wall.

'Oh dear,' said Flora, following the direction of Viola's gaze to Thom walking over to the trestle table where he got himself a slice of cinnamon tea cake.

'It appears the heat has really taken hold. Let's get you to a seat. Thom, bring Viola a cup of sweet milky tea.'

'No, no, I don't need a cup of tea,' protested Viola as she was propped on the seat. She didn't want him coming closer. Connie appeared and plopped herself on the seat next to Viola and leant right into her as though she was claiming her stake. Lydia sat on the other side of her. Thom was already standing in front of her holding out a teacup filled to the brim so that it was spilling over into a moat in the saucer. She tried to say thank you but the words just wouldn't come and she knew she was sitting there, looking up at him open-mouthed like an idiot.

Connie sang, '*Thom and Miss Mitchell sitting in a tree k-i-s*' but she got no further as Flora snapped, 'Be quiet, Connie.'

Viola gently shook Connie off her and reached out her trembling arm for the saucer and her fingers landed over his. He didn't pull away, and with her hand touching his and only the teacup and the world between them, all her sickness and trembling and thumping disappeared. That was when she knew that her world would always be a better place if he was in it. She saw in that moment how kind his eyes were, like his mother Flora's, except everyone knew Flora wasn't really his mother so perhaps he grew the kindness in his eyes. She saw how he was tall like his father, how he would stride through life with purpose, and she realised in that moment that he was not for her. He was too strong, too at ease with the world. He didn't need mending and she needed to mend things and she was filled with an overwhelming disappointment as she sipped his tea, which was already cold and bitter.

When Thom and Lydia think on what could have been

Sunday, 17 December 1939

The bookshelves in the manse ran the length of the hallway so that when you got to the stairs you had to walk sideways between the books and the stairway balustrade to get past. More books took up three walls in Joseph's study from floor to ceiling and there were another two shelves of books in the living room. There were many works on these shelves like Homer's *Iliad*, *Moby Dick* and *Little Women* in worn linen covers with gold or black lettering, but the majority of the books were bibles in various versions, the American Standard Version, the Concordant Literal Version, the Emphasised Bible and the King James. The bibles came in large sizes with bold easy-to-read print, they came small enough to fit in a woman's purse so she could pull it out and read on the tram, and all the sizes in between. They came with notes in the margins; they came with the words spoken by Jesus written in red or with devotional reflections at the bottom of each page. They came separated into 365 sections so that over a year you could read the entire bible, both Old and New Testaments, ready to start again the next year. Along with the bibles were concordances, *Young's Analytical Concordance*, *Strong's Concordance* and books on exegesis, books on interpreting the bible and guides for sermons. Thom knew that in the sea of bibles that lived in his house just one bible wouldn't be missed.

So, in the afternoon, while Mabel Finchley stared at the corned beef not able to eat anything and wondering if Manny was safe at war and Birdie was scratching at her arms and wondering if her boys were safe off playing, Thom slipped from the table, not noticing Connie following him, and on his way up the hallway he took one of the large bibles from the shelves. It was leather bound and the spine was warped inwards, unable to hold the weight of its pages. He went upstairs to the room he shared with Danny, shut the door and sat on his bed under the window with the bible, then he took Joseph's grafting knife, which he'd hidden under his pillow some days ago, and began to cut into the middle of the bible until he heard his father's footsteps coming up the stairs.

'Connie, stop hanging around your brother's door and go back to the table,' Joseph barked.

Thom quickly slipped the grafting knife back under the pillow and opened the bible, pretending to be engrossed in *The Song of Solomon*. Joseph opened the door and Connie peered around his legs.

'Oh, I wondered where you'd got to. I was going to call you back to the table but as you are taking in the word of the Lord perhaps you may be excused.'

Thom made a show of how engrossed he was by holding up his finger then said, 'Sorry, Pa, I just had to finish the verse I was on.'

Joseph shut the door. 'Come on, Connie, back to the table,' and Thom heard their steps recede back down the stairs, so he took out the knife to begin his project again, until Connie, who had taken the first opportunity to vanish from the dining table once again, opened the door. Without waiting for an invitation she entered and started poking around on his dresser as if looking for a secret.

'I hate Sunday lunches,' she moaned.

Thom took her by the shoulders and ushered her back out the door.

'I know you aren't reading that bible,' she said and he slammed the door on her, which was most unlike Thom.

He went back to his task until Lydia came in, flopped onto his bed and lay back, her legs dangling over the side and her arms outstretched. 'Ugh, those women are so dreadfully boring and miserable,' she moaned.

'Connie agrees,' Thom said, and quickly shut the bible and again hid the knife. 'It's time to leave for Christian Endeavour soon,' said Thom.

'Oh, I can't wait,' drawled Lydia, scowling. Then she sat up and looked at Thom. 'You know, when I finally get out of this house I don't think I shall ever set foot inside a church again.'

'Aren't you worried about hell?' he said. He wasn't sure whether he believed in hell or not.

'Don't you ever wonder,' she said, 'how different things might have been?'

Thom knew what she meant. Lydia was always full of what might have been but wasn't. 'Flora is the only mother I really remember,' Thom lied, 'so I guess I don't.'

'Ugh,' moaned Lydia, and Thom watched her. He could see her mind ticking over, then she said, 'I don't believe you. You're older than me and I remember our mother – so you must too.' She sat up and looked intently into Thom's eyes, searching for his allegiance. 'I won't ever forgive him – or her, or that strange brat they had that Flora fusses over so much,' she said.

'I don't mind Flora, or Connie for that matter,' Thom said quietly, but Lydia was staring out the window at what might have been.

He stood up, holding the bible against his chest. He wasn't going to be able to accomplish his task at home; the interruptions were predictably unpredictable. There was no privacy in this house. He took his work satchel from the tallboy and stretched the soft old leather over the enormous bible.

'Why are you taking that brick to work?' asked Lydia.

'I've had a rush of the Holy Spirit come over me,' said Thom. 'I just can't bear to be apart from God's word and perhaps I might witness to the blokes at work.'

'Well,' said Lydia, 'I suppose with that you can hit them and hit them hard. One wallop on the head and they're sure to convert.'

Thom smiled. He reached over with his satchel now stretched into the shape of the bible and hit her on the head with it.

'Oww – you beast,' she cried, and jumped up and dug him in the ribs.

When Connie finds a secret

Monday, 18 December 1939

On Monday Thom woke and lay in his bed thinking of Viola. For months he had been trying to get near her, but every time he did, she ran away, and he could only think that she detested him. There was no other explanation. He thought of her sunshine hair that she held back from her face with a tortoiseshell clip, her eyes that were large and kind like his stepmother Flora's. He thought of the way she smiled when the children in her Sunday school class ran to her and the way she opened her arms to them. With a girl like Viola waiting, you would be sure to come back from the war; her goodness would keep you safe. But even if he was old enough to go to war, Viola wouldn't wait for him; she wanted nothing to do with him and didn't even drink the tea he took her. He saw how she placed it on the floor in front of her. It was left until the milk congealed and the tea evaporated, leaving a stain on the cup where it had once been.

Viola lay in bed thinking of Thom and how she no longer felt a need to flee from him. Her insides had settled with the knowledge that he was not for her. She was sad because he really was lovely and kind to his sister Connie. He had a way of humouring Connie that no one else had. He could question her without upsetting her. Viola knew his ability to understand others was strength and he was too strong for her. With him she would lose herself completely and that was terrifying; she'd seen Birdie lose herself to Aubrey.

Birdie was lying in bed, her arms around her boys, who slept either side of her. She was fretting about how she would survive the coming months until the war ended. It had been a month since Aubrey signed up and not one cheque had come home to her. She would have to move in with his mother or her parents. She felt the dead weight in her chest as it pushed her back into the mattress, trying to make her disappear altogether.

Hazel had been up for a good while and was putting on her uniform ready to start her morning shift in the paediatric ward. She pinned her hair back and ignored the red curls that escaped anyway. She had desperately wanted to say goodbye to Aubrey at the train station but hadn't been able to find him. She had felt as though her beating heart and breathing lungs had left on that train with him. Every night she had written him long yearning letters and he had sent back a short note with a pair of cardboard ballet shoes he had cut out and coloured with a pencil. Then his gift had arrived with a note saying he'd meant to give it to her before he left but he couldn't find her. She had torn off the string and the brown paper and opened the box to find a pair of russet shoes. She held the shoes to her nose and breathed in the leather. They were the most beautiful shoes she had ever owned. *To match the colour of your hair,* he'd written.

Connie was awake and listening to her father moving about in the kitchen below. To anyone else she would have appeared to be staring at the ceiling and muttering to no one, but Connie was chatting with Archangel Mike, as he was now called, and asking him to make sure that when she grew up she got to marry Mike. Archangel Mike said he couldn't promise anything.

Flora was woken by the tiny chinkling bells of bone china. It was the sound that woke her every morning, the sweet soft chime of teacups quivering on their saucers, a song that came from Joseph's heart as he stood at the door holding a tray with two cups, a pot of hot tea and a jug of milk and his shaving cup filled with water. He walked to her side of the bed and rested the tray on her knees while he opened the curtains, letting the already warm sun stream into the room where it settled happily like a child with new toys, then he hopped back into bed on the other side and took the tray, balanced it on his legs and poured the milk first and then the tea into Flora's favourite Royal Albert Imari teacup. They drank three cups each in silence as they gazed out the window, past the silver birch growing in the front yard and onto Dawson Street, wide and empty.

Across the street was St Patrick's Cathedral, many times the size of their church. St Patrick's was bluestone bricks, with high steeples, great arched windows, transepts, golden organ pipes that you could climb to heaven, and shining tiled floors. St Patrick's didn't butt right onto the road like the Baptist church did.

Instead it was surrounded by a lush expanse of grass and bushes that didn't burn and brown like the rest of the town but stayed a succulent green. Joseph sometimes joked that the devil must be sending up water from hell to keep the grass green like that while the rest of the town shrivelled in the summer heat. Wrought-iron gates and fences with bluestone pillars enclosed St Patrick's and its priests declined to be part of the Ecumenical Association for the Preservation of Society in these terrible times. They claimed to be the true church, directly descended from Peter the apostle, but Joseph thought the Catholic church was a stain on Christianity, separating people from direct access to God and making priests unnecessary intermediaries. And to him Peter was never the first of the popes in rich gilded gowns but a humble fisherman in everyday clothes struggling to feed his family.

After their last sip of tea, Flora and Joseph put down their cups in unison and then bowed their heads and Joseph prayed for each of their children, for the day ahead, for the world at war, and asked that God would overcome the evil that the devil was letting loose on the world. They said *Amen* in unison and Joseph got out of bed, pulled the chamber pot from under the bed and took his mirror from the side table, and with his shaving cup and his shaving soap and brush he turned his face into Father Christmas, which he then shaved away, letting his cut hairs fall, like slivers of silver threads, into the urine pond in the pot. Then he took the lot and went outside and emptied it onto the lemon tree.

While Joseph was doing this, Flora washed and dressed. She put on her pink silk panties and her press and lift bra of crème lace. She took her weekday frock, green cotton with little lemon primroses over it, from the walnut wardrobe and slipped it over her head. Then she put on her housecoat, which would protect her house dress as she did her chores, and buttoned it up the front. The housecoat was also floral, light blue with pink and yellow flowers, and it meant that should anyone come to the door she could just slip it off and be ready for them in her clean house dress. To protect her housecoat so she didn't have to wash it so often, she put on her Temperance Union apron. *Lips that touch Liquor shall never touch Mine* the apron said.

Flora stood in front of the dresser and pulled her tortoiseshell comb through her hair. Joseph said her hair was like honey and smelt just as sweet, but when she looked at it all she saw was brown. She dragged out the knots, holding the ends to ease the pain, and satisfied no knots were left, caught her hair into a net and pinned the net along the back of her head. Her natural curls meant she didn't need to curl the front of her hair into tight little circles. Flora looked at herself in the mirror, unaware how round and blue her eyes were and how delightfully her curls danced around her face. She thought her looks were passable and more than adequate to go about her tasks. She didn't wear make-up because Joseph asked her not to, he said he loved her the way God made her, and she didn't bother with stockings, saving their expense for going out and Sundays. She slipped her feet into her flat house shoes and walked to the kitchen where she put the kettle on the Kookaburra stove and sliced bread to toast. She got the butter from the ice chest and the vegemite tin from the cupboard and put them on the kitchen table. Joseph was sitting in his striped pyjamas at the kitchen table waiting for the next pot of tea, which was her responsibility.

Thom was the first to appear in the kitchen and he brought the morning paper that he had collected from the front yard. He was dressed in his overalls ready for work.

'If you read the morning paper you'd think there wasn't any war on at all!' he said and handed the paper to Joseph. 'Christmas ad after Christmas ad and no mention of the war in these ads and Christmas spelt with an X.'

'What is Christmas if you take Christ out, I ask you,' said Joseph, opening the paper over his knees.

'You could make a sermon out of that,' suggested Flora.

'It's not Christmas for our boys. There should be no Christmas presents this year. The money should be donated to the Red Cross and the Comfort Fund for wool and such for the soldiers. They survive on knowing those back home are always thinking of them,' said Thom.

Flora looked over Joseph's shoulder at the ads. Thom was right, you would think the world was at peace and everyone had money to splash. 'That's a very good idea,' said Flora. 'I daresay we could forgo presents for the war.'

'No we couldn't,' said Connie, 'that's not a good idea at all.' Connie had on her weekday dress but it was inside out. Flora sighed. That child was just not in the same world as everyone else.

'Connie, go and call Lydia and Danny for breakfast and put your dress on the right way out,' said Flora, putting the teapot on the table. 'And Thom, tell Mister Jake there is hot tea ready if he wants to join us.' Thom did so and then came back into the kitchen and kissed Flora on her forehead. She looked up at him. 'Are you off already?'

'Early start,' he said and grabbed the cheese and gherkin sandwich she had wrapped in paper, and was out the door to work.

Thom was an apprentice at Jobson Dewar Building. Currently they were commissioned to build an army storage shed next to the army office. All day Thom hammered, held planks, carried planks, sawed planks, and as he did he kept one eye on the men walking in and out of the army office next door in their uniforms, clapping each other on the back, all of them heroes who hadn't hesitated to join up. At lunch break Thom sat on a pile of timber slats next to the three other men working this job. He got out his sandwich and put it on the timber next to him. Then he took the bible out of his satchel. He had to tug hard, but freeing it, he took the grafting knife from the pocket of his overalls. The men sitting near him laughed and Johnno said, 'Following in the old man's footsteps, eh, kid? You gonna convert us all?'

'Nah,' said Thom, 'I'll see you blokes in hell.' The last thing Thom wanted was to become his father. There was a dark seed in his father that all his father's zealousness couldn't bury deep enough. Thom knew he had his own dark hazy void in the middle of his stomach, but he wouldn't use God to suffocate it. He wanted to hold onto his dark place forever because it was where the shadow of his real mother lived. He often lay in bed and tried to remember her. But there was just the grey ghost of her somewhere beyond his consciousness. In those moments he was a little boy waiting for her to come back and blaming his father that she had gone.

He loved Flora but was always aware she was a stand-in. It filled him with a desperate need to be different to his father, the man who lost his mother somewhere and then replaced her with Flora. So he tried to be as different as he could. Where his father was religious and good, Thom tried to be bad, and only pretended to pray in church and at family devotions. Where his father was contained, Thom tried to be unpredictable. By being different he would make his own mark, not realising that his efforts to be different were superficial and that he couldn't escape the goodness and the steadfastness his father and Flora had poured into his bones.

Thom opened the bible.

'Go on then, give us the verse of the day to set our hearts on the narrow road,' said Dazza, scrawny and brown but stronger than he looked and able to carry three planks at once.

Thom flicked to near the back of the bible. '*For you walk in lasciviousness, lusts, excess of wine, revellings, banquetings, and abominable idolatries*,' read Thom theatrically.

'Bloody oath,' laughed Johnno, his belly heaving with emphysema as he lit up another smoke.

The men watched as Thom flipped back to near the beginning of the bible and took the grafting knife and cut deep into the pages, a swift line straight through the words of God. He turned the bible and cut in the other direction and again and again and he pulled out the rectangular cut pages and repeated the process until he had cut a grave into the bible.

'The word of God for you, Dazza, and for you, Johnno,' he said and handed the men the cut pages. Then he put the bible back into his bag and, shooing the flies away, he ate his cheese and gherkin sandwich. The men, curious as hell, said nothing, because after all it was none of their business what the kid did and after a swift glance at the pages he'd given them they screwed them up and tossed them to the ground.

After work Thom walked to the Peter Lalor Hotel that sat proudly on the corner of Doveton and Mair streets. Walking around the corner into Doveton he entered the laneway behind the hotel, and there he met Franko, a tousled-looking man who, when he called himself an artist, everyone laughed and said 'con artist'. Thom swapped a hard-earned crown for a small bundle that he tucked safely inside the bible he had prepared.

And so it was that night that books approved by Joseph were no longer the only books being read in the manse. Because inside Thom's bible, now hidden under his bed, was a banned, poorly printed copy of *Lady Chatterley's Lover.* Some pages were too faint to read, other pages were smudged and too dark. Only one proper copy had made it past the government censors to the sandy shorelines of Australia and that one book was then copied many thousands of times. It was exchanged in pubs and laneways as buyers handed over crowns, quickly grabbing the illicit pages under a table or behind a lavatory door and stuffing them into a bag. Women hid copies under the mattresses in their children's prams and under the silks in their lingerie drawers. Poor old David Herbert Lawrence, his magnum opus was only to be read in dingy, damp corners, but still, he was used to it. His book *The Rainbow* had also been seized and burned and thirteen of his poems were removed from his book of poems called *Pansies* and his exhibition of paintings was raided and every painting with a tendril of female pubic hair was confiscated. If Thom's copy was ever found he was going to swear black and blue that he didn't know how it got there or how the bible had been vandalised. But as far as he ever knew it wasn't discovered and safely slept in the dark under his bed.

Lady Chatterley's Lover wasn't Thom's only sin. Sometimes after work in the lane behind the Peter Lalor Hotel he played illegal two-up with half-drunk men who kept dashing inside the pub to fill up during the six o'clock swill. And if anyone said, 'Hey, aren't you the reverend's son?' he would laugh and say, 'Everyone says that but nah, he just looks like me. Lucky bugger.'

And during the full moon he would wait for Danny to start snoring and then pull out the postcards he had hidden in a dark corner of the tallboy. Pulling the curtain aside, he would look at them in the moonlight before sleeping with torrid dreams.

Thom didn't know that Connie, having worked out he had done something with the bible, had to find out just what he'd done. So one afternoon, before Thom got home from work and while Danny was playing outside with Gabe and Mike, she'd looked under his bed, in his closet, and finally felt under the mattress, where her fingers caught hold of the edges of the bible. Pulling with all her might, she'd dragged it into the light, and it fell open revealing its secret: a book within a book. Connie couldn't read but she knew it was a bad book because why else would Thom have hidden it? Connie touched the book and was sure she felt the tips of her fingers burn. Did she dare open it? Of course she did, but there were no pictures, which made it boring. She closed the bible with its secret inside and pushed it back under the mattress as far as she could and she smiled because she knew something about Thom that he didn't know she knew. And that was power even a five year old could feel.

When Corporal Tuddenham dreams of early retirement

Tuesday, 19 December 1939

Thom lay awake all night and by morning he had made his decision. He got up, had his breakfast, put his sandwich into his satchel without even bothering to ask what was in it, forgot to kiss Flora, and went to work. Then at four, when Johnno said he could knock off, he walked up Sturt Street and down Lydiard to the recruiting office at the School of Mines, a rambling, cold bluestone building, and went inside and stood in line with the other six men and the two more who came in after him. He kept his head down and pulled his cap over his eyes in case someone recognised him. He wasn't the shortest in the row; he had inherited his father's height. He was tall and lanky and that was going to come in very handy when he got to the front of the line. Every now and then he snuck a look at the other men. Luck was going his way; he didn't know any of them – that was not an easy thing to accomplish in a small town of thirty-nine or so thousand people. Which may seem a lot of people but eventually everyone knows everyone and everyone knows your business and who you're related to, and if they don't actually know you they at least have friends or family members who do know you and who can tell them all your secrets whether you want those secrets known or not. But Thom didn't recognise anyone at all.

Corporal Tuddenham was not a good fit for war. He was a man who should have been born in a time of opulence and leisurely, overly rich meals with lots of potatoes and gravy. He was a man who believed in six-hour days, two-hour lunches, and that being a good government employee meant creating as little paperwork as possible, which in turn meant doing as little as possible. His face was round and flaccid, his arms were soft and pudgy and his belly was held in by the bursting buttons of his army shirt. He had only ever worked in administration, where he could sit in front of a typewriter all day and watch the men training outside his window. He dreaded having to do any real fighting.

So it was lucky he had been sent from Melbourne to manage the recruitment office in Ballarat and not to some godawful front where he would have to do actual fighting. It was lucky for Thom that Corporal Tuddenham was from the city and it was doubly lucky that Corporal Tuddenham was only interested in stamping what he had to stamp and moving the line on so he could get to his supper.

Thom got to the front of the queue and found himself standing at a wooden trestle table covered in pastel towers of papers, pink, blue, white and yellow.

'Name,' said Corporal Tuddenham, pulling a sheet of cream paper from the pile and feeding it into his typewriter. Thom said his name.

Corporal Tuddenham adjusted the glasses on his nose and without looking up said, 'Where were you born?

'Are you a natural born British subject?

'Age and date of birth?'

And Thom, prepared as he always was and having practised in his mind while he'd been waiting in line, said the year of his birth was 1921, some three years and three months earlier than it was. It fell off his tongue pretty easily; he was proud of himself for delivering the lie. He was sure his father had never had the courage to lie. The date he gave still made him under twenty-one but together with the letter he had giving permission for him to join up, signed with his father's signature, or as close as Thom could get it, he was eligible. Corporal Tuddenham didn't quiver at the lie. He didn't even look up at Thom. He moved on. As was his habit.

'Letter from parents?'

Thom handed over his forged letter and Corporal Tuddenham stamped it and put it in the wooden box at the end of the table. Then he went on with the form.

'Occupation?'

'Chippie,' said Thom, and the corporal wrote *builder* on the form. Thom was asked his next of kin and gave Lydia's name.

'Have you ever been convicted of a criminal offence?' Thom laughed and Corporal Tuddenham sighed loudly. They always laughed. Even if they did have a criminal record.

'Sign here, here and here,' said Corporal Tuddenham and Thom signed that he had answered every question truly and that he was willing to serve the Australian Military Forces within and beyond the Commonwealth. Corporal Tuddenham witnessed his signatures that attested that Thom had promised his life for the duration of the war and twelve months thereafter unless discharged.

'Take this and this,' said the corporal and he yanked the enlistment form from the typewriter and held it and a blue sheet of paper mid-air. Thom took the papers and stood waiting for his next instruction. Then, weary of his life, Corporal Tuddenham said, 'Next,' and waved Thom on, still without looking up. He had a fair idea a good percentage of the sign-ups were under or over the age requirements. But what he didn't see he didn't know. So he kept his head down and the stamp well inked. Thom went and stood in the next line as he couldn't see anything else to do.

Soon Thom was in his shorts and singlet. He was measured (5 foot 10 inches, four more than required), his chest was listened to and measured (38 inches), he was weighed (150 pounds), his eyes and ears were tested and his feet inspected, and he was stamped fit and able class A1 and his enlistment form went into a box and it was the first A he'd ever got.

Next he was passed on to the uniform trestle table where he stood in front of Lance Corporal Scutcheon, who was his height and looked to be not much older. Lance Corporal Scutcheon didn't want to be handing out clothing like a girl in a shop, he should be off at the front doing something for the war, and his scowl said this to Thom. Clothing spilled off the shelves and Thom could see why they had been asked to build a storeroom down at the barracks. Lance Corporal Scutcheon read the measurements on the sheet of blue paper Thom handed him and then reached behind him and grabbed a slouch hat, a khaki shirt, khaki trousers, brown socks and slapped them on the table, then he walked behind the shelf and came back with a mess tin, cup and plate, which were thumped hard onto the table, making it rattle on its trestles.

'Boots?' asked Thom.

'Don't you read the papers?'

Thom looked at Lance Corporal Scutcheon, waiting for him to explain.

'We're short on supplies – no boots and no gaiters. You have to use your own until the government in its wisdom sorts it.'

'Weapons?' asked Thom hopefully.

Lance Corporal Scutcheon laughed, then he looked at his colleagues sitting at the other trestle tables and they looked up and laughed too, even Corporal Tuddenham had a chuckle. Thom felt the heat rising in his neck and cheeks.

'Let's get you trained first. Then you can go kill Nazis.' Thom stuffed the clothes into the duffle bag he was given and flung the strap of the hat over his arm.

'Do I report next Monday?'

'Hardly,' said Lance Corporal Scutcheon.

Thom was confused.

'It's Christmas Day and then New Year. We'll see you at the army barracks in Shepperd Street at six sharp ready to march to the train station on Monday the eighth.'

And then Thom was out in the evening air, waving his piece of paper and ready to report for duty in what uniform it pleased the army to provide.

Thom walked slowly back down Lydiard Street, past Craig's Hotel, past the Mining Exchange on the other side of the street, planning where he was going to hide his army gear, pleased he was going in his own direction, making his own decisions and that the path he was taking was the opposite of the one his father wanted. Filled with these exciting thoughts rushing around like toy soldiers in his brain, Thom headed up Mair Street to the Peter Lalor, even though it was getting late and, after half an hour of gambling, a sin that would horrify his father, Thom had won a shilling and lost two. He began walking home down Doveton Street and that's when he saw Lydia engaged in her own bit of sinning with his mate George Wilson down Wigton Place alley. Thom leant against the brick wall of the lane and he crossed his arms over his chest and waited for Lydia to notice him.

Finally she sensed his presence and her eyes opened with shock as she realised he had been watching her entangled kissing with

George for some time. She pushed George away and straightened her body and her clothes and her hair.

Thom wagged his finger at her and shook his head. She looked scared, so he laughed and said, 'Don't worry, your secret's safe,' and he zipped his lips.

'There's no secrets in our family,' said Lydia, picking up her school bag and coming towards him with a worried-looking George following.

'George,' said Thom, nodding at his friend, then he turned to Lydia. 'We better get home or they'll be asking where we've been.' He saw George sigh with relief. 'I wasn't going to go you, George. Lydia can decide who she kisses.'

'Well,' said George, 'some older brothers can be overly protective.'

'Oh, by the way,' Thom said as they walked off down Doveton Street. He put his arm around George's neck, pulling George uncomfortably towards him. 'If you hurt her, I'll have to kill you of course.'

Lydia kicked him in the shin. 'Owww,' he said, letting George go and making it sound as though she hurt him. 'I was only protecting your honour.'

They walked on and, reaching Dana Street, Lydia said, 'I suppose we must part here, George,' as though parting was such sorrow and she was the only thing sweet in the world.

'Yes, well, this is it for me,' and he nodded in the direction he needed to go, in the opposite direction down Dana.

'Shall I see you tomorrow?'

'Go on, give him a kiss goodbye,' said Thom, and Lydia kicked him hard in the shins.

'Oww. That really hurt that time.' He rubbed his leg hard while Lydia pecked George on the cheek. Then Lydia and Thom turned the corner and went up Dana.

'How long?' asked Thom as he and Lydia turned into Dawson Street.

'Me and George? A few months,' said Lydia. 'He's signing up next week though.'

'He's too young,' said Thom.

'You all just have to be heroes,' said Lydia.

'Have you told him you'll wait for him?' said Thom.

'I told him I'd pray for him,' said Lydia, mockingly holding her hands together.

'Well, you can pray for me too,' said Thom, putting one arm around her and holding out the duffle bag and slouch hat in the other.

She pulled away from him. 'Why didn't I notice?'

'You were rather busy with other matters.'

'Tell me no, Thom. I can't stand it at home without you there.'

'Oh, and that's the only reason you're worried, is it?' laughed Thom and she punched him in the arm.

'I won't make it into the army if you keep injuring me,' he said and pulled her against him, resting his arm around her shoulders. 'You can't tell anyone,' said Thom, leaning into her ear. 'Not a word – especially to Connie.'

'And you can't tell anyone about George – especially not Connie. Are you really intent on going off and killing yourself?'

'I told you, I'm going to be a hero. Now, where do you think I can hide this stuff for a few days?'

Only Connie, who was sitting in a dark corner of the shed playing with the frogs in their buckets, saw Thom stuff a big bag into the corner of the shed behind the push mower.

When Dr Salter has his Christmas Eve ruined

Sunday, 24 December 1939

Birdie sat in the Sunday service four rows from the front. Joseph's sermon washed over her, barely wetting her. Birdie's heart was at sea, lurching this way then that, fearing for Aubrey's safety, then angry with him because he hadn't sent one measly shilling home to her to feed the boys – not even for Christmas. Her love for Aubrey was a tide crashing in then out, sometimes full and sometimes barely there. Because it was Christmas Eve there was no Sunday school and beside her Gabe fidgeted and she patted his leg every now and then to remind him he was in church and needed to be quiet.

Further down the pew Thom was counting down the days until he had to report for duty and wondered if he should ask Viola to write to him while he was away. She looked so lovely, sitting on the other side of the aisle, two rows back, in her light summer frock and her straw hat with a yellow ribbon, and when the congregation stood and sang 'Hark the Herald Angels Sing' Thom could barely stop from turning to watch her, but she didn't glance at him once.

Lydia was sitting next to Thom, thinking of George and wondering if she actually liked Winston better. George had signed up, as he said he would, and had asked her to write and she said she would because how could she possibly say no when he might be going away to die? It was only letters he asked for, after all, so that didn't stop her from seeing other boys, did it?

Connie, sitting on the other side of Thom, was staring up into the high arched ceiling of the church, then, without warning, she leant right over both Thom and Lydia, her elbow digging into Thom's leg, and said to Flora, 'I think the demons are winning.'

And Flora nodded and whispered, 'It does seem that way for the moment.'

Then Connie sat back up and said to Lydia, 'I saw you kissing Winston behind the fence.' Lydia's face drained of its enthusiasm-for-life peachiness and she gaped at Thom to help her shut Connie up before Flora heard her.

'Connie, you shouldn't be a peeping Tom,' he said.

'Pa will use his belt on you if he finds out you've been kissing boys,' whispered Connie, and Lydia glowered at her and leant over Thom too, so Thom had to stretch right back into the pew and Lydia whispered into Connie's ear, 'One word, Connie, and I'll kill you. I will.'

Joseph took a breath between sentences and looked over his congregation, letting his last words sink in. Normally there would be about a hundred in his congregation, but today the church was packed, people squeezed into the pews, their sweat mingling as sticky arms pressed hard against each other. The women fanned themselves with hymn books and the young children grizzled so that Joseph had to speak over them.

On the other side of the world, where the weather was cold and icy, Pope Pius XII sat in his gilded room with the fires burning. He hadn't been able to sleep and had called for breakfast. On the trolley near him was strong hot coffee in a silver pot and next to the pot was a plate of chocolate and *biscottate* and *amaretti*, more than the pope could possibly eat in a day, let alone at one meal. Beside the breakfast biscuits and chocolate sat a pot of warmed milk. Pius thought of himself as Eugene, which his family still called him when no one else was around. He poured coffee into the gold-rimmed bowl, then the warm milk, and took four of the biscuits and sat down with his feet as close to the fire as he dared. He had issued a five-point plan to bring peace to the world at Christmas. It was his gift. It was filled with beautiful words about human rights and dignity. He hoped it would end the war.

Everyone but Eugene knew that though words could start a war, they could hardly stop one, and so the world ignored him. Joseph, who had a much smaller audience than the pope, couldn't bring himself to preach about peace, which he thought was a pipe dream. Instead he preached about the ultimate war between good and evil.

'In the last days – if everyone stays faithful – good will win out. God will triumph over the devil,' he boomed over the miserable hot babies as they whined. But as lovely as Reverend Starr was, as sweet and reassuring as his voice was, his congregation just weren't sure they could believe him any more than that Catholic pope. All anyone really cared about was the men who were going to be missing from their Christmas lunch.

Joseph finished his sermon and said the benediction and old Mister Hooley, who had been playing the organ since anyone could remember and rarely played the list Joseph gave him, instead playing his own choices, put his fingers to the keys and instead of 'Joy to the World', the chorus of 'Waltzing Matilda' rang out through the church. Flora looked at Joseph, who shrugged, and she sang along as she joined Joseph in walking down the aisle, her voice clear over the organ, and soon everyone was belting it out at the top of their lungs – *You'll come a-waltzing Matilda with me* – and as they sang they thought perhaps, with determination, good could win after all.

Birdie didn't join in the singing; she just couldn't bring herself to be joyful when there was so much threat. She walked past Dulcie and Nola, who tried to catch her eye, and went straight to the back of the church where Flora and Joseph were shaking the congregation's hands one after the other as they passed through the small foyer and she stood in the queue. When it was her turn she held out her hand and Flora's warm hands gently enclosed her own.

'Birdie?' Flora asked, leaning in close.

Birdie hesitated. 'Nothing,' she mouthed back.

'Oh, Birdie,' said Flora.

'Never mind, if worst comes to worst, there's his mother or mine.' The shame of not having a husband who would support her was bitter in her mouth and Birdie swallowed it down, patted Flora's hand and walked out into the morning sun to find her sons. She knew they would most likely be next door with the Starr children. She saw them by the lemon tree in Flora's side garden. They were playing knucklebones with pieces of lamb bone with Danny and Connie. The lemon tree was growing awfully large. It wouldn't bear good fruit if it grew too large. She should warn the reverend about that.

'What does your father feed the tree?' she asked Danny.

'I feed it,' said Connie, coming to stand in front of her and wiping her grass-stained hands across her yellow gingham frock. Birdie noticed the shirring across the bodice had caught on something and was pulling. She should offer to fix that for Flora.

'Tea and pee,' said Connie. 'I feed it pee and tea.' The boys laughed and parroted her, 'Tea and pee, tea and pee.'

'Gabe and Mike, I need to have a word with you, come here – now, please.' Birdie walked away from the tree, out of Connie and Danny's hearing. Mike put his knucklebones in his pocket and got up and ran over to her immediately, but Gabe walked over slowly, belligerently, his hands in the pockets of his shorts, straggling on purpose, resentful she had interrupted his game. She shook her head; he was his father's son. She waited patiently and when he too was standing in front of her, she crouched down, her face level with theirs. Looking over Gabe's shoulder she saw the reverend's girl watching with her intense blue eyes, which sent a shiver running through Birdie's blood. She shook the shiver out of her and looked back at her boys and said quietly, 'Directly we'll be having lunch. You need to eat up big and not go running off to the river or anywhere else.'

'But you tell us not to take more than our share,' said Mike.

'Not today – today you need to fill up.' She looked back at Connie, who was still staring at her. That girl was insolent and spoilt by Flora. Determining to put the child out of her mind, she stood up, moved her bag to the other arm, fixed her hat, and straightened her back so that when she walked into the church hall neither Dulcie Whittaker nor Nola Turnbull nor Viola nor anyone else would see just how alone she was. 'Don't be late for the church luncheon,' she called back to the boys.

Now Birdie and Flora had been friends since primary school and their friendship was built on each balancing what the other lacked. Where Birdie never could grab hold of all she needed and had empty spaces inside her, Flora could sense the unfilled places in people's souls and knew that sometimes all a body needed was another's touch or kind words. Flora was like a spring morning and people were drawn to her freshness and warmth, and in a crowd of people she would be the person everyone's eyes settled on, and her words would be the ones that people quietened to listen to, even though she would be by far the shortest in height. Birdie reminded Flora that life and all it could promise didn't always fall easily into people's laps, and that kept Flora's feet on the ground. Because Flora knew that life had brought her more than her share. They fitted together as friends, each being what the other needed.

And when the last of the lunch plates had been washed and put away, and most of the Starrs' visitors had gone home, Birdie sat at the empty dining table staring at nothing because she couldn't face going home to her house with her nearly empty kitchen cupboards. She had made shirts for the boys for Christmas; she had remembered how they reacted to the sailor suits and she had taken two of Aubrey's crisp white work shirts and cut them down to size and turned them into the same shirts but much smaller for each of the boys. Tomorrow they would go to her parents for Christmas lunch. She had sewn a tie for her father, a small pouch that would hold a lipstick or a few pennies for Viola, and an oven mitt for her mother. She made these out of an old skirt, pink with blue flowers, using the same material for each gift so that even her father's tie was floral. But after Christmas there would be no more food apart from the wild tomatoes in her garden and the apricots and pears on the trees. She didn't know how they were going to manage and she didn't want to move in with Aubrey's mother or her parents. She was afraid if she did she would disappear before she had hardly begun, but perhaps she would have to. Flora came and sat next to her and held her hand and they sat like that in silence until finally Birdie said, 'I'm ready now.'

'Let's go and find what our children are up to this time,' said Flora.

'With my son and your daughter, it could be anything,' said Birdie, and still holding hands they walked outside and she saw the boys were lying on the grass under the lemon tree with Connie and Danny – four little soldiers all in a row.

'There's hardly any shade under that tree,' said Birdie. Her boys would be sunburnt. She would cut open an aloe vera stalk later and spread the stickiness over their faces and arms and legs. She stood over her boys and looked down at them.

The boys put their hands over their foreheads and squinted up at her.

'Come on, we must be off,' she said and she held out a hand to each of them. Their weight in her hands as she pulled them up was reassuring; they were real and were hers and nothing could take them away.

'Come to Christmas lunch tomorrow, after the service,' said Flora.

'We have to go to my parents,' said Birdie, and she let go of the boys' hands and without thinking or knowing why, she threw herself into Flora's arms and for a moment felt her weight being held by Flora and she breathed in the deep headiness of having no concerns or troubles that must be Flora's life all the time. They held each other at arm's length and wished each other happy Christmas and Birdie called the boys to follow her as she went up the driveway.

Going down Dawson Street, the boys dawdled along behind her. Where was the play fighting, the punches just missing each other's cheeks, the jabs in the stomach, the skipping and running? Perhaps they were more sunburnt than she had reckoned on.

'Come on, boys,' she cajoled them, but they slumped and dragged their feet and she took their hands and nearly pulled them home. She opened the back door and the boys walked into the lounge room and slumped on top of each other into Aubrey's big chair.

'Goodness,' she said, 'what have you been doing to be so worn out?'

'Nothing,' said Gabe, and his voice was raspy and had lost all its defiance.

She felt a desperate need to cheer them up, to bring them back to normal. 'Would you like the wireless on? It's probably time for *Children's Hour.* Would you like a cup of tea? Would you like a bath?'

But the boys didn't answer and the prickles on her skin turned frozen and icy and not even the stuffy hot house could melt them. She walked over to Gabe and put her hand against his forehead and then Mike's and bile rose in her throat and she gulped it back down and tried to think. She ran to the bakelite phone; it stared at her, black, dressed for a funeral. She picked up the handset and dialled 9 for the Ballarat exchange and asked the operator to put her through to Doctor Salter. His number seemed to ring forever but finally his voice crackled down the receiver, 'To whom am I speaking?'

Birdie tried to speak but the words were stuck. She took a deep breath and croaked, 'Birdie Mabbett, come quick.' And she dropped the handset and it fell onto the telephone with a thud and rocked to find its place as she ran back to her boys.

She felt their foreheads again; their skin was hot, red and sticky. It could be sunburn. It only took fifteen minutes to burn beetroot red in this heat. Perhaps they had sunstroke. She knew that could kill a person. She ran to the kitchen and got two glasses of water but when she came back the boys were asleep. She picked up Mike and his weight made her grunt; he was heavier than she expected. She carried him up the hallway, bumping into the walls as she tried to balance his weight and almost dropped him onto her bed. Then she walked back to the lounge room and picked up Gabe, who after Mike was light, as if he was nothing at all, and she carried him to the other side of her bed. She went to the laundry and filled the bucket with cold water and got a flannel from the linen press and she dunked the flannel into the water, squeezed it out and wiped the tacky sweat from Mike's forehead and then she rinsed the flannel in the bucket, walked around the bed and wiped Gabe's head. The boys drifted in and out of sleep as she sat beside the bed, watching, watching, and then moved to the other side and watched. How could they be playing one minute and so sick the next? And where was Doctor Salter? It seemed hours had passed before she heard the thumping on the back door.

She looked at the boys and then out the bedroom door to the direction of the thumping; she didn't want to leave her boys to answer it. The thumping grew more demanding and she ran down the hallway.

'Quick,' she said to Doctor Salter, 'this way,' and she ran back up the hallway to her bedroom.

Doctor Salter was a short man with a goatee beard and darting eyes. You would think to look at him that he would be quick and nimble, but to Birdie he seemed to take forever as he walked up her hallway, slowly removed his hat and said, 'You do realise it's Christmas Eve, Missus Mabbett, and I do have children of my own,' and he put his hat purposefully on the end of her bed. Then he looked at the boys, sprawled in her bed, their faces wet with sweat, the pillows under their heads damp and said, 'Mmmmm, did I need to be called out for a bit of overexertion in the sun?'

He turned and his eyes flicked over the room and looked at her with disapproval as if to say, *What else could he expect from a single mother?* And Birdie straightened her shoulders and stood tall. She would do anything, take anything, for her boys and she let his condemnation wash off her. She didn't take her eyes off Doctor Salter as he reached into his bag and took out his thermometer bottle. He unscrewed the bottle, took the thermometer out and shook off the disinfectant and then forced Mike's mouth open and pushed the thermometer under his tongue. Birdie winced as Mike cried out. The doctor swirled the thermometer in the disinfectant bottle and then put it under Gabe's tongue. Then he put the thermometer back in the jar of disinfectant and screwed on the lid and put it back in his bag. He didn't talk as he lifted Mike's arm in the air and again Mike cried out, which made Birdie cry out, and Doctor Salter looked at her crossly to be quiet. She ignored him and stood right over him as he listened to Mike's chest with his stethoscope, straining to hear the thumps of Mike's heart, and she followed him to the other side of the bed as he repeated all this with Gabe. Birdie rubbed her arms and scratched at the itchy spots that were bursting on her skin. Doctor Salter stood up, took hold of her elbow and pulled her out into the hallway.

'Well, Missus Mabbett, I don't think it's sunburn or heatstroke.'

Birdie sighed and tears came to her eyes with relief.

'They might have polio – we've had an epidemic every summer for years now. We keep hoping it will end, that next summer it won't make an appearance, but it's been so hot so early this year and it seems to come despite our best wishes. Keep them cool, remember polio likes heat, lots of fluids, and they'll be better. It can take its time, polio, or it can get better or worse quickly. There's no way to tell.'

'But they're getting worse,' cried Birdie, scratching her arms to red spots of blood, 'they need to be in the hospital.'

'Nonsense,' said Doctor Salter, and walked back into the bedroom, closed his bag and came and stood close to her. 'I know you worry about them more than is a normal amount for a mother. It's because you don't have a husband around to assist you.'

'He's at the war.'

'Well, wherever he is, the result is that you are what I call a *mater incredibili sollicitus.*'

She looked at him blankly.

'You over-worry,' he said crossly.

'Will you come back tomorrow?' she called as he went down the hallway towards the back door.

'It's Christmas Day. Try and enjoy it, Missus Mabbett,' he called back over his shoulder and the door swung shut behind him and she was alone with two sick boys and for the first time she wished with all her will and determination that Aubrey would magically appear. She sat on the bed and tears spilled down her cheeks as her heart split and shattered. At seven the boys were worse and she couldn't even wake Mike to give him water and at eight she rang the exchange who rang the doctor's phone and he said, 'For goodness sake, Missus Mabbett, it's Christmas Eve. Have some respect. I told you, Missus Mabbett, they will be fine. Yours are not the only children to contract polio. They won't be the only ones to recover.' He hung up and half an hour later she rang again. 'I'll keep ringing until you agree to see them again,' she said.

'I'll see you tomorrow, even though it's Christmas Day, or maybe Boxing Day,' he conceded and with this she had to be content.

Birdie left the light on and sat in a chair beside the bed where she could keep an eye on them. Every now and then she woke with a start, not meaning to have fallen asleep. She got up and got fresh flannels and wiped the sweat from their foreheads, she lifted Mike's arm to wipe the sweat from it but he cried out so mournfully that his cry sent sharp icicle barbs right through her skin and she carefully laid his arm back down, gently and softly, hardly touching him as though he was made of the most fragile memories and would disappear on her, and she didn't even try to wipe Gabe. She listened to the carollers out in the street and she sang along, her voice weak and unsure but she sang to her boys until, against her will, she fell asleep.

When Birdie knows better

Monday, 25 December 1939

When she woke in the morning, the room was silent and lit by the sun creeping through the gap in the curtains. She looked at her watch and saw it was eight and she looked at the boys who were both peacefully asleep and she realised the doctor was right after all, they were recovered. There was no more moaning or the smell of sweat. She turned off the light and pulled the curtains open and went to the bed and felt Mike's forehead and it was cool. She breathed with relief and shook him gently to wake him to give him water as the doctor had instructed but he couldn't be woken and she put her hand against his mouth to feel his breath. She rushed around the bed to Gabe and felt his forehead, it was still hot and clammy and she shook him and a small moan left his lips; she put her hand against his mouth and felt his breath hot against her skin. She ran to the phone and dialled 9 and asked to be put through to Doctor Salter immediately. She waited forever to hear his voice and when he answered he sighed loudly and said, 'It's Christmas Day, Missus Mabbett. Do you have no decency?' and she said, 'My boy's dead, Doctor Salter. Mike has died, Doctor Salter, so are you going to save my other son or not?'

Within an hour her house was a flurry of activity. Two ambulances came, white with painted-over windows. They looked like coffins on wheels rather than instruments of salvation. Two ambulancemen in white uniforms held her tight while they lifted Mike from the bed to a stretcher, his body a small hill under the white sheet. It needed only two men to carry his weight and they took him away to a waiting ambulance and the neighbours watching from a safe distance shooed their kids safely inside away from the deathly germs and back to their presents.

When the men released Birdie, she crumpled to the floor. She heard painful howls but didn't realise they were her pain consuming her, flames licking at the far reaches of her soul, her heart, her bones and skin. Then she remembered Gabe, who was struggling to breathe and who could no longer move his limbs, who was being taken to the other ambulance and she tore at her arms as she clambered up from the floor, raced through the hall, the door, the garden and rushed for the other ambulance. She wouldn't let them take her other son as well. She would keep him with her, she would keep him alive if it killed her. His tiny head was poking above the white sheet, his body strapped tight to the stretcher with leather belts. They slipped the stretcher into the ambulance and she tried to clamber in after him but she was pulled back by the men who were stronger than she was.

'Missus Mabbett, Missus Mabbett, look at me. I've rung the hospital,' said Doctor Salter, grabbing her arms and turning her to look at him. 'I've rung the hospital,' he said again, as though he had saved the day. 'They are expecting him and luckily have an iron lung available. He'll be put in it. He has some chance of surviving – though he won't be undamaged, so you must get used to that knowledge. Visiting is at two o'clock. You can go and see him then.' Then as fast as they had all arrived, they were gone and all she was left with as she stood in the middle of the road was – nothing.

Birdie stumbled into the house and sat alone in a hard wooden chair at the hard wooden kitchen table. The house was empty of doctors and nurses and ambulance men. It was empty of her boys' laughter trickling through the house. It was empty of their running footsteps as she told them to walk inside. It was empty of anything that mattered.

Birdie should have known better than to think she could have a happy life.

When there is a commotion

Thursday, 28 December 1939

There had been no presents and no Christmas lunch. No carols were sung around the piano, or games played, there were no crackers or silly newspaper hats or bonbons or bad jokes. There had been no forgetting the war for a blissful few hours, and no one bothered to listen to the king's speech on the wireless. Flora didn't bring out the pudding she had made months earlier and basted with brandy each week so it wouldn't mould. She hid the brandy in the laundry and did it every year and if Joseph tasted the brandy he never said a thing. The pudding stayed alone in the dark, in its calico bag, pegged to the inside clothesline that was suspended from the laundry ceiling. Boxing Day came and went and there were no picnics at the lake in the hot December sun that jeered at them all whenever they ventured out. The boys didn't play backyard cricket in the street in their singlets and shorts with upturned rubbish bins until their skin was blistered and pink from the sun.

Christmas had passed by unnoticed for three days. On Thursday Joseph stood behind the pulpit feeling the weight of all the evil in the world pushing his shoulders into the floor beneath him. His anger, dark and purple, came from deep within him and pushed at the wall of his skin. He was full of questions about why God would add pain to pain, like everyone else, but unlike everyone else he somehow had to find words that would give Birdie – and the congregation – faith and hope at this funeral for her son, and he hoped the words would calm his own rage. Gripping the sides of the pulpit, he fought against the spirits of doom he could feel but not see.

Connie could see them. She could have told him the angels were losing.

Joseph raised his voice and pushed his words out against the foul fog he could feel descending on them all.

'Heaven is the opposite to the world,' he said. 'In heaven there is no war, no death, no artillery, no rations. In heaven aggressors will lie down peacefully with their enemies like lions lying down with lambs. Bombs will be turned into tools like swords turned into spades with which to garden and grow.' Joseph lowered his voice and leant forward over the congregation.

'That is where Michael, Mike, is now. He is smiling and skipping, he is in a place of unending beauty and peace.' Joseph's voice rang out over the small coffin, over the daisies wilting in the heat, over the mothers worrying, sick in their stomachs that their children would catch the dreaded polio too. His voice soared over Birdie, who was consumed with the knowledge that life would never be fair to her, and over Flora, who felt useless in the face of Birdie's immense loss and grief. Joseph filled his words with expectation and still the words seemed to Flora to dissipate into thin promises.

'It's because of the demons,' whispered Connie, who was sitting beside her mother.

'You shouldn't speak during the funeral,' whispered Flora.

'It's the demons,' said Connie quietly, and she pointed at the ceiling. Her mother bent her ear down to Connie. 'The demons are piercing Pa's words with their forks, that's why the words aren't working.'

Flora looked up at the church's high ceiling, at the beams covered in cobwebs that could only be reached on an extended ladder, and shook her head. It seemed to her to be filled with a bleak emptiness. She looked over to Danny, who had barely spoken in the last few days; he was sitting on the other side of Connie. She looked at Connie, who seemed to have buried herself further in her own strange world where Flora couldn't reach her, and she turned and looked at Birdie, her skin so thin Flora could see her bones. It was as if Birdie was made of paper; one decent rain and she would be washed away without a trace. Flora counted the sores that ran up Birdie's arms where she had scratched till her skin bled. Then she looked at Birdie's grey face, staring out at a world that held no future for her. Flora put her arm around Birdie as they stood for the hymn and held her tight.

'I'll hold you up,' she whispered, 'just lean it all on me.' As Flora held Birdie, Birdie's weight fell helplessly into her and Flora stood, her feet apart, digging into the floor for strength and balance and sang for them both *as the darkness deepens Lord abide with me*, and she didn't notice Connie and Danny slip from the church.

Of her three stepchildren, Flora loved Danny the most. She couldn't help it. Thom and Lydia could remember their mother and there was always a sense with them that she was somehow a usurper. That, even though she hadn't met Joseph until after his first wife had died, perhaps she had somehow even caused their mother's death. But Danny was only a baby when Flora began to care for him. She was the only mother he could remember and he loved her with admiration and believed every song she sang to him and every kiss she gave him. And that made it so easy for her to be his mother. There were no memories she had to be better than. When he was little he thought the world became sunnier and warmer when Flora sang and he thought his father could reach into the clouds and touch God.

Danny believed every word his father spoke. Joseph's soft lilting voice settled on Danny's skin like warmth from a fire, making Danny feel safe. But then Danny believed everything anyone said to him without question. If you said to Danny that when he was in his forties a man named Ron Popeil would invent a device that would scramble an egg in its shell, Danny would have no reason not to believe you. Or that when he was eighty-two a woman named Anke Domaske would invent clothes made of milk, he would picture it in his mind and know it could be done, or that one day soon you would not only be able to listen to men far away in your own kitchen on the wireless, but would be able to see them too, Danny would believe it. So Danny had no reason not to believe Connie when they tumbled out of the church into the hot sun and she said, 'My angel Mike has told me what to do with the frogs.'

'Oh, I'd forgotten all about the frogs, Connie,' he said. Since Mike died his world had been a numb hollow place. He and Mike had been bonded not by their differences, like Flora and Birdie, but by their similarity. Neither he nor Mike pulled the wings off ladybirds like the other boys, instead they carried them outside in the safe chamber of their cupped hands and then they would set the petrified ladybirds free on a branch so they could fly away home. Neither he nor Mike teased Connie and when they found other children taunting her, they would put a stop to it and they would take Connie away to a shady corner of the churchyard, wipe her tears, and distract her with their marbles or a story they made up. When, down at the river, Gabe had whispered to them that they should abandon Connie and run home without her, Mike and Danny had said *No* in unison. Then Danny had said, 'Connie is special.' He didn't know if she really was but he knew he was her older brother and he had a responsibility to protect her. It's what his mother Flora would want.

'Like peculiar,' Gabe had said, stumbling over the word so it came out *pecuke-ular.*

'No,' said Danny.

'Like a retard,' said Gabe.

'No,' said Danny. 'Anyone can see she's not a retard, you retard. She's just Connie, that's all.' And they noticed that Connie was watching them from where she stood in the water in her wet Sunday dress, a skipping stone in each hand. She looked like she was about to cry. She knew they were talking about her and Danny had called out, 'Go on, Connie, we'll count the skips,' and she'd smiled instantly, forgetting her hurt, and threw her stones across the water.

But now Mike was gone and Danny knew he could never be replaced, he would never have another friend who knew him without words. Friends like that come once in a lifetime.

Danny and Connie hadn't discussed Mike's dying or Gabe being in hospital in an iron lung. Danny didn't know what that was but it sounded like torture, like Daniel being thrown to the lions or like the Protestant martyrs being burnt at the stake. He couldn't understand why Gabe and Mike had got sick and he and Connie hadn't and wished he had because then he would be in the hospital with Gabe or in heaven with Mike. He knew Connie felt the same because on Wednesday night when everyone was asleep Danny had got out of bed and gone into the laundry at the back of the house. He had a plan to get sick too by sitting on the cold floor all night, but when he got to the laundry Connie was already hiding in the dark. She was curled up in the corner in only her nightie and with only the light from the night sky filtering through the window into the room.

'What are you doing, Connie?' he'd asked, and she'd said, 'Catching polio.'

'You won't catch it here in the laundry, old bean,' he'd said, even though that was exactly what he had planned too, and she said, 'I thought if I got cold enough I'd catch it like you catch a chill.'

'It's too hot to catch a chill,' said Danny, 'even in the middle of the night.'

And he'd sat on the floor next to her and they looked up at the Christmas pudding hanging above them like a moon. Danny knew that there were going to be no more escapes to the river or lying under the lemon tree deciding what animals the clouds were with Mike and Gabe. They knew they would never see Mike again and they had been warned that Gabe, if he lived, would be a different boy the next time they saw him.

'He will most likely be a cripple,' Pa had explained. 'He will be in a wheelchair. He won't be able to run or play.'

Connie and Danny had stood side by side in front of their father trying to imagine Mike in heaven and Gabe in a wheelchair. No amount of straps and buckles could keep Gabe in a wheelchair. Their veins boiled with anger at their father's words and the anger travelled through their bodies to their brains and hearts. And Danny being Danny had pushed his anger and pain to a place in his belly where it turned into a sadness that he thought would never leave him.

As they stood in the driveway beside the lemon tree Danny could hear the congregation inside the church still singing the hymn. He looked at Connie so she could explain why she had dragged him out of the funeral but she looked into the sky and nodded as though she was listening to someone. Then she turned to Danny and said, 'Come on.'

Danny shrugged; the funeral was dreary and Mike's grandfather, Mister Mitchell, had stood up and spoken about Mike but nothing he said actually sounded like the Mike Danny knew and he trusted that whatever Connie needed to do it must be important for her to drag him out of church, so he followed her as she ran to the shed. She opened the rickety door, went to the dark corner and picked up one of the buckets. Perhaps she was going to drink the frog water to try and catch polio again, but instead she handed it to him. He looked inside at the frogs, clambering over each other in panic at their world being shaken by an earthquake. She held the other bucket against her chest with both arms leaving dirty streaks of muddy water on her Sunday best dress.

He followed her, carrying his bucket of squirming frogs down the driveway and back to the church and they crept quietly inside and stood at the back. Their father was praying now and everyone had their eyes shut. Connie nodded at him and he knew what they had to do; he crept to the other aisle and then they both knelt down turned their buckets up and frogs, frogs, frogs slipped and tumbled out onto the church floor. With their sudden freedom they croaked and hopped and leapt into women's laps and they sat on bibles and they perched on the backs of pews and stared with big black startled eyes at the startled people. Mabel Finchley squealed when a frog jumped onto her chest and clung there for dear life and her squeal caught and all the women squealed and Joseph, who had stopped praying, looked about for the cause of the commotion that had interrupted Mike's funeral but all he could see were frogs jumping down the aisle towards him because Connie and Danny were already lying under the lemon tree, the incriminating buckets tossed on their sides not far away.

'Archangel Mike is happy now,' said Connie.

'There's a horse, there,' said Danny, pointing at the clouds.

'Can you see Mike riding it?' she asked and he looked at her and looked within himself and saw that he wasn't going to get the dreaded polio and that no matter what, his life would go on and he said, 'You know, Connie, I think I can.'

As terrified frenzied frogs croaked and jumped, Joseph vainly called for calm. Flora thought only of Birdie – she would be distraught that frogs were leaping through her son's funeral, it would break Birdie into a million pieces. Flora looked at Birdie and Birdie slowly smiled, then, her eyes moist with tears, she began to laugh.

'I can't wait to tell Gabe about this,' she said. 'He'll laugh and laugh and Mike did so much love collecting frogs down at the river.' In that moment Flora realised the children hadn't been by her side in church for some time and with that realisation came the realisation of who had caused this commotion.

'Connie,' she said. The frogs would be Connie's doing. Flora looked around the church. Viola, Claude and Elsie were on the other side of Birdie, all too consumed with the loss of their grandson and nephew to care about the frogs. They huddled together for strength. Flora looked behind her at Dulcie, who always made a fuss of everything, flapping her arms about and swatting at frogs like they were flies. Gertie was holding her hat with its large yellow-centred daisies over her face. The frogs, hoping the daisies were real, had attempted to hide in the foliage. Nola was squealing as though she was being murdered. Indeed, what a commotion.

'Shall we?' Flora said to Birdie and held out her arm. Flora saw that the moment in which Birdie had smiled and laughed was gone and Birdie was again drowning in her anguish. She was scratching at her arms, creating new red scars and she looked at Flora with hollow empty eyes.

'Come on,' said Flora, and she linked her arm through Birdie's, tilted her head up and whispered, 'Keep your head up, Birdie dear, so they can't see,' and together with their heads held high under their church hats they walked down the aisle in their funeral frocks and no one saw that tiny Flora was holding Birdie up. They walked through the parted Red Sea. There was a chasm between them and the screaming women and the shocked men trying to catch frogs in their hands. It was as if the rest of the congregation were locked away behind a great sea-glass wall as an amusement for Flora and Birdie to gaze upon as they walked past, carefully stepping over the bounding frogs. Flora stood outside the church door blinking in the sunlight and then, her arm still linked in Birdie's, she walked them to the driveway of the manse where they saw the two children lying under the lemon tree, pointing at the sky and laughing.

'Don't punish them,' pleaded Birdie.

Flora looked at Birdie, surprised to see how earnestly she was pleading for the children. Normally Birdie's only concern was her own two children. It was an easy thing for Flora to give Birdie what she requested, so she took a deep breath and, trying to sound as stern as possible, said, 'Children, put those pails away immediately.'

She might not punish them, but they needed to think she might, and if Joseph realised it was them, he would. Connie and Danny, shocked at their mother suddenly sounding just like their father when he was furious, jumped up and grabbed the pails and stood looking at her with their mouths gaping open. They looked at the pails and back at their mother and knew that she knew where the frogs had come from. They expected the worst. The strap from their father at least.

'Shut your mouths before you catch flies, children,' Flora said. 'And change your clothes, quickly, and make sure to put those ones in the laundry and make sure you are out the front in time to walk to the cemetery.' And the children ran, not believing their luck and Flora smiled at Birdie. 'I didn't know I had that in me.'

Flora and Birdie waited, two women, the hot sun beating down on their black jersey dresses, their arms linked, their hearts still, as they prepared to bury a boy. Women found their way out through the frogs and were brushing each other's frocks and wringing out their hats to make sure they were rid of the brown amphibians. Joseph came out and behind him four men carried the small white coffin.

Joseph came over and leant down to Flora's ear. 'We'll deal with them later,' he said, and Flora wasn't sure if he meant the frogs or if he had reasoned that their children were to blame. She looked over to where Lydia and Thom were laughing as Lydia mimicked Nola Turnbull's screams and flapping arms, then she looked down as she felt Danny and Connie standing at her elbow and saw they were in clean clothes with wide terrified eyes as they wondered what punishment was coming their way.

'Right then,' she said, 'in line, you two, and make sure you stay right where I can see you.'

Then Birdie and Flora led the procession to the cemetery. Joseph walked between them and Connie and Danny walked meekly at Flora's elbows and everyone said what wonderfully good children, how obedient and compliant, how respectfully they were mourning their friend. Viola, Claude and Elsie walked behind and everyone thought about Gabe, lying alone in his hospital bed, near death and unable to farewell his brother.

When Flora takes advantage of her position

Sunday, 1 January 1940

'I don't know why you have to spend so much time at Gabe's house,' Connie said.

Flora took her by the shoulders and said gently, 'Because, Connie, right now Missus Mabbett needs me more than you do.'

'But it's not fair,' said Connie. 'We barely had any Christmas, no Eton Mash, no presents and now no Sunday lunch.'

'I thought you hated Sunday lunch. And it's Eton Mess, which I can still make one day if we can get some cream,' said Flora.

'Well, why can't I come to the hospital at least?'

'Because they won't let you in on account of that you might also catch polio and it's a miracle you haven't so we won't tempt fate further than we have to. Now, go help your father make sandwiches for lunch and collect any eggs those silly chooks have laid.'

They were in the church kitchen where Flora was overseeing the cleaning up after morning tea. She ushered Connie out of the hall and Connie, angry at the world for taking away the things she hated as much as the things she loved, went next door to the manse and opened the door of the chook house.

'Go on,' she yelled. 'You stupid chooks might as well fly away too,' and she chased the fat lazy chooks to their unwanted freedom until their squawking as they ran in circles in the backyard brought Joseph from the house.

Connie said, 'I don't know how they got out,' and helped Joseph round them up and was promised an extra slice of cake after lunch for her efforts.

Connie was right, though. Flora had been going to Birdie's every day since Mike had died. Birdie had lain in bed unable to move, her bones and sinew racked with the pain of her grief. Her chest crashed in on itself and she breathed in laboured gasps. To Flora's horror, Birdie refused to go to the hospital. She was afraid that Gabe would die too, and she couldn't bear it. So if she didn't go to the hospital they might not tell her and she wouldn't know and she could keep pretending Gabe was alive.

Now it was New Year's Day and Flora stacked up the last three dirty cups and saucers into one hand and looked over at Birdie who was sitting in a kinder chair staring at the black and white linoleum. She had sat in that same chair, Viola on one side of her and Claude and Elsie on the other, all through morning tea. She stared at the floor as people milled about her with their biscuits and tea, barely able to look at them; their sympathetic glances and whispers were like shards of glass in her soul.

Viola got up and came over to Flora. 'Flora, I'm taking Mum and Dad home.'

'I'll look after her,' said Flora.

Viola walked back to Birdie and bent over so her face was level with Birdie's. 'You should move back in. I don't mind us sharing our bedroom again. Perhaps we won't fight over our clothes now we're older.'

But Birdie didn't answer. She didn't know who she was or where she was going. Or how she would wake up tomorrow.

'This is the last,' said Flora and she put the cups and saucers next to the sink full of dirty water where Dulcie was washing and Nola was drying. Every now and then the two younger women had started tittering, whispering and laughing, and Flora frowned at them – this wasn't a time for gossip with Birdie sitting right in the next room, full of raw pain – and they would stop chatting and turn back to the dishes for another five minutes. Flora emptied the teapots down the gully trap outside the kitchen. She could hear the chickens squawking and wondered what Connie was doing to them. She went inside and turned off the urns.

'All done,' said Nola.

'Thank you, ladies,' Flora said, and saw them to the door as if the church hall was her home. She shut the door behind them and walked over to Birdie, took her hands and pulled her up from the chair. Flora tucked a curl away from Birdie's face and said, 'Are you ready?'

Birdie's face was blank, empty of every feeling.

Flora had gone to Humffray Street before church, pulled Birdie out of bed, helped her dress, combed her hair and walked her to church just as she had done the day of Mike's funeral.

'Come on,' said Flora, 'we're going to go see Gabe.'

'But your Sunday lunch,' Birdie said.

'It won't kill us to have one lunch late. I've told Joseph to make sandwiches and to save us two for later,' said Flora. 'I won't take no, Birdie. You know that. I got you to church today, didn't I?'

And Birdie, not having the energy to fight anyone, let alone Flora, nodded.

Flora took Birdie in her arms, supporting her thin bones, and walked her out the door, turned and pulled it locked it behind them, and held Birdie tight as she walked up Sturt Street to the hospital, carrying Birdie's weight the entire way. Flora wondered if Birdie would ever be part of the world again. The small moment in the funeral when Birdie had laughed seemed gone forever. She needed to be reminded that she still had a living son who needed her.

At the hospital Flora nodded to the nurse at the reception desk, and she and Birdie went up the stairs to the second floor, halting at the glass windows and locked doors of the polio ward. The sign on the door said, *Juveniles forbidden from entering this ward. Visiting hours strictly 2 p.m. to 4 p.m. Immediate family only.* Flora knew that being the reverend's wife had some advantages; she didn't have to worry that they were an hour early or that she wasn't immediate family. The nurses knew Flora, the Baptist minister's wife who often visited the sick with her husband, and who had visited Gabe over the last week even though his mother hadn't. So the nurse let them in with a nod to Flora and a look of shock at Birdie. The nurse opened her mouth to say something to Birdie but Flora shook her head and moved Birdie, who could barely walk without her, into the ward towards Gabe.

Inside the ward eight iron lungs were lined up, four each side, and poking out of six of the iron lungs was a tiny head with large frightened eyes and all that tiny head had to view the world with was a small mirror attached awkwardly with screws to the body of the iron lung. Flora and Birdie went to the last iron lung on the left-hand wall.

Gabe tried to smile when he saw his mother in his mirror. It was secured above his immobilised head and what he could see in that small portion of mirror, the size of a car's rear-view mirror, was now his world. Inside the iron lung his arms and legs were plastered and his plastered arms and legs and his torso were strapped down tight with leather straps so that he was completely restrained. Flora crouched down and looked into the mirror and saw the pale, scared eyes and realised Gabe was being crushed and eaten. The iron lung was a huge whale monster, it had swallowed him for lunch and didn't want the last bit – his head. The longer he stayed in there the more he would disappear.

Birdie crouched down beside Gabe and smoothed his sweat-soaked hair and they stayed until the bell rang for the end of visiting.

On their way home from the hospital Birdie said, 'Every night I pray for God to give me polio instead so I will be strapped down, immovable like a stone statue, like Lot's wife. But God doesn't answer my prayer, just like he didn't answer my prayer to save Mike. I don't think God is answering, Flora, because I don't think God is actually there.'

And Flora held her tighter. If she had to, she would walk Birdie to the hospital every day of the week until she decided to live again.

It's the grand old Duke of York

Monday, 8 January 1940

Even though it was the first week of January, no matter how hot and dry or how fiercely the north wind blew, the small city of Ballarat would always cool down at night, and in the night air that was relief from the suffocating heat of the day, the men would forget their anger and guilt and the wives would forget how he had come home reeking of Ballarat Bertie's and they both would forget how the war had them all on pins and needles and throw their arms around each other and hide together under the summer cotton sheets. And the night-time coldness would stay as long as it could, trying not to leave until finally the sun shooed it away.

Thom lay in bed waiting until the first light filtered into the room past the faded floral curtain. He held his watch up to the light and checked the time. It was five-thirty. Thom got out of bed and reached under his mattress and pulled out the bible with *Lady Chatterley* safely tucked inside. He tiptoed across to the tallboy that knew all his boyhood secrets; he had stowed many things in its dark corners. He kept an eye on Danny to make sure he didn't wake, then he slowly opened the door of the tallboy and put the bible in the far right-hand corner where one day Danny would find it and know Thom had left it for him. He picked up his boots from under his bed and tiptoed down the stairs and left a note on the kitchen table.

For a moment he wavered. He put the note down, then picked it up again. He should have had the courage to tell his parents that he'd signed up and was leaving. After all, he was going to be a soldier and soldiers needed to be brave. How could he face the enemy when he couldn't face his parents? But it was too late now, so down the note went again and he pinned it under the edge of the aluminium teapot with its brown bakelite handle.

Connie had been woken by the creak on the stairs. She got out of bed and followed Thom, keeping a distance so he wouldn't know she was there. As he tiptoed out of the kitchen she took the note from the table and held it tight in her fist. Thom tiptoed past the stretchers in the vestibule and disappeared into the shed, then soon he was back, dressed in his soldier's uniform. He bent down and left his pyjamas in a neatly folded pile on the back step. Connie watched all this from the kitchen window. The last she saw of him, as she watched leaning over the front gate, was his back walking down the footpath towards Sturt Street, that big bag slung over his shoulder. Because she couldn't read the note, she had become bored with it and walked into her parents' bedroom and dropped the scrunched-up ball of paper right on Joseph's nose.

Thom was on his way – off to war – off to a grand adventure. As he walked down Sturt Street he swung his arms in straight exaggerated swings, as though he was already marching with his troop. He stomped his feet down into the asphalt pavement so they thumped in a rhythmic drumbeat. He nodded at the milkman who went past, his horses clip-clopping on the road and his bottles rattling in his cart. He passed the window cleaner who was running a squeegee down the enormous Thomas Jewellers windows, creating little rivers that ran down the glass, which he then came back and wiped away. Thom nodded at the man and horse walking up the street with the bakery cart, a manly nod that was barely perceptible because he was a man now and no longer a boy and the baker tossed him a bun, still warm, and Thom tore off a large chunk of the soft white bread with his teeth. This was already a fine adventure. He turned into Grenville Street and then crossed over to the army headquarters. Men were gathering, all in their spanking new uniforms – uniforms to make their mothers proud. You could not imagine that blood and flesh, sweat and tears, would ever stain those shiny brass buttons. Thom joined the men. He stood in the middle of a group he didn't know so he wouldn't bump into someone who did know him, who might give him away, although it was too late now, surely. It was signed and sealed – he was in the army.

'What time is it?' he asked one of the men.

'Shouldn't you be getting ready for school?' the new soldier said.

'I'm older than I look,' said Thom to the man who, with his freckled nose and his eyes that had never seen trouble, didn't seem all that much older than him.

'Sure you are,' said the soldier and he put out his hand and Thom shook it hard to show he was a proper grown-up man.

'Alfie,' said the man, then he turned and yelled, 'Hey, Geoffrey, come and meet this young blighter who reckons he's twenty-one.'

'Eighteen,' said Thom. 'My father signed for me.'

'What? Doesn't he love you?'

Thom must have looked devastated because Geoff slapped him on the shoulder and said, 'It's all right, kid. It's his sense of humour – he hasn't got one.'

At six-thirty Corporal Tuddenham appeared and stood on the steps looking like he'd rather be anywhere else. He had just three hours to whip these men into something that the town could be proud of. He blew a whistle and the men all stopped talking, stood up straight and looked at him.

Corporal Tuddenham nodded to Lance Corporal Scutcheon, who yelled, 'All right, privates,' and that made the men stand even straighter and taller.

'Get into rows, three abreast. Now – pronto!'

The men scrambled into ragged lines. Thom stood next to Geoff and Alfie. Lydia's George, who he'd been looking out for, was right behind him. His heart was thumping against the buttons on his shirt. The sun was getting warmer and already making him sweat. It was going to be another stinker of a day with heat that would send old people to the hospital and drive mothers mad as their babies grizzled and whined. But the sun didn't bother Thom. He couldn't wait for it all to begin. Once the instruction *March* was yelled it would be real – he would be in the army.

'First thing,' yelled Lance Corporal Scutcheon, 'is teaching you men to march.' He paused so his words could sink in. 'In time!' Pause. 'So that when your mothers and sweethearts arrive to see you off they can be proud of you.' Pause. 'Now, on the spot on three.'

The men marched and the ground shuddered under their thumping boots, but Lance Corporal Scutcheon yelled, 'No. No. No. IN TIME! Starting again on three.'

Thom marched on the spot, watching his feet and watching the feet of Geoff and Alfie to make sure they were all together. By the sixth time they had it and he nodded and smiled at Geoff and Alfie but their faces were full of shock and horror as though the fighting had already started. Thom felt a sharp painful yank on his ear as it was grabbed, hard. It hurt; his ear was being ripped from his head, the pain shot through his brain like lightning. His ear was hot and burning like coals as the rest of his body was forced to follow his ear to keep it on his head. His ear was dragged through the men to a sudden halt in front of Corporal Tuddenham.

'You signed up my son, private!' said Joseph, still in his dressing gown, still holding onto Thom's ear so tightly Thom thought Joseph planned to hold onto his ear forever. He had his son and he wasn't letting go. Thom's insides, his guts and his blood and bones dropped to the ground as he realised that every man was watching. The quadrangle was silent – all eyes were on him. He was bent over, the rest of his body following in whatever direction Joseph pulled his ear and Thom looked up, from under his hair, at Corporal Tuddenham, to warn him that he shouldn't antagonise his father, not when he was using his quiet voice. But Corporal Tuddenham didn't know Joseph and said boldly, 'Corporal, actually. Can I help you?'

'Are you the idiot here – I am assuming it was you –' and Joseph looked at Corporal Tuddenham, who reached for his belt and clutched it tight as Joseph's fury hit him in the face and Joseph quietened his voice even more and said in a low growl, 'that signed up my underage boy?'

'He had a note,' Corporal Tuddenham stammered.

'Sorry, private,' said Joseph, acting as though he hadn't heard and knowing full well the man's rank.

'Corporal,' said Tuddenham, and repeated, 'He had a note. He had a signed permission letter with your name and signature. There's nothing you can do now.'

Joseph took a deep breath. 'Obviously it was a forgery.'

'It looked ridgy-didge,' mumbled Corporal Tuddenham.

'Sorry?' said Joseph.

'It looked ridgy-didge,' said the corporal, a bit louder.

'Look,' said Lance Corporal Scutcheon, stepping in to back up his superior; surely they could manage a man in a dressing gown. 'They're just about to leave for the station and they'll go to Mount Martha for training and you don't have to worry. He won't be going to the Northern Territory or New Guinea or anywhere overseas. We don't send the young ones to any of those places. We keep them here safe. He'll stay on Australian soil. Most likely he'll be back here in Ballarat in no time.'

Joseph looked like he was thinking about it and Thom felt hope rise in his ribs and wriggled because his father might finally let go of his red-hot ear pulled to a thin stretch of skin, but still Joseph held tight.

'It'll be the making of him – you'll see,' said Lance Corporal Scutcheon.

Joseph leant forward and, completely ignoring Scutcheon as though he was no more than an annoying fly, he glared at Corporal Tuddenham and Thom saw Corporal Tuddenham begin to shake. Such was the force of his father, even in a dressing gown. The Germans should try and take him on.

'Get me a sheet of paper and a pencil,' said Joseph.

Corporal Tuddenham nodded at Lance Corporal Scutcheon, who scurried into the office and came back with a sheet of paper and a pencil and handed them to Joseph, who finally let go of Thom's ear. Thom could at last stand up straight and he rubbed his ear hard to get rid of the burning. Joseph scrawled *721* on the sheet of paper and handed it to Corporal Tuddenham.

'My phone number. You get my son or any more of my children in here signing up, you ring me. Do you comprehend?'

Corporal Tuddenham nodded. Then in a tiny voice he asked, 'How will we know who your kids are?'

'For goodness sakes, man, it's Ballarat. If you don't know them someone will. Remember the surname. Starr. That's not too hard, is it?'

Thom felt the pull of his army issue shirt collar as it was grabbed firmly by Joseph and he was dragged like a naughty schoolboy past the men going off to war, and someone began to sing and soon the other men joined in, *The grand old Duke of York, he had ten thousand men, he marched them up to the top of the hill and he marched them down again.* Thom grinned at the men and did a little jig like this was all planned for their entertainment – *Enjoy, boys, before you go off to war!* He was dragged past the new recruits' wives and sweethearts, who had begun to gather to cry and to make promises to wait, and he blew them kisses. He waved his arms like a conductor as he passed the band who had held their instruments frozen in mid-air as they watched Joseph order the corporal about, and past Viola whom he'd sworn to secrecy and asked to write to him, who had put on her sunny yellow dress to see him off. Seeing her there watching him being dragged off by his father like a schoolboy, Thom was ashamed. He was dragged past the shopkeepers just opening their stores in Sturt Street and the only marching Thom did that day was his march home, past Connie, who was swinging around the trunk of her lemon tree as if it was a maypole. Thom looked at her and she shook her head.

'You're not very good at hiding things, Thom,' she said. 'I'm much better.'

'That's enough, Connie,' snapped Joseph and he grabbed Thom's ear and dragged him up the stairs, where he was put in solitary confinement in his bedroom while Joseph decided what his fate would be.

Thom didn't think he could ever forgive his father.

When Flora comes to the rescue

Wednesday, 31 January 1940

Nearly three weeks ago, on 13 January 1940, seventy-one people had lost their lives, at least five towns were wiped from the earth as though they had never existed, and Ballarat had been covered in thick, rolling grey smoke that came like a tidal wave and was so dense that you couldn't see your hand in front of your face. Then ash fell like snow. Connie, Joseph and Flora had stood on the front steps of the manse watching it.

'It's beautiful,' Connie said, holding her hands out to catch the ash.

'It's the remains of people's homes,' Flora said, and Connie snapped her hand back to her side.

'As if the war wasn't enough,' Joseph said.

Connie had looked up then, shielding her eyes from the falling ash, and seen how the demons jumped and threw their long barbed forks and yelped with joy. They had it all over the angels.

'The demons brought the ashes from hell,' Connie said.

Joseph and Flora looked at each other. 'Yes,' they said.

Now it was the end of January, Connie had forgotten all about the big fires, except at dinner time, because since the fires Flora had been busy cooking casseroles for needy families, which meant the good food was going to people Connie didn't even know and Connie had to put up with the chicken soup that was left for them. But her mind was filled with more important things than dinner.

Next week Connie would start school. While she wanted to wear her new school tunic, she didn't like the idea of classes, which Lydia never stopped moaning about. Connie had better things to do than school. She tipped the contents of her parents' chamber pot onto the roots of the lemon tree and gazed up at its leaves. Her tree had no thorns. Joseph said this was because it was a hybrid. The tree had grown over summer; it had fruit, lemon-shaped but orange and juicy and sweet, and there was a branch she was sure was strong enough for her to sit on. She reached up to the branch and swung on it. Her angel smiled down at her from where he perched at the top of the tree like the star on a Christmas tree.

Connie could just hear the drone of the wireless in the distance. Inside the house Neville Chamberlain talked about peace as though talking about it would make it happen. But Winston Churchill, the announcer claimed, said the war was the war everyone had to have, that this blood and horror was a cleansing that would rid the world of evil and usher in a new era of everlasting peace. Joseph switched off the wireless; his audience was much smaller than Churchill's.

On the other side of the fence the door to the church hall was open to let in any breeze that might come through the stifling heat. Connie could see women bustling back and forth with the Sunday school chairs, cakes and sandwiches, stopping only to fan themselves with a hanky or a paper fan or a hymnal.

She decided to give her branch a try and clambered up the trunk, putting a tear in her dress as she did so. Perhaps it would mean she'd get a new one. The branch bent under her weight, but it didn't break. She swung her legs and Archangel Michael sat beside her and they watched unseen as Joseph and Flora walked past to join the women in the hall. Soon Connie could hear her father's voice as it floated out the door.

'A new world exists for all in the afterlife as a consolation, a reward for putting up with this life and all its pain and sorrow. We must hold onto hope in the face of the current world, which is so dire for so many of us.' He took a breath and mopped the sweat from his brow with his handkerchief. The air in the room was thick and suffocating and outside the sun beat angrily at the windows like hell-fire and they all felt they were in an oven.

Flora, who sat at the front with Joseph, cast her eyes over the women. Mabel Finchley looked as though without her son Manny the world had already ended and they were all in the scorching pits of hell. Birdie stared out the window not listening to a word Joseph was saying, as though she would quite happily throw herself into hell's fiery mouth. Her mother Elsie sat next to her, tightly clenching her handkerchief as though it was her most precious possession and if she didn't hold it tight enough someone would steal it away. And Meryl Rowbotham had her lace-edged hanky out, dabbing at the tears in her eyes.

Joseph finished his homily and Flora looked up as he turned to her. She was in charge of the women's bible studies each Wednesday morning at ten-thirty. He only came to give the talk. Traditionally the women's bible study was held in the manse lounge room, but that was when Flora was lucky if fifteen women turned up. When it reached twenty-five women Flora realised she didn't have enough chairs.

'Come on, ladies – follow me,' she'd said and moved them into the church hall. Now fifty women came and the number was still growing. Soon they'd have to move into the church, and the deacons wouldn't like that – women speaking in church, acting like their little bible study was a church service. Besides, bible study was less formal and everyone sat, even Joseph. Flora thought the women came to hear Joseph's clear deep voice and his words from God. But they came for her.

Joseph stood up and looked over at the trestle table at the back of the hall and said, 'Well, ladies, I'll leave you to your sandwiches and cake.' He nodded to the trestle table, the food covered in clean tea towels to stop the flies that swarmed like vultures.

'Shall we?' said Flora, and some of the women went into the kitchen to make the tea as others lifted the tea towels off the food, then because of the flies put them back again. The women would just have to reach underneath the towels.

Plates were handed around; the heat was complained about and the air raid shelters being built at Dana Street school were discussed. There were to be three, one in each corner of the school, except the corner that was asphalted for the quadrangle. Then talk turned to rationing and cosmetics, which were getting harder to get, and what would be rationed first. The women agreed it would be clothing, and that was why those with money had rushed to Harry's and Messer and Opie's and Faull's straight after Christmas to buy up clothes and shoes, and to the grocer's to stockpile tins of condensed milk and sardines, which they had then hidden in their rooftops and behind their winter blankets in the dark linen presses in their laundries.

The women talked about beer rationing, which they hoped would happen soon, and how the men who were still at home would have to give it up. *Drink for Need and Not Habit*, said the government's posters, and the women reminded the men of this as they headed off to the Peter Lalor and the men laughed and said, 'A man always needs his beer and, in these times, even more so.' And then they would say back to the women, 'Did you not read that the government posters say, *Natural is smart*, and you don't need to waste money on make-up,' but the women knew better and said '*Beauty is duty*,' and used whatever bits of cosmetics they could find at the bottom of their bags and drawers to look bright and sparkly despite the war, but of course they were only doing it to keep the men's spirits up.

Flora saw Meryl still sitting in her chair, her eyes moist as she held back a dam of tears. Flora had been visiting Meryl last Thursday when John Rowbotham told his wife he'd signed up. His sea-blue station master's uniform was the smartest clothing he'd ever owned. The Rowbothams had married when he was eighteen and Meryl sixteen and they'd had six sons, bang, bang, bang, one after the other, and five of them were now aged between nineteen and twenty-five and those five had turned up all together two weeks prior and stood proudly in front of their parents and announced they had one and all joined up. That left only the baby, Chris, who at sixteen hated being called the baby, behind.

John decided there and then that with his five sons signed up he might as well sign up too and, without telling Meryl, had gone to the recruitment office, given a false date of birth that made him five years younger than he was, which Colonel Tuddenham hadn't disputed, and signed himself over to the British Commonwealth. Most Ballarat men were assigned to the Eighth Battalion, so John thought if he was lucky the army wouldn't cock it up and he'd be assigned there too and be able to keep an eye on the boys. Then he'd walked home with his head held high beneath the beating sun. Seeing Flora sitting in his kitchen he'd said hello, but he couldn't hold his excitement in and blurted out to Meryl and Flora then and there that he'd joined up. Meryl had sobbed into the corner of her apron, dusty with flour, and flour clogged in the corners of her wet eyes.

'Meryl, sweetie, I'm only going to the front to look after our boys,' he'd said earnestly. Really, he couldn't bear his boys showing him up. 'Besides, with all this talk of peace the war is likely to be over in a few months. If I don't go now I might miss the chance,' he added, thinking it sounded perfectly reasonable.

'The chance for what?' Meryl cried.

'The chance to kill a few Gerries,' he said.

Flora had quietly excused herself from the family drama but this morning there was a photo of John and his six sons on the front page of *The Courier* – 'Six Men from One Family Give Their All', it sang. Bobby Winters from *The Courier* had turned up on the doorstep and asked for a photo of John and his sons and so Meryl had carefully taken the one photo she had of them all together out of its frame and handed it over. Mister Rowbotham and his six sons lined up side by side in their swimming suits. It had been taken the day they'd caught the 7.08 train to Geelong to spend Saturday and Sunday camping at Torquay. Mister Rowbotham and his six sons in their bathing suits at the beach, all smiling and not a danger in sight. So now, whenever she could, Meryl kept a hand on the youngest boy, Chris, gripping him tight so no one could take him away.

The number of men in the congregation had shrunk as more and more responded to the government's advertisements – *I've joined up. When will you?* The number of women who came to bible study and church grew as those deserted searched for solace and company.

'They will look after each other, you know,' Flora said to Meryl as she sat down next to her and passed her a lemon slice on a pink plate, 'and they'll look out for John too. They're good boys and if the war goes on longer than we anticipate and young Chris becomes old enough to join up, well, then you can always write to the army that he be excused from duty as all your other sons and husband have gone and so your family has already given more than is due. And if young Chris tries to join up illegally, well, I will send Joseph down to fetch him back just as he did with our Thom.' She put her hand gently on Meryl's trembling hands and Meryl felt warmth and reassurance rest on her skin and she heard herself saying, 'Yes, yes, I'll do that – I will write – that's exactly what I need to do. In fact,' and she stood up with more energy than she'd felt in weeks, 'I'll write this very afternoon and make sure in advance that they don't take Christopher.' And seeing that Meryl was feeling much better, Flora went and sat next to Mabel Finchley.

'Don't worry for Manny,' she said. Mabel screwed her fingers around themselves, then she looked up, her eyes full of grey tears, and in a tiny voice that was no more than a hairline crack in the world, she said, 'I've not heard from him.' Mabel gasped for air. 'Flora, he's my only child.'

Flora put her hand over Mabel's twisting contorted fingers. She felt Mabel's hopelessness enter her like a black vapour that filled her lungs. 'If he was dead you would know it in your heart, and if he's captured the Geneva Convention will ensure he is fed and treated properly, but it's most likely the army is confiscating his letters for our sake, for national security.'

Flora thought her words were thin and hopeless and of no use to anyone, but the women commented to each other how they felt lighter after Flora had spoken to them, and when she tenderly rested her hand on their arms they felt a kind-heartedness and calm fill their veins, and when she lifted her hand away it was as if she had taken some of their burden. Flora was unaware of the women hovering, waiting for her.

At a February meeting, when Jocelyn Lewisham said she was at home alone now, Flora put her hand on Jocelyn's shoulder to comfort her and in that moment she saw Jocelyn walking through the empty tomb that was her home, she saw her cold in the middle of the night searching aimlessly for comfort, and so she said, 'Jocelyn, why don't you move in with us for a few nights? Just for the human comfort.' She saw hope light Jocelyn's eyes and saw her shoulders become straighter, then Jocelyn said, 'Oh, I don't want to put you out; there are so many of you in your house already.'

'Nonsense,' said Flora, 'it will do both our souls the world of good to have you in the house. You and your baby can have Connie's bed.' And later when Connie complained and said it wasn't fair she was always giving up her bed to strangers, Flora, tired and worn out with other people's worries, snapped and said, 'For goodness' sake, Connie, you can be the most selfish child.'

Connie glared at her, so Flora tried to appease her. 'Would you like a slice of the banana bread I made? I was saving it for Sunday lunch.'

But Connie said, 'I don't like bananas.'

'But you liked them last week,' pleaded Flora.

'Bananas aren't on my diet,' said Connie.

'Well, what is on your diet?'

'Potato chips and sausages and lemonade.'

'Good luck with that during the war,' said Flora and Connie sighed as if Flora was the most useless mother in the world and ran off, and Flora was filled with guilt for being so harsh with her in the first place.

The following week Flora invited Frieda Gallway and Lottie Winters to stay for a few nights, and soon many more women were invited to stay so Flora was forced to ask the church deacons for thirty shillings to purchase two new camp beds from Harry's, and she put one under the stairs in the hallway, leaving just enough room between it and the bookshelf to get past if you walked sideways. The other camp bed went in the back vestibule, where there were now three camp beds. At night all four beds were filled with the soft weeping of lonely women who dreamt of the sweet touch of their husbands and when they were empty of women they were filled with the excited breathlessness of men from country areas like Beaufort and Lal Lal who had come to Ballarat to sign up and would be off first thing the next Monday morning.

Flora saw that Connie would barely look at their visitors and she wondered if the child had even one Christian bone in her body. And if she didn't, where had she come from?

When Flora sees Hazel dance

Tuesday, 5 March 1940

Flora was still going to Birdie's every day, helping her bathe and dress. Forcing her out into the world, compelling her to keep living, taking her to bible study, putting food in her cupboard and walking her up to see Gabe. Sometimes Birdie's mother Elsie would be at the little house in Humffray Street, washing the dishes or boiling Birdie's sheets in the copper. Sometimes Aubrey's mother Gert would be there, sitting in her own misery and eating Brockhoff's biscuits. Birdie would look at Flora helplessly and Flora would say, 'We can only keep praying and trust God to heal Gabe,' and the words sounded so stupid and meaningless.

Birdie was wasting away, becoming no more than a ghostly version of herself, a white apparition clothed in black. She couldn't think about Mike because every time she did the pain shattered her flimsy bones and her frail heart, yet he was all she could think of. Flora was afraid for Birdie. One day Birdie wouldn't be able to pick up the pieces and put herself back together, she would just float off into the air and disappear. None of the church women spoke to Birdie about Mike; the women at church knew it would be cruel and rude to mention him, it would be pushing her loss in front of her face so they didn't and they didn't know that this made it seem to Birdie like he had never existed at all. So, Flora reminded Birdie every chance she got that Birdie had a son who needed her and Birdie would nod and for a moment Flora would see her come to life before she vanished again into her grief.

On this afternoon when Flora said, 'I've come to walk with you to the hospital, Birdie – to see Gabe,' Birdie asked, 'So Gabe is safe?'

'Yes,' Flora said as she poured Birdie a cup of hot tea and, despite the escalating price, put several sugars into it to give Birdie strength. She passed the cup over and wrapped Birdie's cold hands around it. 'He's strapped into the iron lung, remember.'

Birdie seemed strangely pleased about this. Flora couldn't understand how her other boy being so sick could be a good thing and Birdie couldn't find words to explain that as long as he was strapped in an iron lung Gabe couldn't fall out of trees or into any old mine shafts, he couldn't drown in the river or get hit by the tram in Sturt Street. He couldn't blow pieces of himself away with firecrackers. He couldn't get lost in the bushes between Ballarat and Buninyong during long dark nights with no moon when he could freeze to death in the icy winter darkness.

'He has nurses looking after him all day and night?' said Birdie.

'Yes, but he needs you. He needs his mother,' said Flora, looking at her wristwatch. 'Shall we?' Even though it was warm out she got Birdie's coat from the hook and helped her into it. She wrapped the red knitted scarf around Birdie's neck and walked up the hall and took an old camel cloche hat from the stand and pulled it tight over Birdie's gold curls. Birdie was so thin the slightest breeze would take her like a falling leaf.

'Shall we get going?' said Flora, looking again at the roman numerals on her gold wristwatch. Joseph had given her the watch as an engagement present instead of a ring. He said he would buy her a ring when he could afford one worthy of her. She had thought him saying that was the most romantic engagement gift he could have given her. Her mother had thought it was cheap.

'We don't want to miss any of the visiting time,' she added, and put her arm through Birdie's.

Birdie picked her bag up from the kitchen bench and slung it over her other arm. And so, as she had done every day for more than two months now, Flora walked Birdie out the front door, up the small cracked path, up Humffray Street to Grant Street until they reached Drummond Street, where the red two-storey hospital sat solidly like a mountain that would never be moved. They went up the stairs to the polio ward and waited next to the closed double doors until the nurse pushed them open and secured them with a kick of her foot and nodded that they could go through. At four the bell would be rung and they would be made to leave.

Gabe was safe in his machine, like a butterfly trapped in its chrysalis. Flora stood back to let Birdie have her time with him; Birdie leant close and spoke to him in soft whispering murmurs. Flora looked at the other children in the ward. There were four of them, last week there had been five. Each week one seemed to die. Their little heads poked out of their iron lungs, worried mothers touched their wet foreheads – the only part of their child they could touch – and tried to smile to hide the fear that filled their bodies. Flora saw that two of the empty iron lungs were new, made of plywood instead of iron. She wondered how many children the disease would take over the next summer.

Flora looked away from the other children.

'When can Grandma and Grandpa visit?' Gabe asked weakly. 'Can I see Auntie Viola?'

'They only let in parents,' said Birdie. 'And Missus Starr because she is an official hospital visitor.'

Flora pulled *Pilgrim's Progress* from her bag and walked over to Gabe.

'Are you ready for the next chapter?' she asked into the mirror. She saw the dullness in his eyes; he was giving up and it made tears well in her throat and hope flee from her chest. The whole world was on the verge of giving up but Gabe was only seven. She opened the red linen covered book to page 51, then she flicked back and held the last picture to the mirror for Gabe to see because he liked the pictures, then she went back to page 51. '*I will yet go forward*,' she began. She was still reading, glancing at Gabe's reflection every now and then to check he was listening when she saw his eyes fill with terror. She turned to the source of his fear and saw two doctors striding into the room. Their heavy steps on the linoleum drummed a warning, but there was nowhere for Gabe to run.

'We're going to start his rehabilitation today,' said Doctor Unsworth, standing over Gabe. Flora had met Doctor Unsworth and knew he was in charge of the ward. She had sat next to Birdie as she shook and scratched when Doctor Unsworth told her that Gabe would be crippled and in a wheelchair for the rest of his life at best. Doctor Unsworth had tried to say this kindly and had spoken in a soft voice, leaning forward as though telling Birdie a secret, but the words were still cruel. He assured them that he had consulted with Health Department Polio Officer Doctor Fitzsimmons on the matter and they were both in agreement that this was the best that could be hoped for. Birdie needed to prepare herself, he'd said.

'And who is going to prepare Gabe?' Flora asked.

'He's a child,' Doctor Unsworth said, as though that was all that was needed.

Now two nurses came into the ward and Flora noticed how the one with red hair came through the door as if she was ready to take flight or dance. 'What a happy person,' she whispered to Birdie, 'in the face of such sorrow.'

'This is Health Department Polio Officer Doctor Fitzsimmons,' said Doctor Unsworth, motioning towards the other doctor and speaking loudly as if addressing everyone in the ward. 'He is here today to watch us take Gabe out of the iron lung, remove his full plaster and start the next stage of his treatment with half plasters. He will be out of the lung for the rehabilitation and then we'll put him back in after. Doctor Fitzsimmons is an expert in juvenile poliomyelitis.'

The nurse who had danced into the room came to an abrupt halt next to Doctor Fitzsimmons. The other nurse stood beside her, nodding in agreement with the doctor's words as though the doctor needed her permission to proceed. Flora looked at Gabe and saw he was afraid of what was coming, he was shaking as much as his restraints would allow and tears were rolling down his cheeks and falling into damp pools under his ears.

Flora looked at Birdie, who said, 'What if he can't breathe on his own?'

'They are probably letting his lungs get strong so they can work on their own, a bit at a time. Isn't that right, doctors?' said Flora reassuringly.

'Yes, you're quite correct, Missus Starr,' said Doctor Unsworth.

Flora put her arm around Birdie. She could feel Birdie shaking in her arms, tremoring more and more like an earthquake getting ready to shatter the earth into dust. She saw Gabe afraid and helpless and her heart lurched towards him and she told herself that surely he was in the best of hands. Doctor Unsworth looked at her and nodded towards the door and Flora understood that Birdie needed to be somewhere else.

'Perhaps, Missus Starr, you could take the mother outside the ward. You can watch through the glass but this isn't pleasant, I warn you. But it is necessary if he is not to be a vegetable for the rest of his life.' He didn't look at Birdie; he was still putting on a show for all the other parents in the ward.

Birdie didn't move.

'Nurse Harbolt, would you please take the mother and Missus Starr outside the room.'

Flora looked over to Nurse Harbolt so she could lead the way, but Birdie still didn't move.

'Now, little man, you need to be big and brave,' said Doctor Fitzsimmons.

'You need to be a brave soldier like your pa,' said Flora.

'Yes,' said Doctor Fitzsimmons, 'like your father. What's his name, this brave father of yours?'

And through his tears Gabe said, 'Dad.'

The doctors laughed and looked to Flora and she said, 'Aubrey Mabbett. His father is Aubrey Mabbett.'

And the red-haired nurse said, 'Aubrey Mabbett,' in barely a whisper, but Flora heard her.

'That's right,' she said and she watched as Nurse Harbolt's face drained of all its peppiness and lightness and Flora understood why.

'Yes,' said Flora purposefully, 'Missus Mabbett's husband Aubrey is away at the war.'

There'll be no dancing now, thought Flora.

'Ohh,' said Nurse Harbolt, her mouth a perfect O, and Flora watched as Birdie's face shot up and through her tears she stared at the nurse and their eyes locked and in that instant Flora saw them recognise who they were to each other and she held Birdie tighter and moved her towards the door.

'Nurse, please,' said Doctor Unsworth, 'we don't have time for pleasantries. Take the two good ladies outside.'

Flora was already walking towards the door with Birdie and she looked back to see Nurse Harbolt taking deep breaths and staring at the floor.

'Nurse, now!' said Doctor Unsworth, and so Nurse Harbolt forced one heavy foot in front of the other as she followed them out with plodding steps that weren't taking her anywhere she wanted to go. She can't look at Birdie now, thought Flora.

'You need to stay here,' Nurse Harbolt said. Still staring at the floor, she walked through the door and shut it behind her and was back at the doctors' side.

Flora held tight to Birdie because Gabe cried out as Doctor Unsworth unclipped the iron lung and forced open its huge mouth. The nurses rolled Gabe out on his gurney and Flora saw the leather straps holding him immobile. Gabe looked at his mother, separated from him by the glass window, and he cried out for her and Flora held tight as Birdie pulled against her to go to him. But Birdie was brittle and not eating and although Flora was shorter she was stronger. The doctors were unstrapping the leather belts. Next they unscrewed the braces on Gabe's arms and legs. Gabe cried out for his mother again like a dying soldier. He had seen this happen to other children in the ward who had come and gone before him. He knew what torture was coming next. Once the discarded braces had been moved out of the way, Doctor Unsworth took the small saw and cut through the hairy plaster casts and they were passed piece by piece to Nurse Harbolt who put them on the small trolley. The two doctors and two nurses surrounded Gabe and Flora and Birdie had to move to see what was going on. Then Gabe's piercing scream bounced from one wall to the other. It ricocheted through Flora's skin and into Birdie's heart, repeating over and over, and Birdie pushed forward and loosened herself from Flora's arms and ran into the ward, yelling, 'Stop, stop! Stop that! Stop it! Stop hurting my boy!'

Flora ran in after her.

The doctors put down the leg whose dead rigid muscle they had been forcing to move violently up and down and in and out. The two nurses kept their hands on Gabe's shoulders, holding him down.

'Move away from him!' yelled Birdie. 'I mean it, move away from him or by God I will, I will,' and she opened her purse and frantically looked for some kind of weapon but all she could find was a half-folded pamphlet, so she waved that in their faces.

'Missus Mabbett, this is quite unnecessary; we are only trying to heal your boy. If you hope for him to have any mobility at all then this is quite, quite essential and you need to be strong.'

'You won't touch him. He has been through enough. I am taking him home,' said Birdie and she looked to Flora for support.

'Are you sure, Birdie?' asked Flora, noticing for the first time in months there was life in Birdie's eyes.

'It will be on your conscience when he spends the rest of his life as a vegetable then,' said Doctor Fitzsimmons.

'You're not touching him again,' said Birdie, waving her weapon, which she passed to Flora, who read it as quickly as she could. Stunned, she looked at Doctor Unsworth, who was muttering that he had never seen such reprehensible behaviour from a parent in his life but it was to be expected he supposed after what he'd heard about Birdie Mabbett from his good friend Beecher Salter.

Flora had to do something to help Birdie and Gabe. Frantic ideas were forming in her mind as she searched for a way for Birdie to become whole again the same way she needed Gabe to mend. She quickly read the paper again then said, 'Doctor Unsworth, perhaps we can have a word?' and motioned towards the corridor.

Doctor Fitzsimmons nodded that he would remain sentry over the child, so Doctor Unsworth walked into the corridor and Flora followed him. A tiny woman with no medical training at all, she stood as tall as she could and tried to sound like Joseph when he was immovable.

'What do you think of this?' she said, gesturing with the pamphlet.

He knew what it was. That pamphlet had been causing him no end of trouble with parents desperate to try any witch's spell to cure their child. 'Quackery,' he said. 'Quackery from the mind of an insane woman.'

'But it's not going to kill the child, not at this stage, is it?'

The doctor had to concede, 'No, he's past the two-week danger stage, but he's still a very sick child, he still needs the lung. We've been building up his time out of it but he can only manage thirty minutes a day and this voodoo – well, it won't cure him either.'

'The new iron lungs,' said Flora, looking over at the plywood lung, 'they must be transportable; after all, they were brought here, were they not?' said Flora.

'Yes, they're quite light,' said Doctor Unsworth.

'So one could be moved into Birdie's home? The local doctor and bush nurse could come by each day to check on Gabe and to provide treatment?' Flora persisted. She knew Birdie and Gabe needed to be together.

'Not possible,' said Doctor Unsworth. 'And who will move this equipment? That's if I was to agree to this ridiculous fancy.'

'The church will organise it,' said Flora. 'Assuredly,' she added.

'Let me think about it,' said Doctor Unsworth, 'and consult with Doctor Fitzsimmons. I will let you know tomorrow.' Doctor Unsworth motioned for Doctor Fitzsimmons to join him in the corridor and Flora watched as, muttering together, they walked off down the hallway. She went back to Gabe and Birdie looked at her.

'You got them to stop?'

The two nurses saw there was nothing for it but to strap Gabe back into the lung and the bell tinkled and parents unwillingly left their sad lonely children to the coldness of the hospital ward.

When changes happen like whispers

Friday, 3 May 1940

It had been nearly two months since Flora had told Birdie her plan as she'd walked her home from the hospital that terrible day when the doctors had been torturing Gabe. They'd gone down Sturt Street, into Grenville Street and down Eastwood Street, where Flora saw the Church of Christ had taken down their sign saying *The Most Powerful Position is on Your Knees* – which had made the men coming home from the pub bellow with laughter – and replaced it with *Come in and Pray for Allied Victory.* The women's heels tapped on the pavement like drips from a tap.

At Birdie's house Flora had put the kettle on, and when the tea was ready she'd stood in the doorway to the living room and said, 'Birdie, just stop. Stop and have a cuppa to calm your nerves.'

'But I have to make space for the machinery. It will have to go in the living room where I can light a fire and keep him warm. As soon as April comes it'll be cold. I must clear out all the other furniture,' she'd said as she dragged Aubrey's favourite armchair to the doorway.

'After we have tea we will do it together. Come on, Birdie.' So Birdie had left the chair in the middle of the living room, the rug scrunched up beneath it, and plonked into the kitchen chair and rested her elbows on the table.

'So, we're going to do the Sister Kenny method,' said Flora.

'Oh, Flora, do you think I'm going to ruin him?'

'I don't see how a method that is kind and gentle can do any more harm than what we saw being done in that hospital today,' said Flora. 'But I think you are going to need some help.'

And somehow Flora worked a miracle, or was it she, Birdie, who had done it? Somehow, the very next day, Gabe had come home, inside his plywood lung. The lung was lifted up into the back of Faull's delivery cart by Joseph, Thom, Claude and the seven other men and boys they had roped into helping.

Doctor Unsworth had watched, shaking his head the entire time. The nurses lined the hospital driveway, their arms crossed under their red capes as they watched Gabe being taken home. Once Gabe was inside the truck Birdie had climbed up and sat beside Gabe. Then the men and boys under Joseph's constant direction had lifted Gabe off the cart and carried him and the lung into her lounge room. And then Birdie had set about her life.

Now it was two months later and Flora could see the changes in Birdie. They had come in such soft whispers that no one else, certainly not Birdie, noticed them but Flora did. After Mike died, Birdie had been drowning in raw pain that scratched at her soul. She would wake and for a moment she'd forget that her beautiful angelic child was buried in the MacArthur Street cemetery. But that split second of not knowing between sleep and wakefulness would be gone before she could grab it, and tight and biting agony with its razor teeth would grind at all her nerves. Drowning, she couldn't move her bones, she couldn't go anywhere or do anything and she would lie in bed staring blankly at the ceiling, dead like Mike, until Flora arrived, helped her wash and dress and then walked her up to the hospital to see Gabe.

Then Gabe had come home and she'd chopped the wood that Aubrey had always chopped and she'd lit the fire to keep Gabe warm as the Sister Kenny pamphlet she'd found in her letter-box instructed and the warmth filled the house and eked into her cold bones, which were becoming as stiff as Gabe's. Every day she spent hours warming towels by the fire and placing them on Gabe's rigid unmoving arms and legs and ignoring the pain in her own frigid bones as she gently massaged life back into Gabe's immobile limbs. Flora came with Connie and Dan and the children played pretending the plywood lung was a submarine, sometimes a German one and sometimes an ally, and Gabe was always its captain. Flora brought soup that Birdie carefully spooned into Gabe's mouth, not spilling a drop, and sometimes without thinking about it she'd have a spoonful herself, and each time she did she felt her bones soften just as Gabe's were slowly softening.

It was six months after Gabe came home, at the end of August, when he was able to spend more time out of the plywood lung than in it that Doctor Salter said that Gabe could try a chair.

When Birdie and Flora helped Gabe off the hospital gurney and into the wheelchair, he'd looked up and smiled at Birdie, and Connie and Dan had danced around him and decided he was now Franklin D Roosevelt, who had been in a wheelchair, even if he wasn't now.

It was that day that Birdie realised he really was going to live. And if Gabe was going to live, she needed to live too.

PART TWO

1941 to 1943

What Birdie did

Friday, 1 August 1941

The year had passed in a haze for Birdie. Her mind was filled with nothing but making sure Gabe lived. She massaged his rigid, contorted limbs long after Sister Kenny recommended, she gave him her share of meat without him seeing. She warmed milk for him every night and Gabe complained she burned so much wood they may as well live in the Sahara Desert it was that hot.

On this Friday morning Birdie woke and, as always, she forgot for a moment that Mike was dead and Gabe was a cripple and had spent the last year in a wheelchair. And as she reached out for the life that used to be when she had two healthy golden boys, it all came rushing into her and she gasped for air as the cruel jagged edges of Mike's death cut into her. But then she heard the squeak of the wheelchair as it came closer and closer up the hallway until Gabe spun the chair, scraping the paint on the hallway walls, and squealed out with excitement as it came to an abrupt halt and Gabe, looking like he'd won the grand prix, sat smiling proudly in his striped pyjamas, his hands still on the wheels, framed by the bedroom doorway. Birdie looked over at the floor and saw the black lines left by the rubber tyres on the floorboards where he'd spun the chair, but she didn't care. She stretched out her arms and noticed the pain had lessened. She stretched out her legs and toes and placed them on the cold floorboards and they didn't cramp up into gnarled balls.

Now Gabe was wheeling the chair back and forth over the ridge in the doorway, creating more scratches in the floor. The chair squealed with every rotation of its wheels. Birdie watched him. The noise was annoying but she wasn't bothered, she only cared he was alive. He could murder someone and she wouldn't care as long as he stayed alive, and this knowledge that she would do anything to keep Gabe alive for the rest of his life set the pattern of how things would be between them. Gabe could do anything he wanted, and he would have her blind and resolute support. She pulled the curtains aside and let the weak winter sun into her room. Something in her shifted as she listened to Gabe wheeling the chair up and down the hallway as fast as he could. There were holes along the hallway where he had careened into the plaster. She loved those holes.

'I have to get things in order,' she said as she grabbed her dressing gown, which was lying across the end of the bed in case she needed to get up to Gabe in the night. She threw it on, tied it around her thin waist and wheeled him down the hallway to the kitchen. She felt light as she pushed him and hoped this new feeling of him being alive against all her expectations would never leave her. She pulled the kitchen chair away from the end of the table and pushed Gabe up to the table. Then she opened the potato bin and took out the bundle of unopened letters she'd been tossing into the darkness of the enamel tin since Mike had died. She looked at the mountain of envelopes with their red angry stamps.

'You open those for me,' she said to Gabe, passing him a kitchen knife, 'and put the envelopes in a separate pile so I can re-use them for the fire lighting. A pot of tea first and then we might think about how we can get on – the two of us.'

'The two of us?' he said.

'Yes, the two of us.'

And her voice broke with pain.

So Gabe clumsily tore at the envelopes with the knife and ripped out the bills and smoothed out the creases and laid them on top of each other in a neat pile while Birdie made tea. Then with a cup of steaming tea for strength, Birdie added up all the bills that she had ignored for so long and only got away with because of the war and because of Gabe. They came to nine pounds. The government had recently introduced child endowment of five shillings a week. It had started a month or so ago on the first of July, but it wasn't enough for Birdie's bills.

After the tea in the pot was drained of its last brown drop and Gabe had eaten the last of the bread, Birdie dressed Gabe in his oldest clothes. She wanted his clothes to look worn and too small, but not scabby, because she was after all a good mother. She wrapped a scarf around his neck, slid gloves over his hands and forced a pair of Aubrey's shoes, many sizes too big, over his contorted feet and, despite his protests, put an old beanie over his dark curls. She stood back and looked at him and nodded approval. They had to look desperate but respectable. Then she dressed herself and covered her funeral dress that she had worn every day since Mike died, with her gardening coat. Bracing the chill breeze that blew from the Antarctic to her front door, Birdie wheeled Gabe up Humffray Street to Albert Street, then on to the corner of Dana Street and Lydiard Street, where she used all her strength to get Gabe's chair up over the two bluestone steps into Bartrop's Real Estate. She stood at the counter out of breath and argued with the desk girl until Mister Edgar Bartrop appeared and then she cried at Mister Bartrop, a kind, softly spoken man who pulled his glasses from his nose and rested them on his balding head. Mr Bartrop took one last puff on his pipe before holding it mid-air and peering sadly at Gabe in the wheelchair. Gabe, having been instructed not to put on any cheek, peered sadly back.

'Well now,' he ran his finger down his nose, 'even with the freezing of rents, and with the money your parents and the church paid, well, you're still six months behind in the rent, Missus Mabbett,' he said.

'But you can't evict me – can you?' she asked. 'Not with the war rent restrictions.'

Mister Bartrop rubbed his long chin and finally said, 'You've been there in that cottage a long time.'

'Would you call it a cottage, Mister Bartrop? It's more like a bedsit, it's so small,' Birdie snuffled through her tears. 'I don't think anyone else would want to rent it or would look after it as well as I have.'

Edgar sighed and looked again at Gabe with his sad face and thought of his own boys who were so full of naughtiness.

'I'll talk to your landlord and see if we can waive a good portion of the unpaid rent,' he said, and then, remembering his accountant, he straightened and added, 'But only, Missus Mabbett, if you start paying and continue to pay promptly from here on. And only because of these sad times and because the government has introduced these new rules. I won't be doing this again, Missus Mabbett, I assure you.'

Birdie kissed him on the cheek and because she was such a pleasant-looking young lady he found he didn't mind one bit and said, 'Oh,' many times and rubbed the spot to make the kiss sink in.

Edgar helped Birdie and Gabe down the steps and she pulled Gabe's coat further up over his chin and wheeled him to the general store and then the butcher's to negotiate paying off her run-up credit, which Mister Fogget at the butcher's and Missus Spence at the general store agreed to do because it would look bad for business if in these sad times they didn't help out a mother who had been through so much and who could obviously barely afford the clothes on her back and whose husband was off fighting for their very freedom. Then Birdie wheeled Gabe to her parents' Californian bungalow in Raglan Street where it sat three houses up from the intersection with South Street. The gate squeaked as she opened it and Viola came out and stood on the front veranda as Birdie struggled to get the wheelchair through the gate, which was only just wide enough.

'Why aren't you at work?' asked Birdie, heaving the chair to line it up with the gate.

'I have every second Friday afternoon free,' said Viola.

'Oh,' said Birdie. 'Do you like it? Nursing, I mean.'

'I listen to the boys cry out for their mothers in their sleep. I wipe their sores clean as they weep and they grip my hand so tight I feel like they are going to break all my fingers, but that's the only time they have any strength. They are so broken, Birdie, they all have bits of them missing, but I suppose we all do now. So am I supposed to like it?' But Viola did like it. The men's emptiness made her feel whole.

'It's going to rain,' said Birdie and they looked at each other and not the clouds and in each other's eyes, they saw themselves.

Then they remembered Gabe, listening to every word, and Viola stepped down off the veranda, leant over and poked his chest. 'Well, look at you, Gabe. This is a to-do, isn't it?' and she took the handles and arched the chair back and up over the steps.

'Goodness,' said Birdie. 'Show me your muscles.'

'I have to lift the soldiers all the time,' said Viola. 'I suppose I've built up some strength,' then she pushed Gabe through the front door and up the hall, calling out, 'Mum, Dad, look who's here.'

In the kitchen Birdie took off her coat and hat and then helped Gabe out of his and hung them over the back of a chair. Elsie was ladling trench stew that was closer to soup than stew into bowls. She took off her oven mitts and bent over to hug Gabe, then stood up and hugged Birdie. Elsie smelt of warm food, of spices and care, and Birdie wondered if perhaps she was doing the wrong thing and she and Gabe should move in with her parents. Elsie put the kettle on and got two extra plates from the dresser, then she split the stew between the five bowls and put a thick slab of bread on top of each and the bread started to soak up the stew and was stained with reds and oranges from tomato and pumpkin.

'Birdie, call your father from the shed. He's hiding in there listening to the VFL forecasts on the wireless. He likes to hear who the experts think will win but he doesn't want the neighbours to know, so he's got it down low.'

Birdie thought about putting her coat back on, but it was a short walk to the shed and she couldn't be bothered, so she crossed her arms against the cold and passed the garden of winter vegetables struggling through the frosts to the shed at the back and flung open the door. Her father was crouched over his wireless, his ear pressed up against the speaker.

He looked up at her. 'Oh, some don't approve of the football continuing,' he said.

'Dad, I don't care if you listen to who might win the footy,' she said, 'but lunch is on the table.'

'Oh, right then, love,' he said and he stood up and patted her cheek as though he still saw her every day. As though she still lived at home. As though she was six.

'It's not much,' said Elsie. 'Mainly pumpkin from the garden to be honest,' and she passed bowls down the table and Birdie took off her bread and it dripped onto the table on its way from her plate to Gabe's.

'I'm not that hungry,' she lied and she stared at the pieces of frayed pumpkin and the threadbare bones in her bowl. 'How's work, Dad?' she said.

'I never counted on being back at work at my age,' said Claude. 'I didn't like the training I had to do as if I'd never done the job before – bringing me up to modern standards they called it, but still, I don't mind it now I'm there.' Claude was working five and a half days a week at the guncotton factory.

'And here is our Viola training as a nurse at the repatriation ward – who'd have thought,' said Elsie and she laughed and said, 'Who knows, even I might end up back in the workforce.'

Claude said, 'Let's hope the war is over before it ever comes to that, dear.' And no one saw the hurt that flew across Elsie's face as she stood up and gathered their dishes and mountained them in the sink for later. Elsie pulled a chair around to the end of the table and sat next to Claude holding his hand and Viola sat opposite Birdie and Gabe and none of them spoke as they waited for Birdie to tell them why she'd come.

Birdie took a deep breath. 'We need to borrow ten pounds.' There was no use beating around the bush. Elsie gasped.

'I know you kept the electricity on for me, I saw you get the quarterlies out of the letterbox, Dad.'

'It wasn't just us,' said Claude. 'The church helped.'

'I know ten pounds is a huge amount.'

'Two weeks' salary for Dad,' said Viola. 'More for me.'

'But we'll all pitch in for you and Gabe,' pronounced Elsie loudly and no more discussion was needed on the matter and soon there were ten one-pound notes on the table, six from her parents and four from Viola, along with a cauliflower.

'Don't know what you'll do with it but at least it's food,' said Elsie, 'and Gabe likes cauliflower, don't you, Gabe?' and Gabe screwed up his face.

Gabe nursed the cauliflower as Birdie wheeled him back down the hall. Viola helped lift the chair down the steps and as she turned the wheelchair into the street, Birdie stopped at the gate and asked, 'Do you ever see a nurse up there at the hospital with red hair? Frizzy, though I imagine she keeps it tied up.'

'Well, the nurses don't like to talk to us trainees except to order us about, but yes, I see her. Why?'

'Nothing,' Birdie said, looking hard at Viola and she realised that all afternoon she'd been trying to work out what had changed about Viola and finally she saw the light that Viola had whenever she saw her nephews or when her Sunday school children ran into her arms, had gone.

'Mike's death has taken a toll,' said Birdie. She looked at Gabe, sitting in the chair holding the cauliflower as though he was about to toss it through a hoop. He was alive and getting stronger every day. She must focus on this or drown.

'Cheer up, Viola,' she said. 'You used to be so happy. Not like me at all. Everyone said so.'

'I'm never going to leave here – living with Mum and Dad,' said Viola.

'Probably not,' Birdie said. 'Not if all our boys keep getting killed.'

'Oh, Birdie, do you always have to see the worst possibility?' Viola said, and she ran off crying.

Birdie called after her, 'But you brought it up, not me.'

As Birdie walked home, ideas formed into plans that would mean she and Gabe could keep their little house. The war was changing things, especially for women, and Birdie could take advantage of that. Her father was at the guncotton factory and Birdie knew Dulcie worked there too. Dulcie said it was dangerous work, soaking cottonwool in acids for munitions. She said she got paid two pounds a week and the men who had worked there before they signed up had been paid four pounds. She'd said all this some months ago to Birdie after church, but at the time Birdie hadn't been listening to anything other than the sombre music of Mike's death. She was sure she could hear someone playing a violin nearby, straining out the death notes. She wasn't listening to Dulcie and Nola chatting about their new jobs. Nola was working at the railway station as a porter and even Mabel Finchley was working at Coutts and Cottingham as a secretary. All the women had to have a medical exam to make sure they had no female weaknesses before they worked.

'But such indignities are what we women have to do to support the war,' Dulcie had said.

As she pushed Gabe across Grant Street, Birdie wondered if she could work and told herself she couldn't possibly. Gabe couldn't go back to school in a wheelchair, he still needed twenty-four-hour care. Anything could happen to him. He could relapse and she couldn't trust him to anyone else, not even her mother. No, unless Gabe was walking by himself she would stay home with him, and in the middle of Grant Street a gust of wind took hold of her coat, blowing it open and a button popped off and flew away. She would have to mend that. She looked down at the coat that she'd mended many times with such neat stitching no one would ever have known it had been torn, and it came to her in a flash. She turned the wheelchair around and pushed Gabe all the way down Sturt Street to *The Courier*, where she placed an ad for next Friday's paper.

The following Saturday morning Birdie got up before the light of the sun woke her. She set her machine up in the lounge room, where the iron lung had been. She collected all her leftover material and clothes of Aubrey's and folded them into neat stacks. She made herself a pot of tea. Connie and Danny turned up to play with Gabe and even though it was too cold, she made Gabe rug up and sent them all outside. She could hear Connie squealing and wished the child wasn't so noisy.

Then she sat and waited and at ten there was a knock on the door and it was old Missus Blackmarsh needing her husband's trousers mended at the crotch, so Birdie mended them right then and there and charged her a shilling. At eleven it was Nola, who said, 'Oh, Birdie, I've always known you have a way with a machine and with working so hard for the war effort, well, I just don't have the time myself,' and she dumped two work dresses into Birdie's arms and washed her hands of them. Birdie uncrumpled them and saw one had torn at the hem and the other's side seams were unravelling.

The Saturday after that four people came with mending, and the following week eight, and each week it doubled until Birdie had to have a waiting list for her mending.

'Oh, but Birdie, it must be you that mends my best frock,' whined Dulcie, standing at Birdie's front door, 'and I know you'll fit me in because we've been friends all these years.'

'There's a two-month waiting list,' Birdie said and she crossed her arms over her chest so Dulcie couldn't dump her apricot frock and run.

'But Birdie, when you mend things they somehow look brand new.'

Birdie stood firm and Dulcie said, 'Oh all right then. I'll just have to wait, won't I?'

Birdie soon paid off her bills and paid back her parents and at night she massaged Gabe's legs and arms with lard to soften the muscles and one night Gabe told her he felt strong enough to try a few steps, so Birdie took him to the chemist the next day and had him fitted for crutches. A few steps became many steps and Gabe no longer needed the chair and could get along on his crutches when Connie didn't steal them from under him. How often she'd gone outside to see Gabe sitting on the cold ground, watching as Connie hopped around on the crutches pretending she was a returned war hero. 'Give them back at once,' she'd say and Connie would look at her as if Birdie was the one who had started the war. Birdie would help Gabe up from the ground and back onto the crutches and order that girl off home. How had sweet Flora bred such a terror?

But Birdie sometimes felt content with her new life, until she thought of Mike dying and Aubrey at the war and then she wondered what was going to come next to ruin everything.

When Thom takes a train or two

Monday, 1 December 1941

A month before the world would enter the year 1942, on the morning of Monday, the very first day of December 1941, Thom left the house at 5.30. This time he left no note. Not even Connie, who heard so many things she shouldn't, heard him go. He boarded the 6.15 train to Melbourne and, after changing his clothes in the men's toilets, which cost him tuppence to use, he found his way out of the madness of Spencer Street Station where women and older men bustled to jobs that had been held previously by men now at war. He caught a tram up Collins Street and got off at Swanston, took a deep breath, then turned right and walked down Swanston until it became St Kilda Road, noticing as he had the last time he was in Melbourne that no one stopped to yarn as they would in Ballarat, no one nodded to say hello as they passed him. Men carried briefcases, *The Argus* tucked under one arm, and women in smart frocks walked by fast, their heads down against the day ahead of them. Thom stopped at the ivy-covered barracks. Here in Melbourne no one knew his father. Just a couple of weeks earlier he'd feigned sickness to his boss and come on the 11.06 and signed up and now he was ready for action. Ready to do or die. Thom stood tall and walked into the barracks and that very afternoon he was on his way to Mount Martha for his four weeks of training.

A week later, on the seventh of December, the sun had woken early and shone bright and clear over the Pacific Ocean and then cast its beams on Oahu so that everyone on the island woke feeling lazy and warm and full of sunshiny optimism for the day ahead. The sun chased away the clouds and with an evil glint it turned on the people of Oahu and opened the skies to three hundred and fifty-three marauding metal birds with red suns on their tails. After their vicious spree three thousand five hundred and eighty-one bodies lay dead or dying in the marshy lagoon called Pearl Harbor. America reeled from the attack and then it turned and retaliated. On the eighth of December America and its young brother, Australia, declared war on Japan. On the ninth of December Germany and Italy each declared war on America. So on the tenth of December America declared war on Germany and Italy. And this is how world wars are built.

Tit for tat.

Day by day.

Thom knew he had done the right thing. The war needed him whether he was twenty-one or not.

On the twelfth of December the government decided that Australia was vulnerable to the Japanese army, which was crawling closer, and was nearly on the doorstep. Prime Minister John Curtin ordered the evacuation of all women and children from Darwin unless the women were nurses or working in other essential services such as the Post Office. Of course, being Darwin, where everything happened slowly, it took a few weeks for this order to be put into action. On the fifteenth of December and barely trained, Thom, along with other boys with soft fuzz on their chins, roses in their cheeks and innocent hope in their eyes, boys who had forged their fathers' signatures or lied about their ages, were put on a train from Mount Martha to Melbourne, then a train to Adelaide, and then on the train to Darwin, '*Where you'll finish your training, lads.*'

So here was Thom, sitting on a rowdy train. You'd have thought the train to Darwin was a party train. The conductors shook their heads and smiled at the larrikin behaviour of the army boys and said to each other, 'Comforting, isn't it, to know our freedom is in the hands of this lot,' and they kept to the gangways and smoked the cigarettes the boys shared with them. Boys leant out the windows and let the soot fill their hair and they whooped and twirled their hats in the sky like rainbow streamers, they joked and fell over each other in the crowded aisles of the carriages. They brought out flasks of illicit whisky; they talked about women as though they had bedded many when in fact they had bedded none. Thom sat in his seat jammed up against the window, bumping and jolting against the other fellows, disappointed he was being kept in Australia and wondering how long his father's reach was. He might not have left a note for his parents this time, but his father would have worked it out. He was amazed his father hadn't turned up in Mount Martha to drag him home.

'Cheer up, old man,' yelled Watson, who had a chubby face with freckles and looked to Thom to be no more than fourteen but was in fact twenty-four. Watson was in the seat opposite, and leant forward over his knees and yelled to be heard over the racket of boys and the rattling train. He held out his flask to Thom.

Thom shook his head.

'Go on,' yelled Mossley, who looked older again and wore glasses so thick his eyes were like two giant fat frogs' eyes looking out at the world. Perhaps his eyesight was why he was going to Darwin, even though he was older. 'You're in the army, man,'

Mossley said and he pushed Watson's flask closer to Thom. So Thom took a good swig of the burning liquid and coughed and the boys around him laughed.

'Ever been to Darwin before?' yelled Watson, then taking a good look at Thom laughed and said, 'Ever tasted booze before, my man?'

Thom shook his head and stared out the window at the flat expanse of empty land that went on for miles and miles. Everyone said the prime minister was overreacting. 'Covering his arse,' said Watson. Japan wouldn't bother with Australia. Most of it was empty nothingness anyway. And Thom knew he would never see any real fighting even though he'd heard that lots of underage boys were sent to the front despite the rules.

Fifty hours after the train left Adelaide the boys arrived at the platform in Darwin, tired and grumpy and out of hijinks. They clambered stiff and sullen out of the carriages and made a motley effort to stand in line and to attention. They were told to get their kits from the luggage van and Thom stood back and waited while the boys scrambled over each other to find their kit, each only identifiable from all the others by its name tag. Once his kit was slung over his shoulder he jumped into the back of the waiting army truck and was taken to the barracks at Larrakeyah.

When Thom learns new skills

Monday, 5 January 1942

Thom had been in Darwin for just over a couple of weeks. The heat was still unbearable and he still couldn't see why he was wasting time in Darwin when he could be killing Gerries or Japs. There were times he wished he'd listened to his father and stayed at home. He missed Lydia and their secret alliance, and sweet Danny who snored, and even strange Connie, who always seemed to be where she shouldn't, listening to things she shouldn't hear and seeing things that were just none of her darned business. And after a breakfast of cold toast and lukewarm beans he missed Flora's cooking.

There was nothing to do in Darwin except think of home and find ways to cope with the heat, so day after day the boys took it easy, got up late, sprayed each other with hoses, dumped buckets of water on each other's heads and sat on the cliff looking over the beach, then dawdled off to the pubs – except Thom, who, after taking a gulp from a flask on the train, wasn't eager to try alcohol again. On Christmas Day the boys had sung *I'm dreaming of a white*

Christmas over and over, each rendition more drunken than the last. They had opened extra cans of corned beef and shared the fruit cakes their mothers had sent. But that was the most effort they'd put into anything.

This wasn't how it was supposed to be in the army.

As he took his last sip of ghastly tea with canned milk, Sergeant Buller walked up to Thom's table, leant on the table top and, looking straight at him, told him to go and wait at the main gate.

'Why me?' Thom said.

'Because I can't resist that beautiful baby face,' said Sergeant Buller and the men at the table laughed, so Thom escaped and did as he was ordered. It was only eight in the morning but the sun crashed down on him without mercy; his sweat dried as soon as it sprang from his pores, gluing his shirt to his skin. He pulled his hat down over his forehead and flapped his shirt to get the flies away from him. He straightened up as he saw the sergeant walk towards him. The man was solid and towered over Thom, his face pink from the heat. Thom guessed that Sergeant Buller was about the same age as his pa.

'They've made you a gunner in the event of an attack,' laughed Sergeant Buller. Who would bother to attack a nowhere place like Darwin?

'But I've never even touched a gun, sir,' said Thom, who had spent his training at Mount Martha doing endless marching. He wondered if Sergeant Buller was going to spend the day teaching him.

Sergeant Buller slapped him on the arm. 'Don't worry, lad, you'll never need to use a gun. The Japs aren't likely to test Australia with Mother England watching over her, and in the meantime you're to assist me with the evacuation. There's some stragglers refusing to go and it's our job to make them.'

'How do we do that, sir?' asked Thom.

'We walk,' laughed Sergeant Buller. 'We walk the streets, if you can call dirt roads a street, in this bloody heat and humidity and we knock on doors and offer to escort the women and children to the port so they can be shipped south and when we're covered in dust and sweat we go back to the barracks and wash it all off. Righteo, son – let's get going.' Sergeant Buller stomped off and Thom ran to catch up with him.

'We'll start nearest the town centre and work our way out. We've been assigned the north side. We don't have to bother evacuating any Aboriginal women and children – they'll run off into the bush if any real danger starts,' said Sergeant Buller.

Thom knocked on doors and some of the women had suitcases already packed and their children in their best clothes ready for the journey. Some of the women refused to be moved and said only the devil would get them out of their homes and Sergeant Buller stepped forward, showing he was the superior officer and said, 'You evacuate willingly and let my private here carry your case to the port or I'll put you over my shoulder and carry you there myself,' and some of the women would sigh and submit to being evacuated against their will and others slammed the door shut, and when that happened Sergeant Buller looked at Thom, shrugged, and said, 'We can only try, son.'

That night Thom, tired from walking all day, lay on his bunk bed, his arm over his eyes, and said again he didn't want to go to the pub. But Watson and Mossley insisted and when he still said no they pulled him off the bottom bunk, forced his boots onto his feet, pulled his hat down over his eyes and dragged him after them through the sleepy dusty town of Darwin, which was home to five thousand civilians, though this number was decreasing every day. They walked past drunken men, too old to sign up, urinating in streets littered with bottles that were piled up against the sidewalks like growing ant hills. Mossley dragged them into a bar.

'This is called the Blood House,' he said proudly, and indicated the bullet holes that decorated the walls. Pointing to the sawdust on the floor, he said, 'To mop up the blood from the fights. Roughest pub in town.'

'Why are we here then?' said Thom. He shouldn't have come and was already regretting it. Mossley knew he was underage, but just laughed and pushed his glasses up his nose and said, 'It's Darwin. No one gives a rat's arse that you're not twenty-one as long as you pay for what you drink.'

'Do as the Romans,' said Watson, and he ordered them all a beer, and Thom, not wanting to be rude, drank. It was warm and bitter and he wanted to spit it out, but that would make him look like a baby, so he swallowed hard and took another slug.

It took Thom just over six weeks to become a seasoned drinker with the best of them. After another hard day of doing nothing, Thom and his mates were at the Blood House this early Wednesday evening and Thom was on his third beer. A hand slapped down onto Thom's shoulder and he turned to see Mister Rowbotham's beer-addled smile not far from his ear.

'Mister Rowbotham,' he exclaimed, surprised he was in the pub, because until then he'd only ever seen him in church or at the barracks. 'And Ronny and Trevor,' and the boys pulled him into bear hugs and called out to the publican, 'Another brave Ballarat soldier, mateys – the Japs can't beat us boys from Ballarat.'

'The other two boys are somewhere as well, except Johnny, who they declared a sapper and he was sent off today – who knows where. Somewhere to build a bridge I expect – they won't tell us. How's your father, son?' said Mister Rowbotham.

'I haven't had mail since I joined up, Mr Rowbotham,' said Thom.

Thom felt Mister Rowbotham sizing him up and he looked hard at the ground.

'Well,' said Mister Rowbotham, 'it's John here, son, we're all in the same boat now. We sink or swim together, eh? No more of this Mister Rowbotham business,' and he slapped Thom hard on the back. Looking at the others standing around them, he said, 'You heard the Japs are in Malaya,' and they took a large swig for luck for the Allies and another and another.

Just before midnight Thom stumbled back to his barracks. Mossley held him up. He and the others would wake late tomorrow with swollen brains, dried-out veins and unseeing, blinking eyes. None of this was allowed, of course, the leaving of barracks at night, the drinking and the drunkenness.

But it was Darwin.

When Thom takes a shower

Thursday, 19 February 1942

On Bathurst Island, Father John McGrath, a giant of a man with a long bushy beard, got out of bed on Thursday morning as he did every morning and got down on his bare knees in only his boxers to pray on the small rug beside his bed. He asked God to bless each member of his small flock by name and finally he asked God to help him get through another day of this bloody stinking tropical heat.

After his breakfast he sat at the trestle table that was pushed up hard against the window. A wooden box with two speakers sat on it and at his feet were two pedals just like on a bicycle. Every now and then he would scan the skies as he had since the war began. John was reading the Book of Revelation, *each of the four living creatures had six wings and was covered with eyes all around, even under its wings.* He could actually hear the creatures with their six wings flapping furiously as they hovered over the earth. He stopped and read the passage again, and again he heard the creatures, and being practical and not inclined to interpret the bible literally, he leant forward and saw the sky was filled with metal birds, more than he could count, the sun glinting off their shining wings, and he put his hand over his forehead to get a better look and then fell back into his seat and pedalled madly, bringing the wireless to life.

At 9.47 Thom was in the shower block trying to wash away his hangover. The showers only had cold taps – the cold water came out warm anyway. The hum of the machines in the distance was making his head throb. It would be the Yanks returning from their flight to East Timor, so Thom dismissed the background noise and held his face to the water with his hands over his ears. Thom didn't hear it coming. You don't when it's close. If you can hear the scream then it's too far away to cause you harm, but if it comes without warning, you're right under it. The timber shower walls burst open like an overripe fruit in the hot sun and suddenly Thom was standing there stark naked like the statue of David among the splintered palings, but no one noticed. All around him men and women were screaming, yelling, and running, their arms waving. He could see dust and flying timber, he could see the sky filling with black smoke and there was the noise of machines and bursting buildings crumpling to the ground. All the noise in the world had gathered up into this one place.

Thom saw Mossley pick his glasses up from the ground and put them back on his nose, then Mossley in his pyjamas ran and so Thom pulled his towel from the debris and in his bare feet picked his way over the remains of the shower block and ran after him, wrapping his towel around his hips as he followed. Mossley ran towards the one anti-aircraft machine gun the barracks had. It was one of the six around Darwin that the army in its wisdom had decided were sufficient to protect Australian soil.

Thom ran after Mossley, past bodies and past boys crying out for yesterday when they were whole, past fires dotted across the earth like camp sites, past pieces of buildings, past Major Barrie's desk chair lying dead on its side and Major Barrie's glass dresser in which had been locked the two .303 rifles along with their ammunition that were left over from the last war. The glass was shattered and gone and Thom stopped and reached in and pulled out one of the rifles and a handful of bullets that were scattered on the ground. Sergeant Buller came up to him, panting and gasping, then, gathering his breath he took the other one and what he could find of the ammunition. Sergeant Buller with his greying hair and enormous smile that spread slowly across his face like he knew all the jokes there were to know.

Sergeant Buller had given Thom some postcards saying, 'They'll want to know you're safe, boy. It's the least you can do. I'm a father of four, so I know.' So Thom had sent a postcard to his pa and ma and one to Lydia and one to Viola, and he wrote the same in each because he couldn't think of what to say that wouldn't be censored. *I'm utterly safe*, he wrote, *here on home soil in Darwin. Though I dare say it's more dangerous walking down Mitchell Street than being in the army. Don't worry about me, folks. I'm right as rain.* The army censors cut holes in the postcards, neat rectangles made with small sharp scissors so they looked like doilies and all the recipients in Ballarat got was *I'm utterly safe* in the top corner and *I'm right as rain* in the bottom corner. And the kangaroo on the front of the postcards was just ears and eyes at one end and toes and tail at the other end of the holes.

With the .303s slung over their shoulders, Thom and Sergeant Buller ran on. The bombs were falling madly now like silver hailstones pelting from the sky without mercy. The morning sun, taking part in the ferocity, glinted silver shafts of light from the bombs as they fell, turning the bombs into beautiful evil comets.

In minutes the sky turned black with smoke and Thom tried to push it aside like a curtain.

The 3.7-inch anti-aircraft machine gun sat on its wheels for easy removal at the edge of the cliff, where a thatched canopy had been built over it to shade it from the sun and it spent its days lazily looking out over the vast blue sea. No one ever expected to have to use it. No one had been trained to use it. Not one practice had been held because, Major Barrie had explained, they didn't have enough ammunition for practices and practices were noisy and that might upset the townsfolk. So they hadn't even taken the wheels off. Thom came to a halt next to it. Mossley was there with ten other men all crowded around the machine, frantically removing the wheels. His glasses were cracked, splitting his vision in two. Even in all the mayhem, smoke and death, the men stopped and laughed at Thom, ready to fight in nothing but an army-issue towel. Thom held his arms out and the towel fell off and they laughed harder as he scrabbled to secure it around his thin hips. Thom looked at the ammunition lying on the ground in its worn cardboard box – there wasn't much of it. 'Should I go get more, sir?' he yelled above the noise.

Major Barrie looked at him and yelled back, 'That's it, son,' and they all crouched and put their hands over their ears as another bomb fell. Then they stood as though bombs falling was an everyday part of life and with the last wheel removed the men got to loading the machine and because he had been an arithmetic teacher, Mossley was given the job of trying to calculate the height they would need to set the gun to and Major Barrie turned back to Thom and saw the rifle slung over Thom's shoulder.

'That's a relic,' he said, 'probably hasn't been used in twenty years. But it's all we've got. I was going to send someone for them all the same.' They all crouched down as the squeal from another bomb cut through the thick grey smoke and when they stood

Major Barrie dug into his pockets and pulled out a handful of extra bullets and emptied them into Thom's palm.

'We'll shoot at the bastards the best we can,' said Sergeant Buller and Thom looked at the bullets and back at the major and then at Sergeant Buller and back to the major, but Major Barrie was concentrating on the anti-aircraft machine gun and Thom realised that what he held in his hand was it.

He grabbed his towel to keep it on and followed Sergeant Buller further down the cliff edge, away from the anti-aircraft machine gun in order to get a go at the aircraft before they got to blow up their one defence.

'You get the bastards from here,' said Sergeant Buller. Thom looked at the rifle. He'd never held one. The army was short on everything.

'They got the Red Barron with one of these buggers. They can hit a mile away on a good day.' Sergeant Buller pulled a bullet from his pocket and showed Thom how to load the rifle and how to shoot it.

'I'll go down there, but not so far that you can't see me,' and Sergeant Buller ran off and Thom was on his own. Thom knelt, prayed quickly and took aim. He realised kneeling made him that much farther away from his target so he stood, one leg in front of the other, his towel falling from his hips, so he stood there naked as the day he was born, shooting for the first time in his life at the enemy aircraft. Even though there were hundreds of them he couldn't hit anything. The rifle, not used for twenty years, hadn't been calibrated for tropical conditions, and his first two shots went nowhere. A Japanese pilot saw him standing there in his naked glory and like an eagle seeing a small helpless baby magpie fallen from its nest, it swooped in for him. Thom could see the pilot laughing at him and he took aim, slightly to the left, to account for the gun and an instant later blood splattered against the windowpane and the plane swerved and dived and tipped away from Thom, falling into the burning sea.

Thom had thought that if he killed an enemy he would be yelling with heroic joy, he thought he would leap and jump and feel like a man, but there was no time for feeling anything. Bombs were still falling, men were still dying, buildings were still being splintered into woodchips.

He turned and waved to Sergeant Buller, who he could just make out through the smoke as Sergeant Buller was shot into a million fragments. Thom looked out to sea; the harbour was red and bubbling with hot burning oil from dying, drowning ships and red with blood from burning, dying boys. So Thom put Sergeant Buller from his mind and fought on, carefully aiming and shooting his handful of bullets with his wonky rifle from the First World War until the world went black. He felt himself falling through the blackness, down, down into the sea alight with the flames of hell.

All his failures fled past him as he fell and his last living thought was that he had never kissed Viola Mitchell in her pretty lemon dress.

When something is stolen

Sunday, 12 July 1942

Connie was sure that if she saw the lemon tree grow in her mind then it would obey her and grow as she imagined. She saw the tree reaching up over the ground-floor windows, then growing up past the ivy growing through the brickwork, past the tin of the veranda roof and past the second-storey windows until it reached up over the tiled roof of the manse. Connie was sure that if she was brave enough to climb to the top of the tree she could have stepped down easily onto the roof and gazed out over Ballarat and waved at Mount Buninyong staring back at her through the misty clouds. But she never went further than her sitting branch, which was high enough now for her to easily see over the fence between the church and the manse. She could hide there among the leaves and hear secrets.

Everyone admired her lemon tree. On Sundays, lunch visitors would pat their stomachs full of Flora's creamed cabbage and kidneys followed by butterless lemon rock cakes. They pretended the meal had been just as good as anything they ate before the war and would say they must get going, wanting to get home for *Dad and*

Dave, but would instead sit in their seats, waiting, dropping hints, saying, 'Oh, Joseph, how did you manage to grow such magnificent sweet lemons?' or 'Goodness but the lovely desserts you must be able to make with those lemons, Flora – even in these times of want. Those lemons would need barely any sugar to sweeten them. The rock cakes were the best I've tasted.' They would continue until Flora said, 'Why don't you take a few of the lemons on your way out?'

'They're mine,' Connie would blurt and Flora would hand the visitors a paper bag to put the lemons in. Birdie would look at the lemon tree, size it up and say to Connie, 'My, what did your father do to grow that tree so tall?' then without waiting for an answer she would call Gabe to come home and Connie would holler after her as she walked down the drive, 'I 'spect he prayed over it like the loaves and the fishes.' But Connie knew the real reason the tree had grown so large was because she, Connie, had wished it and so her angel had made it happen. When the tree was still small and thirsty she had watered it when she remembered and Flora had watered it when she hadn't and Joseph had emptied the chamber pot onto it so it got lots of nitrogen and magnesium.

Connie, sitting on her branch, picked herself a lemon and sucked out the sweet juice and sat there, hidden, watching the world from her secret place.

Because that was how Connie was in the world: apart. She didn't care for the day-to-day things of life – what was for lunch or that they had no butter and only lard for the bread or what the Japanese might do next or whether the girls at school were playing elastics or rounders this term. At school she sat and gazed out the window and got the cane across her upturned palms six times because she didn't know her multiplication or had blobs of ink over her writing, or because she had cracked her chalk on her slate yet again. At lunchtimes she sat alone in the shelter shed and watched the other girls playing hopscotch on wobbly chalked-out squares as though she was watching on from behind a thick pane of glass.

Connie didn't think about who she would become when she grew up or what she might do. When people asked, 'And what do you want to be, Connie?' she would shrug her shoulders and walk away and not see the confusion and sadness in Flora's eyes that she couldn't even teach the girl to be polite. Connie gave the things of life no thought at all. Instead she was separated from the world and all the people she knew in it and she watched them go about their lives from her special hidden spot in the lemon tree as if the people below were ants scurrying about without any realisation of how small and insignificant they were.

It was the space between Sunday school and lunch when the women were still tidying up after morning tea. Connie was now eight and her mother had knitted her a cardigan from scraps of wool so the cardigan was a patchwork of colours and thicknesses. She'd given it to Connie in April for her birthday. It was now July and it was cold; the wind blew nastily but Connie didn't notice and the cardigan lay in a crumpled heap on the grass below her along with her shoes and socks. Connie was kicking her bare feet through the air. She saw Missus Mabbett and her mother come up the driveway and go in through the back of the house. Gabe hopped along after them on his crutches. When he was in the wheelchair, which he was for such a long time, she had pushed him up and down the road outside his house or hers and spun the wheelchair in circles making the loose gravel fly into the air and she had climbed on the back and held on tight and they had both spun until they were dizzy and holding onto their heads and the chair was nearly tipping over and spilling them onto the hard road. Now Gabe was on crutches they had to walk everywhere slowly so he could keep up. It was a pain in the neck. Lydia walked past the tree next and Connie watched as she went into the house and Connie remembered that during the hot summer when she was up in her tree she had seen Lydia pressed up against the church wall kissing a boy in a uniform and even though it was still January the boy must have cold hands because he had hidden his hands under Lydia's dress to keep them warm. Connie couldn't see who the boy was.

But now there were no boys.

Ballarat was empty of boys.

The only men who walked the streets were the young, the maimed and the old, and every night at dinner Lydia complained the war was going to kill all the boys and she would never marry and Flora would say she was far too young to worry about marriage just yet.

Connie looked down and saw her white socks and her mary jane shoes that had once been Lydia's and had all the black patent leather scratched away at the toes leaving rough brown like dirt showing through. She looked over into the church and saw Danny scratching his name and the date *12 July 1942* into the bluestone block of the church and she could see how empty the space around him was. He had shrunk since Mike had died. She'd tried to tell Danny that Mike was still here but was an angel now and Danny had looked at her for a moment and she'd seen for the first time that he hadn't believed her and he'd walked away without saying a thing. Connie felt as though Danny had stuck her with a sharp knife. Well, Danny would get their father's belt if Pa ever saw what Danny was doing to the church wall and perhaps Connie might tell him.

'Connie, I have a joke for you,' said Angel Mike, distracting her from spying on Danny. He was sitting on the branch next to her, swinging his legs with his gown pulled up around his knees.

Connie looked at him. 'Go on,' she said. 'I'll laugh if I like it. But you'll have to be quick. I'll have to go and see Gabe soon.'

'What sort of shorts do clouds wear?' said the angel.

Connie shrugged her shoulders like she wasn't really interested even though she did want to know.

'Thunderwear,' said Archangel Mike and he bellowed and snorted with laughter, loud like an earthquake and the tree shook and Connie held on for dear life.

'You nearly shook me out of the tree,' she said when Angel Mike had stopped making such a racket.

'Do you want another one?' asked the angel, recovering himself enough to speak.

Connie nodded and the medal pinned to her chest tinkled against the buttons of her dress.

'Oh, Connie, I see you have won a medal,' said Angel Mike, forgetting all about his next joke.

'Yes, I was terribly brave. Pa calls it the PC medal,' she said, flipping the medal up and down on its striped ribbon.

'What does PC mean?' asked Mike.

'Paltry Compensation for Thom dying,' said Connie, mimicking her pa.

'Why can't I come and sit up there?' asked Nero, suddenly standing below them, his golden hair shining and his green eyes pleading to be part of their game.

'Because you've got no undies on and you would get splinters in your bum,' said the angel. Nero lifted up his tunic and was disappointed to see his bare skin underneath.

'And because you're bad,' said Connie. 'You kill Christians. This branch is only for good people.' Nero pouted and wandered back up the driveway, playing on his fiddle.

'Back to work,' said the angel. Sighing, he put his finger on the medal. The medal had a wreath on it and was inscribed *For bravery in the field*. He flipped it over and on the other side was a picture of an old bearded man.

'Ma and Pa got it down in Melbourne. They put on their best coats and their best hats and they went on the early train last week and I wanted to go and Pa said it would be too boring and Ma said it would be too sad. They came back just before dinner and Pa had the medal in a velvet box and he said it was a paltry compensation medal and he said "Here, Connie, you're brave, you have it",' said Connie, but her angel had flown away and was back at his endless war between good and bad.

Connie slithered down out of the tree, scraping her knee as she went. She unpinned the medal from her frock and slipped it into her pocket. She would have to put it back in Pa's top drawer later when no one was looking. She'd be in awful trouble for taking it. Then she sat on the grass and put on her cardigan, shoes and socks and went in for lunch.

Lydia was taking the opportunity of her parents being busy getting Sunday lunch ready to look for the PC medal. She knew her father put it in his top dresser drawer and she was carefully lifting up his handkerchiefs, which Flora had ironed into neat flat squares, his boxes of cufflinks, and his medals from the Great War to find it. She had to have it. She would pin it on her slip near her heart and keep it there. It would be safely hidden under her dress and no one need know she was wearing it. She would keep Thom alive there next to her heart.

She had nothing left now from the life that had been her, Pa and Thom and her real mother. Under the last handkerchief she saw the scalloped edge of a photograph and she pulled it out. It was small, just big enough to put in her purse. She held it to the light coming in through the window and gazed at the image of her mother, expecting she would look young and ready for the world because that was how Lydia always imagined her, but the young woman in the photograph looked sad and alone, even though she was holding Lydia in front of her obviously swelling stomach. Lydia must be about three or four years old in the photograph. Her mother sat next to her handsome young husband, who held their son Thomas. Joseph looked oblivious to the pain in his young wife's face and Lydia was surprised to find him handsome, because she had only ever imagined her father at the age he was now. Thom, who was about five, was looking away in the photograph, as though there was a whole other life for him just outside the edge of the picture.

Lydia touched Thom's face with her fingertip and then held the photograph to her lips as tears fell down her cheeks. How could he not come back? How could he be dead? How could she go on without him? She heard Flora call her for lunch and wiped away her tears and slid the photo gently back where she found it. The medal wasn't in the drawer. She made sure everything was smooth and neat and as she closed the drawer she shut up her life as it should have been, a life with her real mother, her brother and her pa before Danny was born, before Flora and Connie. That would have been a happy uncomplicated life. She took a deep breath. She thought for a moment where the medal could be and she knew instantly who would have it.

When Lydia walked into the kitchen Connie came in from outside at the same time. She was squalling and held out her leg and drops of red blood landed on the black and white linoleum floor in splatters like petals breaking from a rose. Connie was wailing like there would never be an injury worse. Connie always had to be the centre of attention. Flora spoilt that child as though she was made of glass and the slightest wind would knock her over and smash her to pieces.

'Oh for goodness sake!' said Lydia. 'You haven't been in the war and you're not dead.'

Oh God, she shouldn't have said that, she shouldn't have said the word 'dead'.

Connie stopped squalling and everyone held their breath and Lydia whispered, 'Thom,' and they all thought of Thom except Birdie, who thought of Mike. Even though soupy steam filled the kitchen the air turned icy and no one knew how to move forward into the next space of their lives until Flora, her eyes filling with tears, said, 'Dearest Thom.' Lydia looked to Joseph. His eyes were sad, tired, and she saw how he was a completely different man to the young husband in the photograph. He bowed his head so she did too and they all bowed their heads and prayed silent tears for Thom and for all the boys who would die in the war.

Connie broke the silence. 'Thom was a hero; he went and shot down two Japanese airplanes and he didn't have a stitch on, not a stitch.'

'I don't think anyone needs to know this, Connie; it's just enough that he shot down two enemy planes, thank you,' said Lydia, taking the opportunity to scowl at her again. How dare Connie speak about Thom so flippantly. He was only her half-brother, whereas he and Lydia were bound by their mother and father. After lunch she would make the stupid girl hand over the medal.

'Lydia, can you put a bandage on Connie's knee and fix the floor while I start serving the soup,' asked Flora and Lydia buried her anger at Connie and swallowed the enormous bundle of loss in her throat and it sank and settled like a dead thing under her heart. Even though Flora had asked kindly, Lydia glared at her and watched as she shrank. Lydia couldn't return Flora's love, no matter how much Flora tried. If Flora said kind words to her, Lydia would let them land on the floor; if Flora made her a skirt, Lydia would say it didn't fit properly or was the wrong colour. If Flora asked her for help, Lydia would do the task without a word, sullenly and resentfully, knowing her father would always back Flora if she just outright refused.

Lydia went to the enamel medicine chest in the laundry and took the iodine, cotton wool and a bandaid and cleaned up Connie's knee, dabbing too hard so Connie cried and Lydia said, 'If I don't put on the iodine it will get infected.' Then she cleaned the floor with the dishcloth. 'I should be called Cinderella,' she muttered. She wrung out the bloody cloth under the cold water tap and watched as the red ran down the drain and disappeared leaving no memory of its existence. Lydia wiped away a tear, put away the medicine things, went to the dining room, sat opposite Connie and ate her thin watery soup and drank her thin watery cup of tea and Flora said, 'I'm so sorry, everyone. Everything is thin and watery these days and rations are to be announced any day.'

'Oh, you've done an amazing job with very little to work with, love,' said Joseph and he reached over and held Flora's hand and Lydia, seeing his hand gently over Flora's, felt her heart break open and the bitterness buried beneath it seeped through. Lydia focussed her bile where she could and looked over to Connie, who was staring back at her as though Lydia was a complete stranger. Lydia pushed the look from her mind. Connie was always doing odd things and she nodded towards the back door.

'Can we be excused?' Lydia asked, still looking sternly at Connie, and when Joseph nodded she pushed back her chair with a scrape and Danny and Gabe took it that they were also excused and got up from the table. Lydia grabbed hold of Connie's arm. 'I can't go, I have homework to do. I have to make family trees,' said Connie.

But Lydia ignored her, pulled hard on her arm and dragged her out of the back door and into the shed, not caring one bit that she was hurting her, then she stood Connie opposite her in the darkness among the smells of oil and damp rotting timbers. The boys watched from a safe distance. Summoning her deepest, quietest voice, just like her father did when he was furious with them, Lydia said, 'Hand it over!'

'Hand what over?' Connie sniffled and rubbed her arms.

'The PC medal. Hand it over.'

'I haven't got it,' said Connie.

'Stop lying, Connie,' she said.

'I'm sure she's not,' said Danny from where he and Gabe stood in the doorway peering into the darkness.

'Oh yes, she is,' and Lydia held out her hand for the medal.

'I don't see why you get to have everything,' said Connie and she pulled her pockets inside out and a used handkerchief fell to the floor in a ball but nothing else and Lydia saw that Connie was more shocked than she that no medal fell out.

'You've lost it,' she spat.

Connie looked up at her and for a moment Lydia saw real fear in Connie's face.

'I just wanted to be brave like Thom,' cried Connie and Lydia realised that was what she wanted too and tears fell down their cheeks.

'Let's go to the river,' said Gabe.

'You can't,' said Connie, 'not on crutches.'

'I reckon I can,' said Gabe. 'Come on.'

Lydia looked at Gabe, so eager to be whole again, she looked at Danny, so sad since he lost Mike, and she looked at Connie, who was still whimpering as she wiped tears from her eyes.

'Stop sniffling, Connie,' she said. 'Well, come on – the river will be well up with the rain this last week.'

'Why don't we take the rubber raft?' said Gabe, and he pointed to the raft, folded neatly into a square sitting on the tool bench.

'Why not?' said Lydia and she carefully made her way past buckets and tin boxes and reached for the oars that were standing against the end of the tool bench and passed an oar to Danny and one to Connie and she got the bicycle pump from the shelf near the door and she passed the pump to Danny and she pulled the raft from the shelf and tipped it into the wheelbarrow and they helped Gabe climb on top and soon three children and one barely seventeen-year-old girl were heading towards the Yarrowee River with a wooden wheelbarrow that squeaked as its wheels turned, two oars and a pump and a boy holding onto crutches and they had completely forgotten about the PC medal.

Birdie had gone home and Joseph was busy in his study where he was supposed to be writing his evening sermon but was instead bent over his desk, his head in his hands that were moist with his tears, watching memories of Thom. Flora went and looked under the lemon tree; she'd seen the glint of the medal under Connie's cardigan when she'd gone out and noticed it missing when she'd come back in for lunch. She bent over and brushed the grass this way and that searching for a glint catching the sun. Finally she spied it, picked it up and brushed it off and took it to her bedroom where she slipped it back into its box and shut the drawer on the awfulness that was Thom's death. And she sat on the bed and wept into her handkerchief for him.

Joseph heard her weeping and came and sat with her. He took her hand in his and let her cry. When Flora stopped crying Joseph patted her hand, stood up and got the medal out of the drawer. He carried it cupped in his hands to the middle of the backyard and stood there for a moment looking for the right place. Flora followed.

He decided on right near the back door and slipped the medal into his pocket, then got the spade and his knife from the shed. He walked over to the rose bush that sat neglected in the corner of the back fence and sliced off a branch, making sure to take at least three nodes. He dug a hole beside the back door and carefully placed the medal in the hole. Then he held the cutting in place and gently pushed the earth back over the rose cutting, making sure to cover two nodes.

'Every time I enter our home and every time I leave I will take him with me,' said Joseph, and he thought that when the rose bush prickled him on his way in and out the door it would prick him with the pain of Thom's death. He would prune this rose bush until it grew thorns as long as the ones of Jesus's crown.

He was scooping over the last of the earth when Flora heard the doorbell ring. She left Joseph with the rose cutting and found First Constable Jobson, who should have retired but couldn't now because of the war, standing at her front door with her three bedraggled children, stringy and shivering in their wet clothes as they tried to hide behind the first constable and hide their shame.

'Fished them out of the river, Missus Starr,' he said. 'They could have drowned at this time of year.'

'Gabe?' she asked.

When Birdie gets a visitor

Sunday, 12 July 1942

When Birdie got home from lunch at Flora's she went straight to her sewing machine. She lifted the lid of her sewing table and the machine glided up easily and clicked into place. The machine was black with a gold painted paisley pattern up the side, over the top and on the base, where she fed the material through the needle. The word *Singer* was also painted in gold along the top and sides of the machine. She slid her hand along the smooth shiny enamel paint as it gleamed in the light from the window. Her sewing table had three small drawers one under the other, each drawer engraved with scallops around its handle. The top drawer held her pins and needles, then the next her bobbins, and the bottom drawer held her cotton reels. The legs of the table were wrought iron, again spelling out the word *Singer*, and between them sat the wrought iron foot pedal shaped into diamonds.

Birdie scratched at her arms; it was impossible for her to relax when Gabe wasn't near her. How could she know he was safe if she couldn't see him? But Flora said that wherever the children had gone, Lydia had gone with them and she seemed a level-headed girl and seventeen, so surely she'd have the sense to make sure no harm visited itself on Gabe. Birdie scratched at her arms again, peeling off scabs that had just formed, then shook herself. She had so many orders, six months' worth at least; she must take the opportunity of Gabe being out playing to get on with her sewing.

The arrival of rationing in June had been a boon for Birdie. Adults were allocated 112 coupons per year for clothing, and those coupons were soon used. It cost five coupons for a boy's school shirt, thirteen coupons for a simple women's frock and thirty-eight coupons for a man's suit.

'A person could own the Reserve Bank,' Prime Minister Curtin said, 'but without those pink ration coupons you can't buy a thing, so don't even think about flouting the ration laws.'

It was most unfair because now women were working they needed presentable clothes to go to work in. And how were they to stay optimistic about the war if they had to wear dreary old clothes?

Mending was no longer enough for Birdie's customers. Women wanted new dresses for themselves and shifts for their daughters and shorts and shirts for their boys.

Birdie spread newspaper over the floor, then taking her dressmaker's chalk she got down on her hands and knees and drew out white shapes over the newsprint and then cut the shapes with her enormous haberdashery scissors. She took her pins from the top drawer and put three between her lips and pinned the newspaper pieces to each other over her dummy until it resembled the tailored dress she wanted to create. All the women wanted tailored dresses, similar to the uniforms the Land Army women wore. She stood back and looked at it. No, it was too big at the waist, so she unpinned the paper, snipped a little off at the waist and pinned the newspaper tighter and she took a little off at the neck and the hem. She stood back and looked again and decided she'd got the measurements correct this time.

She sighed because now came the difficult part, finding the material. It had to be just right and it couldn't be bought because bolts of cloth were rationed along with clothing, and even if you had the coupons there just wasn't any to be had as the factories had turned their machines to producing khaki and navy wool and cotton for the forces. She had to find her material from something she already had. Birdie looked up at the curtains hanging in the lounge room but they were green with red roses and just not right, the material was too heavy. She went to Gabe's room but the curtains in there were blue and had children fishing and playing with paper boats in a pond on them and the ones in her bedroom were salmon pink with bouquets of flowers and would be perfect for someone but not for her sister.

Viola had pleaded and pleaded for Birdie to make her a dress and Birdie always said she was too busy with orders. But then she had remembered how Thom's death had made Viola so sad and how Viola had been so kind when Mike died and she was filled up with love for Viola, so Viola's dress had to be the best she'd made yet. It had to be a dress that would make Viola happy again. She flicked through her dresses and Aubrey's shirts but none of them were what she wanted. She went to her linen press and put her fingers on the cotton sheets, the flannelette sheets and then she looked down to the shelf below to the embroidered tablecloths and knew she had found what she was looking for. She selected two tablecloths. She would have to cut around the tea stains on both of them but with two tablecloths she should have enough material. One had two birds embroidered into each corner; the birds sat on a bird bath and sang to the beautiful blue daisies that floated between them. The other tablecloth was embroidered all the way around the edges with yellow, pink and blue daisies as though they had just been picked from the garden on an idle sunshiny afternoon and gathered into a bunch. Birdie laid the tablecloths on the lounge-room floor and smoothed out any creases, then she carefully unpinned the newspaper shapes from the dummy and laid them over the tablecloths and pinned the two together and cut the material. She fed white cotton through the machine, spun the silver wheel and pedalled until the machine came to life and skated over the material. The hum of the machine in her ears and the vibration of it spreading through her fingers and feet was soothing, like sitting in a train that lulls you to sleep as it takes you home.

Birdie had sewn three pieces together when she heard the rapping at the front door. She groaned; she had expressly put in her advert that she would only take new jobs on Saturdays. She let the machine come to a stop, removed the pins from her mouth and stuck them in the pin cushion and walked to the front door. She opened the door and there was a police sergeant standing in front of her, so tall she had to look up at him, so broad he filled up the entire doorway and she couldn't see past him. He had his hat on and it shaded his face but she saw his eyes were severe and his mouth held firm and she knew instantly he had come to tell her Gabe had perished and her world span and a discordant cry rang out from her heart as she fell. She felt her head land against the doorjamb and her skin open up, she felt the floor crash into her body and then everything was black.

When she opened her eyes, the world was blurry and the pain in her heart screeched out so she shut her eyes tight to keep the pain out. The right side of her body was aching, someone was dabbing a handkerchief on her forehead and there was an annoying breeze in her face and a voice in the distance calling, 'Missus Mabbett, Missus Mabbett.' She had forgotten about the sergeant being at her door and she had forgotten she had lost her only other son.

'Bother,' she said and she forced her eyes open to see who was calling her and what was causing the annoying breeze. His face was right in front of hers. His eyes sparkling and his mouth trying not to smile. What he could possibly think was so funny that he had to hold it in? She was in the bridge chair and he was squatting beside her, she could smell him. He was waving one of Gabe's western story books in her face to create the breeze and she pushed his hand and the book away.

'Missus Mabbett, you fainted,' he said. 'You've got a bit of a cut there on your head but a bandaid should fix it up.'

The reason he was there came back to her in a rush – he had come to tell her that Gabe had died and her entire body convulsed and vomit churned in her stomach and rose to her throat and she gagged.

'It's okay, Missus Mabbett, he's just been a very naughty boy.'

She blinked and looked at him, confused.

'Gabe, we fished him out of the river. He might have drowned but he's okay. Just very cold and needing a hot bath, some hot soup and likely as not a sound caning.'

'No one canes my boy!' she said crossly and the force of her words pushed him back onto the floor. She lifted herself out of the chair. 'Where is he? I must see he's all right,' but she was wobbly and the world spun around her. She'd had a terrible shock. The sergeant picked himself up and, taking her shoulders firmly in his hands, he lowered her back in the chair.

'He's fine, just hiding from your wrath, I imagine. Gabe, come and show your mother you're alive and well. Now, whether or not you deal out suitable punishment, well, that's up to you of course. You're his mother and I take it his father is off helping the war effort. Me of course – I couldn't join up. Exemption for essential service personnel but I'd go in a flash if I could …'

She wished he would just shut up and called, 'Gabe?'

The sergeant went to the lounge-room door and peered up the hallway. Then he looked back at her and said, 'Oh he's hiding in the hallway, too ashamed, I'd say, to face you. Of course boys will be boys and I know myself when I was a boy oh the worry I caused my poor mother on many an occasion and of course once …'

'Gabe,' she called again. 'Here, now.'

Gabe had never heard his mother sound so forceful and he obediently hobbled into the lounge room, holding onto the wall and he stared at the floor as though he was ashamed, which he wasn't, the river had been great fun. He and Danny, Connie and Lydia had had a right old time pumping up the raft and then lowering it into the river. They had three goes at clambering in and someone always managed to tip them over into the water at some stage but finally they had managed to get all four of them into the raft, including Gabe's crutches. Off they had sailed down the Yarrowee to China, until the river upended them and they had clung to rotting tree branches as the river rushed on by as though they were just more debris to be washed away. Then someone had heard their screams, the police had turned up and fished them out and, really, Gabe had never had a better time in his life.

Gabe was never ashamed of his antics; he was just like his father in that regard. All he could see was how much fun something was and never the danger or the hurt to others. She looked him up and down, studied the scratches on his face, the dripping hair, the wet muddy clothes, the way he shivered under the police blanket. He wasn't okay, something was missing, and she realised what it was.

'Your crutches?'

'Oh yes,' said the sergeant. 'Well, we fished Gabe out of the river and the other Starr children but we couldn't find those crutches. I suspect they're at the bottom and of course when the river dries out in summer, well, they'll most likely be rotten by then or perhaps washed away to Magpie.'

'I don't need them, Mum,' said Gabe, and he tottered drunkenly towards her like a toddler learning to walk, and when he lost his balance the sergeant put his strong arm out and caught him and had him upright again in no time. Birdie looked up at the sergeant and saw how solid he was, how reliable and how he observed everything and how his face belied the rest of him by being covered in a million boyish freckles.

'Thank you, Sergeant –?'

'Fortunato,' he said.

'Why aren't you interned?'

'Well, it just so happens my family are Swiss Italians that immigrated here way back in –'

She didn't need his family history. 'Gabe, thank the sergeant for saving you,' and she stood up to see the sergeant out but wooziness overcame her and he was there in an instant with the same strong hand he had provided Gabe, and she felt his hand wrap around her elbow and take all her weight and for a moment it was as though she had no burdens, no worries, and she felt light like a cloud and he gently lowered her back into the chair.

'Gabe, show me where the kettle is,' he commanded and he helped Gabe into the kitchen.

'And then change into warm clothes,' called Birdie.

Birdie laid her head back and tormented herself to push away the dangerous lightness she was feeling. She saw Gabe thrashing about in the rushing river with his useless limbs and tears rolled down her cheeks and the fear of the worst happening was a much more comfortable feeling for her.

'There, there,' said Sergeant Fortunato, and he put her Royal Albert teacup and saucer that she only used for best into her hands and watched her intently until she obediently sipped at it. 'Now

I must be going, crooks to catch. Gabe, be good to your mother or I'll have you locked up in no time,' and she saw him look at Gabe like he meant it and Gabe looked at his mother and she saw that for the first time he was terrified of what punishment could await his antics. Birdie looked back at Sergeant Fortunato and his boyish face full of the happiness she couldn't get hold of smiled back at her.

She stood up and said, 'I'll walk you to the door.'

Sergeant Fortunato leant over and ruffled Gabe's hair. 'I hope not to see you again unless I'm off duty.'

At the door he put out his hand and Birdie put her hand in his and he shook it hard and she winced.

'I'll be going then,' he said and he turned and walked down the path.

Then without warning he was back; his arm was around her waist pulling her tight to him and his lips were pressed hard against hers. His mouth was soft and kind and when he pulled away she had to stop herself leaning forward for more.

'I'm married,' she protested but it was a whisper he didn't hear as he strode down her front path.

She walked back inside, covering her smile with her hand. She looked at Gabe and said, 'Well, I suppose I need to go buy you some new crutches tomorrow.'

'No, I can manage without them,' said Gabe.

'But what if you fall? There won't be any Sergeant Fortunato to catch you.'

'If I fall – I fall,' he said. 'But I really want to give it a go. You can go buy crutches if you want, Mum, but I won't be using them ever again.'

Birdie sighed; she wouldn't argue with him. 'You get changed. I have to get back to my sewing. No leaving the house or I'll call Sergeant Fortunato,' she threatened and they both knew she wouldn't and then she said, 'If you want to be without crutches you have to be able to walk the length of the hallway unaided.'

Birdie sewed, and when the machine stopped its humming song she could hear Gabe practising walking up and down the hallway without his crutches, his better leg pulling his worse leg along in a limp. Birdie sewed the last panel of cloth and then she pulled the cotton out of the sewing machine needle and bit off a long thread. She held the sewing needle to the light and threaded it through, then she sat in the bridge chair and hand-sewed the hem with tiny delicate little stitches and as she sewed she smiled because Gabe was walking. Doctor Unsworth had said he would never walk again – well, it only went to show.

When Joseph is given an ultimatum

Sunday, 2 May 1943

For nine months the Americans fought off the Japanese, who, having failed to invade Australia after the Darwin attack, were now trying to invade Australia through its eastern seaboard via the Pacific Ocean. By December 1942 fifteen thousand American marines and soldiers were worn out from the ongoing fight in the Pacific islands. They were ragged starvelings. Their once-smart uniforms were torn, their shirts hung heavy over their thin spines, crusted with months of dirt, their lungs coughed up green phlegm, their bones could barely hold them up. Their spirits wafted above them, waiting for them to give up and die.

'What my boys need is steak, eggs, ice-cream and the congenial company of Australian girls,' their commander, General Vandegrift, said, rubbing his handsome Cary Grant cleft chin. And Brisbane answered his call.

The Americans were rich and starved of girls and Australia had plenty of those. The Australian girls were starved of ice-cream and chocolate and the American boys had plenty of those. So a mutual exchange was advantageous to both. They called the Aussie girls *ma'am* and the girls who were used to the Aussie boys dismissing them as soon as their beer or their mates were around, fell into the Americans' waiting arms and pressed their red lips against the soft wide American mouths. The Americans were happy and brash and thought nothing of swinging a girl back over their arm and kissing her feverishly right in the middle of King George Square. Parents watching this excess of wealth and amorousness were horrified and frightened and forbade their daughters to fraternise with the Americans, and of course their daughters ignored them.

Girls were happy to eat in cafés, shop in stores and go to dances and movies with any paying American no matter his skin colour, and the American soldiers came in two varieties. The Aussies, seeing their girls out and about with the Americans, lashed out and brawled with the Americans and, as wars do, everything escalated so that fists were replaced with guns and the brawls grew from lasting two hours to lasting two days. Shots were fired and boys died at the hands of their allies on allied soil and everyone realised that eighty thousand hot-blooded Americans was too much for a small town of three hundred thousand. The American boys were moved to Melbourne and again a war broke out, this time on the MCG; shots were fired and lives were lost. The only thing for it was to spread the Americans across the state.

And so in February 1943 nearly five thousand of them arrived by the trainload into Ballarat, where they camped at Victoria Park in neat rows of tents. Four stretchers and one small kerosene burner to a tent and the promise of Aussie army-issue jackets to keep them warm when the cold winter chill descended.

At first the people of Ballarat happily welcomed the Americans. In fact Mister George Banks, who lived virtually opposite Birdie in Humffray Street, even ferried them around in his car. A short trip up Sturt Street cost the Americans six shillings and cost Mister Banks a three-pound fine for illegal cabbing. Mister

Horace Green from Sebastopol was fined forty pounds for selling the eager Americans illegal grog at three pounds ten per bottle.

'Whisky, lads,' he'd told the marines, holding the brown bottles so they caught the moonlight. 'You won't get a better brew anywhere,' and taking their money he handed them bottles filled with a dash of sherry and plenty of Ballarat water.

The girls were thrilled with the American invasion and giggled and skipped and put on their best frocks and extra make-up because once again Ballarat had boys and not just boys but five thousand of them swaggering up and down Sturt Street or whooping and whistling at the girls as they leant out the tram windows, or lining up out the door and down Lydiard Street at the Regent Theatre. The girls were given chocolates and stockings and were kissed, bent backwards over the marines' arms in front of the council chambers. They were taken to the movies to see *Casablanca*, which had finally come to Australia, and as the girls cried at the sad parting of Ingrid Bergman and Humphrey Bogart, the American boys kissed up their tears. Oh how Lydia wanted to be one of those girls, but Joseph would never allow it.

Ballarat parents were not pleased and gathered on street corners and tutted and harrumphed. When the Americans walked past they all stopped talking and glared at the boys. They stood in huddles discussing it after church.

'They fill the back of the church pretending they're here to worship but we all know they are here to collect our girls.'

'They pluck them up like they're swooping up handfuls of yellow daisies.'

'They are reprobates and debauchers!'

'And some of them aren't even white!'

'The girls must stay away!'

By May the parents had had enough. Two months was long enough to be welcoming and tolerant. The boys just weren't respectful of Ballarat ways. The church parents sent a deputation to Joseph. Three of the deacons went, including Cecil Finchley. And for no reason he could see, since he didn't even have a daughter, Cecil became the spokesperson.

'You must do something about it,' said Cecil, and the other two men nodded.

'What do you expect me to do?' Joseph said, slowly filling his front doorway. He didn't like Cecil making demands of him. Out of all the men in the congregation, Cecil was his one friend.

The men leant forward and pushed white-clenched knuckles into the doorframe.

'You must forbid the girls from fraternising with them before we have half-breed babies popping out in Ballarat. Just imagine if some of those babies started coming out black. Our girls' lives would be ruined.'

Joseph sighed, looked at Cecil and said, 'Are you coming in for lunch? Mabel's already here.'

And Cecil, shamefaced, stepped through the door.

When Joseph gives an ultimatum

Sunday, 9 May 1943

The following Sunday, Joseph, thinking of his own Lydia, stood in the pulpit gripping its sides and preached fervently about the dangers of carnal sin, of getting in trouble with a boy who may not stay around to see his trouble through, and of the lure of treats unavailable to Aussie girls that the Americans had in plenty. He raised his voice as he preached about the sin of dancing, which was the starting point of seduction, for in dancing boys took the opportunity to pull girls' bodies up against their own and hold them tight. He raised his voice against St Patrick's over the road, which held dances for the Americans every Saturday night, but what could you expect of Catholics who didn't understand God's true word? He wanted to see none of his flock there. He looked sternly at Lydia the whole time he was preaching and while he was preaching, the girls decided they would never set foot inside the St Patrick's dance again. But of course, once they were outside the church, watching the American boys with their loud laughs, their winks and their elaborate bows, they would forget all Joseph's warnings.

Lydia sat there looking at the floorboards. She might as well be the only person in the congregation because she was the only one Joseph was preaching to. She was sitting next to Flora. Viola had been sitting on the other side of her but Viola had taken the children out to Sunday school. When Flora had asked Lydia to teach a Sunday school class she'd said, 'But I'm teaching during the week. I think that's enough of children for me.' She'd seen Flora about to press and she quickly added, 'I need to be in church listening to Pa's sermons so I have the spiritual fitness needed for my teaching duties during the week.' And Flora had let it go.

With the war there was a shortage of teachers, so more women were accepted and you could go straight into the classroom on a six-year apprenticeship. Lydia was teaching at Dana Street Primary, and like most teachers had gone straight from her Leaving Certificate to teaching. She had the bubs class, the five year olds. By the end of the day she couldn't get 'Incy Wincy Spider' out of her head. The thought of teaching on Sundays as well made her stomach churn. She wasn't like her friend Viola, who smiled and laughed when the children clambered all over her good frock. Lydia wanted her frock intact, her hair unmussed, and the children with their snotty noses and dirty sticky fingers to keep their distance. Lydia's whole world had become the two-minute walk from the manse to the school in the morning and back again in the afternoon – with Connie for company. It was far too small a world for her. Ballarat was too small for her and her need to fly away sometimes made her bones clench up tight and her arms would start flapping against her sides like a bird about to take flight and her feet would start aching as they tried to carry her somewhere else. But she'd never get anywhere on her own. She had a little money that she was able to keep from her wage but most of it went to Flora for housekeeping. She wasn't left with even a train fare to Melbourne.

She looked to the back of the church where the Americans were standing two-deep along the back wall, their arms crossed over their chests, their heads down to hide their smiles as Joseph preached about their evil influence. There was no room for them on the pews. One of the boys lifted his eyes and met hers. He winked at her and she smiled back. His skin shone in the yellow sun that came through the leadlight windows. He was taller than any of the others and she felt his black eyes weighing her up, seeing her hunger for something she didn't yet know and she felt bare. She couldn't look at him any longer; she turned in her seat and slunk down, her heart pounding, her cheeks hot and red, and hoped Flora wouldn't notice.

When Joseph said the benediction and he and Flora walked to the church door, Lydia bolted out the other way through the door to the hall, through the hall, out of the church grounds and down her driveway. She stood under the lemon tree in the May sunshine, oblivious to Connie above her, and took deep breaths to calm her beating chest.

She felt Viola come to stand beside her.

'Connie climbs up in that tree and spies on people,' Lydia said, nodding her head towards the top of the tree.

Viola laughed. 'I bet she does.'

'It's time you and I went to the dances,' Lydia said.

'You mean the one your father just forbade all of us to go to? The reverend will have a right royal fit. He'll lock you away forever if he catches you.'

Lydia looked at Viola; her light brown hair, gathered at the side into a tortoiseshell clip, glistened in the sun. 'Your hair is so pretty,' she said, touching the flyaway strands. 'Mine is too dark and too straight. It won't ever go where I want it to. It's like my father's. When I was little it was light like my mother's. Then it turned dark. See, look at my eyes – I could say I was Italian and no one would be the wiser. So, we'll go to the dance next Saturday night.'

'What about your father?' said Viola. They watched as some of the American boys walked down the street. The boys saw them and waved and the girls fell into each other giggling. The tall one stopped and looked at Lydia and a slow smile spread over his face. Lydia stopped giggling as the danger of him filled her up. She took a deep breath and said, 'Next Saturday. I'll get out somehow. I'll meet you there.'

On Monday after dinner Lydia was sitting at the kitchen table preparing the activities she would do with her class the next day. There was going to be an air raid drill and that would take up most of the morning but she still needed to fill the afternoon. Connie was in bed on a mattress on the floor of her parents' room, and Flora was in the living room chatting with Missus Forster, who was staying in Connie's bed. Lydia hated having to share her room with a constant trickle of strangers. She blamed Flora. Her father would be a different person if he hadn't married Flora. She didn't know what sort of person he might be but it would be better. If she didn't blame Flora, she would have to blame her father, and she couldn't do that because he was the last one left now because she didn't count Danny, who had helped kill her mother.

A shadow rested on her before she looked up to see Joseph standing in the door.

'A word, Lydia, when you're ready. In my study.'

Her stomach lurched and she put her hands over her belly to calm it. If her father wanted a word in his study you were in enormous trouble. Had he discovered her plans for Saturday night? But how could he? Viola would never tell. Lydia left her exercise book and pen and ink and walked into the study. He looked up from his bible and motioned to the chair opposite him. Lydia was glad the desk was between them, a fortress. It gave her a good two feet advantage if she decided to run.

He took a deep breath and said, 'I expressly forbid you from fraternising with any American boys.'

Lydia rolled her eyes.

'I mean it, Lydia. I won't have it. It's not up for discussion.'

'So, I can't even speak to them? I can't even be polite and Christian and say hello if I pass them on Sturt Street? Not that with work and church I ever get to stroll up and down Sturt Street any more.'

Joseph leant forward. 'No, as a matter of fact you can't. You can nod and walk on by. Especially the blacks – they might not even believe in God, they might practise voodoo for all we know.'

'If I don't talk to the Americans, who do you expect me to talk to? Because there isn't anyone else around.'

'You can talk to me and your mother,' he said, as though it was a perfectly reasonable alternative.

'Ugh, you really are just so exasperating,' said Lydia and fled to her bedroom.

When Lydia dances

Saturday, 15 May 1943

On Saturday Lydia waited until Missus Forster was gently snoring in Connie's bed and her mother and father were in their room and she could hear the mutter of Joseph reading their nightly bible passage, his voice murmuring up through the ceiling to her room. The curtains were all drawn and only dim lights were allowed so that the Japanese couldn't see you from their planes. Joseph and Flora would be praying soon and would have their eyes closed, so she'd have a double safety net. They wouldn't see her run across the street to St Patrick's. She threw her coat on over her dress, and carrying her best Sunday shoes she tiptoed down the staircase and through the kitchen. Danny was sitting at the table with an open bible and a sheet of paper, wearing his coat and a scarf because the May night was cold.

'What are you doing?'

'Studying for bible school,' he said. 'I can't decide what to do when I matriculate so I thought I might as well be a missionary.'

'You've got a couple of years to think about it before you decide.'

'I thought maybe Africa or India,' he said.

'Anywhere has to be better than here,' she said.

'Where are you off to?' he asked.

She looked at him. Danny would believe anything, so she said, 'The lavatory,' and shot out the back door. Her coat caught on the growing rose bush. 'I don't know why Papa put you so close to the door,' she growled. Her coat tore as she pulled it free and she dashed across the street in her bare feet.

Viola was waiting for her outside the hall.

'Did you bring it?' she asked and Viola held up a tin of vegemite. They ran to the toilets and in the dim light smeared the vegemite all over their legs and they danced about waiting for the sticky vegemite to dry. Then Viola took out her eyebrow pencil and drew a line up the back of Lydia's legs and Lydia did the same for her.

'It looks just like nylons,' lied Viola. 'Well, it doesn't look any worse than gravy, which is what most of the girls are using.'

'Lipstick?' said Lydia, waving her hands in the air. 'What are we going to do?'

'*Voilà*,' said Viola and she pulled out half a beetroot she'd taken from her mother's vegetable box.

Lydia smiled and rubbed the dirt from her feet and slipped on her shoes. 'Come on – let's go do our duty for the war and dance with these Yank lads. Who knows, maybe one will propose on the spot and whisk me away to America.'

With her beetroot lips and cheeks, her hair combed and pinned, her legs stained amber, she was ready to be swept off her feet.

The windows of the church hall were covered in masonite. Australian and American flags hung on the walls either side of a crucifix from which a sad and lonely Jesus, nailed to his cross, unable to come down and dance, watched as the band played and young men who might be having the last happy days they were to ever have, laughed as they twirled girls in giddy circles.

The band played 'Don't Sit Under The Apple Tree' and suddenly Lydia, who realised she had no idea how to dance, felt herself pulled out into the middle of the hall, where she was twirled and swung and dipped. Breathless, this was the way to go through life, with someone taking you by the hand and dragging you along at a furious pace before you even knew where you were going. When the band finished he stopped swinging her about but held tight to her hands. She was bent over catching her breath when she looked up and saw it was him from church, his black eyes shining at her.

He smiled and said, 'Ready? Here we go again.' And before she had time to answer, they were off and dancing to 'Chattanooga Choo Choo' and they formed a line that wound around the walls and she threw her arms up in the air and yelled 'Choo choo!' with the rest them.

At the end of the song he said, 'What's your name?' but the band had started playing 'Frenesi' and he pulled her close up against his tall body. She could feel the hard muscles of his chest as she rested her head there. She could hear the beating of his heart slowing, seeming to match the rhythm of the music, she could feel his arms holding her weight and his feet guiding them both across the floor. The lilting clarinet softly soothed her deeper into him and she let it carry her away to somewhere else, where she could be someone else, and when other boys tapped on her shoulder, she opened her dreamy eyes, shook her head and stayed wrapped in him.

Finally, the band played 'Waltzing Matilda' and he stood tall, still holding her hand and sang loudly as though it was his song. Then he said, 'I'll walk you home.'

She laughed and said, 'No need.'

'No really, I don't mind at all,' he said. 'No distance is too far.'

'Oh believe me, the distance is not far enough,' she said.

She pulled away from him and she felt a wrench as if she was separating from part of herself.

'Hey – what's your name?' he called after her as she ran off to find Viola.

'Lydia,' she called back over her shoulder. She saw Viola, exhilarated, red cheeked and shiny-eyed, leaning into a marine, his sandy hair wet with sweat and his smile spread right across his face so that all Lydia saw was white teeth.

'He's going to walk me home,' Viola said and she nodded towards the marine. Lydia looked harder at him to see if Viola would be safe and she saw his freckles and his kind eyes and he smiled at her and she saw Thom.

'I better go,' she said, and taking off her shoes she ran like Cinderella from the ball straight into her father, waiting in the dark, under the lemon tree, his arms barricaded across his chest.

'In my study,' he said, his voice barely even a whisper.

She felt her bones turn to jelly so she reminded herself of the worth of disobeying her father, of the one who held her so safe as he danced her away, and she straightened and walked through the house and into the study.

'You disobeyed me,' he said. He was in his slippers, pyjamas and dressing gown. 'I had a good mind to go right over there and just drag you home in front of everybody. I've done it before and I can do it again.'

Yes, and you got Thom killed doing it, thought Lydia bitterly. She wanted him to scream and yell so she could scream and yell back. But she knew it was useless to wish that so she fought back on his own ground and speaking even more quietly and more calmly she said, 'You can't stop me. I'm working now. And besides, the government wants us to entertain the Americans. It's our duty.'

Joseph leant forward, right into her face, and said, 'Not my daughter. Not my daughter who lied to me. You are grounded henceforth. You will go to work and you will come straight home. I will be monitoring your every move.' And he stood up and she knew nothing she could say would change his mind. For him the conversation was over. She looked at him in his dressing gown and slippers and slowly realised he was just a tired old man who wanted to be in bed. She could get around his rules. She would take a leaf from Connie's book, and if she couldn't get around the rules she would just ignore them because, she realised for the first time in her life, what could he actually do to stop her?

When Lydia takes flight

Saturday, 15 August 1943

Lydia put the mop and broom back in the laundry. Flora was in the kitchen in her housecoat and apron making a cake. Danny, now fourteen, was at the kitchen table studying his bible. Lydia flipped the bible shut as she walked past.

'What a waste of a perfectly good Saturday morning,' she said in his ear so Flora wouldn't hear.

Connie was hanging about Flora, waiting to lick the bowl and wooden spoon. 'Where are you going, Lydia?' she demanded.

'Nowhere that you need to know,' said Lydia.

'I'm going fishing at the river with Gabe this afternoon,' Danny said. 'If the weather clears up.'

'Can I come?' asked Connie.

'I don't know why you want to be a missionary; just become a pastor like Pa,' Lydia said.

'It's more years of study to do that. I only have to do two years to be a missionary. I just have to decide which language I'm going to learn.'

'I've done my chores,' said Lydia to Flora.

'I know where you're going,' said Connie, 'She's going to ...' but Flora cut her off.

'The bath and the basin and the floor?' said Flora. The *Women's Weekly* was lying on the kitchen bench open to the cooking page. Lydia, taller than Flora, looked over Flora's shoulder at the page of recipes and a government advertisement running down the side of the page saying, *Mrs Housewife! You are hereby appointed controller of food. Yours is an all-important war job now! All spare food is needed for Britain, whose people are facing worse conditions than our own. Issued by the Commonwealth Food Patrol.*

'Look here, they ran a contest for best ration recipes,' said Flora, not looking up as she ran her finger down the list of ingredients. 'Two and six this woman won for her cake. No milk, no eggs and no butter. You boil it all together before baking it.'

'Does that mean I don't have to collect the eggs any more?' Connie asked. 'I hate collecting eggs.'

'I'm going to meet Viola,' said Lydia, glaring at Connie, daring her to contradict her. She wasn't lying exactly, she probably would see Viola some time during the day.

'No, she's ...' started Connie and Lydia reached over and squeezed her arm tight and when Connie started to squeal Lydia squeezed tighter until Connie clamped her mouth shut.

'There's a recipe here for meatloaf that is made of cabbage and vegemite and no meat,' said Flora.

'Disgusting,' said Lydia.

'You and Viola are awfully thick these days,' said Flora, looking at her.

Lydia shrugged.

'When do you expect to be back?' said Flora. She carefully tipped a cup of sugar into a saucepan so as not to drop a single rationed grain. 'Remember your curfew, I don't want you in further trouble with your father. What will I tell him?'

'Tell him you've sent me to the store.'

'But …' said Connie and Flora handed her the wooden spoon and Connie, distracted, began licking.

Flora put down the measuring jug. 'Not mentioning you are out is one thing but I can't lie for you, Lydia.'

Lydia grabbed her coat and hat from the hook. 'Then tell him the truth. Tell him I'm at Viola's and I'm going straight there and will come straight back,' and she glared at Connie again and walked out the back door, making sure to dodge the thorns on the rose bush.

The August wind beat at her face and snapped at her cheeks as she walked in the opposite direction to Viola's house. She buttoned her coat, pulled her scarf up over her nose and put her hands in her coat pockets. She went down Grant Street to the corner of Humffray Street and came to a halt at the end of a line of women. She stepped out into the road and saw the line went further than she could see. Women were lined up in coats, hats and scarves that flapped and beat about them in the wind. They chatted with those in front or behind them and ignored their boys, who chased each other on the street with sticks, and their girls, who clung onto their legs or played hopscotch on the road. Women jiggled babies on their hips or rocked prams back and forth over rough bits on the path to lull the babies to sleep. Lydia walked past them all. Up the line she went, past Nancy who worked in the shoe shop and past Dulcie and Nola who she saw each week at church and past the women she knew by face but not by name and the women who were mothers of her students. She followed the queue all the way to Birdie's front door.

'You can't push in,' June Burchmore snapped at her as Lydia reached for the door handle. June Burchmore was a large woman standing nearly five foot ten with breasts that she pushed into a separate and lift bra. The two pointed cones stared viciously at

Lydia. Other women when confronted with those breasts were aware only of their inadequacy as their breasts shrivelled to flat invisible things. Lydia would not be so easily subdued. Lydia had fought with her father and not even June Burchmore's breasts could outdo her father.

Without moving any other part of her body June pushed her enormous breasts forward. She wasn't about to let anyone get in front of her; she'd been standing in this line since seven, that was nearly three hours ago, and she didn't care if the girl was her daughter's teacher, she wasn't going to barge her way to the front like that.

'What's going on here – why the queue?' asked Lydia, pretending she didn't know.

June hoisted a large carpet bag up under her breasts and opened it. Lydia peered inside and saw it was filled with tablecloths and doilies.

'There's no accounting for what Birdie can do with a sewing machine,' June said. 'She takes people's old dresses, takes off the outdated puff sleeves and takes out the bodice seams and makes them into something modern and completely new, something tailored and military. She uses old tablecloths, curtains, doilies, anything she can get her hands on and turns them into the most superb frocks for dancing. She has a waiting list a mile long. But – and she's really strict about this –' Lydia pulled back from the finger waving in her face, 'she only takes new orders on Saturdays. There's always a queue. She stands and looks at you and then she knows exactly what you need, she doesn't even measure, and you wear that new dress and you feel like a different person in a different world. The war seems forever away.'

'Hmmmm, well I'm here to see Gabe,' lied Lydia, and she brazenly opened the door, pushed past June and walked in. As she walked through the hall she could hear voices and followed the sound to the living room where Birdie was standing against the wall in her dark grey funeral frock, her arms crossed over her chest as she looked hard at Winnie, who was standing in front of her.

'Faull's,' said Lydia to Winnie, 'you work at Faull's.'

Winnie twirled her auburn hair around her fingers and opened her mouth to reply.

'Don't talk,' said Birdie and both girls' mouths shut instantly, then Birdie moved forward and looked through the old dresses and the lace curtain that Winnie had brought with her. 'I need this and this,' she said, and she took a piece of paper from her table and wrote 'Winnie – Faull's' on it in pencil and pinned it to the two pieces of material. 'I'll send Gabe down to Faull's when it's done,' said Birdie. 'I work on need, not your place in the queue.'

At this Lydia felt herself stand taller with hope. Her need was enormous. She needed a dress that would make him take her away.

'Okay, you can go; tell the next person I'll come let them in as soon as I can.'

'That will be June Burchmore,' said Lydia as Winnie left.

Birdie looked at her and Lydia wriggled. Birdie knew she'd pushed in.

'Did Flora send you?' she asked.

'Yes,' said Lydia, 'she said I needed a new dress now that I'm working.'

'Did you bring material?' said Birdie. Lydia squirmed and shrugged and then she spotted Gabe, whom she hadn't noticed till now, sitting in the corner reading *Raiders of Spanish Peaks.* The cowboy on the front cover held a gun that emitted a stream of white smoke.

'If you make me something,' said Lydia as the thought formed, 'I'll look after Gabe whenever you want – you know, after school and on Saturdays. You could get more sewing done.'

Still Birdie looked at her and Lydia felt she was being judged and if she was being judged it wouldn't be favourably.

'No,' said Birdie. 'You've seen the queue and I can't make you what you want. I'm sorry, Lydia.'

'I really need ... I really need to be something different,' said Lydia.

Birdie shook her head.

Lydia turned and walked out the front door and she motioned for June to go in, which June did with a harrumph and a swaying of her shoulders. Lydia walked past the queue of women and was almost at the corner of the street when she heard her name being called. She turned and Gabe came towards her in his half-limp half-run. He was puffed when he got to her. She waited as he got his breath back.

'Mum said to give you this,' he puffed. 'And she said you have to make sure I don't get into any more trouble and she says if I do it will be on you and you'll have to live with it for the rest of your life,' and he took a deep breath and placed a bundle of material into her hands.

Lydia held the material to her chest. She felt its gentleness and its lightness, she felt it trying to fly away and knew this dress was exactly what she needed.

'It's one of Mum's,' Gabe said. 'She doesn't wear it any more.'

Lydia hugged the dress tight to her chest and walked back up Grant Street. She walked down Dawson Street and into her driveway past Connie sitting in the lemon tree.

'I know where you've been,' Connie called down to her.

'Aren't you too old to be sitting in that tree?' Lydia called back and walked past the empty stretchers in the vestibule where Missus Gibbons and her daughter Jenny had stayed for the last three nights, past the empty stretcher in the hallway, and up the stairs to her room, where she shut the door and wedged the chair under the handle. Then she pulled off her Saturday dress and slipped into the dress Birdie had given her and stared at it in the chipped dresser mirror. The dress had two layers; the underneath layer was satin blue like a spring sky and over this was a lace layer that had once been a filet lace tablecloth and woven into the lace were angels, their wings stretched out as they hovered ready to take flight. She took the dress off, carefully folded it and hid it in the top dresser drawer beneath her underthings. Then she put her Saturday dress back on and walked into the kitchen.

'Can I help with the cooking?' she asked Flora.

She saw Flora try to hide her shock as she said, 'Well, yes, that would be lovely. Perhaps you could help me set out lunch first; we're having the mock meatloaf I mentioned.'

Lydia nudged Danny to pack up his bible and notebook and he sighed and gathered up his things and she heard him going up the stairs to his room. She set the table and called Connie from the tree and Danny from his room and her father from his study where he was writing his sermon.

In the afternoon she helped Flora make onion rolypoly and savoury cabbage jelly mould and mock cream for the cake. All for tomorrow's Sunday lunch.

Flora was filled with hope that perhaps things had finally turned around with Lydia, perhaps her father's firm hand had been just what she needed. They chatted as they cooked and Flora didn't know that Lydia was balancing the disobedience she planned for that night with some obedience now.

After dinner Lydia lay on her bed reading and every hour either Joseph or Flora checked on her and finally, satisfied that she had learnt her lesson and was safe, she heard them saying their prayers and then there was quietness and she assumed they were asleep. She listened to the house, to its whispers and groans, to Connie's snuffling snores in the other bed, and she tiptoed to her drawer, slipped off her flannelette nightie and slid the dress down over her arms. She combed her hair and pinned it back on the side with her clip, then wrapped the blanket from her bed around her in a shroud and with her shoes in her hand, she crept down the stairs in bare feet, trying to avoid the steps she knew squeaked. She went into her father's study and took the church keys tied up with string from the hook on the wall, holding them tight in her fist so they didn't jangle, and she stole through the living room, through the kitchen and through the vestibule like a thief past Jonnie Johnson asleep on a stretcher, who had arrived during the afternoon after travelling from Ararat to join up. She was out the back door, her shoes on and running down the driveway and past the lemon tree.

Lydia stood in the street looking for him. She saw the moonlight playing on his skin as he stood in the empty road waiting for her as he had done for the past three months since she had met him that night in May.

He grabbed her and held her to him. 'We're being shipped out soon – maybe next month. Who knows what could happen,' his husky voice whispered in her ear.

'Who knows,' she said, realising that this was her life – her future was an unknown quantity where death played with people's lives. People as young as her, people like Thom, died every day in this dreadful war. She knew she couldn't risk missing out on him; she had to let him take her where he wanted. Sometimes they had walked around the block, pressed hard into each other and not saying a word for fear of someone in the houses hearing. Sometimes they had sat on the church porch pressed together for warmth and she'd rested her head on his shoulder.

Now she felt the weight of the keys in her pocket, grabbed his hand and pulled him to the front door of the church. She quietly closed the door behind them and led him down the aisle, past the communion table in front of the pulpit and up the steps to the platform where her father's pulpit perched, with the baptismal bath beneath it where she had been baptised by her father when she was deemed old enough to understand the significance of it, just after she turned sixteen. She had come out of the water spluttering and feeling nothing.

'I have to be back at camp before reveille,' he said, and he put his marine cap on her head and she saluted and he laughed.

'Me too,' she said.

'I'll be in so much muck if we're caught.'

'So will I – more than you, I expect.'

'I don't know where I'll be sent next,' he said, and the urgency of their world, the shortness of their lives, filled their lungs and they breathed deeply and thought it was their only chance to step into the future.

'I watch you in church, I watch your black hair like night, your eyes dark like …'

'Like night?' she laughed at him.

'Yes,' he said. 'Your eyes are darker than mine.'

She smiled up at him, at his own dark eyes and his skin that was warm in the moonlight coming through the leadlight windows and he took the blanket from her and wrapped them both in a secret world inside the blanket where time stretched out for them. He put his hands around her face and held it to him, then he kissed her and her heart flew into the sky.

'Take me away,' she whispered as he buried his head in her neck. He reached under her dress and his fingers played up her leg, one note after the other, and his touch on her skin left hot tingling traces of the music he played. He laid her down on the blanket. He took off his jacket, his shirt and trousers and then peeled off his white singlet. She watched his muscles stretch and contract with each movement. He was strong, he would have the force to stand up to her father. He leant forward and slipped her dress up over her arms.

'Your arms are so slender and pale I can see the moon dancing on them,' he said, 'there and there and there,' and he kissed the moon-spots and then he kissed the warm inside of her elbow. She shivered, and thinking she was cold he wrapped her up in him and their heavy breaths mingled and warmed their blanket cocoon. He pulled up her slip and kissed the bare white skin of her stomach. She arched her back and pressed herself into him and he looked down at her and said, 'Marry me.'

'I can't,' she said. 'My father would never give permission.' She sounded pathetic and young; she would never get away if she listened to her father, so she gathered her determination and said, 'Yes, yes,' thinking she would find a way. And he, knowing he now had a future, pushed her knickers aside and entered her and she cried out at his thrust, she became a small fragile thing because it hurt and she hadn't expected that.

'I'm sorry,' he said, and he gently moved inside her, all the time kissing her and whispering, 'I love you – we'll be married,' and it took her where she wanted to go and she said she loved him back.

The weight on Lydia's shoulders

Sunday, 16 August 1943

Joseph lay in bed unable to sleep. He lay still and straight and he felt the rise and fall of Flora sleeping beside him. He held his arms by his sides and squeezed his eyes shut, holding in his tears. If he let go, the flood of his agony would be unleashed and he would drown. He blamed himself for his unbearable pain.

How had he let Thom slip off to Melbourne like that? How had he not seen how the boy had been cast in his mould? How had he not seen that the boy, just like him, would persevere in his plan to join up? Once Joseph had decided on something, even Flora's pleas couldn't stop him, and Thom was the same and he just hadn't seen it. He opened his eyes and looked into the dark of the room trying to see Thom, to reach out to touch him through the veils that separated earth from heaven. He stretched out his arm and pointed his finger, trying to reach the heavens, but no angelic finger touched him back. He had lost his first wife, Lydia, whom his daughter was named for, and now Thom. He should have taken control. His bones ached with his pain and his soul was dried and frayed.

He scolded himself for thinking only of his own pain and forced himself to think about Manny Finchley, listed as missing in action and presumed dead. He was a clever boy but soft and gentle and not cut out for war. Joseph remembered how Manny made people laugh because he was quick-witted and he laughed at everything. He thought of the Rowbothams, whose five sons at war were now just three as Ronny and Trevor had been killed in the Battle of Darwin along with Thom. He thought of young Michael Mabbett, so unlike his good-for-nothing father, a sweet fair boy who had shown such promise and slipped away overnight with only his mother clinging to his soul.

Cold hard stones hit his heart with a rhythmic sound and he let them as his heart was already battered. What more could be done to him except to give him the punishment he deserved? Then he realised the sound wasn't coming from within him, it was from outside the house. Someone was tossing stones on the road. He took his feet from under the warm covers and put them on the cold floorboards and reached over, pulled aside the curtain, and peered out.

The night was dark and shadowy apart from the occasional glint of the moon on leaves. He stood and looked out for some time but he couldn't see anything or anyone and sighed. Perhaps it was his own guilt hammering at him after all. He slipped back in under the blankets and quilt and wrapped his arm around Flora, who murmured at his touch. Then he thought he heard the tinkling of a girl's laugh out in the street. He rolled away from Flora and held his clock to the moonlight eking its way through the curtain. It was past midnight. No one should be out on the street at midnight, let alone a girl.

He got up and took his torch from his bedside drawer. He padded quietly out of the bedroom, walked up the stairs and checked Danny's room, shining the torch past Thom's empty bed until the light fell on Danny, sleeping with his bear that he kept hidden under his bed during the day and took out to hold each night. Joseph walked to Connie and Lydia's room and swung the torch over Connie's sleeping body and wondered how he and Flora had created such a strange child. He moved the torch over to Lydia's bed and saw her there, so soundly asleep that there was no movement in the blankets. He held the torch there for a moment, knowing something wasn't right, then lifted up the blankets, laying bare the two pillows and jumble of clothes.

'She's flown away,' murmured Connie sleepily but Joseph didn't hear her.

He walked out into the hallway and gasped for breath.

'Lydia, Lydia,' he said to the darkness but no one answered.

He ran down the stairs and out, in his striped flannelette pyjamas and bare feet, into the street that was covered in black ice. He swung the torch up and down the street but he couldn't see her. He walked around the block and didn't notice the frost forming on the soles of his feet and his toes or his skin turning purple and he still couldn't find her so he went inside, sat at the kitchen table, lit the stove for warmth and waited.

He heard her come in through the front door and he looked at the kitchen clock. Three-thirty. She must have taken the key for the front door from his office. He heard her quietly pad up the stairs and he went and stood at the bottom.

'Lydia,' he said.

She was at the landing, wrapped in her blanket. She turned and he saw the fear in her eyes.

'In the kitchen now!' he yelled and she jumped and walked hesitantly down the steps. He stood back so she could go past him.

Flora came out in her dressing gown and said, 'What's going on, Joseph? Surely whatever it is we can deal with it in the morning.'

He looked at her, she was worried for him and he put his hand on her shoulder but she shook her head at him.

'Oh, Joseph, I know. She's been going out these past two months that I know of.'

'Why didn't you say?' he said. How could Flora have kept this from him?

'She hates me already,' said Flora. 'I hoped it would stop of its own accord. That she would find what she needed and stop.'

Joseph glowered, then turned his back on her and walked into the kitchen. Everything was crashing in on him; he couldn't control anything – not his wife, not his son who was now dead, and not his daughter. The noise in his ears was deafening and he had to shout over it. He saw Lydia standing in the corner, still wrapped in the blanket but she was shivering as if she was standing naked in the middle of the street in the middle of the August night.

He walked over and shut the door to the vestibule and then he shut the door to the dining room. He stood on the opposite side of the room to her. There was only him, Flora and Lydia in the room. And Lydia's rebellion shouting in his head.

'Where were you, Lydia – in the middle of the night?' he yelled.

'I was safe,' she yelled back.

He saw her gather herself up to fight him, and she glared at him through black angry eyes. He didn't want another war; he tried so hard to be a peaceful godly man. He took deep gasping breaths. He placed his hands at his sides and held them there clenched tight.

'How can you be safe in the middle of the night in the middle of a war in a town full of godless oversexed Americans? Answer me that, Lydia! Answer me that!'

Lydia looked over to Flora. He followed her gaze and saw Flora was crying and he felt guilty he had done that to her and forced himself to take slow steady breaths and the noise quietened in his head.

'You know what sort of girls are out at night,' he said, lowering his voice. Lydia lifted her shoulders and jutted out her chin and he saw that she didn't care about his anger, she saw it as a challenge. He had to compose himself. 'I want answers, Lydia,' he said quietly, 'and I want them now.' And he watched her wilt and give up and Flora walked over and put her arm around the girl as though she'd merely had some sort of nasty accident that needed a good bandage.

'I'm not like you,' said Lydia in a small voice that he hadn't heard since she was six. 'I'm not all godly and good. I just look like you but I'm really like my mother.' She pushed Flora away and he saw Flora crush and bruise like a stepped-on rose petal.

'You don't even remember your mother,' he said, 'so how do you know you are anything like her?'

Lydia cried for a few minutes and he waited until she said, 'I do remember. I do. More than you think.'

'Lydia, this isn't the way to find what you need,' Flora said gently.

Lydia, crying, looked at Flora and for a moment Joseph thought she was going to rush into Flora's arms where she could return to being a little girl, safe from the world, safe from growing up. He so much wanted to protect her from the world and from herself.

'Lydia, your actions reflect on the whole family,' he said.

'Family? I didn't choose this family!' Her eyes brimmed with salty, bitter tears, her voice scathing. 'This isn't my family. My family was you and Mama and Thom and Mama and Thom are both gone and I have no family. But that's all you care about, Pa, isn't it? How my actions reflect on you? How about your actions, Pa?'

'What are you talking about?' he said.

'You killed her. I know you killed her,' she said. 'Oh, I heard, Pa. I heard the doctor say, "No more babies, Reverend Starr. There must be no more babies." I was little but I remember. But did you listen to him? No you did not! And you let Danny kill her and then you married so quickly, as though she had never existed. One year, wasn't it – that's all you waited or was it less? – just one measly year and you had found a replacement wife. Well, Danny might have been too little to remember but I've always remembered.'

He saw Flora flinch at Lydia's words and grip the kitchen table for support. But Lydia didn't care that she had hit Flora in the gut.

'She's only the mother of that brat Connie,' Lydia spat, and then knowing she had gone too far, she stepped back into the corner of the room as though she had hit a fatal blow and was waiting for the referee's bell.

'Lydia, how can you say such things? This is a devil speaking through you,' said Joseph.

'I am not a devil!' Lydia sneered from her corner. 'I am your daughter! I am a person. Mama was a person! I'm a person and I detest you and it's not a devil making me do it!' She took a deep breath and said quietly, 'I have to get away. I have to get away from you, both of you.'

Joseph saw her change then. She smiled as though she had found something she was looking for, she had unpicked a lock, and she walked past him triumphantly and opened the door. He felt powerless to stop her. If he stopped her he might force her to do worse than she planned, he might kill her as he had Thom. Lydia walked out through the dining room past Connie and Danny, who had been listening with their ears up against the door, and Joseph, not having a clue what to do, with the wind completely knocked out of him, didn't call her back but shrank into a chair.

A moment later Lydia came back in, Connie and Danny following her, and he could barely lift his head to take whatever she threw at him next.

'Oh, and by the way,' she said, 'I'm getting married.'

Joseph looked up at her. She was blurry, he couldn't focus on her through his tears. 'He's American?' he said, already knowing the answer.

'Yes,' she said.

'You're not old enough,' said Flora with a gasp.

'Yes, she is,' said Joseph. 'Twelve for girls and sixteen for boys, that's the law in Victoria.'

Lydia smiled. Her father had just handed her a gift.

'But you still need my permission until you are twenty-one and you'll get that over …'. He couldn't finish the sentence. He couldn't say *dead body.* It was no longer just words. Instead his brain filled with an image of Thom, shattered, and sorrow filled him up. He couldn't lose another child.

Lydia knew Thom had forged a letter, he must have, so why couldn't she? It was already forming in her mind.

'Don't go down that path,' said Joseph quietly. 'Look where it took your brother.'

'So, you plan to leave us. To go with him to America,' said Flora.

'Is that your plan, Lydia? To go to America when this war is over? When you're twenty-one?' He made it sound like a stupid plan, a childish plan. 'Well, that's a good three and more years away. Anything can happen in three years.' He felt his constricted chest loosen.

'Oh, and,' Lydia said, and Joseph pushed himself to his feet, instinctively knowing another punch was coming and that he needed to be braced for it.

'His name is Flynn Murphy and he's black,' she said triumphantly.

'The tall boy,' said Flora, remembering him from church.

'In that case you can't ever go to America, Lydia,' said Joseph sadly. 'You can't possibly understand what pain is there for you if you go with a black man. Do you not realise they won't serve you in shops, you'll be an outcast not wanted by his family and not wanted by your own kind, your children will be half-castes and will have no place and no people.'

'Which,' said Lydia slowly, 'is why after the war he is coming here.'

'Do you really think it will be any better for you here?' asked Joseph, shaking his head.

'He says it is,' she said. 'He says he gets treated better here than anywhere else he's ever been. He gets served in shops like a normal person, he can go to the cinema and sit anywhere he wants. He can hop on any carriage on the train. Shopkeepers call him sir.'

'He's a novelty, Lydia, and he's a soldier doing his best for the war. After the war he'll just be another black man and no one will want him. And if you get pregnant to him before you're married – well, you know what disaster that will bring you. You – not him. He can always walk away. It's different for girls. You don't have to do this, Lydia.' He should take hold of her, lock her in the shed and keep her prisoner. If he'd done that to Thom, would Thom still be alive? He saw she was decided and nothing would move her and it terrified him that he was unable to control his children.

He looked at the clock and saw it was five and the night had gone. The sky was lightening to a melancholy grey that cast a shadow over the world. He was exhausted so he got up, patted Flora's shoulder to let her know he wasn't angry with her and went to his bed and lay down and Flora came in and quietly lay beside him, her hand resting on his heart. They lay in silence until Connie stood in the doorway of the room. He tried to ignore her but her presence was insistent and demanding and Flora said, 'What is it, Connie dear?'

Connie walked to the end of the bed and stood there in front of them waiting for their attention. He opened his eyes and looked at her and she announced, 'Lydia is gone. She has flown away. I tried to tell you but no one ever listens to me.'

And she walked out.

Joseph looked out the window at the sun as its thin beams struggled against the grey clouds. He sat up and so did Flora; she took his hand and held it in both her own.

He looked at her through tears and said, 'How have I lost two children, Flora? Two. Neither of them struck by disease. Neither of them even left our soil.' He got off the bed and walked to the kitchen where Connie was sitting at the table and Danny was filling the kettle. Connie was silent and drawing pictures. Normally you couldn't stop her inane chatter about nonsensical things. The silence filled the kitchen.

He looked at Connie and then Danny and they looked at him and he whispered, 'No more. The devil will take no more.'

Lydia stood at the corner of Sturt Street and Dawson Street and pulled her coat up tight under her chin. Quiet filled the streets; it was a silence she hadn't heard before and it felt empty and alone. She didn't know where to go. She kept looking back over her shoulder, expecting her father to come after her, to grab her by the ear and drag her home as he had Thom. She realised she was waiting for him to do just that. But the street behind her was empty. No one was coming for her and the freedom she had felt in walking out of the house now seemed like a cage. Exhaustion washed over her and she remembered she hadn't slept the entire night. She looked at the old school bag in her hand stuffed with her brush and a dress and a bra and pants. She looked at the grey clouds that stared back at her. She thought about where she might go. She wanted to sleep, to curl up and forget the vicious words with her father. She walked up to Raglan Street and turned left and walked to Viola's front door.

When Lydia gets a promise

Sunday, 15 August 1943

'I've run away from home,' she said when Viola opened the door, and she heard how childish it sounded. 'I haven't slept all night. Can I?' She knew Viola wouldn't say no and before Viola could answer she stepped forward into the hallway. Lydia fell into Viola's arms and the knowledge that they alone understood what it was to be a young woman bound them. Together they squeezed through the door into Viola's bedroom and Lydia never thought Birdie's old bed looked so good. She fell onto it and smiled as Viola gently laid a blanket over her.

When Lydia woke there was a note on the bedside table that had seen better days. Viola wrote she was at work and would be back in the afternoon. Lydia went to the kitchen. Elsie and Claude were sitting at the table. She could hear their minds wondering why she was sleeping in their home during the day.

'Cup of tea, love?' asked Elsie and she poured a cup and pushed it across the table without waiting for an answer.

Lydia sat down and took a big slurp. 'I'm getting married.'

Elsie took a deep breath.

'War makes people act rashly,' said Claude, shaking his head.

But Lydia had no choice. His life could end soon. This might be her only chance.

'There's a fresh towel in the bathroom,' said Elsie.

Lydia washed, put on her clean frock, brushed her hair and looked at herself in the mirror and only then she realised that it was Sunday and she had missed church for the first time in her life and it was another fraying of the ropes that bound her to her life with her father and Flora.

She walked up to Victoria Park. He would be back from church soon. Two American marines, bulky and healthy, were posted at the entrance and they smiled and asked, 'Who's the lucky marine to score a Sunday afternoon date with you?'

'Pick me instead,' said the one with the blue eyes.

The taller one pushed in front. 'No way, I'm off duty in an hour, ma'am, choose me.' She laughed because they were so sweet and charming and the word ma'am tickled her ear. She saw Flynn walking towards her with his friends and she waved and the marines saw who she was waving to and in that instant they changed from angels to demons.

'Disgusting,' said blue eyes as he glowered at her, his large round eyes now dark slits.

'You Aussie girls seem so tickled pink to get one of the blacks. You must be the ugly ones who can't get anyone else.'

She stepped back from their assault and Flynn stepped forward and put his arm around her as though he would never let harm come to her.

'Let's walk around the lake,' she said. She wanted to get away from the hatred and she wanted to show him off. The marines were right: the Australian girls loved the black marines, they were glorious and their skin shone like a black pebble wet with river water caught in the sun. Other girls would be jealous she had a glorious, exotic fiancé.

Flynn looked at the sky. 'It might rain.'

She smiled up at him and he bent down and kissed her and the two marines pretended they were vomiting.

The wind whipped over the top of the water and blew cold against them. They sat on a bench and looked out over the lake, sitting close together for warmth. She knew she would be safe with him. Lydia stared at a black swan that was challenging a canoe for right of way.

'My father was up waiting for me when I got inside last night,' she said. 'Now I can't go back home and I don't know what to do.' She felt her breathing stop as she waited for his response.

He put the tips of his fingers against her cheek and said, 'I'll be shipped out soon. Next month or the one after. We're all going. After the war I will send for you or I will come and live here.'

He got down on the ground in front of her, plucked a long piece of knobby club rush grass and tied it around her finger. 'Lydia Starr, will you marry me?' he asked.

And oh how his eyes shone at her. No one would ever look at her like that again.

'Yes,' she said and she bent over and kissed him. He brushed off his knees and sat next to her again. She looked at the grass around her finger and said over and over to herself, 'I'm engaged.'

Then she said, 'My father says if you really loved me you wouldn't subject me to a life with you.'

'Did he?'

'Practically.'

'What do you think?' he asked, turning to study her answer.

'I will go anywhere you want to take me,' she said.

He pulled her tight to him. 'I just love the ducks,' he said. 'Look at them diving under the water until they nearly disappear and all you can see is their backsides.'

'But in the meantime?' she said.

'In the meantime, you work, so if you don't give your parents your wages surely you can afford your own place.' He took her face in his hands so she was looking at him, and leant in close as if he was going to kiss her. 'I promise I will either send for you or come back for you. I won't desert you.'

PART THREE

1945 to 1947

When Gunter's long journey begins

August 1945

Gunter Schmidt didn't know that one day, in another part of the world, his life would be entwined with a young girl named Connie. He couldn't even imagine it. Gunter had grown up in the sun, in a home filled with light and intelligence where new ideas were always waiting to be explored. But the happiness was cruelly chased away and he was left in the dark, crouched under the cloud of a demon that hovered above him and it changed him.

Gunter's father Ernst was a theologian who had gone to university in America with Dietrich Bonhoeffer, and they studied under Reinhold Niebuhr. Ernst came back and started a local chapter of the Fellowship for Peace, and Gunter would sit in a corner and listen as adults talked in whispers about the horrors of Hitler. After the peace meetings, Ernst taught his only child English and read Johannes Müller to him. Müller had been branded a friend of the Jews and was rotting away somewhere in one of Hitler's dungeons along with Ernst's friend Dietrich Bonhoeffer, whose conspiracy to murder Hitler had been discovered.

Gunter had lived all of his life in the Sudetenland, which was in Czechoslovakia but full of Germans like him. The Sudetenland was heaven on earth, that's what Ernst said. He'd stop explaining inconsistencies of English grammar and lean over in his chair, his elbows on the kitchen table, and ash would fall from his pipe onto Gunter's English letters scrawled in pencil across a notebook.

'Ahhh, Gunter,' Ernst would say, 'I have travelled the world and seen the grand city of New York, but it is here, our homeland, that God has touched. This is heaven on earth,' and he would wink at Gunter's mother Ilse who was making *leberkäse.* Her *leberkäse* was better than any his friends' mothers could make. Ilse said it was because of her secret ingredient and she would whisper in his ear, 'speck,' and then put her finger to her lips and say 'shhhh.' Gunter would look from his mother to his father as they forgot him for a moment and gazed at each other in the wonder that they had ever found each other at all. Such was the happiness of his life. But they were gone now – both of them – and he was totally alone in the world, running in darkness, never reaching a place that was sunny and warm. The darkness was bitter on his tongue so that nothing he ate tasted right.

Germans and the Czechs had been fighting over the Sudetenland all of Gunter's life. The Germans said it was theirs because it was largely populated by Germans, most of whom had a Czech ancestor in there somewhere, but the Czechs said it belonged to them because it encompassed their verdant rolling hills, their snow-capped mountains, their villages and towns and castles. The Czechs had built concrete and barbed-wire fences and forts around the border to keep the Germans out, as if a fence was all that was needed to do the trick. Hitler had said he would look after his fellow Germans despite a fence because that was just the sort of good bloke he was. England, always seeing itself as the benevolent dictator of the world, stepped in and decided for everyone. They held a meeting because meetings solve everything. Both Britain and Germany forgot to invite the Czechs.

In March 1939 Germany invaded. Jews were killed, their synagogues set on fire. Gunter and his parents hid Jews in their attic and spoke in soft whispers that not even their walls could hear. They tried not to attract attention when they went about their lives. When Ernst was stopped in the street and asked why Gunter hadn't joined the Hitler Youth, Ernst would step forward in front of Gunter so he couldn't be whisked away and say that Gunter had a bad chest, bad hearing, bad eyes – in fact, bad everything. He was a poor example of Aryan manhood.

In May 1945, Czechoslovakia was freed from Germany. Now Gunter was forbidden to call his homeland by its name. It was now the Border Territories. The Czechs said that Germans, all Germans, even the children, were collectively responsible for the atrocities of the war and so were due the harshest punishment.

Germans were expelled from the newly named Border Territories. On 12 June 1945, three days after Gunter turned sixteen, Ernst threw books into pillowcases while Ilse filled their picnic basket with bread and cheese and sewed her jewellery into the hem of her dress. Gunter fitted as many clothes as he could into his small leather suitcase, he wore pants over pants over pants and four jumpers and as many shirts and socks as he could so he was rolypoly and had to walk with his arms held out over his fat sides and he forced his feet into his boots. He picked up his most precious possession from beside his bed: a tunnel book that Ilse had made for him before he was born, filled with the animals going into the ark. Each little animal ready for its long journey at sea, painted by her. He tucked it into a pocket in the inside of his shorts, and into his heart he tucked bitterness at being forced out of his home and losing everything because of crimes he hadn't committed.

He joined the long line of Germans marching out of the only home they'd ever known. Crowds lined the streets to watch them go. Girls dressed in dirndl and boys in lederhosen ran and skipped barefooted alongside the marching line, thinking they were part of a celebratory parade, not knowing this parade would go on for days until the marchers' feet were bleeding and their toes falling off. Gunter hadn't marched at first. He had sat up high on top of cases and bags and furniture on their cart, which was tethered to their neighbour Fritz's horse. Ilse sat up there with him and Ernst walked at the front with Fritz, who pulled the rein of the unwilling horse. As Gunter sat up on that piled-high cart he could see the line of Germans stretching for a mile in front and a mile behind. Ilse waved to her Czech friends who had come to see them off, and Gunter could see she was trying to be brave. The Czech friends cried.

'We'll see you soon,' they called, knowing it was a lie. Gunter waved at the boys he'd gone to school with and one threw him an apple, which he gave to his mother. And so Gunter rolled out of his country.

After an hour of travelling, Czech soldiers on horses and motorbikes appeared from nowhere and rode up and down the line of pilgrims, ensuring they kept moving and didn't try to return to their homes. The soldiers had been issued with instructions, *Ten Commandments for Czechoslovak Soldiers in the Border Regions*, that said, *Do not cease to hate the Germans. Be harsh to the Germans. Deal with them too in an uncompromising way.*

The soldiers directed which roads they took and Gunter saw bodies laid out on the grass on the side of the road. The procession was made to stop and look at the dead bodies. Skeletons with barely any flesh, open empty eyes that had seen only horror. It was hard to imagine they had once been alive or ever been happy.

'You killed these young Jewish women!' yelled the soldiers. 'You filthy Germans did this! You all deserve to die.'

Then finally they moved on, but not far, so that those behind them were forced to stop and look as they had. And so the day passed, stopping and starting. As the sun went down on the world and the soft grey of dusk rolled in, Gunter hoped at last they might stop to sleep and this day would be over, but shots echoed through the thick smoky air. There was screaming and shouting and Gunter sat rigid on top of the cart, unable to move, and gripped his mother's hand. Ernst looked back at them and shook his head; they should do nothing, so they sat still and invisible.

Gunter felt rotten stinking death in his stomach and he wanted to vomit. When the shooting stopped he looked to his mother who was sitting beside him and she stared back at him with the empty hollow eyes he had seen in the women on the side of the road. He saw her chest was red as though she had been carrying raspberries and they had smashed against her heart. He looked to his father and Fritz but they were nowhere and so Gunter squeezed Ilse's hand tight in his and felt the dark demon step into his soul.

The horse clopped on the road following the procession without either Fritz or Ernst to guide it, so Gunter clambered down and walked up to the horse's nose and took its lead in his hands. The ground was covered in a layer of muddy slush. His boots became soggy and he could feel his toes bleeding. He got hot and pulled off his jumpers and threw them onto the cart. But still he walked because word had spread up the line that if you couldn't keep up you were shot where you stood.

When darkness overcame them, they stopped and Gunter reached in the moonlight for one of the loaves of bread his mother had packed but as soon as he took it out a soldier shone a torch in his face, grabbed the bread from his hand and spat at him, 'You don't deserve to eat, German pig.' The soldier shone his torch over the luggage to see if there was anything else worth confiscating and he opened cases but was disgusted to find only books. His torch landed on Ilse's frozen face as she sat on the cart, propped up against bags. The soldier clambered up and tipped her body off the other side of the cart and she fell with a thud face down onto the ground. Gunter did nothing, he felt nothing other than the dark demon inside him, and stood there until the soldier, bored with playing with him, moved on. Gunter ran around the cart and dragged Ilse's body up the slope and he knelt down in the wet dirt and scraped frantically with his hands trying to cover her as best he could but doing no more than smearing mud across her. As he scratched at the dirt he could hear the muffled sobs of women and girls and the grunting of the soldiers raping them and anger with nowhere to go buried itself in the pumping arteries of his heart.

Exhausted, he lay on the baggage in the cart, too afraid to sleep, and then the sun broke through the night; it came with no warmth and no hope and the marching began again. At midday they stopped at a fork in the road. Gunter was told to follow the line to the right, his horse and cart and possessions were sent to the left and he reached for his case and his jumper and was told to leave them. He didn't know that the road to the right was the better option and he didn't know that after another day of walking he would arrive in the American zone. The other line would be marched back up to the border where the adults would be told to dig their own graves and then shot. The children would go on trains to Theresienstadt and there they would die of starvation. But what were thirty thousand Germans compared to six million Jews?

Gunter didn't know that this was happening all over the country. Had this sad, sad world learnt nothing? He stood dumb and watched as people after him were sent to his line or the other. He looked for his father until a gun was pointed at him and he was told to move on. He could hear parents and children crying as they were forcibly parted. Gunter reached the American internment camp in the late afternoon. He was lined up. A number on a rectangle of yellow paper was pinned to his chest by an American woman who smiled as though all was right with the world. Under no circumstances was he to remove it. He was given a bowl of sickly-sweet porridge and a blanket. He wondered if this was to lull him into a sense of security before he was taken out in the night and shot. Germans had a lot to answer for. Would he have to dig his own grave? He had never dug anything.

He lay under his blanket and his exhausted bones rattled and shook. He tried to stay awake, keeping vigil for his death, but he slept and in the morning was given bread and strong coffee and then lined up again. He got to the head of the line and stood in front of the trestle table. On the other side sat a chubby American with an orange moustache and next to him was a thin angry Czech. He didn't trust the Czech to interpret his words. Neither of them had looked at him so he bent down and said to the American, 'English, some I can speak. An interpreter is needed not.'

The American's head snapped up and he said, 'Okay, Sonny Jim,' and nodded at the interpreter, who went off to assist with another line at another table.

'You understand you are a displaced person,' said the American. 'You have no country or citizenship. We are arranging your transfer to a host country. I can't tell you which one yet. It's the luck of the draw. But because you speak English, you will have priority. In the meantime you'll live in a transit camp.' The words echoed in Gunter's head. He knew there and then that the world did not want him, so from now on he would take whatever he wanted from the world. Papers were stamped and Gunter was so relieved he wasn't going to be shot that he cried and the American waved him on and so began his journey across the world that would end in the town of Ballarat where Gunter told everyone he was much older than he was and that he was a Baptist minister because it was the only job he knew about from watching his father.

He changed his name to Greg Smith and said he was Czech because by then he knew how hated Germans were. And inside his soul the dark demon was just biding his time.

One day Connie Starr would say to him, 'You and me, we are the same.'

'No, we are opposites,' he'd say and take a piece of his white hair in one hand and a piece of her black hair in the other and hold them against each together.

'No, we're the same,' she'd persist. 'We can both see the demons.'

When Birdie and Aubrey dance

Monday, 1 October 1945

Mothers, fathers and lovers expected their boys home the day after the war ended with the Japanese surrender on 14 August 1945. *The Courier* declared *Our Boys to Come Home* on the front page. But getting the boys home turned out to be an arduous process. Ships had to be organised, men had to be documented, injuries had to be assessed, and it all took far longer than expected. Eventually, and for the first time in almost exactly six years, Aubrey stepped onto Australian soil. He did this at ten-thirty in the morning on 1 October 1945. He had signed on to the army for the duration plus twelve months thereafter. Well, the army had taken all they were going to get from him. The war was over and bugger their twelve months thereafter. He had a life waiting for him. Aubrey had faced death during the war and it had changed him. He had become a larger version of who he always was. He stood on deck as the ship pulled into dock, he and a shipload of men who were the lucky ones, the survivors. With their kits slung over their shoulders, they waved at the crowds below with their relief and guilt that they had survived and wondered if their women had been faithful and if children born while they were away were really theirs.

The gangplank was lowered and Aubrey worked his way towards it. He was pressed tight between the men in front and behind as they shuffled towards their loved ones and getting down the gangplank seemed like the longest part of the journey home. Aubrey didn't have anyone waiting to meet him. He'd sent no letter or telegram to Birdie, his mother or Hazel. He would surprise them all. He loved surprises; he didn't think about whether or not Birdie would like a surprise – it was what she was going to get.

When he got off at the Ballarat station he stomped his feet on the ground and touched the bluestone walls painted white, then he walked down Sturt Street. The tram rattled past and he took off his hat and waved and the riders waved back and cheered him like he was a real hero. Nothing in Ballarat had changed, it felt like he'd never left.

Birdie had known he would turn up some day, she just didn't know when. At night she lay in bed and said all the things to the empty space in her bed that she would like to say to him when he finally came home. Why had he never sent any money? Why had he never taken leave, not even to come to see his sick son, not even to come to Mike's funeral? Why had he never written, not even a postcard or birthday card? Why had he never sent her the beautiful shoes? She imagined telling him she had fallen in love with Sergeant Fortunato, that he had kissed her. But it was only once, because she refused to see him after that. He came to the door several times but she would say, 'I'm married. My husband is fighting for our freedom,' and she would shut the door and lock it.

For nearly six years Aubrey had been a ghost, but when she opened the door to him all her angry thoughts flew away. He stood there with that sheepish boyish grin of his as though they'd had one of their tiffs and he'd merely been gone a couple of days and she remembered again why she'd married him and that she belonged to him.

'Birdie,' he said, holding out his arms for her to fall into.

She held onto the doorframe instead. 'Who?' she said.

'My love,' he said.

'And who might you be?' And she crossed her arms over her chest. Of course, she would stay with him, he was her lawful husband, but that didn't mean she had to make it easy for him.

'Those are lovely shoes, Birdie.'

'Coupon busters,' she said, but made no effort to show him how the shoes could turn into three different pairs.

'Come on, Birdie – you haven't forgotten me.' He took off his hat and ruffled his hair. 'Too short, army cut. But it's still me,' and he grabbed her waist, pulled her to him and kissed her and she felt herself melt back into him like she always did.

'You missed that, didn't you, old girl,' he said and he kissed her again. His kiss laid claim to her, he owned her. He dropped her suddenly and walked past her to the kitchen and was calling out to her.

'Where's Gabe?' He sat down at the table.

She walked past him to the stove and put the kettle on.

'At school,' she said.

'How bad is he?'

'He walks – with a limp.'

She saw him thinking of Mike and her heart wanted to flee, to go wherever Mike was. It was still too much for her to bear. *Come on, say something about our lost son.*

He smiled at her. 'God I've missed you, Birdie.'

And Mike was gone as though he'd never been and she quickly convinced herself that Mike's death was just too much for him to speak about. He walked over to her and swung her into his arms, lifted her up onto the table.

'Let's take off this tattered old grey thing. It doesn't suit you one bit.' He pulled her dress up over her head and arms, then he reached down and slipped off her shoes; he studied them for a moment and then tenderly put them on the floor. He took her foot between his warm hands, his fingers gently pressing between her toes.

She remembered his tricks and the russet shoes she never got and pulled her foot away.

'Come on, Birdie,' he murmured in her ear, 'don't resist me. You know we are only for each other.'

She supposed that was true. She'd never really had anyone besides Aubrey, just a wayward kiss. It had only been him and his fingers were gently pressing and working away the swelling in her ankles, then her tired calves, and then he was kissing the inside of her thigh and she supposed that it really would be good to no longer have to face everything alone. So when he slipped off her knickers she arched up off the table to let him and he put his fingers into her warm moist body and she moaned so he pulled down his trousers and gently and slowly entered her and she leant back on her arms and accepted the loving she had spent six years without.

'Are you leaving again?' she asked as he took his last ragged breath.

'Why would I do that?' he said, and he looked at her, puzzled. He pulled away from her and reached to his ankles for his trousers. She hopped down from the table and picked up her knickers from the floor and put them back on and slid her feet back into her new shoes.

'Tea?' she said and she watched him peer through the door into the lounge room.

'Looks like a tornado hit in there,' he said, looking back at her.

'It's my business, I'm making clothes. Though I daresay it'll stop as soon as rations stop. I had to find a way to support us somehow.'

'Well, you don't need it now I'm back,' he said. 'You can pack this lot away and I'll have my living room back thank you.'

'You never sent us anything!' She put the kettle on the stove with a clang and lit the gas, which burst furiously into flame. She turned it down.

'Birdie, Birdie, I was lucky to get paid at all, love. I reckon the army owes me heaps, Birdie. We'll be rich when they pay me what they owe me and you won't have to sew a thing. You can get shop-bought dresses once rations are over. If I'd had it I would have sent it. You know I would.'

She felt unease slither through her bones like a worm. She didn't know whether or not to believe him. She tried to smile to show him she believed him but she knew her smile was weak. He reached to the mantel for the teapot and got two cups from the dresser. Then he took her shoulders and turned her to him; she could see herself in the intense blackness of his eyes.

'I've changed, Birdie,' he said. 'Trust me.'

'I'll try, Aubrey. I will,' she said and she meant it. 'For our remaining son. For Gabe, if nothing else.'

He put his kit in their room and came back into the kitchen. 'I have to nick out, Birdie, but I'll be back for dinner. Cook me something nice, love.' He took her hand, opened her palm and closed her fingers over four shillings. Perhaps he was changing if he was giving her this much?

'There's still rationing,' she said. 'I don't know what I can get.'

'Hey, it won't be army issue so it will be grand,' he said and he pulled four crumpled coupons out of his trouser pocket and handed them to her.

She held them up to the light.

'They're not counterfeit, Birdie, if that's what you're thinking,' he said. He'd picked them up at Spencer Street Station from a bloke who called them a work of art.

'Where are you going? Gabe will be home soon.'

'I'll see him at dinner. I just have to go see Mister Faull about starting my job.' She kissed his cheek. Perhaps he really was ready to settle with her.

After he left she put on her summer hat and got her basket and walked to Sturt Street to the butcher's. She was tempted to walk past Faull's and see if he was really there. 'Oh, Birdie,' she scolded herself out loud for thinking the worst of him. She should be more like Flora, who always saw the best in people.

Aubrey stood smoking beside the rose bush. He had to wait half an hour before she spotted him out the window. She nodded towards the nurses' quarters. He stamped his smoke out in the grass and walked to the back door.

'Aubrey,' she said when she opened the door.

She looked not a day older than when he'd last seen her. Her gold pin said Matron Harbolt.

'Hello, love, I wrote you I'd be home soon.'

'You never wrote you were married, though,' she said and started to close the door on him. He took a step back to get some space to think quickly. He reached out and stopped the door.

'Ah, Giselle, my Giselle,' he said as his mind frantically searched for more.

'It's Hazel, actually,' she said, 'which you'd know if you'd read my letters,' and started to shut the door again.

'But we're getting divorced,' he said. 'It's nearly finalised. It was never any good between me and Birdie.' He opened his arms and said, 'I promise. You're the only one that means anything to me, Giselle. You make my heart dance.'

He stood back to watch her, to see if she would come to him.

She looked behind her, then at her watch, then tucked a strand of her red curls back behind her ear. 'Come back at nine-thirty tonight.'

He leant forward and kissed her. 'We belong to each other, Giselle, no others,' he said.

He walked off to the Unicorn to spend a few hours until he went back to the nurses' quarters and he didn't get home for dinner with Birdie and Gabe.

When the war fails to end

Monday, 5 August 1946

In a whitewashed timber bungalow in Nightingale Street, Mabel Finchley sat at the kitchen table in front of the speckled green enamel Kooka stove with the door open for warmth. The old black labrador Snowy lay with his fat lumpy body on the chipped tiles in front of the stove. Cecil sat opposite Mabel and the lemon tart she had made with dripping and Flora's lemons sat untouched between them, staring at them and reminding them that Manny wasn't there to share a piece and he so loved lemon tart. Other boys were coming home in dribs and drabs but not theirs. The war had been over for a year and there had been no word about Manny. He was still missing in action, presumed dead.

Manny had been born when Mabel thought it was no longer possible for her to have a child. He had been born on Christmas Day, a gift from the angels, so she had named him Emmanuel. Cecil didn't care what his name was, he was just deliriously stunned that they had produced a baby at all. He'd stood looking at the tiny pink thing sleeping in Mabel's arms and he'd breathed in the powdery baby smell and his brain turned to a wonderful strawberry mush. Mabel held the baby tight to her chest and promised she would never allow any harm to come to him as long as she lived. She hadn't counted on him joining up and going to war.

Now the war was over and he should have returned to the safety of her love. She had watched the number of men in the congregation grow. She had seen man after man return to his family. Some came back whole and some came back with parts missing. But at least they were back. She should have Manny back in her kitchen helping himself to another slice of lemon tart no matter what state he was in.

Without saying a word to each other, Mabel and Cecil both held tight to their hearts as they tried to acknowledge that Manny was never coming home.

Mabel wiped the tears from her eyes and said, 'Put the kettle on, shall I?'

'Yes, love,' Cecil said, but even he could hardly hear his voice.

Mabel rested her hands on the table for strength and lifted her thin frame from the chair. She walked to the dresser to get the cups and saw the cup that Manny liked to use. They hadn't used it since he had gone. It was a plain simple cream cup with a single green band around its middle. It hung patiently on its hook with its saucer resting behind at the back of the dresser. There was no painted bouquet of flowers on the cup, no gold gilt around its edges, and it had a hairline crack that ran down the side and she had warned Manny that one day he would have a cup full of hot tea and without warning the crack would just open up and hot tea would spill out and burn him. And he had laughed and said, 'That, Mum, is a risk I'll just have to take. I like this cup, Mum. You know I don't like change much.'

Mabel tried to look through the tears that filled her eyes but she could no longer see the cups in the dresser. She felt Cecil's arms enclose her and they stood together in front of the empty cups, two old people in a shell of a house that had holes everywhere their son should be. And a dog that was their last link to him but was now old and tired. For them the war would never be over.

But the rest of the world didn't notice that Manny was missing and after six years of war the world expected peace, fluffy white sheep frolicking over fluffy white clouds and white daisies that caught the golden sunlight in their yellow stamens, the lion lying down with the lamb. This was not what they got. The world was battered, bruised purple and braced for the next onslaught of evil. The yearning for supremacy was now familiar and had become safer than reconciliation. Besuited men sitting in the United Nations were asked to give up their power in honour of the new world and they declined the offer, which shocked no one in the timber cottages that lined the streets of Ballarat.

The Americans accused the Chinese of sabotaging their policies. Israel and Palestine accused each other of everything. Moscow played football against Britain. It was a draw, but Moscow claimed it had won and in doing so had proved that Britain was no longer the power it once was. John Curtin, the prime minister, worn out from seeing the Australian people through a war, died, and as quick as you could blink Frank Forde jumped into Curtin's shoes and was pronounced prime minister only to be replaced a week later by Ben Chifley. Chifley announced that Australia must grow so it could fight off any future invasion by the ferocious Japanese and the gates were opened to any English-speaking immigrants who could pass as white and Lydia fretted that her man, not being white, would never come back for her.

When there are cuts and bruises in Ballarat

Saturday, 10 August 1946

In Ballarat, Sebastopol played footy against Redan and the boys who had been away for so long and seen terrible things no one could imagine, could no longer keep their pent-up rage and discontent inside of them and out it spilled in an uncontrollable deluge into the mud and slush of the football oval. The teams, who were friendly neighbours living happily side by side over shared beers and sausages, slipped and skidded in the mud and bitter rain. They bruised their knuckles and split the soles of their boots open as they hit and kicked until their faces were red with blood. They gashed each other's skin and cracked each other's bones until the match was declared a bloodbath and people wandered back to their cottages, their feet scuffing the pavement, feeling the war was perhaps not over after all.

And so the world clumsily crawled towards peace.

Men returned to jobs they thought were waiting for them to find a woman doing the task they thought only a man could do. The woman would be reminded she had only been a fill-in and was no longer required and, having had a taste of working and her own money even though it was only half what the men earned, went resentfully back to her home. Magazines and newspapers told women it was their responsibility to provide adequate meals and clothes for their families and to enhance their beauty to keep up the men's spirits, but this was impossible with continuing rationing, and so they lined up outside Birdie's house on Saturday mornings with their scrounged cloth while their children ran off and dropped fire crackers down the mine shafts they had been told to stay away from.

Birdie took in the orders despite Aubrey standing in the room, his arms crossed over his chest, scowling and muttering about wanting his living room back.

'I've been home for nearly a year now and still she insists on taking in sewing. And if she insists on sewing I don't see why she can't make something more pleasant for herself first. She looks like death warmed up and not what a hero needs to come home to, eh?' The men at the pub nodded in agreement. Aubrey had a hard life.

Lydia's fiancé had not come back.

Lydia was living with Viola in a little half house at the bottom of Webster Street where it met Creswick Road. The house was two-storey, one of three brick terraces in a row, each sharing a brick wall and divided into two. Lydia and Viola had the top half of the end one. You had to climb up seven steps to get to the front door. The half house had one bedroom, which they shared, a kitchenette with a gas bottle and burner, and a sitting room. She and Viola could hear everything that happened next door, every time Janice and Digby Woolcutt fought and every time they made up. They were woken when he came home late, drunk and singing, and they heard him when he got up at four in the morning for work at Berry Anderson printers. Sometimes Lydia buried her head under her pillow so she didn't have to listen to them. When they chatted, she and Viola chatted in whispers because if they could hear the Woolcutts, the Woolcutts could hear them.

Joseph never visited Lydia. It was his protest at her leaving home before she was married. At her giving herself to a man she wasn't married to. He was sad and disappointed that she no longer went to church; she was baptised and had given her life to Jesus so she should at least keep that pledge. But beneath all this was another reason he didn't visit her: he knew his heart would break if she slammed her door on him. However, it was Ballarat and he couldn't help but pass her in the street as she walked home from work. Especially if he ran out when he heard the school bell go and walked around and around the block hoping to catch sight of her.

It was on his fourth attempt to run into her that they pulled up in front of each other and he said, 'Lydia, have you fallen so far that you don't even come to church now?' Which wasn't what he'd planned on saying at all. He wanted her to come back home, to be her old self again. But for her the cut had been made good and deep and she would never go back.

'He'll be back for me. He promised,' Lydia said. Then she turned abruptly and walked off down the street. And pain seared him as he thought she would walk in the wrong direction if need be, as long as it was away from him.

Connie caught the look that passed between Flora and Joseph when Joseph relayed this short conversation. They knew different. Lots of Ballarat girls had been deserted by American marines they thought loved them. Lydia's man – dead or alive – was gone. Connie, realising Lydia was an idiot, would have to explain it to her. But she'd be gentle, because Connie was grateful to Lydia in a way because Connie was sure she was now the favourite daughter.

Joseph and Flora included her in their discussions of the news and sometimes Joseph asked what she thought, for example about the new airline TAA. Would she ever like to fly in a plane and who did she think should win the election, Labor or Liberal? But Connie didn't care about these things. She was twelve years old and taller than anyone in her class. The only person taller than her was Gabe. She tried everything she could think of to stop herself growing. She'd sat for hours with a heavy bible on her head, and tried scrunching down when she walked so she wouldn't look so tall until Flora told her to stand up straight.

She ate as little as possible so she was not only tall but thin. She refused to wear the new Sunday dress Flora had Birdie make for her. It was yellow with green spots and had a hem of lemons around the bottom. 'Because I know how much you love your lemon tree,' Flora had said. It was made from an old tablecloth and had darts in the chest for a bust. She was growing breasts, tiny little pointed things budding from her chest. She went everywhere with her arms folded high over her chest to hide them. There was absolutely no way she was going to ever wear a dress with places for breasts, so on Sundays she squeezed into her old yellow dress that was far too short and too tight and made Flora sigh and fret and say, 'Oh, Connie, we all have to grow up some day. Soon you will need rags. You can't stop it from happening.' And Connie put her hands over her ears and sang 'Jesus Wants Me for a Sunbeam' as loudly as she could.

When Connie can't see what's right in front of her face

Monday, 2 September 1946

It was the second week of the school holidays. Gabe, who at fourteen was nearly as tall as his father, sat in the kitchen carefully gluing together the soft plywood pieces of the model Halifax bomber Aubrey had given him for his birthday; Aubrey had said he would help Gabe build it but never had time. Gabe looked at the clock, stopped gluing and, without a word to his parents, he picked up his school satchel and walked to Connie's house. The constant pain in his leg reminded him that he still couldn't run. His legs and feet were twisted things, his feet deformed with protrusions and lumps that shouldn't be there and his calves, which should have been muscled and strong, were thin wasted sticks. He had to have special shoes made and that was the one good thing Aubrey had done for him. He'd watched Gabe pushing his feet into normal shoes that were two sizes two big.

'Why such enormous shoes?' Aubrey had said, putting down the tuna sandwich he was eating.

'He has to wear shoes that are too big so they go over the polio damage,' Birdie had said.

'No, no, no. Not my son,' said Aubrey, and he'd gone and got the tape measure that hung over Birdie's sewing machine and he'd made Gabe stand up while he'd measured both his feet in different directions and then made him sit down and put his feet out straight. 'He has one leg shorter than the other,' he said to Birdie. He'd left then and a week later he came back with a parcel for Gabe wrapped in brown paper and string.

'Here, try them on,' he said, and Gabe had taken out the shoes and turned them this way and that. The shoes were black and decorated with a row of punched holes around the eyelets and over the toe cap. One shoe had a larger heel than the other.

'Go on,' said Aubrey. 'Put your feet into them, son.' Gabe put his feet into the shoes and Aubrey knelt down and pulled the laces so the shoes sat snug on Gabe's feet. 'Stand up, son. Stand up straight and proud.' And Gabe had stood and walked around the kitchen table without limping and on his fifth turn of going around the table, he'd gathered up speed. He stopped only to kiss his crying mother on the cheek and she said, 'I never knew such shoes could be got.' Gabe looked at his dad and smiled and Aubrey said, 'It's all right, son. You'll have the shoes you need from now on.'

Gabe clomped rather than walked, one boot always louder than the other. Connie was in the garden shed washing vegemite jars and their tin lids with water she'd got in the metal bucket from the garden tap. For weeks she had been collecting them from where Flora stored them in the laundry. The water gushing from the tap was freezing cold and Connie stopped to flick her fingers in the air to dry them before giving up and going back to rinsing the black vegemite from the jars. The front of her tartan wool skirt and her shirt and cardigan were soaked and the water trickled down her clothes and pooled inside her shoes. Once Danny would have been busy helping her with her plan, to make sure she didn't get into any real trouble if nothing else, but he had gone off to bible college in February.

Connie sang 'Down by the Riverside' at the top of her lungs, pleased with what a great singer she was, and didn't hear Gabe coming down the driveway or opening the back gate until the light coming through the door was blocked by him leaning against the doorjamb, his arms crossed over his chest. She looked up and stopped singing. He was smiling as though catching her singing out of tune at top volume was the funniest thing he'd seen in years.

She threw a lid at him.

'Did you bring them?' Connie asked him. She was lining up her washed jars with their matching lids in front of them. The jars were opaque white glass and their screw-on lids said *For tasty nutritious sandwiches Vegemite most economical.*

'Of course,' and he reached into his school satchel and pulled out a large paper bag full of rationed sugar. They had decided he should ask for the sugar because his mother would give him anything without question. He tipped up the satchel and bulbs of ginger root fell to the floor. He bent down and picked up the lid she'd thrown at him and threw it back.

'Oww,' she cried, even though the lid hadn't hit her.

'What do you want me to do?' he asked, sitting on the concrete floor of the shed, the jars lined up between them.

'I found the recipe in *The Courier* on the "Entertaining during rationing" page,' said Connie and she pulled a package out of her pocket. 'It's the yeast. It's best to keep it warm,' and she put it back into her pocket.

She handed him the grater she had taken from the kitchen. 'You grate the ginger and put it in the jars. I'll put in the sugar and yeast.'

Gabe brushed dirt away from a patch of concrete and grated the ginger onto the cleared patch. They worked for some time in silence. Gabe had faced death and it had changed him. As he lay in that iron lung for all those months, as he wept for his brother who had died, and as he cried out with pain as his useless limbs were stretched and massaged, Gabe's heart had stretched and opened and it had opened to no one more than Connie, whom he had previously tormented. When he looked at Connie he no longer saw pigtails that could be pulled or a girl who could be pushed into the river. He no longer saw a girl who told lies so bad she deserved whatever he could throw at her.

Instead he saw a girl who was alone and unable to find her place in the world. Gabe had friends at school. The boys in his class made allowances for him; they always bowled the cricket ball a bit slower for him, and waited for him to begin his walk before chasing after it and going for the wickets. But Connie, who had no physical disabilities, had no allowances made for her. He often saw her sitting alone, chatting to herself at lunchtime in the shelter shed while the other girls kept their distance. He would stop and talk to her, sit beside her for a moment until the boys called him away and he made it clear to everyone he was on Connie's side. Connie was his one true friend. She never made allowances for him and she took him out of the confines of his body and sometimes showed him glimpses of her strange world.

'I have a friend at school now,' she said as she tipped sugar into the jars.

'Righto,' he said, grating the ginger until the grater scraped his skin.

'Heather,' she said.

Heather was the most popular girl.

'She told me that we are now bosom sisters,' Connie said. 'She just can't tell anyone else because they will be too jealous. I have a new joke. My angel told it to me.'

He had heard Heather laughing about Connie with Beth and Monica. She wasn't Connie's friend.

'Let's have it then,' he said as he divided the grated ginger between the jars.

Connie licked the sugar from her fingers and sat up straight to tell her joke. 'A man walks into the records office and says he wants to change his name. The clerk says "What's your name then?" The man says "Adolf Stinkybumbum". "Well, what do you want to change it to?" says the clerk.

'The man says, "Frank Stinkybumbum".'

Gabe laughed and Connie, pleased he liked it, laughed too. Then they went back to the bottles.

With ginger, sugar and yeast in the bottoms of the jars, they filled the jars with tap water, screwed the lids on tight and stacked them in the corner of the shed where the frogs had once been.

'How long do you think we have to leave it before it will become beer?'

'I think we should taste it each week,' said Connie.

So for three weeks after church on Sundays they opened a jar and tasted it and then on the fourth week they forgot all about the ginger beer and left it to itself in the dark. As September became October which became November which became a hot

December, the sun burnt the grass brown, fried the leaves to lacy skeletons so they fell in brittle crisps to the ground and in the humid heat of the dark shed the yeast and sugar fermented and bubbled and came to life and exploded one Sunday in the middle of Joseph's sermon, sending everyone rushing into the street, sure the Japanese had come back.

The dribs and drabs

Friday, 6 December 1946

The nurse stood over him in her white starched apron and her white starched nurse's triangle cap that she had pinned carefully over her hair and he just wanted her to go away and leave him to his slow death. It was too much white. Underneath her apron she was wearing a red checked trainee nurse's dress with white starched collars and white starched cuffs pinned to the short sleeves. It was still too much white and he turned away from the brightness of it and then looked back at the gold gilded watch pinned to the top of her apron. The watch hung from a blood red porcelain poppy pin. He turned away again and stared at the far wall that gave him nothing to focus on. When he looked back at her again, the poppy taunted him. It grew bigger and smaller and now he couldn't move his eyes from it. The poppy began to bleed. A single blood-red drop fell down her chest; it blasted red against her sterile white apron. He'd seen enough blood. He turned away and could feel tears trying to force themselves from inside him, but he was dried up and he would not cry. He heard her voice in the distance and something was familiar about it, so he forced himself to peer back at her, just for a moment, being careful not to look at the poppy, and a distant memory pushed into his mind. He looked back to the blurry wall and felt her whisper his name in his ear. Her breath was warm and sweet and he looked back at her and it came to him.

'Miss Mitchell the Sunday school teacher,' he whispered, not sure if he was talking out loud or only to himself.

'Yes,' she said, and held his wrist in her hands, feeling for his pulse. Her fingers enclosed his paper-thin skin that stretched over twig bones.

'Go to sleep now, Manny. I'm here to look after you,' she said.

He must have looked unsure because she bent down and whispered, 'You're safe now and I'm so good at looking after injured things.'

'What date is it?' he asked.

'It's Friday the sixth of December 1946,' she said, and as she walked off to tend to other men he felt the wetness of a tear sliding down his face. He had cried a lot at first, at night in the dark. Then he hadn't cried at all. Not for years. He shook his head against her. No one would be able to ever mend him. He was broken like a fledgling sparrow that has fallen from its nest onto the harsh asphalt road. His insides were crushed and he would never be a man again.

Manny had entered Australia quietly; not even his parents were told he was found and coming home. That was because Corporal Matty Edwards, who was typing up the list of returning injured, was distracted by Sergeant Louisa Evans, who had leant against his desk while she talked to Warrant Officer Class One Scott Watson about their Saturday plans. Her bottom had rested right on his sheet of paper, in front of his eyes and he didn't know whether to sit tight and just enjoy the sight, or whether to say something. Given they both ranked above him, he chose to say nothing. When she stood up his eyes followed her pleasant bottom to the door and he heard her chuckle sweetly at something the warrant officer said and as the door closed behind them Matty Edwards shook himself and went on to the next name of recovered soldiers on his list and missed Emmanuel Cecil Finchley and so no telegram was sent to ease Mabel and Cecil's pain.

Manny did not triumphantly set foot on Australian soil. He did not march down Swanston Street bellowing 'Waltzing Matilda' in front of cheering crowds, he did not caress eager girls who threw caution to the wind with excitement that the boys had returned. He did not drink to the king's health or world peace. Manny was pushed over the gangplank in a squeaking wheelchair. He was unable to put his thin legs to the ground because they would crumple and break even beneath his meagre weight. His bones poked through his transparent skin, his mouth was dry and his lips split and his eyes, empty of tears, were dark hollows from which he looked out at the world and saw only terror. If he opened his mouth to speak a whisper floated over his swollen tongue. His blood was malarial and for a long time his temperature had stayed stubbornly above the 103 degrees required for him to be admitted to the repatriation hospital. Manny had lived with death. It had stared him in the face day after day and reduced him to nothing. When food was put in front of him his stomach churned and rejected it and bile rose in his throat. His bones refused to fatten and his cheeks didn't fill out.

He had been found in Changi and when the Australian and American troops walked into Changi he and all the other men who were prisoners of the Japanese had gathered their last ounce of strength and sent up a cheer. He had lifted his wasted arm into the air, he had smiled at the other men with his rotten yellow grin. At last they were saved.

Then he was told he wasn't going home.

None of them were.

He wasn't well enough. He was disease-ridden and starving; he had broken bones and a broken soul. He needed to be documented and debriefed. There were fifteen thousand men just like him. It was going to take a while to process them all. The fittest would go first. He would stay longer in this terrible prison. He would be treated right here in Changi, staying on the very stretcher in the same dormitory where he had seen things he would never speak of.

Of course, they would treat his mattress for vermin.

To be saved, to be helped out of the pit of snakes only to get to the top and be thrown back in, was crueller than anything the Japanese had done to him. Manny had fallen back onto his flea-ridden stretcher and cried dry empty tears that stung the corners of his eyes. He wanted a meat pie but was given soup and penicillin. He wanted beer and was given water and Alka-Seltzer. He wanted to be home in his parents' timber bungalow in Ballarat and was kept imprisoned in Singapore. He had to be marked fit for travel by the army doctor first. So he tried to eat, he clamped his thin lips shut over the chicken soup until it forced its way down his throat and slowly his temperature returned to normal and he was able to leave his stretcher and sit in a chair. One day the army nurse carefully slipped a new shirt over his arms, one limb at a time as if he was a baby. She smiled at him as though the new shirt was a remarkable achievement on his part. She called for help and with the other nurse holding him up she pulled new shorts up his stick legs and, supporting his elbows, helped him into a wheelchair.

'Where are you taking me?' he asked.

'You're going home, mate,' she said and he was taken in the back of an ambulance to the port, put on a ship and sailed home. In Melbourne he was put on a medical truck and driven to Ballarat and every bump in the road ricocheted through his unprotected bones until his spine was rigid with pain. Then he was put onto a stretcher despite him telling them he could manage a chair now and he was carried into the repatriation hospital and lifted into a bed and he lay there, invisible in the cast iron hospital bed, swallowed up by the white sterilised sheet, wondering if he would ever be a living thing again. And still no one in the army realised Corporal Matty Edwards' mistake so Mabel and Cecil still hadn't been told he was alive. And Manny, who was surprised they hadn't come, didn't ask for them because he didn't want his dear mum to see him like this.

When Viola got home from work she dropped her nurse's cap on the small hall table they used as a dining table. She took the green wine bottle sitting next to the oven and opened it and took a gulp.

'You'll never guess who came in today, army transfer,' Viola said to Lydia.

'Who?' said Lydia, hoping stupidly that somehow it was her Flynn, though there was no logical reason for him to end up in an Australian hospital.

'Manny Finchley,' said Viola, passing the bottle to Lydia, who got two teacups and split the wine.

'Has he got bits missing?' asked Lydia.

'No, nothing missing but you wouldn't recognise him if you saw him. When I took his pulse my hand wrapped right around his wrist and you remember how chubby he was.' Viola held her fingers up forming a circle so Lydia could see how small his arm was. 'Lydia, you really should come and volunteer at the hospital – it would cheer you up. Besides, you might meet someone.'

Lydia held up her ring finger and wiggled it in the air. Flynn had given her a ring before he left, a small band of silver with a heart in the middle which he'd had engraved with *L & F*. It wasn't an engagement ring but it was as good as. It made her furious that no one, not even Viola, would take her engagement seriously.

'Yes, but how many years since you've heard from him?' said Viola. 'Not even a letter. Nothing.'

'You don't think I'm busy enough teaching brats all day?' said Lydia. 'When would I volunteer?' But Viola was right. She hadn't heard anything from Flynn, though she had written millions of times. The thought that he had used her and then fled was bitter inside her. But the very fact that no one else believed in him made her determined to believe in him all the more.

She filled her teacup with more wine and held the bottle towards Viola.

'You could meet someone nice,' said Viola.

'It can take four years for a letter of transportation to come.'

'Lydia, there are so many girls who've been left high and dry by the Americans. Attorney-General Evatt is trying to do something about it, he says the American boys aren't being very nice to the Australian girls. The girls just wait and wait and then even if they're married the next thing they know they're divorced by an American court without any say-so from them. At least you didn't marry him.'

'He's nice, he'll send for me,' said Lydia. 'My parents still don't know I drink.' She held the teacup up in the air.

'I'm surprised you remember him at all,' said Viola, and Lydia leant over and walloped her arm.

'Oww,' cried Viola, rubbing her arm even though it didn't hurt. 'I'll never marry,' she said. 'It only leads to sorrow and disappointment. For women at any rate. You only have to look at my sister.'

'Hmm, Aubrey Mabbett,' said Lydia, and they both broke into giggles. Something slammed against the wall next door and they giggled more and filled their glasses and it didn't occur to either of them to let Mabel and Cecil Finchley know about Manny. Until Sunday morning at church when Viola said to Mabel, 'Isn't it just wonderful?'

'Isn't what wonderful, dear?' asked Mabel.

'Manny arriving at the base and being on my ward. I get to look after him.'

And Mabel fainted, her thin body collapsing like dropped paper to the new linoleum floor in the church kitchen.

PART FOUR

1947 to 1948

When a journey ends

Saturday, 4 January 1947

Gunter Schmidt stood in the grey foyer of the migrant hostel in Wendouree. It was stinking hot outside, hotter than he'd ever known it could be. A man and a girl were sitting waiting for him in the corner where one hard wooden bench met another. They were the only people in the room apart from the secretary behind the counter. No one came to visit migrants. He took a deep breath and reminded himself to be who they needed him to be, to be someone new. He was no longer eighteen-year-old Gunter Schmidt who had his education interrupted by war. He would now be Greg Smith, twenty-four years old, who would have completed his Bachelor of Theology if not for the war. He was tall and lanky. He could get away with it and already had.

He smiled too widely, too eagerly, and held out his hand towards the man.

The man stood up; he was taller than Greg expected and looked down on him. The man's handshake was strong, taking in all of Greg's slender hand, and Greg was reminded of his own father, whose handshake had been just as certain, and a crack opened in his soul and the demon who hovered over him pushed a finger through the crack and Greg almost gasped.

Greg focussed on the girl still sitting on the bench. Sulky, she didn't want to be here. She looked to be about sixteen, and didn't get up but looked up at him through her curly fringe. Her black hair fell to her elbows in eight or so ringlets. Her thick lashes outlined her black eyes as if someone had carefully drawn around her eyes with black ink. He smiled at her and she blushed but didn't break her gaze and looked back at him with wide open eyes as if he was the first boy she'd ever seen.

'You'll catch flies, Connie,' the man said and she shut her mouth. Gunter didn't understand what he said but the girl did. They were two opposites, him and the girl. Her hair black and thick like sin; his hair thin and white like the feathers on the snowy chest of the barn owl that had lived in the tree outside his house in the Sudetenland. The home he would never see again.

The tall man nodded to the hard wooden-slatted bench and so he sat down against the wall where no one could come for his back and the man sat on the bench the girl was already sitting on. The bench tipped with the man's weight at one end and the thin girl at the other and they had to reposition themselves.

'Reverend Starr,' said the man, 'and this is my daughter, Connie. And you are … Greg?'

'Yes, reverend,' said Gunter. 'Greg Smith.'

'That wasn't the name your parents gave you, surely?' said Joseph, eyeing him suspiciously, but Greg had practised his answers and was ready.

'They liked English names,' he said.

'How old are you?'

'I'm twenty-four,' he said.

'The congregation has grown since the war and I have approval from the deacons for an assistant pastor. It's part of your residency requirement that you work in a regional area like Ballarat. You'll have to finish your study. There will be some resistance amongst the congregation to a refugee as a pastor, but once they see you're committed and a true born-again Christian they'll come round. What nationality are you?'

'I'm Czech,' Gunter lied. 'Study I'm good at,' he said quickly to stop any further investigation.

'I'm good at study,' muttered the girl.

'Are you?' said Gunter.

'No, it's what you should say: *I'm good at study.*'

'All in good time, Connie,' said the reverend.

'My father under Reinhold Niebuhr studied and his knowledge passed on to me.'

'I don't know who that is,' Joseph said dismissively.

The girl hadn't once taken her gaze from him. He looked away and looked back; her gaze didn't falter and he felt unsettled by her. He wriggled on his seat.

'Dietrich Bonhoeffer – good friend,' he said.

'Ah,' said Joseph. 'We know of him. The whole Christian world knows of the martyr for peace. Well, your salary is subsidised by the government – that's the only way the church can afford you. We can move you into the manse now if you're able.'

'You mean this day? Right now?' said Gunter.

'That's what we've come for. To pick you up. Can you manage it?' said Joseph.

Gunter jumped up; he couldn't wait to get out of the cramped hostel, to leave the humans who meandered around in circles with their eyes dim and their mouths pressed shut as if, were they to open them, they would let out a scream that would never stop.

Connie jumped up too and he saw she was as tall as him and her dress was indecently short for her.

'A moment,' he said and ran through the dim narrow corridor to his dormitory. He threw the few clothes the Red Cross had given him into a cotton bag. He reached under his mattress and took his tunnel book and put it in his pocket. It was all he had left of his parents, Ilse and Ernst.

When he walked back into the foyer the reverend was leaning on the desk handing the phone receiver back to the secretary.

'I just called us a cab. The church is getting a car next week but for now it's the cab.' He looked at the bag in Gunter's hand. 'Is that all you've got?'

'Yes,' he said, looking at the scruffy bag.

The reverend sat in the front of the cab, Gunter sat in the back with the girl, who was still gazing at him.

'How old are you?' he asked.

'How old do you think?' she said, and she sat up and pointed her nose in the air and tried to look older and sophisticated and he tried not to laugh at her.

'Mmmm … sixteen?'

'She's tall for her age, she's thirteen,' said the reverend.

'I'll be fourteen soon,' whined Connie, slumping back down into the seat.

'Not for four months you won't,' said Joseph.

When the cab pulled up at the manse, Gunter took a deep breath. It seemed forever since he had lived in a house, in a home with parents. He would do and be whatever it took to stay here. To stay safe. It didn't matter that he didn't believe in God. He believed in the devil and that was close enough. He would be the most upright Baptist to ever walk on Australian soil. He would give them no reason to send him away. From this moment he would be Greg Smith.

'Connie will show you your room,' said Reverend Starr as he reached into his trouser pocket and took out his wallet to pay the cab driver. Greg looked at Connie, who said, 'This way, Greg,' and skipped down the driveway, past a lemon tree. She stopped and pointed. 'That's my lemon tree – see how it reaches to the top of the manse roof. It's the largest lemon tree in the entire world and not one thorn.'

'Impressive,' said Gunter, peering to the top, 'but does it quite go that far upwards?' It was true he'd never seen such a tall lemon tree. Perhaps that was how things grew in Australia, where there was no snow to kill things during winter. But all the same, the girl could obviously exaggerate. He followed Connie into the kitchen and could smell something sweet baking in the oven. Connie went straight past the cooking smells that begged him to stay and eat and he followed her upstairs and she stood at the doorway.

'It was Danny and Thom's room but Danny won't be back until the end of the year. You'll probably have to share then. We all have to share in this house.'

'And this Thom?' he said.

But she turned on him with a flounce and walked away and then was back standing in the doorway staring again.

Greg walked into the room. He blinked away the tears forming in his eyes. He sat on the bed and realised that after nearly two years his tormented journey had reached an end.

When Connie dances

Saturday, 4 January 1947

When he got up from Danny's bed and closed the door on her, everything inside Connie stopped and she stood staring at the dark wooden door not able to understand why he didn't want her company. She shrugged it off and ran to her bedroom and took off her dress that pulled her breasts hard against her chest and put on the new dress that Birdie had made, the one that allowed her breasts to fall naturally and gathered at her tiny waist to cascade out in pleats over her hips. She looked in the mirror. What would Pastor Greg think about her in her dress? And how was it his hair was whiter than the flour Flora baked with and fell to his eyebrows in light wisps that moved with the slightest breeze? She had softly blown at him when he wasn't looking just to see if his hair could fly on her breath and it was so light it could. His eyes were pale blue, so pale they were almost like glass that you could see straight through, and there wasn't one freckle on his skin. She could tell he was nearly an angel. She watched in the mirror as she ran her hands over the dress and shrugged, put him from her mind and ran downstairs. Flora was in the kitchen taking the lemon suet pudding out of the oven.

'I'm going to Gabe's,' Connie said as she flew past.

'Have you done your Saturday chores?' asked Flora, not looking up. 'Have you got a cardigan for when it gets cold later?'

'Of course,' Connie lied and she twirled in the middle of the kitchen so the skirt of the dress blew out like a cloud. 'What do you think? It passes the twirl test.'

'Lovely, but it's supposed to be for Sunday best,' said Flora, smiling at her. 'If you insist on wearing it today, well, just don't ruin it. Don't sit on the grass with it on.'

But Connie was already out the door and down the street.

Gabe was in the back garden, sitting on the grass, fiddling with wires. 'I'm making a crystal set,' he said, not looking up at her. There were bits and pieces of silver stuff everywhere, sparkling in the grass. She had no idea how he could make sense of it all. She sat down cross-legged in front of him, pulling her frock down between her legs.

'We have a new assistant pastor; he looks like Gregory Peck but with blond hair and his name is Greg which is short for Gregory. He's in Danny's room. He's much older than you.' In the distance she could hear the hum of Birdie's sewing machine.

'Pass me that bit,' said Gabe. He had heard every word and every meaning but he didn't look at her. Even though he had pointed, she had no idea which bit, and so picked up a handful of wires and bits of silver things and held them out to him and he took the piece of red wire that he wanted.

She watched as he melted bits together with a soldering iron that was attached to electric leads that ran into the house.

'It's quite simple,' he said. 'This is the capacitor and that bit is the detector,' but already he had lost her attention and she was thinking of Pastor Greg.

'Do you think he will preach as good as Pa? He has an accent and mixes up his words; perhaps no one but me will understand what he says.'

Gabe didn't answer and she watched as he attached more bits and finally an old knob that he twiddled until a crackling sound echoed weakly through a carbon amplifier. Now she was fascinated.

'How did you do that?'

'I told you,' he said, and tuned the wireless some more until the sound became clearer and turned into a crackled voice singing *Rumours are flying you got me sighing.* They laughed and stood up and she twirled so he would notice her dress. He looked at her and saw the dress falling softly over her body. He saw that she had changed. She stopped twirling and he began dancing as best he could with his gammy leg. She knew he hadn't noticed her dress. He was just a boy. Pastor Greg was a man.

'Remember me?' said Sergeant Fortunato.

They came to a dizzy halt. Gabe stood next to her, their arms touching.

'Well,' laughed the policeman, 'you've both shot up. You'll both be taller than me soon. I remember when I was shooting up my mother couldn't feed me enough. I expect you're the same young …'

'We haven't done anything wrong,' said Connie firmly, cutting him off, 'but you missed his crutches when you got him out of the river.'

'That was years ago.' He slapped his wrist and said, 'Well now I've been ticked off soundly, Miss …'

'Starr.'

'That's right. One of the reverend's children. I had cause to speak to him just this morning as a matter of fact. Is your mother in?' he said to Gabe. 'Well, of course she's in, I can hear the sewing machine going. She's a whizz on that thing I hear. The other men tell me their wives …'

'She's inside,' said Gabe.

'Well, I'll just be having a private word,' said the sergeant, and he walked off to the back door. Connie looked at Gabe.

'Come on,' she said, and they followed the sergeant inside to the living room.

Birdie stopped sewing when Sergeant Fortunato walked in, and looked over to Connie and Gabe at the doorway. She started to stand up but then sat down again as though she didn't want to get too close to the policeman.

'Missus Mabbett, you might want to do this in private,' Sergeant Fortunato said and he looked at Connie and Gabe. 'There are some things that are not right for young people's ears and this may well be one of those times. In fact, I think it definitely is one of those times.'

'It's all right, sergeant,' Birdie said. Connie watched her eyes settle on Gabe. 'You can't be here because of Gabe so I can't think of anything else that would rattle me.'

'It's senior sergeant now and no, it's not your boy, it's your husband,' said the sergeant and he closed his lips tight and put his hands on his hips and Connie waited for Birdie to send them out but she didn't so Connie stood there by the door with Gabe. Sergeant Fortunato looked at her again to send her out and Connie stared defiantly back at him.

'What's he done?' said Birdie, sighing.

'We've had a visit to the station from the Methodist minister. He was concerned because a young lady came to him with her plans to marry.' Sergeant Fortunato took a deep breath. 'It seems her intended is one Aubrey Mabbett,' the sergeant whispered. 'And, well, the Methodist minister talks to the Baptist minister and the Anglican minister, whom she'd also visited, and the Presbyterian minister and the Lutheran minister and see all these ministers get together once a month and pieces get put together and I spoke to Reverend Starr to confirm the one and the same and …'

'I get the picture,' said Birdie.

He looked at Connie and Gabe again as though he wanted to say more but couldn't because of them and then looked back to Birdie.

'Oh dear,' said Birdie from behind the sewing machine. 'Poor girl.'

When Gunter chooses his path

Saturday, 4 January 1947

Greg watched as Flora moved about the kitchen chopping vegetables at the bench, then she pulled something steaming out of the oven, and Joseph sat at the table with his bible laid out in front of him.

'No, no, put that away. I'm ready to serve up as soon as Connie comes back from the Mabbetts,' said Flora. Joseph closed the bible, slid it up the table and set four places. Now, Greg had choices. He could have thanked God for keeping him safe and at last bringing him into the Starr home, a home so like the one he had grown up in. But instead he chose the other road. Rather than comforting him, the similarities were barbed swords that cut right through him and reminded him of all he had lost and that was what he chose to think and breathe on. So he sat at the table, his mouth bitter and salty.

'Might as well throw you in the deep end, Greg,' Joseph said as Flora put a bowl of steaming potatoes on the table.

'I don't think we can wait for Connie any longer,' she said.

Greg leant towards the bowl and let the steam warm his face and he breathed in the smell of the potatoes and then saw they were just potatoes. No herbs or seasoning, no onions or cream through them. His mother would never have served a bowl of bare potatoes. Flora went to the oven for more and came back with a dish steaming with robust meatiness that made him want to grab it from her and fill his empty body with its goodness, but when he looked it was rabbit in a watery soup and there was no speck and no rich gravy. And it was stinking hot. Who eats such food in the heat?

'Is it always this hot?'

'Oh, it'll get much hotter in February,' laughed Joseph.

'But it can snow in winter,' said Flora. 'I saved up some sugar so I've made lemon pudding for dessert. But I'm awfully sorry this is all we can offer you for your first proper meal with us,' Flora said.

Greg wanted his mother's *rouladen*.

'Who knows when rationing will end,' said Flora.

'If it will ever end,' said Connie, flopping into the seat beside him. She wriggled her chair so she was touching his elbow.

'Have you washed your hands?' asked Flora and Connie held them up in the air.

'You'll never guess what I heard,' said Connie.

'We don't tell tales,' said Joseph, and he looked at her sternly. Greg was disappointed. He wanted to hear what the strange girl had to say.

'Joseph caught the rabbit, didn't you, Joseph,' said Flora.

'With my bare hands,' he said and laughed and waved his hands in the air. 'Actually, Deacon Finchley gave it to us. He shot the poor blighter and probably several of his brothers to boot. I hope you got all the pellet out, dear.'

'It is a good meal,' Greg said. To him it should have been a feast. It was the best he had eaten in two years, but the bitterness wouldn't let him enjoy it. These people were soft and flaccid and didn't know true heartache. They had waltzed through the war with barely a scratch.

Joseph reached in his shirt pocket and pulled out a piece of paper, he unfolded it and held it out towards him. Greg took it and looked at it. It was a list in elegant cursive blue ink that made it hard for him to work out the English words.

'The order of service for tomorrow,' said Joseph. 'I think the best thing is that I preach the sermon but you do everything else and that way the congregation will know I am behind you. There will be no confusion. It will be clear right from the outset that we work together, you and I, and that we are both leaders of this church. You will call me reverend and I will call you pastor. That way everyone will know where they are.'

Pastor – his father would have been proud. 'Thank you. I will learn by heart.'

'No need for that,' laughed Joseph. 'Just keep it in front of you at church so you can remember what comes next.'

But after dinner Greg practised the list over and over, trying to get the pronunciation perfect.

In the morning he put on his best clothes and stood in the hallway waiting for Joseph.

'Have you had some breakfast, man?' said Joseph, slapping him on the arm.

'I'm not hungry,' he lied.

'Have some tea at least,' said Joseph, and he stood behind him and ushered him into the kitchen. 'Flora, do you have a cuppa for our new assistant pastor?'

He gulped the tea down and it tasted nasty on his tongue. He watched as Connie put two big spoons of honey on her porridge when her parents weren't watching. The honey turned into sickly rivers.

'Righto,' said Joseph, 'let's you and I go into the church so you can get acquainted. You have the order of service?'

Greg tapped his shirt pocket.

'Good man,' said Joseph.

They walked the short distance from the manse to the church and Joseph introduced him first to the deacons gathered in the vestry. Joseph prayed and after the prayer the deacons went into the church. Then Joseph nodded at him and he followed Joseph as they walked to the seats behind the pulpit. They sat in unison and Joseph nodded to him again and he walked up to the pulpit. He heard the deafening silence as the congregation stopped breathing and he announced the first hymn. His speech was so different to theirs. They wouldn't accept him, but he would show them. He would be more devout than any of them. He would give them no cause to doubt him. After the service he stood at the door with Joseph and Flora to shake everyone's hands. The young girls held his hand tight and said, 'Oh I'd just love to show you round Ballarat.'

'Perhaps a walk along the river,' offered another.

'A tram ride down Sturt Street.'

'Pleasant idea, very,' he said to all of them, and the girls giggled so they had to rest their heads briefly on his arm to contain themselves and Connie flounced past him and out the door as though he wasn't even there. The women asked where he was from and he said, 'Czechoslovakia,' and they said, 'Oh yes,' as if they knew exactly where that was and they smiled at his white hair that reflected the light like crystal and imagined him giving them glorious white-haired grandchildren and pushed their daughters in front of him so he was almost face to face with their breathlessness.

But the men. The men were a different story altogether. Many of the men had served in Europe and they recognised his accent and it made their hearts turn to stone, their eyes darken and in the warm sun their skin turned icy. Greg held out his hand and the men pushed past without even looking at him. And afterwards when everyone had filed past and the church was empty apart from old Mister Hooley picking up the hymnals, he stepped out onto the porch and saw the men huddled in the street having furious muttered conversations with Joseph, and the tension of the words he couldn't hear but could see, plain as day, filled the air. He detested the men for their rejection of him. He couldn't help who he was born. These soft, sun-freckled Australians who thought rationing was the same as starvation had no idea.

When Hazel knows a thing or two

Friday, 7 May 1947

Viola had felt Manny's pulse strengthen beneath her fingertips, and listened to his heart as it beat stronger. She had felt the fever in his cheeks cool. She had snuck her mother's mutton stew into the hospital in her father's thermos and had given it to Manny for lunch instead of the soggy liver paste sandwiches the hospital kitchen provided. Over summer she'd helped him hobble on his walking stick to sit on the cane divans in the cool evening air. She had wheeled him out to sit on the veranda on autumn afternoons, where the sun played with shadows and the sweet smells of the lavender bushes filled the air. At the end of her shift they would sit on the veranda and watch as the red sky faded and the southern cross shone over them. And when his parents came to visit, as they did every afternoon, she would give them a little extra time after the visiting bell rang.

Now he was strong enough to walk unaided, and if the weather was pleasant enough she wandered in the garden alongside him as he took slow, careful steps in his hospital pyjamas and his dressing gown and she in her new crisp white nurse's uniform, no longer a student. Their hands brushed past each other as they walked and even though his hand hadn't touched hers, she could feel the warmth of his skin in the air between them. She would watch carefully for the slightest hint he might fall; she was there ready to reach out and give him the support he needed to regain his balance.

Matron Harbolt had seen her walking in the garden with Manny through the second-floor window and on Friday morning caught her in the corridor.

'Don't worry,' she'd said, 'I wasn't spying on you. We're going to be married soon, me and Aubrey, so you and I are going to be practically sisters-in-law.'

'No we're not,' spat Viola. 'I'm not in the slightest bit related to Aubrey.'

Viola felt a bit mean because Matron Harbolt was a kind woman. She flounced flamboyantly around the sick men and made them smile even if it hurt their chests. She didn't think matron was the kind of woman to dally with a married man, but she was wrong.

'I know a thing or two about love,' said Matron Harbolt. 'After this bloody war we need love and a lot of it.' She moved closer and said, 'You know, I didn't think that boy had any chance of surviving. You saved him, Viola.' Matron clapped her hands and did a weird little flip in the air with her feet and landed with a thud. 'That's the sort of nursing I like to see.'

'But I'm not in love with him,' protested Viola. 'He's in love with my friend Lydia and she with him.'

'Oh, that girl who visits sometimes?'

Viola nodded.

'Pfft,' said Nurse Harbolt and off she walked down the cold sterile corridor and Viola watched as she did a little pirouette before turning the corner.

When Birdie takes what's hers

Saturday, 8 May 1947

On Saturday Viola had the day off and walked with her mother to her sister's house. Flora was going to bring some of her lemons and they were going to make a batch of lemon and carrot marmalade for the church fete in November. The women took six months to crochet coathanger covers, sew tea towels, and make jams. They had been saving sugar coupons for months to collect enough for the marmalade. She had invited Lydia but Lydia said she didn't want to be anywhere Flora was and that most likely Flora would bring that brat Connie and Lydia didn't want to see her either, so she would visit Manny at the hospital instead and when she'd said that Viola had felt a lurching in her stomach as though someone had kicked her and she wondered if she was coming down with something. It was the curse of being a nurse – picking up viruses from patients. But she was glad that Lydia seemed to have finally accepted that her American man was not going to send for her.

Birdie sent Gabe outside to the garden shed. Gabe had taken out all her gardening tools and stacked them against the wall of the house and filled the shed with his wires and valves and globes.

'I'll be busy all day,' she said. 'We're making lemon and carrot marmalade and I'll save a jar for you.'

Flora brought Connie and a basket of lemons, shiny like tiny little suns. The women crowded around Birdie's kitchen table, their sleeves up and aprons on. Viola halved lemons and removed the pips, getting her fingers sticky. Connie dug her fingers into the jar of sugar before anyone could stop her and licked the sugar off finger by finger.

'Go out to Gabe,' Flora told her. Connie went for one last dig in the sugar and Flora stopped her just in time. 'Wash your hands before you go.'

Connie scowled at her and disappeared outside. Every now and then they heard a squeal from Connie and assumed Gabe was teasing her.

But Gabe was saying, 'Connie Starr, you better get used to the idea because I'm going to marry you one day.'

Connie grabbed a handful of wire cut-offs and threw them at him. And when she stopped laughing, she said, 'I can't marry you. I'm going to marry Pastor Greg.'

'These will be great sellers at the church fete,' said Flora, carefully pouring sugar into a glass measuring jug so as not to spill one rationed grain.

'How long since there's been a church fete?' asked Elsie, and then answered herself, 'Not since before the war I 'spect,' and she grated another carrot.

'The new pastor says he doesn't approve of church fetes,' said Birdie. She didn't like the new pastor. Something about him didn't fit together. 'He said it in his last sermon. He said churches weren't in the business of making money and that a fete was the same as money changers in the temple. He said if it goes ahead he will upend all the trestles like Jesus in the temple.'

'Hah,' laughed Elsie, 'that I'd like to see.'

'I'd like to see Reverend Starr's reaction if he tries it,' said Viola.

'Perhaps he's just too good for his own good,' said Flora. 'I imagine Joseph will keep him in hand.'

'That's the lemons done,' said Viola, and she began washing the jars that would be sterilised in Birdie's two biggest pots.

Once they were out of the pot the sugar went in and Birdie kept an eye on it to make sure it didn't burn as it melted into syrup.

'Time for the lemons and carrots,' she said, and Viola tipped in the lemons and Elise the grated carrots and Birdie slowly stirred the caramel syrup, then she hung her thermometer over the side of the pot and the women watched as the temperature slowly rose to 222 degrees.

Flora tested the syrup on the back of a spoon and it was declared thick enough.

'Who has the steadiest hand?' asked Birdie.

'You,' the women said, so Birdie, in her thickest oven mitts, lifted the pot with the scalding hot syrup into the middle of the table. She dipped in a jug and carefully filled each jar to just below the rim. Flora burst the air bubbles with a fork.

'We can't put the wax on until it's cooled,' said Elsie.

'Which means cup of tea time,' said Birdie.

Flora was lining up the jars of marmalade so they were safe on Birdie's shelf, Viola and Elsie were cleaning the table of sticky lemony juice and jellied marmalade blobs and wayward pips and Birdie was just filling the kettle when Aubrey said 'What's this? Afternoon tea and I'm just in time.'

All the women stared at him.

'I feel like I just walked into the war room,' he said and laughed.

Birdie put down the kettle. She took careful steps past the women towards Aubrey. She took his arm firmly, pinching him on purpose so that he let out a yelp; she saw him look back over his shoulder at the women and saw the silly grin he gave them as though he knew he was in trouble for some petty thing and like a good boy would take his punishment to make her feel better. She pulled him up the hallway to the front of the house.

'I haven't seen you in months,' she said, still pinching his arm. 'But I've heard about you. See, way back in January I had a visit from the police. So excuse me if that's the last I thought I'd ever hear from you. After all you're marrying that nurse, aren't you? She thinks you are. She told Viola you are. But it's curious because I haven't had any divorce papers arrive in the mail.' She tried to speak quietly but she knew the women in the kitchen could hear every word in such a tiny house. She didn't care. He made a fool of her so often. They would do this here and now.

'No, Birdie, don't be so ridiculous. Why would I do that when I have you? I've been in Melbourne all these months. Trying to set up my own shoe shop. I wanted it to be a surprise – I know how you love surprises.' He wriggled his arm free from her grip and saw she didn't believe a word so he tried again. 'The problem, Birdie, is that I just love women too much. But I love you the most. You'll always be my number one, Birdie.'

'Aubrey, I'm done,' said Birdie.

'Birdie, love, you need me – we've got the boy to think of.'

'No, Aubrey, I don't need you,' said Birdie, and she realised how exhausted he made her. 'I earn more from my sewing than you ever gave me for housekeeping. Gabe and I are quite fine on our own.'

He glowered at her then and she saw that he was shocked. He had expected her to crumble as she had always done before. He leant in close and she saw a demon in his black eyes.

'It's my house, Birdie. It's rented in my name. If anyone's leaving it's you.'

She sighed. 'No, Aubrey, it's you. I started buying this house a year ago. I don't know why I never told you. Self-preservation, I expect.'

'You can't buy a house,' he scoffed. 'No one lends money to a woman.'

'Lucky I wasn't already divorced, isn't it? It's a private sale, between me and the vendor. It's only my name on the deed and as long as I keep paying on time, which I do with my sewing money, it's mine. Only mine.'

His fist came out and before she had time to duck, he had hit her chin and pushed her into the wall. She wanted to cry but she hated him, she wouldn't give him her tears; she wanted to rub the welt coming up on her skin, but didn't even want to give him that, so she stood and looked at him as though he was no more than a bothersome fly.

Birdie reached for the door and opened it and with all her might pushed Aubrey through. 'If you ever set foot in my house again, I will separate your head from your neck with the wood axe, which, by the way, I am quite handy with these days, and I won't be sewing you back together.' And she slammed the door shut on him.

She took a deep breath. She walked into her bedroom and tore off her old dress that she had worn since Mike's funeral. In her bra and undies and slip she walked into the lounge room and took the frock she had sewn for Jocelyn Trebilcock from the hanger that was hooked over the lounge-room door. The voile dress was pale pink with scattered black peacock feathers and a striking neckline where Birdie had embroidered peacock feathers falling from the neck to the breast. Birdie had lined the dress with red satin. She undid the side zip and slipped the dress over her head.

'That's one thing of mine you won't be taking, Jocelyn Trebilcock.' Birdie pulled the teeth of the zip closed over her body and walked into the kitchen.

The women gasped. The dress was far too wonderful to wear around the house. Birdie threw her old dress into the bin.

Flora smiled at her and poured her a cup of tea.

When lemon marmalade is not enough

Monday, 10 May 1947

Viola called goodbye to Lydia and walked out her front door at six. Her shift began at seven. The grass was wet and glistening and early fog filled the air so she couldn't see more than a few feet in front of her. She pulled her scarf tight around her neck and up over her cold numb nose. Her breath formed white frosty clouds. When she got to the hospital she walked in one of the side doors and through the whitewashed brick corridors to the repatriation ward. She put her coat on her hook in the small nurses' cloakroom that was off the nurses' station and hung her hat and scarf over her coat that was damp from her walk in the wet air.

She reached into her bag and pulled out the jar of lemon marmalade she had saved. She turned her gloves inside themselves so they were a ball and put them into her bag where the jar had been. The lemon marmalade had set perfectly and when Viola held the jar to the light, the sun shone through the jelly, casting a warm glow on her skin. She wanted to give that glow to Manny. Not that she loved Manny, it was just that she was a nurse and she would do anything to see him restored to full health. She wouldn't get between him and Lydia.

Viola clasped the lemon marmalade in her hands as though she had captured a precious thing inside the jar and she almost ran to Manny's bed. She didn't know why she was so eager to give him the lemon marmalade, it was just jam after all, and she forced herself to slow down, to take respectably nurse-like steps. She smiled at Matron Harbolt as she passed her and kept up her even pace so she wouldn't have to stop and talk. She walked into ward 4 and looked around the room at the men in the three other beds sitting up at their breakfast tables. Leon in bed 1, with one arm missing and one leg missing and the remaining ones still in splints, every bone shattered as though someone had deliberately beaten him to a pulp. Leon had said to her through tears, 'Terrible things happen at war. I wasn't expecting it when I went.' Bobby in bed 2 stared out the window at a world he no longer belonged to and wouldn't speak; Doctor Blagg said he had no remedy for Bobby's brain. Frank in bed 3 coughed blood into tissues every day and no amount of heroin cough syrup was helping. She looked at Manny's bed, bed 4, and it stared back at her – empty.

It was stripped down to the bare grey mattress and the lumpy striped pillow lying on top was missing its white starched case. Perhaps he was in the dining room. She went there and the three men sitting eating porridge at the dining-room table smiled and waved to her. She didn't feel like waving back but she forced herself to smile and wave even though all she could feel was increasing fear, like someone was sticking her with pins. She went out to the veranda but it was empty apart from the cane divans painted cream with a thin layer of frost. She walked out into the garden and looked around the rose bushes but all she succeeded in doing was wetting her shoes in the frosty grass. She went to the nurses' station. Doctor Blagg stood bent over the desk scribbling prescriptions for heroin hydrochloride one after the other and slapping the sheets of paper into a motley pile. Sometimes if the men were in pain Viola let a little extra slip down their throats and Doctor Blagg never questioned why the bottles were empty before they should be. Doctor Blagg looked up at her. His face was tired and bored.

'Ready for rounds, nurse?'

'Yes,' she said, controlling her voice. 'But patient Finchley doesn't seem to be here.'

'No, apparently he discharged himself last night,' said Doctor Blagg. 'We can't help those that won't help themselves,' and he picked up his clipboard and walked into the ward with no thought for the comings and goings of patients and Viola followed him, suddenly feeling as miserable as Doctor Blagg looked.

At three that afternoon, when Viola finished her shift, she walked to Nightingale Street, to the clinker brick bungalow Manny's parents owned, and knocked on the front door, hoping he and not his parents would answer, and sighed with relief when he opened the door.

'I brought you this. I made it. I took it to work but you left without saying goodbye.'

'I used to see you at church each week, Viola,' Manny said and he leant against the doorjamb, watching her with those soft eyes of his that made her feel there was no man in the world who could be more gentle or kind. But though his eyes were kind, his words were cold and fell cruelly against her skin. She flinched and when she had swallowed her tears and dared to look up, she saw that he knew he'd hurt her, he looked so completely lost.

'Why did you come?' he said, as though he had physical pain because of her.

'I really don't know,' she said, looking up at him and she remembered Lydia. 'It's not as if you're special. You're just another patient. I guess this is a home visit then. Just a check-up.'

He reached out and tucked her hair that was falling across her eyes back behind her ear and it took them both by surprise and for a fleeting moment she saw kindness again in his eyes.

'You don't want me, Viola,' he explained softly. A dog pushed its head between his legs and the doorjamb and he rested his hand gently on its head.

'Of course,' she said. 'I didn't expect. I mean, I know you and Lydia …'

'It's not Lydia,' he said. 'I'm old, and more importantly I'm broken and no doctors or nurses can fix it. Not even your excellent nursing, Viola. Oh, I might look all right on the outside, nothing visible is broken, not like poor old Leon. No, that's not what was done to me,' he said, moving his arms and legs like a scarecrow. 'It's what you can't see that is broken in me. I can never give you what you need, Viola.'

She didn't want his pity, it tasted harsh and she was crying and wiped the tears away with her fingers and they evaporated into nothing. She hadn't realised until he said all this that what she wanted was him. She knew she could depend on him, he was true. He would never cheat on her like Aubrey did on Birdie. He wouldn't be brazen or careless. He was the opposite of Aubrey and that made him everything she wanted. And he needed her. He was scratched and dented and she could look after him if he let her. She might not get rid of his cuts and bruises but she could soothe them.

'I don't mind,' she whispered so he had to lean forward to hear her. 'I thought you loved Lydia, but I think now that you don't. It's you, Manny, that I love. Not the Manny that was before the war. I like everything about you. I like the way you talk in quiet whispers as though an enemy is listening.' She did not see him flinch at her words. 'I like that you don't flirt with the nurses like the other men. You don't make jokes about sponge baths or ask for kisses. I like the way you do everything slowly and carefully as though you may never get to do it again.'

He sighed from somewhere broken deep inside him and stood back and his eyes narrowed as he looked out to the sky as though he could see some far-off danger and was preparing himself for it. The visits from Lydia had been exhausting for him. The girl was full of noise. He looked down at Viola, at her soft brown hair and her quiet eyes. It was her tenderness that had made him stronger, her thermoses of soup and her gentle fingers washing his skin as if baptising him and making him new. He couldn't do it to her. He couldn't throw himself on her. He would wear her out eventually and then she would hate him.

'I can't do it, Viola. It wouldn't be fair to either of us. You must leave.'

He looked at her. 'Go.' And the dog, thinking Manny meant him, turned and padded back into the house.

'Go,' Manny said again, and he shut the door on her.

When Manny looks at death

Saturday, 5 July 1947

Snow covered the grass as if clouds had fallen to the ground and decided this was where they would stay. Inside the manse the seven o'clock news declared it was the fifth of July 1947, and Flora and Joseph strained to hear the announcer over the sounds of Greg's fervent praying that wafted down the stairs from Danny's room. The announcer told them a new computer had been created, and a perfectly ordinary brown household moth, ignorant of the mark it would make in history, had flown into the relay switch. So, a simple bug had brought the new computer to a stunning halt and Flora and Joseph agreed that progress wasn't always a good thing.

Connie was outside in her pyjamas, dressing gown and gumboots building a snowman, not caring at all that her dressing gown had become a soggy mess on the corners as it dragged through the snow. White covered the road and the grass and the fence around St Patrick's, so the road between the two churches no longer separated them.

In the little house in Humffray Street, Gabe sat in bed drinking the tea Birdie had brought him on this very cold morning and he looked out at the snow and thought about throwing snowballs at Connie when she least expected it and Birdie sat at the kitchen table gazing at the flowers Sergeant Fortunato had left on her doorstep next to the milk and thinking that she really should find out what his first name was.

Lydia stared out her kitchen window and in the absolute still quietness of the earth when it has snowed, she felt deafened by her loneliness.

Danny at bible college in Belgrave also saw snow outside his window and he stood and watched it softly fall. Charlie stood beside him and their arms hung down by their sides, their hands a hair's breadth from touching each other's.

Viola looked at the snow through the window of the hospital ward and wondered if Manny was rugged up enough and Manny stood in the front yard of the house in Nightingale Street, Snowy beside him. Manny wore nothing but his striped pyjamas, his bare feet sinking into the snow and each shiver that ran through his veins reminded him of another time when he had stood out in the cold, naked, for hours after hours, desperately wanting sleep and warmth but every time he began to close his eyes, letting sleep take him, a shot rang out and he knew another of his friends had fallen and it was his fault for letting his eyes close. As he stood there in the front yard tears fell down his cheeks in rivers.

'Mum, Mum,' he called out and Mabel ran out to him in her dressing gown calling, 'Manny, Manny, whatever are you doing? You'll catch your death. Come inside,' and she put her arms around him and motioned the dog to follow and pulled Manny inside with all her might and sat him by the fire and Cecil quickly threw extra logs on it and Mabel poured him sweet milky tea using up all that was left of their sugar ration and Snowy sat on his feet and none of them knew this was Snowy's last day on earth.

Manny's hand didn't fall gently on Snowy's head and he didn't touch the tea. He stared out at nothing but horror.

When Greg shows Connie his treasure

Sunday, 6 July 1947

Greg stood at the upstairs window of the room that had been Thom and Danny's and tears wetted his skin that was as white as the falling snow and the tears dried in harsh salty crusts. He remembered his home in the snow and his mother's bean soup and his father's wire glasses resting on the table fogged up with the steam from the soup. This was not his life. He was living a lie, being a different person with a foreign name and it chilled his heart and froze his blood like the snow.

He saw Connie in the garden below him. As if she sensed him watching her, she looked up and waved and he waved back enough to satisfy her. She should be getting ready for church.

He took off his pyjamas and put on his trousers, shirt and jacket and with each item of clothing he put on, he became Pastor Greg Smith and Gunter was buried deep within him under his enormous loss that ate the edges of his soul until it was a frayed battered thing barely alive. He took a deep breath and picked up the sermon he had written. He preached every third

Sunday to give him practice and give the reverend a break, and just as he put on his woollen vest, he remembered to also put on goodness, as though integrity was something that could be worn and discarded at will. Now he was Pastor Greg Smith, but he didn't understand goodness existed in a person's being and was not something that could be just put on when you felt like it. He walked into the kitchen. Joseph and Flora were sitting at the table drinking tea and Joseph was dunking his vegemite toast. Greg had tried to like vegemite toast but it smelt and tasted like something you would find in the bottom of the sewer. Women in the congregation gave him tins of the stuff saying, 'It'll make your bones strong.' If they only knew what he'd survived they'd know he didn't need any black stinking paste to make him strong.

'Enjoying this cold morning?' said Joseph as he sat at the table.

'Did you see the snow?' asked Flora.

'Brrrr, it's freezing,' he said, rubbing his arms being Greg. Gunter wasn't cold at all. Gunter had grown up with winters that were day after day of snow at least three feet deep. This slurry outside they were all excited about wasn't snow. By eleven the snow would be melting away leaving slushy ground that stuck to shoes and bogged car tyres.

And at eleven Greg preached the same sermon he preached every month. He looked down on the young girls sitting in the pews below him and in his crisp English words that seemed chopped at the ends, he reprimanded them. They were responsible for retaining their purity, it was up to them to deny boys' advances. The boys, he said, couldn't help their natural urges, but it was the girls' duty to keep them both pure. He told the girls that make-up was an insult to God – who were they to think they had the right to change the looks God had given them? He told the girls that he would personally chastise any he found trying to get into the Saturday night dances in St Patrick's hall. Dancing, he said, leads to boys' hands wandering to places they shouldn't go, and then he remembered the older women and again stated his disapproval of the upcoming fete they were all spending so much time and energy preparing for.

He was exhausted when he finished and fell back into the hard wooden chair with its pointed back that sat like a throne on the platform and his chest wheezed.

The congregation stood and sang 'And can it be' and Birdie leant over to Flora and whispered, 'He's always rather harsh, don't you think?'

There was only one person in the world Flora didn't like and it was Greg. She couldn't put her finger on why because she hadn't intensely disliked someone before. But every time he came into a room she felt the hairs on her arms bristle, her heart thumped against her chest and her brain became muddy as though there was something she should know about him but couldn't quite see. She didn't like it when she saw him and Connie huddled together, giggling and whispering.

But Flora didn't say any of this. Instead she said, 'He's learning. Joseph says he'll relax when he finds his way.'

After the hymn Cecil Finchley walked to the front of the church to read the announcements. He thanked the women for the work they were doing for the fete and reminded the men they had tasks to do too. The men were thinking about the treats the women would make. They hoped for an array of cakes not seen since the war. The profits would be divided between the church, the orphanage, and sending Danny to India when he finished missionary school at the end of the year. The congregation nodded their heads. Despite the new pastor, things were going back to normal after the war.

Greg stood and shook people's hands after the service. They shook his hands with pursed lips and dark frowns and he hoped it was because they were pondering his sermon. His sermons were harsh, yes, but the world was harsh and these pudgy people didn't know that. So of course they weren't going to say, 'Oh lovely sermon today, Pastor Greg,' like they did after the reverend's sermons. But the reverend's sermons were designed to make people feel better about their puny lives and Greg had learnt that people didn't matter at all. The only thing that mattered was justice, and that was hard to get. Greg didn't go in to morning tea; he couldn't bear the thought of spending more time with the pushy mothers and the eyelash-fluttering girls. So when he had shaken the last hand, he walked up the side of the house and saw Connie sitting in the lemon tree, a tear ripped in the hem of her coat.

'Can I come up there with you?' he said.

She looked down at him and then muttered to her side as if talking to someone he couldn't see. Then she wriggled along the branch to make room for him. It certainly was an enormous lemon tree, he had to give her that. He climbed up, brushed the wet from the branch and flung it from his fingers into the air and sat next to her. They sat in silence listening to the chatter of the congregation and the tinkling of china cups on saucers in the church hall next door.

'We are opposites, you and I,' he said. He studied her. She was a strange girl; she walked as though her feet barely touched the ground. There was a flickering about her; you couldn't be sure she was really here.

She looked at him through those black eyes of hers. 'No,' she said, 'we are the same. We are both afraid of missing out, so we both take what we want.'

He reached in his pocket for the treasure he kept safe there and pulled the tunnel book out and showed it to her.

She ran her finger along its edges and when he opened it her eyes came alive and she smiled at him and he felt some of the ice inside his soul melt.

They stayed up there, side by side, hidden from the world in the branches and watched as the three Finchleys and Birdie and Gabe and Joseph and Flora walked down the drive and into the house for lunch. They only clambered down when they heard Flora calling.

When Flora makes a mistake

Sunday, 6 July 1947

Flora put the pot of broth on the stove to warm up and put the rice pudding into the oven to bake. Mabel had told her that rice pudding was Manny's favourite before the war, so she'd made it specially, even though she wasn't supposed to bake on a Sunday. This was for Manny. Manny was drifting like a rotting branch floating on the river. He needed sugar to fatten him, to sweeten his pallid cheeks and bring colour to his dull eyes. She put in sultanas and lemon zest and sprinkled nutmeg on top.

Flora put her head out the back door and called Connie and Pastor Greg. She had seen them sitting together in the lemon tree on her way in from the church. It was like he was two different people. In church he was a rigid, relentless preacher, and then not an hour later he was sitting in the lemon tree like he was still just a boy. When Connie and Pastor Greg were seated at the end of the table on the piano stool, Joseph said grace and Flora poured soup into everyone's bowls and made sure to give Manny extra, then she watched as he played with it, swirling it into a whirlpool until you could see the painted flowers on the bottom of the china bowl. He looked up and saw her and took a spoonful and put it to his lips but she saw that he didn't really sip any of the soup.

'Tell us about where you went during the war,' said Connie.

'Connie,' said Joseph, 'that's private. We don't talk about wars once they are over.'

Perhaps Manny would eat the pudding Flora had made for him. She cleared away the dishes and put the pudding in the middle of the table and smiled at Manny, expecting to see the delight in his eyes, but all she saw was terror. She lifted the ladle of creamy rice towards his bowl. He began to shake and tears poured down his face and she held the ladle mid-air, not daring to push it any closer to him.

'It's just rice,' said Connie, 'it's not going to hurt you.'

Manny stood up shaking his head and backed away from the table and from the rice sprinkled with nutmeg and he knocked Connie's bowl and cup and they clattered to the floor with a bang and he cried out.

'It's just crockery,' said Connie.

Manny didn't hear her and he backed all the way to the door and then he shot through it, not noticing the thorny rose bush ripping his pants, and when Flora and Mabel went out into the driveway after him, he was gone.

'He has the most terrible nightmares,' said Mabel, wiping her tears for her son. 'He screams out every night. But then in the morning he won't say a thing about it. If only it could have been me instead.'

Flora put her arm around Mabel.

Manny ran, stumbling over his steps, his long six-foot body falling over itself as he buried his head in his collar against the cold and pushed through it. He ran for his life, which he knew would vanish if he didn't find something to cling to. He ignored the people who looked out their windows as he leant on their fences catching his breath. It was five blocks to her house; he counted them as he went and when he arrived he fell onto the bottom step and sat heaving for air. When he had got his breath back enough to speak, he went up the steps and knocked on the door and called out her name as though he was in a desert calling for water, for one last drop that would save his life. The neighbours stared at him through their front window.

Viola opened the door; Lydia stood behind her.

'Manny,' said Lydia. 'Come in.'

And thinking he had come for Lydia after all, Viola stepped back.

'You'll catch your death out there, love,' said Lydia.

He kept his eyes on Viola, pleading with her until she realised he was there for her.

'Just give us a minute, Lydia,' she said.

He waited until Lydia had disappeared into the little kitchen at the back.

'Viola, I can't do it without you. I thought I could but I can't.'

'Do what?' she said.

'Live,' he said.

He looked in her eyes to see if he could find love or pity or anything that would say she would stand by him. She moved forward and put her hands on his face. Her fingers were warm and he felt that warmth travel through him to his heart and he stood up straighter. Then, as if remembering something from a past life, he leant forward and kissed her, just a peck, and he stood back and smiled and realised that after all the death and torture and starvation, he had seen something good.

'I'm broken,' he said.

'I know,' she said. 'But remember – I'm good with things that need mending.'

'I can't eat rice,' he said. 'Can't even be in the same room as it. I can't look at the stuff. And I have nightmares and I can't cope with loud noises. I don't know if I can give you children. I don't know what the war did to me.'

'No rice and no loud noises. Anything else?'

'Most likely,' he said. 'But they come without warning.'

'You're freezing,' she said. 'You haven't got a coat.'

She stepped forward and kissed him and then she stepped back as though waiting for something and he put his hands around her warm face and pulled her to him and kissed her and he breathed in the air she breathed and it warmed his empty chest.

When angels make an almighty racket

Saturday, 22 November 1947

Connie put on her best dress, pulled her long ringlets into a ponytail on top of her head and secured it with a green ribbon, and put on her oxford shoes. She scowled at the shoes; they were ugly things like nurses' shoes. Connie hated them and desperately wanted a pair of shiny baby doll shoes. But oxfords were cheaper and practical and could be worn to school and Flora had reminded her she was the only person in the family who actually had new shoes and only because her feet were still growing. She was sprouting up as though she'd never stop, and they couldn't keep up; she had already grown too tall for Lydia's hand-me-downs.

Flora called out to her to hurry up, so she skipped down the stairs two at a time and out the back door to the lemon tree. Flora put her arms out to embrace her and Connie nestled in and leant her weight against her mother. She could hear birds gossiping in the distance, a tram rattling down Sturt Street, and the noise passed. She looked up to the sky but couldn't see any angels or demons.

At this wedding there was to be no music, which could suddenly rise in volume, no crowds cheering, which could sound like the screams of tortured men, no clapping, which could sound like guns going off without warning, no confetti that could fall like the dirt flying off the spade as a grave was dug. When Connie had been told all this she'd said, 'Sounds more like a funeral than a wedding.'

But Flora had said it was what Viola wanted.

The wedding was to be under the lemon tree because Viola said it was lemon marmalade made with lemons from the enormous tree that made her realise she loved Manny and Connie thought that made perfect sense because her tree could give people their wishes. She looked up to her branch and it was empty. She wondered where her angel was; usually he was blathering away in her ear about everything and nothing. It was eleven-thirty in the morning, the exact same time the princess Elizabeth had married two days earlier, and the sun had kindly chosen to remember it was still spring and sent down a dappled warmth that filtered through the leaves of the tree and fell in soft spots on Connie's skin. She looked over at her father, who was standing apart from the rest of the gathering and holding his bible in front of his chest. Birdie, Mabel and Elsie were standing next to her and Flora. Opposite the women stood Claude, Cecil, Gabe, Sergeant Fortunato, Manny and Danny, who was back from missionary bible school and had brought his friend Charlie with him.

Connie looked at Pastor Greg, his hair and skin so white in the golden sun that he was almost not there at all. He went in and out of focus, translucent in the sunshine. He winked at her and she leant further into her mother, almost pushing Flora over. She glanced at Gabe and he winked at her too and she poked out her tongue at him. Then she looked at her father, but he had his eyes closed and was still grasping his bible. Manny stood between his father Cecil and his soon to be father-in-law Claude, his hands behind his back, not moving at all. He stood stiffly as though something was holding him up. Connie saw Sergeant Fortunato wink at Missus Mabbett and turned to see Missus Mabbett blush and look at the ground as a quiet smile spread right through her. She was wearing a yellow frock with green trim on the collars and sleeves. Her hair shone golden in the sun.

'Lot of winking going on here today,' Connie said loudly and Flora said, 'Shhh,' so Connie went back to studying the men standing opposite. Danny's face was still covered in boyish freckles. He looked just like he did when they were little, but taller. She saw a fleeting moment when Charlie nudged Danny and Danny took Charlie's fingers in his own – just for a second. A lemon fell to the ground with a thud and they all jumped. Connie swooped and picked it up and held it in front of her like a bouquet. Joseph nodded towards the back gate and Connie turned with the others and watched as Lydia, followed by Viola, came through the back gate and up the driveway towards them. Connie gasped at Viola's dress. She knew Missus Mabbett had made it for Viola from old white tablecloths and given it to Viola years ago, but Viola had never worn it. There were embroidered birds on the bodice ready to take flight into happiness and the daisies embroidered around the hem of the dress looked as though they had been freshly plucked for the wedding. In that dress, Viola was sure to have happiness.

Joseph said, 'We are gathered here to witness the marriage of Emmanuel Cecil Finchley and Viola Melody Mitchell.' He spoke so quietly they all shuffled forward to hear him. He said the vows and Manny and Viola repeated them after him and then he pronounced them man and wife and Connie was disappointed because it was the plainest, quickest, quietest wedding she'd ever seen her father do and she looked up and saw Archangel Mike making the most almighty racket as he whooped and clapped and behind him all the other angels blew their horns and plucked the strings of their harps, and standing at the end of the driveway was Nero playing his violin. She looked further behind her and saw the demons gathered in a huddle sulking, and she realised that, no matter what, they were always there, just waiting for their moment.

Everyone went inside and had the lunch that Flora, Mabel, Birdie and Elsie had prepared. There was lemon chicken casserole and lemon coconut cake covered in white icing as a wedding cake and lemon biscuits. Connie had helped make the biscuits and cut them with the star-shaped cutter and iced them. After the lunch they stood at the end of the driveway and waved the bride and groom off as they walked to Craig's Royal Hotel on Lydiard Street before driving to Queenscliffe the next day, where they would honeymoon.

And Connie saw her father reach out and put his arm around Lydia. Did that mean she would no longer be his favourite?

When Joseph loses everything

Saturday, 22 November 1947

That night Connie lay in bed and peered at the moonlight coming through her window. She closed her eyes and dreamt of her own wedding. She would marry in a white gown that sparkled like Princess Elizabeth's. She would have a ten-foot cake like a fairytale castle made with fifty-five pounds of sugar and three hundred pounds of dried fruits and forty lemons from her tree and there would be a choir of angels singing for her, there would be white daisies scattered over the aisle. There was supposed to be something else in a wedding but she couldn't think what it was and she drifted off to sleep until a vicious pain tore through her.

She opened her eyes and saw a ghastly demon hovering over her; his eyes flashed red and his grin was a toothless hollow to hell. He held his sharp three-pronged pitchfork above her ready to strike. He gripped it with two hands and brought it down hard and the steel arrows went right through the soft fleshy middle of her belly, cutting viciously into her skin and muscle. He yanked out his pitchfork and struck again and again and the pain of his stabbing took her breath. She tried to fight him off but was helpless against the weapon he thrust into her and she gasped furiously for air and screamed out for her mother. The demon lifted up his pitchfork and brought it down again into the softness of her belly and she yelled, 'Stop, stop,' and threw away the blankets and looked down to where she'd been struck and in the moonlight she saw dark spots of blood like oozing roses on her cotton nightie. The light went on and she shut her eyes against it because its whiteness hurt and Flora was at her side.

'Connie, Connie, what's wrong?'

But Connie was in too much pain to answer. She felt her ma take her nightie and hold it up in the light. She kept her eyes shut against the awfulness of the pain and the blood.

She heard Pa's voice, 'I'll call Doctor Salter,' and she felt his shadow standing over her. But his voice sounded far away, even though he was right next to her.

'Why him?' said her mother. 'Call our Doctor Quimby, be quick.'

'I'll call Doctor Salter,' persisted Joseph.

With the light on and her mother in the room the demon had stopped stabbing her and Connie curled up into her ma's arms, but Flora's arms weren't strong and Connie knew she wasn't safe.

'It's all right, Connie dear, it's all right, a doctor is coming,' said Flora over and over.

'Am I dying?' Connie asked and she squinted up at the ceiling to see if the angels were there to collect her.

'I think you might have appendicitis,' said Flora. 'We'll have you at the hospital in no time.'

'I'm going to die,' cried Connie. She knew with pain this bad she was going to die and she clung to Flora to keep her in this life. 'Don't let me go,' she cried. 'Don't let the demons take me.' She would go to hell for sure because she had not been good. She fibbed and she caused mischief, she was disobedient, she hated and didn't turn the other cheek and she was a right handful.

It didn't seem very long before the shadow of a strange person was standing over her and Joseph said, 'Connie, this is Doctor Salter. He's going to see what can be done for you.'

'I need to examine her alone,' said Doctor Salter and he sounded angry that his good night's sleep had been interrupted. Connie didn't like him at all and rolled away from him.

'I'll just be in the hallway,' said Flora. No, her mother couldn't leave her. Connie grabbed Flora's hand and held it tight to her chest. She didn't want to be left alone with Doctor Salter. What if he was really the demon in disguise? People weren't always what they seemed. But her ma wriggled her hand free and Connie saw the tears in Flora's eyes as she pulled away.

'I'll talk to you in a minute,' said Doctor Salter to Joseph. Joseph leant over so his face was near to her ear. 'Connie, you do everything Doctor Salter asks. There's nothing to be afraid of.'

But there was, Pa just didn't know. There were demons hiding everywhere and Connie had been afraid of them for such a long time.

Doctor Salter shut the door behind Flora and Joseph. Connie was too sick to run away. She frantically looked for a weapon and picked up her tortoiseshell hair brush from the bedside table.

He walked over to her, one slow step at a time, took the hair brush and put it back on the bedside table. 'Now, what do we have here?' He pulled up her nightie and prodded her stomach up high, down low, over on one side then the other and even though his hands were cold, his prods were like being stabbed with the red-hot fire of the pitchfork. He said, 'Bend your knees, Connie,' and pushed her legs up and without warning he pushed his fingers inside her and she cried out with the indignity and shock of it.

'Hmmm,' said Doctor Salter. 'When was the last time you had the rags?'

'I don't know,' spat Connie. Why should she tell him she'd only had two periods and then none? Horrible messy things they were that meant she had to walk around with a wad of cloth between her legs like a baby with a wet nappy. She'd thanked God she'd only had two and then forgotten all about them.

Doctor Salter walked over to the door, opened it just a sliver and called, 'Reverend,' and Pa stepped into the room. He looked over at her and she saw his face full of worry for her. She was going to die. She wasn't even fourteen yet and her life was over. She would never marry in a beautiful white gown. She would never have her own children to love her or her own home where she could eat creamed biscuits whenever she wanted. Joseph stood with Doctor Salter in the corner of the room, as far away as they could get, which was at the end of Lydia's bed, and they hunched over each other and mumbled and she couldn't hear them but she could see her father scraping his hands through his hair and Doctor Salter crossed his arms over his chest and broke their quiet mumbles saying loudly, 'I am sorry but I'm not mistaken, reverend.'

Doctor Salter came back over to her and took a brown bottle and a spoon out of his bag and poured some clear liquid into the spoon and said, 'Here, drink this,' and the sickly syrup dribbled down her throat leaving a bitter aftertaste. She looked up at her father and saw he was crying. She had never seen her father cry ever and then she felt awfully tired and she was back at her wedding, in her white gown, dancing while the angels played for her.

When Danny gives Connie what she needs

Sunday, 23 November 1947

Connie woke in the morning and saw her nightie and the sheets on her bed had been changed and she wondered if she had dreamt all the pain and Doctor Salter's visit. She got up and walked downstairs to the kitchen and a strange man was sitting at the table and that wasn't unusual so she sat on the other side and looked up and saw the strange man was her father and his black, black hair had turned white overnight and there were scraggly lines on his forehead and around his eyes that hadn't been there yesterday.

'Connie,' said her father quietly, peering at her as if meeting her for the first time, 'Connie, who did this to you?'

'Who did what?' she said.

'Connie, don't play games,' he said.

'The demons hurt me and made me bleed,' she said.

Joseph shook his head slowly and raked his hands through his white, white hair. 'Connie, you're pregnant,' he said very slowly and quietly, 'and we want to know whose baby it is. We need to know whose baby it is.'

'Am I going to have a baby?' She turned to her ma who was standing in a corner of the kitchen hugging the teapot close to her chest like it was a baby. 'Like Mother Mary?'

She remembered that the archangel had visited Mary and told her she was going to have baby Jesus. She looked back at her father and said, 'An angel must've put the baby in me.'

'Connie, don't be ridiculous. Who did you do this wicked thing with?'

Joseph slammed his fist on the table and she jumped and he said, 'Stop this nonsense, Connie. Yes, you are going to have a baby and you nearly lost it last night but Doctor Salter saved it and you.' He turned to Flora and muttered, 'And I don't know if that was God's mercy or punishment.'

Connie looked over to her ma and saw tears fall down her face. Connie didn't like seeing Flora cry, so she cried too. Flora pulled a chair back from the table and sat next to her and gently patted her hair and said, 'Connie, what was the angel's name?'

Connie thought about which angel had visited Mary to tell her she was going to have baby Jesus. 'Archangel Gabriel.' And she watched as her father's face turned white like his hair and then black like the darkest storm as realisation came to him. He stood up from the table and walked out of the house.

Connie stared at nothing as Flora got up and made a pot of tea. Then she poured a cup for Connie, put in three sugars and passed it to her. Connie sipped the tea.

'Can I have another?' She hoped she'd get three sugars again. But Flora didn't seem to hear her. Flora sat beside her softly weeping and Connie put her arm around her. 'It's okay, Ma, an angel put this baby inside me so it's God's will.'

'Oh, Connie, I've done everything wrong,' said Flora through tears that made her face shiny and soft. 'Why did I let you live inside these fanciful ideas?'

Connie could see her reflection in her mother's tears.

'Connie, the only way to have a baby is to have sex and sex without marriage is a sin. An awful, awful sin that gets a girl into the trouble you are in now. It's a sin that has ruined many a girl's life.'

'But I haven't had sex without marriage,' said Connie and she felt all the rolling and crashing seas in her body well up and spill out of her and she burst into waterfalls of tears and Flora, her voice shaking, said, 'Connie, were you forced?'

Connie shook like an earthquake getting ready to split the world in two and she cried, 'It was an angel, it was Archangel Gabriel and the demon tried to kill it.'

Then Connie and Flora looked up because Joseph burst into the kitchen, he was black with anger that raged out of him like shots of lightning. He had hold of Gabe's arm and was dragging Gabe behind him. Connie laughed at Gabe still in his pyjamas. Behind Gabe came Birdie, who was crying. Joseph stood Gabe in front of Connie and she looked up at him and saw he was frightened and her pa was a man to be frightened of.

'Did you do this? Did you do this to my daughter?' seethed Joseph.

Connie hated her father's anger, it made her feel smaller than the tiniest ant and she looked to Gabe to save her even though she didn't know what she wanted him to save her from.

Gabe looked at her and said nothing.

'Joseph, we need to all sit down,' pleaded Flora.

'Yes, yes,' said Birdie. 'Please let's all sit down and find out what this is about.'

'Did you make my daughter pregnant?' Joseph demanded, a dangerous hot whisper in Gabe's ear.

Connie reached for breath as her father's anger hit her skin.

Gabe still looked down at Connie. 'You were supposed to wait,' he said at last.

'Right,' said Joseph, grabbing Gabe's ear and bending him in half. 'I knew it would be you. Who else could it have been?'

'What?' said Birdie. 'Of course he didn't do such a thing. Joseph, have you gone mad?'

Joseph turned to Birdie, still holding Gabe's ear down by his side. 'You wouldn't have a clue what your son does or doesn't do. You've always been blind. You know he's cast in his father's mould but you refuse to see it. You always have. He could have been saved if you'd taken him in hand but you let him run wild having anything he wants. You let him blow up our shed and half-drown our children in the river on more than one occasion. You let him do what he chooses when he chooses without any thought for others. You bred a selfish boy who thinks he can take what he wants. You've never controlled his behaviour.'

Birdie straightened her shoulders and gathered her strength. She grabbed Gabe's arm and one by one she loosened Joseph's fingers from Gabe's ear and, glaring back at Flora as though somehow Flora controlled Joseph, she walked Gabe out the back door and away from the house.

Flora remembered the other people in the house. Danny and Pastor Greg upstairs in Danny's room, and Charlie who was sleeping in the back vestibule. She got up from the table and put her hand on Joseph's arm to still him. 'You and I need to talk about this in your study. Connie, go to your room. Doctor Salter said you are to stay in bed.'

'And stay there,' said Joseph, pointing at her.

Connie walked up the stairs and sat on her bed in her nightie, pulled her blankets around herself and stared out her window looking for Angel Mike. Nero was down there playing his violin in a sad, drawn-out melody as though something had died. Connie watched him until she became bored. She opened her book,

What Katy Did Next, to page 56 and read until an hour later Flora came in and put a plate on the bedside table.

'Come on,' she said, 'let's get you properly into bed.' The sadness in Flora's voice made her cry again. She wanted her ma's normal voice that sounded like a girl skipping along the street. Connie let her feet be tucked under the blanket and Flora handed her the plate with a cheese sandwich on it.

'I haven't had breakfast yet,' said Connie, pushing the plate away and throwing the hot blanket off her legs leaving just the sheet.

'None of us have, Connie.' Flora sat on the bed beside her. 'Your father and I were awake all through last night. You slept because Doctor Salter gave you something. But in the study now we've prayed about this matter and we've come to a decision – it's not a pleasant decision but it's the only decision. Your father is taking you to Collins Street in Melbourne on Monday, Connie, to see a special doctor. You will have to be brave. Until then you are not allowed out of this room. In fact, I feel I will never let you out of my sight again. You are not going to school or church – oh my gosh, church.' Flora looked at her watch and rushed out.

Connie opened the sandwich to see how much gherkin was in with the cheese and closed it again.

She had finished her sandwich and several more chapters of her book when Danny came in, wearing his Sunday clothes – his knitted Fair Isle vest and his white shirt and good black trousers. He sat on her bed and she shuffled over to make room for him.

'I just got back from church. Pastor Greg filled in,' he said. 'Ah, look at that screwed up nose. You don't like Pastor Greg?'

'Do you?' Connie asked.

'He's all right. A funny accent he has,' he impersonated Greg.

She looked at the sandwich crusts scattered unwanted on the green plate.

'You heard everything, didn't you?' she said.

'It was a bit hard not to; you were screaming loud enough to wake up people in Brisbane.'

'The doctor came.'

'I know. Charlie and I were standing on the stairs the whole time. I was so scared for you, Connie.'

'Because I was sick and I'm in trouble. Big trouble. Do you hate me?'

'Why would I hate you?' He pulled her close to him.

'Does your friend hate me?' she said.

'No, Connie,' he said, 'he's not going to judge you.'

'I'm sick. Pa is taking me to a doctor in Melbourne who can make me better. I haven't been on the train to Melbourne before.'

'Oh, Connie,' he said. 'I'm sick too in a way. What a pair we are.'

'Pa's hair has gone white.'

'I saw that,' said Danny. 'Well. Goodness.'

When Flora sees everything

Monday, 24 November 1947

On Monday morning Flora stood in the middle of the kitchen and stared at where Joseph would normally be sitting at the table reading the paper after having heard the news on the wireless. Instead the wireless had been left silent and Joseph was on the train to Melbourne with Connie to see the doctor that Doctor Salter had recommended. He would go to the bank first and clear out their savings. Doctor Salter said the cost would be considerable. Flora stared into space and saw only her own failings as a mother. She had always known she was missing something important about Connie, she just hadn't known what. And she knew that no matter what she gave of herself to Connie, the girl needed more. Flora's failure filled her to the brim. It had never entered her mind that Connie and Gabe were up to such sinfulness at such a young age, and yet it should have. She should have seen some clue. She played memories of Connie over in her mind. Connie lying under the lemon tree with Gabe, so close, so close, the length of their bodies nearly touching. Connie going to Gabe's house every chance she could. The two of them disappearing off for hours, doing who knew what in the secret darkness of the garden shed or off down at the river. Connie refusing to change into a dress that fitted her properly for such a long time then suddenly the new dress was all she wanted to wear.

Pastor Greg walked into the kitchen and Flora watched as he poured himself a cup of tea. She had made it and forgotten it and it had brewed to a dark bitter brown and was thick and soupy as it fell into his cup. He looked up at her and she saw something flash across his face as he quickly looked away. She remembered seeing Connie sitting on her branch with him, sharing some secret that they were both laughing about, and when she had said, 'What's got you two in a tither?' they had leant into each other and giggled and she had wondered at Pastor Greg sitting up there suddenly seeming so young. She saw them laugh at dinners over a shared joke that no one else understood. Connie fussing over whether Greg had a fair share of the food or had had enough cups of tea. But then Connie had changed, imperceptibly, and now Flora thought about it she should have seen it. Connie would sit on the other side of the table to Greg. When Flora told her to go and find him for dinner Connie would yell out from the kitchen door and Joseph would say, 'Your mother said find him, not scream out through the house.' When Greg offered to stay home with Connie during the evening service she protested vehemently that she was old enough to stay on her own and didn't need a babysitter and ran to her room and slammed the door shut.

Flora looked at Greg. She studied every pore and twitch and saw the tremor of his hand as he held the teacup and saucer and the cup rattled out of its place and he unsuccessfully tried to steady it with his other shaking hand and the tea spilled on the floor into a dirty brown pool. Flora stared at the puddle for some moments.

Then she looked up at him and she saw it all. Everything except that he was an orphaned boy, barely nineteen.

'It was you who got her pregnant, wasn't it? It wasn't Gabe at all,' she said. 'For God's sake, she is only thirteen. Did you force her? Did you?'

He carefully and slowly put the empty cup in its saucer filled with a puddle of tea down on the table and took a deep breath.

'Missus Starr,' he said slowly, kindly. 'How could you think such a thing? I am here for one purpose only and God's service. Your daughter is a sinful girl who has seduced some poor boy.' He'd been too harsh so he said kindly, 'Perhaps you should be one to sit and I'll make you a cup of tea. I'll make fresh pot.'

She heard the kind words but also the coldness in his voice and wondered why she'd never noticed it before.

'She's only thirteen,' she said.

He turned the teapot around in a full circle, slowly as though he could control it and everything else in the world. He looked at her and his blue eyes were frozen.

'Connie is wild, uncontrolled – that's your fault,' he said.

'She is thirteen,' said Flora.

'Huh,' he said. 'I have seen so many girls – yes, younger than her – have their way with men.' And his brain filled with the screams of the girls being raped by the soldiers on his terrible journey. 'You people have seen nothing. You people know nothing.'

'You think that makes it all right,' she said. 'You've seen terrible things and so now you do the same terrible things to others. Revenge is not a road you want to travel, Greg. Vengeance won't let you be who you should be.'

'And who should I be?' He took enormous soldier steps and stood right in her face so she was afraid but she dug her feet down into the linoleum and held her spot.

'I have nothing. Your daughter has everything,' he spat at her.

'Not any more. You've stolen it from her.'

As Flora was battling Pastor Greg in the kitchen, above her in the upstairs bedroom Danny stood wiping tears from his eyes as Charlie threw his suitcase on the bed.

'I just can't do this now. I really can't,' said Danny and he crossed his arms over his heart.

'You're willing to throw away all our plans,' said Charlie, 'all that we dreamt of together because your kid sister has got herself in trouble.'

'It's not that simple,' said Danny, 'and you know that. You saw my father, his hair turned white overnight. I can't tell them I'm not going to be a missionary. Any more will break the camel's back.'

'I'm not talking about being missionaries and I don't see why I can't stay,' said Charlie and he clasped the edges of the suitcase and looked up and Danny felt his chest heave. His arms fell to his sides and the accusation in Charlie's eyes speared straight through his chest and the sharp point landed in his heart and stayed there. He rubbed his chest to budge it.

'We all have to have our secrets. But at least I could stay.'

'You know why you can't stay,' said Danny. Even the tears in Charlie's eyes wouldn't deter him.

Charlie walked over and clasped Danny's arms. Danny could smell Charlie's warm breath, he could feel the grip of Charlie's fingers tight around his arms. He wanted to lean in and kiss away Charlie's tears.

'Because,' Charlie whispered, 'if I stay here you won't be able to resist brushing your hand against mine. If I stay here you will crawl into my bed at night and in the shelter of my arms you will forget to wake and we might be found. If I stay here you will sit too close to me at the table, you will look at me a moment too long and you will …'

'I will give us away,' said Danny. 'And we,' he said, slowly and cruelly, 'are a sin.' He saw his words scorch Charlie and tears spilled from his eyes. 'You know we are a sin. We are an abomination before God and if found out we would be arrested. Thrown in jail to rot. I can't do that to my father.'

'Is that your father the holy reverend speaking or you?' said Charlie.

'God smote the sodomites,' said Danny.

'Yes,' said Charlie. 'So he did. But he wasn't too worried about those same sodomites raping the two virgins they were offered as an alternative. Is that the god you want to follow? Because I don't any more.' Charlie grabbed the stuffed bear lying on the bed staring lifelessly at the ceiling. He shoved it hard into Danny's chest. He picked up his suitcase, put on his hat and, without looking back at Danny, said, 'Well, this sodomite has been cast out,' and Danny heard Charlie's steps disappearing down the stairs and he sat on Thom's bed and let his tears cascade down his face and into his heart. He cried for all the men like him but mostly for himself and Charlie.

Flora was stirring custard on the stove when Joseph and Connie walked in the back door at six. Joseph looked at Connie and she pouted but went straight to her room as he'd told her to do on the train. Danny was sitting at the table pretending to read the paper but really wondering if he should go and search for Charlie. Joseph sat at the table next to him and his arms landed on the table top with a thud and he fell into them.

'Where's your friend?' he asked Danny.

'He had to leave; promised he'd visit his mother in Sandringham,' said Danny.

Flora sat opposite Joseph, waiting for him to tell her what happened in Melbourne. But he sat there, his head hanging over his arms.

'I couldn't do it,' he said at last, and he looked at her and he looked so old that if he wasn't her husband she wouldn't have recognised him.

'It was a miserable place with sad crying girls, wailing girls, lost girls, some with their mothers and some with their lovers and there was a cold nurse with a harsh voice. I thought about all the stories I've heard of girls haemorrhaging afterwards and I couldn't take the risk of losing her. Girls die from this procedure, Flora. They die. And then I thought, who were we to take a life, to murder a child because it's inconvenient to us? If this child is born it will most likely ruin us. I'll lose my job. I'll have to learn another craft at my age. But how can I stand up each week and tell people how to live their lives when my own family have delved into such sin? How can I preach to people about how they should be and act when I can't control my own children?'

He looked hard at Danny for a moment as though there was something he should know about him but couldn't grasp. 'It's not the child's fault. It's Connie's fault and Gabe's fault, it's their burden to bear not the child's. So, we will save the child's life. It's the least we can do.'

'But she is a child herself,' Flora said.

'That she is,' Joseph said with a weary voice, 'but she is old enough to get herself in this trouble.'

'It wasn't Gabe.'

Joseph looked at her, not believing her, but when he looked at Danny he didn't seem as surprised.

'It wasn't Gabe,' she said again. 'It was Greg.'

Joseph stormed through the house, slamming doors so they bounced back hard against the walls leaving doorknob bruises. Flora, following his rampage up and down the stairs, said five times, 'Joseph – he's gone,' before Joseph heard her. She took his hands, which were shaking with rage, and held them tight and led him back to the kitchen table. Flora sat opposite him, still holding his enormous hands in her stronger small ones. They sat in silence, the kettle whistling like wind through trees in the background. They each played in their minds all the inconsistencies in Greg that they had seen and brushed aside. Danny had found him distant and wary, and Joseph had wondered why it sometimes seemed that Greg's fervent devotion was actually driven by hate. Flora thought about how young he sometimes looked.

Joseph got up from his chair. 'Where is he?'

'Gone,' said Flora. 'Gone this morning. I don't know where but I told him not to stay in Ballarat. I told him if he stayed you would likely kill him.'

'I would, I think, mortal sin that it is. And oh, what I said to Gabe and Birdie.'

'They'll forgive you,' said Flora.

Joseph sat down again. 'Well, it doesn't change our plans. I had plenty of time to think on the train, Flora. I have a plan. Danny and I will take her to the Catholics in Daylesford. We'll go tomorrow in that new Vauxhall I haven't even used yet. Danny knows how to drive the thing.' He looked at Danny, who nodded. 'We'll take Connie to the convent. You'll tell the school she has – I don't know, measles or undulant fever or something else that means she won't be back at school for a year. We'll tell everyone she came down suddenly and has gone away to convalesce and afterwards we will make sure she never even so much as breathes without one of us watching her. But we'll go on as if it never happened and I won't lose her.' He looked at Danny and said firmly, 'I love my children more than I hate their sin.'

He put his head back in his hands for a moment to gain strength then looked at Flora and said, 'You make sure her things are packed. We will go about our business as if nothing has happened. Don't look so sad, Flora – it's only Daylesford; we can drive over and visit her each month.' He put his head back in his trembling hands.

Flora knew she had lost the husband she once had. He was no longer stronger than any man she knew. He was drained of everything that had made him young. He had striven so hard to retain everything, to keep everything in its place, but bit by bit all the things he tried to hold tight had loosened, unravelled and slipped away. Her mind raced as she thought of options and she held his two large hands in her small ones.

'I have another idea,' she said. 'We can keep her closer.'

She went and got her hat from the stand in the front entrance and Joseph and Danny followed her. 'I'll be back soon.'

'Where are you going?'

'I'll be back in a jiffy,' she said and she walked out into the light evening air. The weather was still warm from the hot day. People were sitting on their front porches in the coolness or watering their gardens to bring them back to life. She forced herself to wave to people as she passed even though her mind was focussed only on her mission. On she walked to the little half house in Webster Street where she knew Lydia was sad and lonely, especially since Viola had married. She stood and talked to Lydia at the top of the steps. They held each other and then the two of them walked back to Dawson Street, each of them carrying a bag of Lydia's things. Even though Flora had warned her, Lydia was shocked by Joseph's white hair and she gulped her shock back and sat at the kitchen table in front of him. She put her hands in his and said, 'You're going to need some help, Pa.'

'I'm going to plant a weeping willow,' he said. 'Right plum in the middle of the front yard.'

'It will dig up the drains,' said Flora.

'Yes,' said Joseph, 'it will most likely uproot everything else in the yard.'

When Connie turns fourteen

Friday, 2 April 1948

Keeping secrets, even in a town of forty thousand people, isn't an easy task. But if the secret got out and anyone in the congregation or even the town had guessed Connie's condition or linked it to Pastor Greg's disappearance, they also knew not to say a thing.

Lydia never let Connie out of her sight. She stood outside the bathroom door when Connie was bathing or brushing her teeth or using the chamber pot. She slept with a scarf flung over her bedside lamp at night so she could see if Connie got up in the night. She slept lightly so that if Connie tried to leave their room she would wake as soon as Connie's feet touched the floorboards. When Lydia went to her teaching job at Dana Street school, Flora would watch Connie and then as soon as Lydia got home she would resume the task. Connie fumed and railed at Lydia and called her a jailor. Flora and Lydia took a break when Danny said he would stay with Connie while Lydia and Flora took in the Saturday afternoon concert at the Regent Theatre. Connie wailed and cried enormous tears when Lydia said she couldn't go with them.

'But I want to hear the famous pianist Eileen Joyce so desperately,' she cried, even though she would normally have been bored to tears by the recital and would have begged not to go.

Connie stamped her feet and wailed when she was told she couldn't go to the side garden and sit in her lemon tree or even go into the backyard in case the neighbours happened to look over the back fence and see her.

'Only Danny is kind to me,' she said, 'the rest of you don't have a Christian bone in your bodies the way you treat me.'

Danny now worked as a teacher at Ballarat Secondary. When he told Joseph he wasn't going to be a missionary and had taken a job as an English teacher at the high school, Joseph had merely nodded and then patted him on the back and said, 'At least you're home, where I can see you, son,' and went back to reading his paper. Danny had looked over to Flora; worry was spread across her face. Joseph was no longer the man they knew.

After Danny got home from school in the afternoons he would try to entice Connie into a game of Monopoly or Who Am I? because he knew she was bored silly, but Connie would always rebuff him and instead choose to sulk in her room. She stomped up the stairs when she was told for the umpteenth time she was confined to the house and was not to answer the door.

'Why can't I?' she demanded, and Lydia wondered if it had sunk into the stupid girl's head at all that she was thirteen and pregnant. Did she not have any understanding of the enormity of the situation?

Flora tried to make up for Connie's confinement and cossetted and fussed over her, making any food she wanted, which was usually lashings of lemon butter on toast with pots of tea, despite tea and butter still being rationed, making the lemon butter prized. But Flora gave it all to Connie and no one else was allowed to touch it. Connie was scrawny and lanky with a barely visible bulge in her tummy so you might think she'd just eaten too big a dinner. But still neither Flora, Lydia nor Joseph were willing to take the risk of someone seeing her and guessing Connie was pregnant. Flora worried that neither Connie nor the baby was getting enough nourishment and gave her bigger servings of meals, saying, 'Eat up, Connie. You're eating for two.'

She made Connie eggnog and as soon as Flora turned her back Connie tipped it down the bathroom sink. When Connie got to seven months Birdie let out her dress. Birdie never doubted Gabe's innocence in the whole matter for a minute and was somehow relieved to see that Joseph could be just as volatile as other men and not the man she'd held up as her gold standard. So she had forgiven Joseph when he apologised for his cruel words and sworn her to secrecy. She always knew that Connie was trouble. But she loved Flora and made another dress as Connie's belly rounded and swelled.

Connie asked what they would dress the baby in because they had no clothes for it and where would it sleep and what would it eat and most of all, how were they going to get the baby out of her? But no one would answer her.

Joseph might once have thought to explain this to her, but when Joseph wasn't off visiting his congregation he sat in his study, old and withered, and wondered how they had all changed so much. Finally, he had all his children home, excepting Thom. But not one of them was the person he'd meant them to be.

Flora might have told Connie but Flora had never been told herself, and so she hadn't known how babies were born until she'd given birth to Connie and she thought the shock of this information might just be too much for the girl, and Lydia assumed that if Connie knew how to get herself pregnant she would know how to have a baby.

So when, over breakfast on her birthday, the one day she should surely get whatever she asked for, Connie said, 'So how's this baby going to get out of me?' they all looked at her and didn't know what to say.

'Well, come on, one of you answer,' she said.

Joseph said, 'I have to visit old Missus Gleeson this morning and take her communion.'

And Lydia said, 'We have an early teachers' meeting before school.'

And Danny said, 'Me too.'

Suddenly it was only Connie and Flora sitting at the table. And Flora said, 'Shall we make a batch of Anzacs for your birthday dinner?'

'Some birthday,' said Connie, and stomped off to her room for another boring day in which she could do nothing.

That afternoon Danny came home later than usual and had a brown paper package tucked under his arm.

'Is that for me?' asked Connie, pushing away the arithmetic Lydia was making her do on the kitchen table to make room for the parcel.

'As a matter of fact it is.'

'Oh, a present,' she said.

He put the parcel on the table in front of her and she tore the paper away.

'*Revelation of Childbirth* by Dr Grantly Dick-Read,' she read the cover aloud.

'The salesgirl in the bookshop said to me, "Oh, so your wife's expecting – congratulations, sir," so I said, "Oh yes, due any day now. We're hoping for a boy",' said Danny and he laughed.

But Connie had already discarded the book with its pale pink cover and was drawing over her arithmetic to hide the tears in her eyes.

'It's okay, old girl,' he said. 'We all got you something else; we're just waiting for Pa to get home.'

After her birthday dinner they gave her a new dress. She held it up against her body and said, 'It'll never fit.'

'It will soon,' said Lydia.

Connie took the dress to her room and put it on a hanger. She left the book on the kitchen table.

Flora picked the book up and gingerly opened it to the first page. When she finished reading at midnight, she padded up the stairs and left the book at Connie's and Lydia's door, and the next morning Connie stepped right over it and it lay there unnoticed all day until Lydia came home and picked it up and began reading it leaning against the hallway wall as she waited for Connie to finish her bath, because they still couldn't trust her not to try and run off or just wander the streets.

When so much is invisible

Wednesday, 12 May 1948

It was a cold May night right in the middle of the school holidays when Connie's baby was born.

They ate meatloaf with gravy for dinner and Connie, standing in front of the stove, traced her finger around the inside of the pot, scooping the leftover fatty gravy into a glob that she sucked off her finger. Lydia and Danny were doing the dishes and she was staying out of their way. Licking out the gravy pot was a much better job. Joseph had gone to his study and Flora was preparing breakfast for the morning. Suddenly Connie felt a gush of water leave her body; it splashed over the green tiles in front of the stove and formed a huge puddle at her feet. Pain shot through her pelvis and she bore down over the puddle. She'd be sure to get in trouble for that. But she forgot the puddle because something needed to come out of her. Another pain shot through her and Connie cried out and Pa came running from the study and stood in front of her looking worried.

'I'm going to die,' Connie cried, 'this time I'm really going to die.' The pain was rotten and it would never end but it did, quite suddenly, and she stood up and smiled. She was going to be okay. Pa could stop looking so worried. Ma could stop crying. But Pa looked at Ma and then he ran to the front hallway and Connie heard him dialling the phone and asking for Doctor Salter, whom she hated.

'Oh,' cried Lydia, 'let's get you to your bed.'

'I don't need to go to bed and besides my socks are wet,' said Connie. 'I peed myself.'

'That wasn't pee,' said Lydia. 'I know because I read Danny's book.'

'I don't think Connie should be going up the stairs,' said Flora, 'put her on our bed.' Flora reached down and lifted Connie's foot and pulled off one wet sock and then the other.

'I don't think I can walk.'

'You can lean on me,' said Flora, and she lifted Connie's arm over her shoulder and walked her in halting steps to the bedroom. Joseph had flung back the quilt and the blankets and the top sheet and, because Flora was insistent on it, Connie lay on the bed she was born in, on the same yellow flannelette sheets, though they were worn now with age and patched by Flora with mismatched colours.

'We'll be right,' said Flora to Joseph, but Connie didn't think she was. She watched Pa go from the room and she could hear him and Danny talking quietly just outside the door and then another pain ricocheted through her body and she screamed out. Flora took her hand and lay beside her in the bed and said, 'Try and keep calm.'

Connie had no intention of keeping calm. How can you keep calm when you are dying? As another pain took her she yelled out her fear. 'I'm dying. I'm really dying this time.'

'No,' said Lydia, 'if you'd read Danny's book you'd know that you're not dying and this is perfectly normal. If you'd read Danny's book you would know what to do and this wouldn't be hurting. But you never do as you're told and you wear the consequences.'

'I don't think it matters now,' Flora said, and wiped the sweat from Connie's forehead with her hanky.

'How – would – you – know?' Connie glared at Lydia as she spoke in rasping breaths. 'You – never – had – a – baby – inside …' And a pain took her last word away with it so that *you* became a wolf's howl.

The banging on the front door was so loud it nearly drowned out Connie's next scream.

'You go,' said Flora to Lydia, but Joseph had already opened the door.

'The weather is miserable,' said Doctor Salter as he handed his hat and scarf to Lydia. 'I would have arrived sooner but I had to take it slow on account of the ice on the roads.' There was frost on the sleeves of his coat. 'Oh yes, I had to wash off the windscreen to see.' He handed the coat to Lydia and she brushed off the sleeves with her fingers before hanging it on the hall stand. Another pain came and Connie thrashed about.

Doctor Salter walked over to the bed and began prodding Connie's stomach. He held his hand there as the pain came and went.

'She should go to the hospital,' he said. 'She's too young to give birth at home.'

'No,' said Joseph quietly.

'We're doing the Doctor Dick-Read method – birthing without fear,' said Flora.

'No. If you're insisting on doing this here then you're doing the Twilight method,' said Doctor Salter.

'But Doctor Dick-Read says the Twilight method doesn't stop the pain,' said Flora.

'I disagree and even if it doesn't we know for a fact it wipes all memory of the labour.' He took out his needle and two bottles and from one bottle he pulled a dose of morphine into the needle and from the other bottle a dose of scopolamine. 'Morphine for the pain and the other is to prevent vomiting. She will wake with no memory of this. None at all.'

Four hours later Connie's drugged and pained body pushed a healthy baby girl into the world. Doctor Salter gave Connie another dose of the Twilight concoction and while she slept the baby was washed and bundled into a thick rug. Flora held her granddaughter tight and cried. Danny kissed her forehead and whispered, 'Goodbye, little one.'

'Go on, Ma,' said Lydia quietly, so as not to wake Connie. 'You know we have to do this.'

Flora nodded.

'Go, go, we're here with Connie and I don't think Doctor Salter is leaving until you get back,' said Lydia.

Flora held the baby close to her heart as she followed Joseph out to the car. He took three tries to back out of the driveway. He drove up Dana Street, over Drummond and turned left at Pleasant Street. She felt ill. To do this they must tell a terrible lie.

Flora, Joseph, Doctor Salter and Lydia had huddled together in Joseph's study on three occasions to discuss what to do with the baby. Danny had taken on the job of distracting Connie as they talked in hushed whispers. Doctor Salter had the most to say, being the most experienced in the matter of unwanted pregnancies, and he counselled them most stringently that Connie should not be allowed to bond with the baby. He would give her a sleeping draught so the baby could be removed from the house and that way when Connie woke she wouldn't remember a thing and could get straight back to being a fourteen-year-old girl. Joseph prayed and then they had all agreed that Doctor Salter was right. This was the best outcome they could hope for.

But now they were actually doing it Flora felt dirty and cruel as salty tears stung her eyes. Joseph pulled the car up outside the cottage in Essex Street. He turned off the lights and the engine.

'Come on,' he said. 'Give her to me. I'll do it.'

'No,' said Flora. 'I want to hold her as long as I can.'

'You'll get more chances,' he said. 'She's not going far.' But Flora knew that wasn't true because the baby would never be theirs again.

Flora carried the nameless baby girl to the front door of her new home. Joseph pressed the bell. It took some time for the door to be answered but when it was Flora passed the baby over.

On the way back home, in between crunching the clutch, Joseph patted Flora's knee.

'She'll have a good life, Flora, she's in safe hands. We all agreed on this, remember.' But Flora felt numb.

When Joseph pulled into the driveway Flora ran inside and sighed with relief to see her only daughter, fourteen years old, still lying asleep in the bed. Flora and Lydia changed Connie's limp body into a clean nightie and she was so drugged she didn't stir once. Joseph and Danny lifted her as they fitted the bed with clean sheets and then lay her gently back on the bed.

'I'll stay here,' said Flora, 'by Connie. Perhaps you could sleep in Thom's bed tonight, Joseph?'

Flora crawled into the other side of the bed. She held Connie's hand in her own all through the night and was still awake when Joseph brought in the tray of tea. She sat up and took it and he perched on the end of the bed and so as not to wake Connie they drank in silence. There were no prayers. When they had finished Joseph took away the tray and Flora waited for Connie to wake.

Connie stirred at eleven. She sat up and looked at Flora for a moment with those unnerving blue eyes and said, 'Did I have the baby?'

'You did,' said Flora. She got out of the bed, walked around to Connie's side and sat on the edge and took Connie's hand in her own.

'Can I see it?' said Connie, looking for it.

'The baby has gone,' said Flora. It was the best she could do. It was the truth and not a straight-out lie.

'No, it can't be gone,' cried Connie, and she tried to get out of the bed and Flora was too tiny and tired to stop her, but Connie was drowsy from the drugs and fell against the bedside table. Joseph caught her.

'I heard her wake,' he said and lifted her back into the bed and pulled the blankets around her. Flora tucked them in tight to hold her safe and sat back on the bed.

'Where is the baby?' asked Connie again. But neither Flora nor Joseph could say what they had agreed on.

Lydia stepped forward and, taking Connie's hand in a way she never had before, she squeezed onto the bed between Flora and Connie and said gently, 'The baby died, Connie. It's gone to heaven.'

Flora nodded. She had never realised how brave Lydia was. She had stepped forward and done what needed to be done. What Flora had been too cowardly to do.

'Was it a boy or a girl?' whispered Connie.

'Does it matter?' said Lydia, and she took Flora's tortoiseshell brush from the bedside table and gently pulled it through Connie's hair, which was knotted with sweat.

Flora took her hand again and Connie stared at her as though she knew she'd been told a lie and she blamed Flora for it.

'You'll be back at school soon. In six weeks, Doctor Salter said,' Lydia told her. Doctor Salter had also said, *Best to look to the future.*

At the terrible news that she had to go back to school, Connie fell back against the pillows with a thump, mussing up her hair and ruining all Lydia's work.

'I don't see why I have to go back to school,' she pleaded, and Flora smiled because it seemed that after all this she had her old Connie back. Perhaps Connie could forget the past nine months and get on with being a young girl after all.

When the manse is a prison

Monday, 17 May 1948

Despite Connie's protests, every morning Flora, with Lydia's help, wrapped Connie's chest up in bandages, and once that was done Flora would give her a bundle of clean rags for the bleeding.

'How long do I have to wear these?' said Connie, pulling at the bandages.

'Ten days inside, then you can go out, but you have to convalesce for six weeks,' said Flora. 'Five more days to go inside. They'll fly by.'

'And the stupid rags?'

'The same,' said Flora. 'Now, turn around so I can pin the bandage while Lydia holds it tight. Then you can get dressed and sit by the stove.'

The day after what they all now called The Day, Flora had told Danny to pull the armchair from the living room into the kitchen and put it by the stove, and so there Connie sat while Flora made her cups of beef tea and albumenised milk. She cooked Connie chicken broth and fish custard and made arrowroot pudding and junket. She fed her and fed her but Connie would take a few mouthfuls, say the eggnog made her vomit, the soup was bitter and the arrowroot lumpy and push the food away.

'When can I go outside?' Connie asked every day. 'It's not healthy, you know, to be kept inside as long as I have. At this rate I'll never be free again. I might as well be in prison like Manny was,' said Connie.

Flora looked up from mixing cake batter. The spoon fell out of the bowl and splattered batter over the floor. 'As soon as the ten days is up,' she said, and picked up the wooden spoon and tossed it in the sink and got a new one.

Connie fell back into the armchair and she was so thin the armchair swallowed her up. Flora held out the new spoon covered in batter to Connie. Connie shook her head and Flora's fingers gripped the spoon tight. The old Connie would have licked the spoon clean and asked for another. The old Connie always thought her serves of food were smaller than anyone else's even if they weren't. The old Connie always wanted more of everything. Worry filled Flora's head. Perhaps Connie would never be her old self.

When the ten days passed, Connie made no effort to leave the house. She sat at the kitchen table and drew. When Flora glanced over at her she saw that Connie's grip on the pencil was so loose it was only just balancing in her hand, and the lines on her drawing paper were thin and barely visible. Her head rested in her palm and her eyes gazed into nothing and she was not at all interested in what she was drawing. It seemed to Flora that Connie had become as thin as the lines on the paper and as invisible as the nothing she was staring into. And Flora didn't know what to do to help her own daughter and that was a cruel and bitter thing that filled her with despair.

When Connie had been convalescing for three more weeks she said, 'If Gabe won't come to me, I'll go to him. I haven't seen him since the day Pa dragged him here by his ear.'

'Not without me and I can't go this afternoon,' said Flora.

'Why? I'm not having a baby now. I'm back to normal. I can go out, can't I?'

'You're not to go out of the yard on your own under any circumstances,' said Flora. 'Your father's orders. He doesn't order much any more but on this I agree with him. Connie, we're keeping an eye on you so you don't get yourself into trouble again. Besides, it's wet and freezing cold out.'

Connie put on her coat and came back into the kitchen. 'Don't worry. I'm just going to see how the lemon tree is.'

Flora wrapped her housecoat tighter around her chest and followed Connie out and watched, shivering in the cold, as Connie climbed up onto her branch.

'An hour,' said Flora. 'I don't want you catching a chill.'

Connie watched her ma go back into the house. She clasped her hands around the branch. It was cold and wet and when she lifted her hands up there were specks of bark and dirt all over them and she wiped it off on her coat. She felt the damp from the wood eking its way through her coat and her dress into her skin. But she didn't care because her world was a lonely place with just her in it. She didn't see her angel any more, or any other angels or demons. They had all left her.

When a million frogs sing

Monday, 5 July 1948

It was Monday morning and Pa stood in front of her in the kitchen. Connie saw how thin his white hair was getting. She could see his pink scalp underneath. She could see each individual hair.

'There are strict instructions that must be adhered to,' Pa said as she stood holding her school satchel, wrapped up in her coat, scarf, gloves and hat. 'You must tell everyone you've had undulant fever. Say it, Connie.'

'Undulant fever,' murmured Connie.

'And you must meet Danny at the school gate and walk straight home with him.'

Connie nodded and Pa looked sad.

'Ah, Connie, once you would have argued with me. I almost miss the old Connie.'

Connie shrugged. She felt too tired to argue. It had been determined this was as good a day as any for her to go back to school. She really didn't feel up to it.

'Righto,' said Danny, looking at his watch, 'we best be off. Don't worry, Ma. I'll keep an eye out for her.' Connie followed Danny out the back door and down the driveway. She kicked at the stones on the pavement and didn't hear or answer when Danny asked her questions. Ma had asked if she was nervous about going back to school but she felt nothing. She was empty.

'We'll find out where you need to go,' said Danny when they got to the school and he took her into the office. There was a line of students at the window. They murmured, 'Sir,' and it took her a moment to realise they meant Danny.

'Come on,' said Danny. She followed him through the door that said *Staff Room*. 'My sister,' he said to the other teachers. 'She's been away for a year. Undulant fever.'

They looked at Connie and nodded sympathetically. She stared back at them; they looked like cardboard cut-out dolls. Danny read a sheet on the wall and said, 'Form Three B, Room 14, English. You like English,' he smiled at her. Then he sighed, 'Come on, old bean,' and she followed him to Room 14 where he nodded for her to go in and she did. 'See you at the gate. At four; wait there while I pack up my things.' He waved and disappeared into the sea of uniformed bodies filling the corridor.

She sat in the last row, in her coat and hat and gloves like they were armour, and stared out the window.

Connie looked for Gabe at morning recess but couldn't find him. She couldn't find him at lunchtime either and she sat alone in the shelter shed and watched the girls giggling and laughing and putting on lipstick which wasn't allowed and she felt no compulsion to try and be one of them. If they looked towards her she would look away. She saw Danny walk past with one of the other teachers and he waved and smiled at her but she didn't wave back. In the afternoon the girls went to typing lessons while the boys went to the machine shop. She sat in front of the grey typewriting machine and looked at the buttons. She rubbed her hands together to warm them up and put her finger on the soft ribbon and when she pulled her finger away it was blue.

The teacher walked into the classroom and said, 'All right, ladies, type this,' and he handed out letters they had to copy. Connie put her finger on 'D' and pressed it down. The clunk of the key echoed inside her. But there on the crisp white sheet of paper D appeared, as if by magic. She typed the letter. The keys of the typewriter clicked and chirped, a million frogs all talking at once, and Connie typed faster, hitting the keys and the space bar and slamming the carriage return lever so that the machine croaked to the beginning of the next line. The noise filled the nothingness inside her. Then the 45-minute period was over. The shrill bell cut across the music of the typewriter. She pulled out her letter, put the typewriter to bed in its linen cover and left her letter on the pile of others on the teacher's desk to be marked.

As she waited for Danny at the gate, girls pushed past her as though she wasn't even there, boys sniggered at her and she glared at them.

She kicked at stones as she walked home with Danny.

'You'll ruin your shoes. You know Ma and Pa can't afford new ones.'

She kicked a big stone into the fence they were passing.

'How was the first day back?'

'All right,' she said, even though it wasn't. Her world was full of devilish tricks. There was trouble everywhere. No one was what they seemed. 'Typing class was good.'

He patted her on the back and said, 'It'll get better, things always do.'

'Not for Thom,' she said.

While Danny and Connie walked slowly home from school, Inspector Fortunato stood at Birdie's door in his best suit.

'Birdie, this is the last time I'm going to ask you. If you don't marry me I'll move in here anyway, even though I bump my head on the lintel of your door, and we can just bloody well live in sin. I spend most nights here as it is.' He rubbed his forehead.

Birdie couldn't tell him she was afraid of happiness. That getting married was announcing her happiness to the world and if she was too happy, it would rain some horrible misfortune down on her. If she married him he would most likely die on her. She pursed her lips and shook her head.

He knelt on the ground and held the ring under her nose. She'd never had an engagement ring. He twisted it this way and that. She shook her head again.

'Birdie,' he said, 'I can't for the life of me work out what the problem is. Are you not happy with me?'

'I have no complaints,' she said. 'You never beat me. You never lie or cheat on me. Why wouldn't I be happy?'

'Bleedin oath! Such high standards for a man to live up to,' he said.

'I'm so happy with you,' she whispered.

'Then why can't you marry me?' he asked, standing up.

'You're Catholic,' she said.

He laughed. 'Not very Catholic. Only when I'm with my ma. I'll convert. My ma will die with the horror of it but I'll do it for you, Birdie.'

'I'm afraid.'

'Of me?'

'Of us.'

'But, Birdie, we've been together for a long time now and nothing bad has happened, and besides I have the full weight of the Ballarat police behind me. I can keep any danger at bay.'

Birdie loved him despite the fact he wanted a pound of garlic in everything she cooked, that he broke into Italian when he was happy or angry and she couldn't understand a word, and that he never stopped talking, and she stepped towards him before stepping back into the safety of choosing disappointment over happiness.

'Come on, Birdie,' he coaxed her and he stepped forward and filled the doorframe as she backed into the hallway. 'It's freezing out here – it's July for God's sake. Say yes so I don't die of cold right in front of you.'

'It would have to be a proper wedding in the church.'

He laughed and slipped the ring on her finger. 'As long as we don't wait. I've waited long enough.'

'The Baptist church.'

'I know,' he said. 'My mother will die of shame but a church wedding in Dawson Street it is. But I can …' And he pulled her to him and kissed her, then he pulled back and said, 'Come on, Birdie, you're engaged to the best copper in Ballarat, there's nothing to worry about.' And he kissed her again and his lips were so warm and sweet on hers and she held up the ring on her finger and the diamond caught the winter light and soft rainbow beams danced on her skin.

When the world is a lonely place

Saturday, 28 August 1948

It was the last Saturday of August and the sun had no warmth and in the night the temperatures dropped below zero, sending everyone scurrying to the top shelves of their linen presses for more woollen blankets for their beds. Car engines wouldn't start in the mornings and were flooded with too much choke in the effort to get them going. The milk was delivered frozen in its bottles, water wouldn't run until the weak sun slowly defrosted the pipes. The puddles were glassed over and then smashed with sticks by boys who muddied their school uniforms. But inside a little house in Essex Street a fire roared and everything was toasty and warm. Viola was bathing a baby, nearly three months old, in an old enamel tub on the floor in front of the fire, but far enough away that sparks couldn't land on the baby's bare skin. Every now and then Manny poked at the coals to bring them to life and a rush of heat would wash over Viola and the child. The baby had tufts of cloud-white hair that hovered over her pink head and eyes like sky that never stopped and she cried in soft little mews.

Viola thought she was the prettiest thing she'd ever seen. She lifted the baby from the water, which was turning lukewarm, and lay her on the white towel embroidered with her name: Emmaline. Carefully Viola dried under her arms and around her groin, making sure to softly wipe the towel in her folds of puppy fat. She smoothed vaseline into the folds then took the nappy she had lying ready and folded it into a triangle and pinned it over the baby's bottom. She gently pulled the fat little arms through the singlet and then the sleeves of the dress Birdie had made, and then again through a cardigan her mother had knitted. She put the baby's feet into the matching booties. Viola passed the little white bundle that smelt of Johnson's baby powder to Manny, and he wrapped his arms tight around the little girl and smiled. Viola looked at the clock. It was ten in the morning.

'My turn,' said Viola, and she went to their bedroom where a painted lamb bounced across the head of the cot. The cot was jammed up against their double bed. She pulled her wedding dress out of the wardrobe and put it on and then her coat, hat and gloves and when the baby was rugged up in the pram with a knitted cap pulled down over her head they walked to the church for Birdie's wedding to Inspector Angelo Fortunato.

Connie sat in the pew and stared out the window. There was nothing there. Just grey clouds that wanted to rain. The groom was standing at the front of the church in his uniform talking to her father. Mister Hooley was playing Bach just like at Princess Elizabeth's wedding. She saw her pa motion for the groom to stop chatting but Inspector Fortunato just kept going and her father nodded at bald old Mister Hooley and he stopped the Bach and began the bridal march and Connie turned to watch Birdie walk up the aisle on Gabe's arm. The sight of Birdie shut the groom up.

She was wearing a yellow satin suit that shimmered like sunshine and sky-blue leather shoes. She was holding a bouquet of daisies as though she had plucked them on the way into church. Connie didn't think she'd ever seen Missus Mabbett smile before, but it was Gabe her eyes rested on – so tall, walking with his back straight and no sign of his limp, he had become someone Connie didn't know. She desperately wanted to catch his eye but he looked straight ahead as though Connie wasn't even there.

Joseph started the wedding ceremony and Connie stared out the window until she heard her pa pronounce them man and wife and all the uniformed policemen in the church hoorayed and threw their hats up to the ceiling and the enormous confetti of hats fell down, were caught and thrown again and again. Connie looked at the hat confetti flying up and down and that was all she saw.

Just hats.

'Cheer up, old bean. It's a wedding,' said Danny, and she tried to smile. 'Ugh, Connie, that's not a smile, that's a grimace.' He took her hand and they followed the congregation out into the frosty August day and their breath turned into tiny white puffs of smoke when they breathed out. The policemen stood in two rows, holding up their hats to form a guard of honour that Birdie and Angelo walked through as everyone cheered and threw paper confetti.

Connie stood next to Flora. 'This was a long time coming,' Flora said.

'Was it?' said Connie.

Birdie came over and put her arm through Flora's and said, 'Make sure you catch the bouquet later, Connie.' Connie touched the yellow everlasting daisies Birdie was holding. They were crisp like paper and when she held up her finger there was yellow flower dust on the tip and she blew it away into the thick air.

'Oh, I'm sure there's someone in line before Connie,' said Flora.

Connie looked past Birdie, whose smile could dim the sun, and saw Viola holding a baby wrapped up in a bundle of white crocheted wool. Viola held the baby tight against her chest.

'If she lets go the baby will fly away like an angel,' whispered Connie, but no one heard her. Connie watched as Viola rocked the baby from one side to the other. Connie's blood stopped running in her veins and her heart stopped beating, her legs felt heavy as though she would never move them forward. There was something she knew about Viola's baby but she couldn't find it and the fleeting moment was gone, pushed away by the persistent tugging on her sleeve.

Connie turned to see Gabe standing behind her. He pulled her away and down the side of the church and her feet got wet in the damp cold grass that needed cutting.

'You don't come to church any more,' she said when he came to a standstill.

'Excommunicated myself,' he said, smiling.

'You look passable in that suit,' she scoffed.

'Single breasted – newest style,' he said, holding out his hands. 'But not warm enough for this cold day.'

'Aren't you afraid of hell?' she said. 'I am.'

'What? For not coming to church? Goodness, if that's the criteria for heaven, hell will be filled to the brim.' Even the air was grey and damp, but his black eyes caught all the light there was and sparkled at her.

She wanted to throw herself into his arms to see if she could feel him against her. When anyone else touched her, she felt nothing.

'I haven't seen you at school lately.' Connie leant against the church wall to appear nonchalant. The bluestone bricks were cold against her back.

'I'm doing an apprenticeship. I'm making televisions,' he said. 'Soon everyone will have them in their homes and wireless sets will be a thing of the past.'

'You expect to make money from something no one knows about?' she said.

'They have them in America. They'll come here too.'

'I don't think I could make them,' she said, looking at her shoes. The toes were covered in mud.

'You don't have to do anything if you don't want to, Connie,' he said and he put his hands on the wall either side of her. She expected to feel caged in by him but instead she felt as though he had created a fort for her. She stood up taller and said, 'How would I do nothing?'

'I will marry you, Connie,' he whispered, 'and instead of nothing you can do what you like.'

'My father said I will probably never marry. I will live at home with Ma and Pa and Danny and Lydia. Maybe none of us will ever marry.'

Darkness fell across Gabe's face and he took his arms away and she felt exposed. He turned in a circle, moving his hands as though he was trying to wind his anger like rope into a controllable ball.

'Why is that? For what archaic reason does the reverend say you can't marry?' he spat.

She looked away from his anger, thinking it was aimed at her and said, 'Pa said a good Christian man expects something I can't give him.'

He laughed.

'This is serious,' she said and she folded her arms over her chest because his laughing at her was hurting.

'Well, it's lucky I'm not a good Christian man, isn't it?' he said.

'It's no good,' she said and she turned away from him and looked at the solid immovable bluestone wall.

'Connie.' He pulled her back. 'You can't disappear. You're not someone who's meant to be invisible.'

'It's too late,' she said, and she walked away from him because no matter how hard she tried to be someone else, she had already disappeared.

'I'm leaving,' he called after her.

She turned and looked back at him.

'I've saved up. I'm going to America to learn about televisions,' he called. 'I'm going to Boston, I've got an apprenticeship at General Electric.'

She turned and walked off.

Now she really was alone.

PART FIVE

1950 to 1952

When Connie makes a decision

Monday, 17 July 1950

In July of 1950 there was celebration in Ballarat when the government announced the end of rationing. Women cooked luxurious meals of roast lamb and crispy caramelised potatoes with lashings of gravy and the men, filled with meat and potatoes and less worry about their finances, brought home chocolates for their wives which resulted in more worry about their finances nine months later. But it went to show that good fortune can't be trusted and neither can the government, because just two months later electricity restrictions were announced. And so the new world of freedom and flowers and plenty for everyone was still just out of reach and hardship prevailed.

The Courier posted the restrictions on page two. There were to be no electric radiators between seven-thirty in the morning and five at night. So cold winter days were spent huddled under blankets and coats. There were to be no exterior lights, so torches were balanced on bare knees as people sat on cold nights, shivering in their outside lavatories. Only one light in any room could be turned on and, worst of all, there was no hot water if you happened to be a poor sod whose hot water was generated by electricity. When Connie and Danny came home in the afternoon the manse was just as cold inside as outside, so Connie thought she may as well be outside as stuck in the house that had been a jail, so she sat in the lemon tree. She was sixteen and too big to be sitting in the tree according to Joseph.

'Even a tree that big isn't made for a sixteen-year-old girl. Especially one as tall as you,' he'd said.

She sat there alone.

She would finish school in December and then get a job as a secretary, perhaps at the council with all the council men running around in their robes and gold chains. They would all depend on her. Without her typing, the whole town would come to a standstill. Connie looked at the watch around her wrist. It was rectangular with tiny marcasite stones in it and roman numerals. Joseph had given Flora a ring and Flora had given the watch to Connie for her birthday and said, 'Time is always moving forward, Connie. The past is the past. It's gone and it can't come again.'

Connie had put the watch on not realising how important it was to Flora. The watch looked pretty on her thin bony wrist. She slid down from the tree and went to her room and took off her weekday dress and slipped on her white shirt which she tucked into her new pleated tartan trousers. She had pleaded for a gabardine suit like the winner of Miss Clunes 1950 whose photograph filled half of the front page of *The Courier*, but she had got the trousers, which Birdie told her were the latest thing. Connie had cut out the photograph, chopping off Miss Clunes's head, and stuck the picture of the gabardine suit on her dresser mirror with tape and she'd cut her own head from her school photo and stuck it in place of Miss Clunes's. Flora said the trousers were perfectly suitable for going out and didn't tell Connie she'd already asked Birdie to make a suit for Connie's next birthday.

Connie sat on her bed and put on her socks and shoes. She stood in front of the mirror and brushed out her long ringlets. She picked the chopped-off head of Miss Clunes from the floor where it had dropped and been left for the past weeks and looked at it. Then she pulled her own hair into a ponytail and tied it tight. She swished her hair this way and that. She went to the kitchen and got the scissors out of the drawer. She walked back up the stairs to the mirror in her room, took her ponytail firmly in her hand and cut right through it and her long black curls fell to the floor, on top of Miss Clunes, and there they lay unmoving, the life cut right out of them. Connie swished her cropped hair and it flicked across her cheeks. She pinned it up each side and smiled. Now she looked like somebody. She looked like Elizabeth Taylor in *National Velvet*. Maybe this was who she wanted to be.

When she walked downstairs into the kitchen, Joseph looked up from the paper, saw her hair and harrumphed, folded the paper, got up and walked away. Connie paid him no mind; he was just a white-haired old man. She stood in the middle of the kitchen flicking her hair from side to side. It felt free – and just try sticking cockroaches in it now, Gabe Mabbett.

'You better go get me those scissors,' said Flora.

'Why?' said Connie. 'What's done is done. What's past is past.'

'Let's just neaten it up a bit, shall we?' Flora said. 'Go on.'

So Connie got the scissors and took them back to the kitchen.

'I'm not doing it in here where the hair will get in the butter. Go outside.'

Connie stood close to the gully trap and Flora, standing on the step stool so she could reach, cut away hair that wafted into the air to fly for only a moment before landing on Connie's neck where it itched.

'There, that's it I think. It's straight at least,' said Flora.

'I like it,' said Danny, when he was called to dinner.

'I do too,' said Lydia. 'Very grown up, Connie.'

'Well, that settles it,' said Joseph. 'We all approve of your hair, Connie.'

But by Monday Connie had changed her mind about her hair and when she and Danny parted at the school gate she kept her head down, hoping no one would notice her hair. The girls who never noticed her before now noticed and gathered around her and trailed their fingers through her shoulder-length curls.

'It looks much better,' announced Rhonda.

'It's so bouncy,' said Barbara, and Connie wondered if she could be part of them after all. But then, why bother, when school was almost over? Just four more months.

When Connie goes to the pictures

Saturday, 4 November 1950

November brought the sun. Retaliating for being shunned throughout winter, it burnt bright and hot and women lined up in the chemist shop to buy red sunglasses to match their red shorts with white polka dots. Men reached for beers and gave thanks for the women's new fashionable short shorts. The days were long and light and where they had been cold in their homes, they were now too warm and instead of hovering around one little radiator they now hovered around one little fan.

This Saturday evening Joseph stood watering the weeping willow, which was growing too fast. He could see its roots stretching out in all directions, hard twisting ridges just under the grass. He thought about his sermon for the following morning. Sermons just didn't come to him as easily as they once had. It was harder for him to preach about a sure world when his own world had been so unpredictable. He thought often of the words of the evangelist George Whitefield, *To preach more than half an hour, a man should be an angel himself or have angels for hearers*, and Joseph knew he was no angel and neither were most of his congregation.

Danny was down by the Yarrowee with Lionel Lewellyn, who taught science. The two men sat side by side in the tall grasses on the bank. They sat in silence and watched children splashing and yelling and fighting, drowning out the crickets and cicadas who wanted to sing in the night. They laughed when the children pushed each other into the water and Danny thought of Mike and Gabe and the days he'd spent with them fossicking for frogs.

Lydia was in a dither in the kitchen. She had been invited to go and see *Samson and Delilah* at the Regent Theatre with Stuart Bingley, who was the new headmaster at Dana Street. At work he was Mister Bingley but when she wasn't at work, Lydia called him Stu. They were going to the Saturday evening session. Lydia was wearing her new circle skirt, yellow with a black poodle frolicking on the bottom of it. It had a wide red band around her waist.

'It's a bit garish, don't you think?' said Flora. 'The new fashions, I mean, not your skirt necessarily.'

'It's supposed to be a terrific movie,' said Lydia. 'It has Hedy Lamar. I look like her a bit, don't you think? We can't go to the matinee because it's full of school children.' She swished her skirt again and touched the red bow in her hair. 'The holidays can't come soon enough for me.'

Connie was at the kitchen table watching Lydia swishing the skirt about her knees. It was bright and sunny, but she said to Lydia, 'If you do that you'll be showing the boys everything. You'll be a slut.'

Lydia and Flora turned on her. 'Connie, how could you?' said Flora. Connie didn't know why she had struck out like that. She began to cry.

'You can take Connie with you,' said Flora and she put the silverside in the pot to boil. 'And you can invite Mister Bingley for lunch tomorrow after church. You will bring him to church?'

Connie sat up straighter and wiped away her tears.

'For goodness sake, Ma, I'm twenty-five and I don't need a chaperone,' said Lydia, and she stamped her foot on the black and white linoleum. Connie slumped back down into her chair. She never got to go anywhere. Home, school and church, home, school and church. That was her life.

Flora looked at Lydia and said, 'Please,' because she felt bad Connie had cried and she wanted Connie out of the house and out from under her feet but she couldn't let Connie out alone. It was really Lydia chaperoning Connie, which Lydia knew.

'Oh, okay then,' said Lydia, and she picked up her shiny red vinyl handbag and on her way past Connie at the table she said, 'Well, are you coming or not?'

Connie looked at Flora, who nodded and reached up to the mantelpiece and pulled down the old Rosella biscuit tin, prised off the lid that always stuck, and gave her a shilling. Connie held it tight in her fist and ran after Lydia.

'We're meeting Stu there, so keep up because we're late now,' said Lydia as they walked down Sturt Street.

'What's he like?' asked Connie, puffed with trying to keep pace with Lydia. 'Is he a good one or a bad one?'

'Who? Stu? He's nice, he's handsome and he's single,' said Lydia and she stopped and rounded on Connie. 'So be nice and behave and don't talk about bloody angels and demons.'

So Connie shook Stu's hand and kept her mouth shut and she sucked on Fantales as Delilah sucked the strength out of Samson and Stuart's other hand snuck up Lydia's skirt. They could do anything they wanted if they took her with them and he seemed nice enough for Lydia.

When the mayor gets a shock

Friday, 15 December 1950

The invitation had arrived on Monday. It said *15 December* and *speeches beginning at seven sharp.*

'I'm not going,' said Connie. School was over and she was done with it and they could keep their intermediate certificate.

'You must,' said Joseph, but he had lost all his stamina and Connie knew she could ignore him.

'Your father's right,' said Flora. 'You must make an appearance.'

'I won't win anything,' said Connie.

'It says here you won typing,' said Flora, and she held up the letter from the school and read it out: '*Dear Mister and Missus Starr. We are proud to inform you that your daughter Constance Starr has been awarded the first prize for touch typing. Please ensure she is at the school hall at six-thirty sharp in full uniform to receive her award during the graduation ceremony.*'

Connie knew the letter by heart but she still wasn't going.

She ran upstairs and shut herself in her room and pushed the dresser across the door.

Lydia stood against the door, getting cross. 'Connie, I need to get changed. I'm already late for Stu. He's coming to see you get your award.'

'Stu, Stu, Stu pooo,' sang Connie, and she sat on the floor and stared at the blue flowers in the carpet and listened as Lydia told Flora, 'You need to do something about her.'

'I'll go if you go,' said Danny. He was going anyway and sitting with the other teachers.

Connie pushed the dresser aside enough to open the door. 'I'm not wearing the putrid uniform.'

Flora produced a brown paper package. 'It was for your birthday next April but now it's a graduation present instead.'

At six Danny drove them to the school in the Vauxhall that Joseph had only ever driven once. Connie wouldn't sit with the other students, she sat with Flora, Joseph, Lydia and Stu. Finally after many boring speeches her name was called and she walked up onto the stage in her Miss Clunes suit, taking her time so everyone could admire it. The mayor handed her the prize and she was supposed to say thank you and walk off the stage but instead she opened the envelope right there and then. She ignored Principal Everett motioning for her to leave the stage, whispering that she was holding up the ceremony. She ignored Mayor Rowe, who was handing out the prizes as he put his hand on her back to move her on. The hall was silent. Everyone watched her.

She pulled the award out of the envelope. There was a certificate saying First Prize and a voucher for two pounds to spend at Taylor and Taylor Chemist on cosmetics.

'I'll keep the certificate,' said Connie into the microphone and she tucked it back in the envelope. 'But I don't wear cosmetics.' And she handed the voucher back to Mayor Rowe. 'You can give that to someone else.'

Mayor Rowe rocked back on his feet. 'Well, ahhh,' he said into the microphone, but Connie had already left the stage.

The next Monday Joseph took the phone call from Cottingham and Coutts Lawyers offering Connie a job, which he accepted on her behalf. She was to start after the Christmas holidays in January. But she would have an interview, just a formality, so the following Monday Flora walked her to the office in Mair Street.

'What do I do in this job?' she asked and Old Mister Coutts said, 'Well, we'll start you on letters and once you're settled in we'll be giving you the legal documents to do.'

'Oh, I can do letters,' said Connie.

She followed Mister Coutts into his office and sat in the hard chair and he dictated an old letter like he did for all potential clerks to see if they really could type the words per minute they claimed. When Connie had finished the letter he smiled and showed her the desk that would be hers. She looked at the gleaming typewriter sitting there as though it had spent its life waiting for her. She sat down and fed in two sheets of paper with a piece of carbon between. She hit the letter 'D' and the typewriter sang. Mister Coutts stood over her in his old-fashioned suit, with his hands behind his back, and through his large moustache said, 'My, Miss Starr, you are by far the noisiest typist we've had, but you're the fastest, too, so no complaints from us.'

And Connie smiled.

When Connie can't tell one voice from the other

Friday, 29 August 1952

By the time the world had moved into 1952, America was blowing up the Nevada desert with nuclear bombs just for practice. The rest of the world asked what they were actually practising for. North Korea and China had captured Seoul and the United Nations troops had captured it back again. Bolivia was taken over by the military and Tibet pleaded for its peaceful liberation from China, a request China declined. King Abdullah of Jordan was shot as he said his prayers and in Australia everyone became terrified of communists. No one in Ballarat actually knew a real communist. Well, you couldn't count the ten or so people who met in the old mining exchange where they sat in a circle blowing mountains of smoke from their cigarettes and drinking wine in enamel camping cups like real working-class heroes and never came to a decision about anything. The politicians railed about them, though, like parents threatening their children with bogeymen if they didn't behave, so even though no one in Ballarat had ever actually seen a real filthy red communist, they knew they must be lurking somewhere nearby and it was terrifying because what were the Japanese if they weren't reds? Compulsory conscription for all eighteen-year-old boys was introduced so the threat of the communists – and any ideas Japan might get to join them – could be fought off, and that made everyone, except the eighteen-year-old boys, feel much safer.

June came and Inspector Fortunato, with Sergeant Lister sitting beside him, chased Lawrence Malady in pouring rain down the slippery wet Ballarat highway. They chased Malady over the dangerous gorge at Bacchus Marsh, where they had to build up speed to get up the hill, even in the new Ford Zephyr police car. They caught Malady when he tried to do a U-turn and head back to Ballarat and became bogged on the side of the road. In August Inspector Fortunato testified in court that he'd had to reach 90 miles an hour to catch Malady, who was travelling at the highly dangerous speed of 70 miles an hour in his FJ Holden. He further testified that when they opened the boot of the Holden they found the implements with which Malady had broken open the safe of Thomas Jewellers and there was no shadow of a doubt of Malady's guilt because in addition Malady had taken his wallet out of his pocket during the heist and left it on the shop counter with his driver's licence folded neatly inside.

Inspector Fortunato drove home in the Zephyr that night to the house Birdie insisted she would never leave in Humffray Street, where she had material resting in piles on every seat in the lounge room and lamb stew and honeycomb pudding waiting for him on the table. The oven door was open to warm the kitchen and Angelo sat where Aubrey used to sit opposite Birdie, and Gabe, who had come back from America, sat between them.

'The lounge room is still unusable for sitting and reading or listening to the radio set,' said Gabe, and Birdie and Angelo looked at each other and said, 'Uh-huh,' in unison.

'You'll soon need to clear it out for a television,' said Gabe.

Birdie heard the material and the orders she had written on sheets of paper fluttering anxiously in the breeze coming through the window.

'A whole room for doing one thing? No, I don't think so,' said Birdie, and all the material lying in piles and the tower of orders settled down, knowing they were safe for a very long time. And so, the room stayed cluttered because no one could sell dresses of the quality and style that Birdie could make.

In the house in Essex Street, Viola had finished bathing her daughter Emmaline, who was nearly four, had put her in her pyjamas covered in snowflakes and her dressing gown and slippers and was settling into the couch with Emmaline on her knee. *The Poky Little Puppy* was open to the first page when Manny came in through the front door and dropped his briefcase to the floor.

'How was work?' said Viola.

'Same as always,' he said, reaching for Emmaline. 'Accounting never changes, and neither does Berry Anderson Printing.' And he sat on the couch and picked up the Little Golden Book and said, 'Now, where are we up to?'

In Raglan Street, Claude and Elsie were listening to the Sunshine Singers coming live through their radio set on ABC Radio. Their lamb chops were steaming on plates balanced on their knees as the women's singing filled their home. The fire was roaring and on the wall above the fireplace were five photos. One was of Gabe on the day he left for America. The next was of Emmaline on her third birthday. The photo in the white scalloped frame was of Birdie and Angelo on their wedding day. Elsie, Claude, Viola and Manny stood next to Birdie and on the other side was Angelo and his enormous family and his mother glared into the camera and next to that was a photo of Viola and Manny on their wedding day. But the largest photo, sitting above the others in a beautiful redwood frame, was of Mike.

In Nightingale Street Mabel and Cecil were listening to 3BR which played re-runs of *Dad and Dave* and as they listened Mabel gazed at the photo of Viola, Manny and Emmaline sitting on their mantel next to the radio.

Further away in the Melbourne suburb of Sunshine, in a double-fronted timber cottage, Aubrey was fighting with Hazel. He'd been gone for three days and she threw pots at him as fast as she could grab them.

'Disappearing for days on end is no way to treat a pregnant wife. Your last wife might have put up with your shenanigans but you have another think coming if you think I will,' she yelled and as he ducked another plate, he thought it was time he curbed his ways once and for all.

In a little flat in Darling Street in Redan, Lydia was wearing an apron over her good work frock. The apron was covered in flour that stuck to it in wet globs. She should have been preparing lessons.

'I'm making you my mother's famous lemon tart,' she told Stu. He came up behind her and wrapped her in his arms. She wriggled away. 'I can't cook if you do that.' She swatted him with the flat of the knife. 'You'll walk me home later?'

'If I have to,' he said.

'You have to,' she said. 'You know my father.'

'Mmmm, we'll have to change that,' he said and he held up her ring finger and kissed it.

And Danny, where was Danny? He was sitting with Flora and Joseph in the sitting room. They were all reading and Danny looked up from page 54 of *The Problem of Pain* and said, 'I'm glad that Lydia has finally found someone. Stu seems like a nice fellow and perhaps one day the right girl will come along for me.'

Flora and Joseph nodded, knowing there would never be a right girl for Danny, even though they couldn't face why, and they went back to their books.

Just outside the window Connie, now eighteen, sat in her tree not caring one iota about the ice coating the branches.

The night was coming and Connie was so afraid of the night. She shook the branch she was sitting on and watched snowflakes of ice fall to the ground like lost souls. She looked at the dirt below her and wondered whether, if she dropped off the branch, she could just melt into the earth. She thought she caught a glimpse of a demon and she sat up straight and repositioned herself. She peered into the dusky air and saw nothing and thought of Pastor Greg who had looked like an angel. He had sat with her in her tree and shown her his tunnel book and she had laughed at the magic of it and put her finger carefully into the tunnel to touch the beautiful doves that flew there, seemingly suspended by nothing, and then he had snapped it shut and she had pulled her finger out just in time, but still the covers of the book had nipped her skin and she'd cried out, surprised. He'd taken her finger and put it to his lips and kissed it and said, 'There, there. I didn't mean to frighten you.'

That night she had woken, and knew someone was in the room. She opened her eyes and he was bending over her and he bent down and kissed her mouth and she pressed her head back into the pillow away from him. He put his hand over her mouth so she couldn't make any noise and in the moonlight he looked so white, like he was made of frosted glass, and she couldn't see his eyes just his iciness and she was scared and cold and shivering. He leant down close to her ear and whispered, 'You are my Mary Magdalene.' She'd nodded, afraid of how cold his fingers were against her skin. He lifted the blankets and slid into bed beside her, pinning her between him and the wall and she couldn't move away. He slowly took his hand from her mouth and when he saw she wasn't going to shout out, he put his finger to her lips, reminding her to keep quiet. He pushed up her nightie and rolled on top of her and every part of him was so rigid with cold as though he was just an enormous chunk of ice without a beating heart and she was surprised he was so heavy and she was trapped under his weight and couldn't run away. He put his hand back over her mouth and pushed himself hard and hurting inside her and he moved and it hurt more and she felt his wet chilling tears as they splashed cold onto her hot cheeks, then the real Connie was gone.

She flew high high high. Angel Mike had taken her hand and swept her far above the bed until she could barely see it. Up, up they went, twirling in circles through the ceiling, through the roof, through the high branches of her lemon tree. She looked down and the Connie in the bed was just a dusty speck of a thing that was barely there. The real Connie soared and tumbled through the clouds holding tight, tight to Angel Mike's hand. They soared over the world, higher and higher they went, dancing through the clouds until Ballarat was just a green spot on a blue round earth. They tumbled and turned and laughed and he called out over the noise of the clouds, 'Why did the angel lose his job? Ah, come on, Connie, you have to say *Why?*'

'Why?' she called back and he said, 'Because he had harp failure, hahahaha.' Then he somersaulted and took her with him and never once let go of her hand until slowly he lowered her back into her bed and Pastor Greg was whispering in her ear and his breath was wet like frost and stung her skin.

'I'm your angel,' he whispered, 'and this is our secret.' His voice was so quiet she could hardly hear it; it was quiet like her father's when he was really angry and it cut right through her. She felt like she would split in two and bleed into nothing and she knew Pastor Greg was furious with her.

'If you tell anyone,' he said in her ear, his head resting on her neck, 'they will kill me and my death will be on your conscience, Connie Starr.' Then, changing in an instant, he said, 'I will wait for you to grow up and we will marry – we are married already in God's eyes.' And so, she had known she couldn't marry Gabe. Pastor Greg came to her bedroom again and again and she had lain awake shaking, knowing he would appear in the dark of the night and each time Archangel Mike would come and take her away and she would fly to the clouds where she was safe.

As she sat in the cold night in the lemon tree, seeing it all, tears spilled down her face. They dropped onto the branch she was sitting on and then spilled onto the dirt below her, forming a pool on top of the earth. Connie climbed higher than she ever had before and looked around the world. Through the dusk she could just make out Mount Buninyong. She could see the willow tree in the front yard, its branches falling with the weight of its tears. She could see where Danny had scratched his name in the church wall, in the same spot where she had last spoken to Gabe and then lost him forever. She could hear the murmur of her parents' and Danny's voices, muffled by the closed window. The sounds were foreign to her; they came from a world she wasn't a part of. She saw the distorted shadow of her mother get up and disappear from the room, then she heard Flora call her inside and she slid down from the tree, picked up her shoes and walked into the kitchen.

'Goodness,' said Flora, looking at her, 'you must have been freezing out there with no coat and your shoes off.' Flora rubbed Connie's arms to warm them up.

Connie shrugged out of Flora's arms and didn't see Flora crumple just a little that her daughter didn't want her warmth. Connie went to her bedroom and pulled off her wet clothes and changed into her nightie and crawled into her bed. She lay, rigid and straight, and listened to the darkness as it pestered her. She heard footsteps and she stopped breathing. But then the steps went to Danny's room and she started to breathe again. Night after night she had lain like this, trying to stay awake, trying not to sleep, being ready and alert and afraid in case he came for her, and she was so so tired.

Suddenly she heard the murmur of voices and thought perhaps it was her parents and Danny chatting at the bottom of the stairs. But the voices became louder and she realised they were talking to her.

'Come on, Connie, come on,' they called and she thought it must be Angel Mike, who she hadn't seen in so many years. 'Come on, come on,' they pestered.

She got out of bed and crept down the stairs in her flannelette nightie and bare feet. She crept past her parents and Danny reading in the sitting room. She went silently through the kitchen and out the back door, letting it close softly behind her. The long thorns of the rose bush reached out desperately to hold onto her but she flew on, leaving a shred of material dangling in their spiky nails. She was out in the cold night. The air was wet and the grass frozen to crisp shards and it crunched as the ice broke under her bare feet and she didn't notice her toes turning blue. She stopped at the lemon tree and looked for Mike, but instead she saw the demons smiling at her and they flew off, beckoning her on, so she followed them down Dana Street and over the road.

Walking back from their dinner, Lydia and Stuart didn't see the eighteen-year-old girl in the white nightdress flash across the black empty road chasing demons.

Connie ran down Dana Street and into the bushes and weeds, not noticing the bleeding scratches on her legs. She pushed through the weeds and grasses until she was standing at the river and she watched it rushing past without a care in the world, without a care for her. The rain had fallen at twice its normal rate for the entire month of April they'd said on the front page of *The Courier*, and it had not let up through May, June and July, so now at the end of August the river was full and overflowing its banks. But above the racket of the river she still heard the demons.

'Come on, Connie. You are broken and tainted and you belong with us where it's warm.' They cartwheeled on top of the water and their splashes wet her skin and her nightie.

The river swirled and gurgled around the playing demons and it yelled and drowned out the silence inside her and she felt peace fill her up. She hadn't been baptised when she was sixteen. Joseph had said he didn't know if she would ever be ready to be baptised.

Now she would be baptised by the demons. She would be born again. Everything in her past would die. She stepped into the water, first one foot and then, getting purchase on a rock, she put the other foot in, and one step after another she walked out into the noise of the river and she felt the weight of her flannelette nightie pulling her down and down into the icy water. The river raged about her and she gave herself to it. She plunged under the water and in an instant the freezing iciness of the racing river took her breath away.

When the Yarrowee flows fast

Friday, 29 August 1952

Gabe never knew why he woke up. He thought he heard crying. He lay in bed and listened. At first he thought it might be a cat, but he realised it was a woman and it was outside, perhaps out in the street. He switched on his bedside lamp. The stand was a porcelain giraffe that he'd had since he was a child. Birdie had bought it for him when he had come out of hospital. He put his bare feet into his shoes and tied them up. He put on his woollen dressing gown, tied the cord tight around his waist and went out through the front door into the street and stood in the middle of the road and listened. He heard the crying again and realised the sound was coming from the back of the house, and went back inside and took his stepfather's police issue torch from the table where it got plonked at night.

He went out through the back door, back into the cold night and made his way down through the small vegetable patch, past the lavatory and out through the back gate to the vacant land beside the canal. The canal was full and rushing and almost drowned out the sounds of the crying but he could still hear the faint sounds and he followed them, walking at first and then running as urgency built inside him. He ran in awkward, clumsy leaps, his bad leg not wanting to go fast. He ran past the houses that were asleep, past the factories and workshops, to where the canal became the river, to the spot where they used to play as kids, where his crutches lay rotting somewhere on the bottom of the riverbed.

He shone the torch over leaves in the trees, over frogs who, frightened by the artificial light, buried themselves hastily in the mud. He shone it over rabbits that sat stunned in the weeds and grasses as though the light of the torch had the power to immobilise them. Silly daft rabbits. Then he shone the torch out into the river, over the rushing and coursing water that bubbled and hissed and caught a glimpse of something white floating on the water for the briefest moment, before it was pulled under and disappeared. Gabe kept the torch on that spot and sure enough the white surfaced again. Then he caught an arm flailing about in the torchlight and he threw off his dressing gown and shoes and plunged into the icy black water holding the torch high with one hand so it wouldn't get wet and die. The coldness of the river took the air from his lungs. His chest constricted and wouldn't allow the air in and he floundered about gasping for breath. He caught it and plunged on towards the white. The water became deeper as he worked his way against the currents to the middle of the river and soon it was up to his waist and the strength of its rushing meant his feet were frantically searching for the riverbed beneath him. He saw the white was a piece of cloth, floating and drowning in the water. What an idiot to risk his life for a piece of cloth. But he was here now, so he reached out helplessly towards the white cloth, grabbing at it until he had a handful and he yanked the cloth up to his chest and with it came Connie, limp and dead.

He lost the torch and grabbed for her body. The torch sank, just another thing eaten by the river. He held her up out of the water and yelled, 'Don't give up on life, Connie! Connie! Don't give up!'

Then he pushed through the dark, cold water and as soon as his feet found the rocky bed of the river again he stopped and heaved her body further into his arms. He dragged her towards the bank and as the river became shallower she became heavier and he stopped again to get a better grip on her. Finally, he pulled them both onto the mud and rocks. He heaved and gasped and then rolled her onto her side and she spluttered and coughed.

He got his breath back and crawled up on his hands and knees and knelt over her.

'Connie, what were you doing besides catching pneumonia?' he yelled.

She opened her eyes and looked at him as though he had ruined everything. 'Dying,' she yelled back.

She had scratches on her face and her arms and legs, they were bleeding in watery stains as the blood and river water mingled on her body. The nightie was in tatters. He pulled her to sit her up and they both sat side by side and she heaved to get her breath back.

'I remember it being deeper,' he said.

'It's deep enough to die in,' she said.

When he felt strength return to his limbs, he stood up and leant over and took both her hands and pulled her to her feet. He reached over and felt around for his dressing gown that he'd thrown into the tall grasses and wrapped it around her. He realised he'd lost his shoes in the mud and he no longer had the torch to find them. He put his arm around her and walked her back up through the grasses and away from the river. The grasses prickled his feet and scratched at his ankles. He didn't know where to take her. There was nowhere apart from his bedroom, so slowly they walked to his house through the moonlit darkness, both shivering and wet and strung out like things that had been battered by storms. They walked up the side of the canal and then through the vacant lot. He held open the back door for her and then took her hand and led her to his bedroom where the bedside lamp waited and glowed. He had to use his feet to swipe away valves and wires and screws covering the floor to make a path to his bed.

'Stand here,' he said, stopping her near the bed, and he looked to make sure she wasn't going to try and run off back to the river. She nodded and he went to the linen press and got a towel and he pressed it to her wet hair to dry it.

'You cut your hair,' he said. He started to dry the woollen dressing gown and realised that was stupid so he slowly pulled it from her body and tossed it to the corner of the room where it fell in a damp matted mound. Next he gently lifted the torn white thing that had once been her nightie off her. She was naked now but he saw only that she was tender and blue and bruised and he patted at her skin, softly as if the towel was a piece of cloud and her skin was the feathers of an angel and he dried her arms and then her back and then he moved around the front of her and dried down her chest and finally to her legs where he made sure to dry between each toe and he did not know that his careful pats were the kindest thing she'd ever known.

Satisfied she was as dry as he could get her, he threw the towel on top of the dressing gown and said, 'Sit on the bed,' and she did and he went to the bathroom and opened the enamelled medicine cupboard that was painted with a little red cross on the front. He took out the tin of bandaids and the bottle of iodine and the cotton wool. He knelt in front of her, dabbing the opened iodine bottle to the cotton wool, then held her leg gently in his hand and wiped each scratch with the red iodine and taped a bandaid over the worst scratches and then he did the same with the other leg and with each arm. Only when he had finished did he realise she was still naked and he reached into his wardrobe and took a shirt off its hanger and helped her into it and then he buttoned it, one shell button after the other, and he took a pair of pyjama pants and slid them up over her legs and she stood up to let him pull them up to her waist where he tied them at her stomach. He moved her back towards the bed and held open the blankets and she lay down and curled up on her side and he pulled the blankets up over her.

He stood there for some minutes before he realised he was shaking violently. He was wet, his skin was covered in purple goosebump pimples, so he turned his back to her, hurriedly took off his wet pyjamas and dried himself on the towel and got a dry shirt from the wardrobe, buttoning it up quickly so that it was longer on one side than the other, then he pulled on his last pair of pyjama pants and crawled into the bed beside her. He lay flat on his back and reached out and turned off the giraffe light. They lay side by side listening to the beating of their hearts and staring at the moonlight that danced across the wall. He lifted up his arm and she twisted over and cradled into him so that her head was resting against his heart.

After some minutes he felt her look up at him and so he moved so he could see her in the moonlight.

'Connie, I have loved you since we were five years old – well, you were five and I was seven. Why do you think I put cicadas in your hair and threw you into the river? Why do you think I pulled your pigtails and put your hair in the inkwell?'

'Because you hate me?' she said.

'Oh, Connie,' he murmured. 'I love that you see things other people don't see, that you write your own story. I love your dark tumbling hair, even if it is now cropped short. I love that we will have children with the blackest hair and the darkest eyes and that you will tell them about all the things you see. You are the person I see most in the world.'

Connie cried then.

'What is it?' he whispered. 'I don't want to make you cry.'

She couldn't tell him that she wanted that baby with the dark hair and dark eyes so much that the yearning for it grabbed at her and caught her breath. She needed that baby more than she needed her own life.

He held her tighter and said, 'I know, Connie, I know what you need.'

'How can you want me after all I've done?' she said.

'I've been broken, Connie,' he said softly. 'I couldn't even breathe on my own and my mother and your mother had to make my ruined limbs work again. I know what it's like to become something from nothing.'

'I can hear your heart beat,' she said.

'Sorry,' he said.

'No,' she said, 'it's all I can hear.'

Connie looked up to the ceiling and saw straight through to the stars and to the kind lemon moon off to the right. She could make out the Southern Cross and saw the slippery slide of the Milky Way. And she saw Archangel Michael tumbling and twirling as he struggled with a demon in the long, long war of good and bad.

Acknowledgements

The people who had a helping hand in bringing *The Secret World of Connie Starr* to life (in no particular order) are my spirited and ever-nurturing agent Selwa Anthony and the lovely Linda Anthony who have stuck by me no matter what – thank you for your love. My husband Pete for reading a first draft and helping research the historical events (I may still have got some incorrect and if I have, I apologise to history buffs). Thank you to Pat Gleeson, perhaps Ballarat's greatest-ever piano teacher, for your story about sweet Joseph and the Yarrowee River.

Thank you to the makers of *The Bombing of Darwin: An awkward truth* – your film was educational, inspiring and sad and filled my mind with images – especially the naked boy, which I have used here. A big big thank you to Linda Funnell, my editor, you are always so kind and gentle with this insecure writer, so encouraging and brilliantly pedantic; as always you have gone above and beyond in helping shape my conglomeration of ideas and yarns into something cohesive.

I thank Annabel Blay for tenderly watching over everything Connie Starr, Andy Warren for the cover of my dreams and Natika Palka for promoting Connie here, there and everywhere. I cannot thank Annabel Adair enough for a brilliant proofread – best I've ever had. And everyone else at HarperCollins whom I might not have mentioned, but especially I thank Jo Mackay for seeing potential in Connie Starr and me as a writer and for giving me Linda as an editor.

I thank my writer friends Kim Kelly and Rebecca Burton, you picked me up when I felt down about my writing.

I thank my dearest sweet family: Pete, Maia, Zane, Indea, Seth, Asher, Kylie, Clara, Ellie, Mitch and the darling little boys Sterling, Jules, Sorin and Remy.

You never fail to believe in me even when I don't.

And I especially thank you, the reader, for daring to go on Connie Starr's journey.

talk about it

Let's talk about books.

Join the conversation:

facebook.com/harlequinaustralia

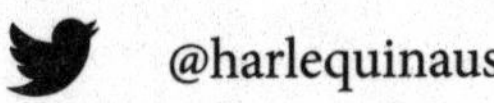

@harlequinaus

@harlequinaus

harpercollins.com.au/hq

If you love reading and want to know about our authors and titles, then let's talk about it.